D0208369

LIE
BESIDE
ME

LIE BESIDE ME

A NOVEL

GYTHA LODGE

RANDOM HOUSE

NEW YORK

Lie Beside Me is a work of fiction. Names, characters, places, and incidents are the products of the author's imagination or are used fictitiously. Any resemblance to actual events, locales, or persons, living or dead, is entirely coincidental.

A Random House Trade Paperback Original

Copyright © 2021 by Gytha Lodge

All rights reserved.

Published in the United States by Random House, an imprint and division of Penguin Random House LLC, New York.

RANDOM HOUSE and the HOUSE colophon are registered trademarks of Penguin Random House LLC.

Originally published in hardcover in the United Kingdom by Michael Joseph, an imprint of Penguin Random House UK, London.

LIBRARY OF CONGRESS CATALOGING-IN-PUBLICATION DATA
Names: Lodge, Gytha, author.
Title: Lie beside me : a novel / by Gytha Lodge.
Description: New York : Random House, [2021] | A Random House Trade Paperback Original.
Identifiers: LCCN 2020052375 (print) | LCCN 2020052376 (ebook) | ISBN 9781984818102 (trade paperback) | ISBN 9781984818119 (Ebook)
Classification: LCC PR6112.O275 L54 2021 (print) | LCC PR6112.O275 (ebook) | DDC 823/.92—dc23
LC record available at https://lccn.loc.gov/2020052375
LC ebook record available at https://lccn.loc.gov/2020052376

Printed in the United States of America on acid-free paper

randomhousebooks.com

2 4 6 8 9 7 5 3 1

Book design by Victoria Wong

For Rufus, the most excellent and ridiculous of sons.
I hope you can forgive the lack of Fortnite references.
And you're still too young to read this. Sorry.

LIE
BESIDE
ME

Prologue

LOUISE

I felt cold. Cold in the way of night sweats. In the way of a slow waking to damp sheets that stuck to my skin. It was like that time when I thought I had lymphoma but was, in fact, falling to pieces mentally instead. Do you remember that? I would wake up every night, drenched and shivering, having sweated so much that it had soaked half the mattress.

I fought waking up. I was too tired, and too aware of the hangover that was about to descend. I was hating myself before I'd even opened my eyes. Well, hating Drunk Louise, anyway. That irresponsible, crappy version of myself who always seems to screw everything up, just so she can have a good time.

So I was half-awake and hating it. And I thought that maybe if I shuffled back onto your side of the bed, then I'd find a dry area and possibly even the duvet, and I'd be able to go back to sleep.

I couldn't seem to find the duvet. So instead, I squirmed farther back to tuck into your body. It's always the warmest way to sleep, with you wrapped around me. But it didn't make me warmer. What had been dampness became shivering wetness. Something was soaking into my nightshirt.

And I remember working out that it wasn't, in fact, a nightshirt. There were thin, hard straps digging into my shoulders and the restrictive feeling of tight fabric. So, clothes. Drunk Louise had gone to sleep in her clothes. And that made me feel a little afraid of what else she might have done.

I opened my eyes a slit and turned over. I saw you as a shadow at first. A reassuring humped silhouette. The window behind you was lit with the orange glow of the streetlamp down the road. It wasn't dawn yet.

That light confused me. I've never known you to go to sleep with the curtains open. Not once in five years.

I remember I put a hand down to the mattress and then looked at it. I wasn't quite sure whether I could see a darker mark on my palm, but it occurred to me quite suddenly that the wetness might be blood.

It didn't shock me yet. Not even when I saw a . . . *spread* of it between us. It was a dark circle that stretched almost as far as the pillows and down to my knees.

And then I felt a creeping understanding. A realization that there were none of the normal sounds of sleep coming from you. No breath. No familiar squeak high up in your nose. No gurgling stomach, which always seems to feature in the early hours.

I touched you on the shoulder. And for some stupid reason, I whispered at you instead of speaking properly. "Niall. Niall." Like it was possible to check you were OK without actually waking you up.

Two things hit me, and I don't know which one came first. I can't quite remember either one being clear before the other.

The first thing was that you were cold. Colder than the sheets. Colder than the feeling of my dress on my skin. A coldness that made your skin feel alien.

And the second thing was stranger. It was realizing that *you* were strange. Your silhouette was too big. It was wider at the shoulder than you are. Perhaps thinner at the waist.

By the time I turned the light on and saw the bleached-white face of a stranger looking back at me, I already knew.

It wasn't you. It wasn't you.

1

The call reached Juliette Hanson at 6:46 A.M. It was an ice-cold first of March, early enough that there were still stars out beyond the gap in her badly fitted curtains and cold enough for an overnight fall of snow to have frozen into bright, glittering crystals. It was also a Saturday, but Hanson was wide-awake now. More awake than she'd been on any day this week.

Unidentified male found dead, the DCI had said. It was the most piercing of alarms. She was already swinging her feet out of bed as he went on to read the address.

She'd never heard of Saints Close, but the chief added that it was northeast of the city center. She was likely to be on-scene before him.

She dragged a clean pantsuit out of the wardrobe, grabbed her toothbrush and toothpaste, and took them all downstairs with her. She snapped the kettle on and dressed quickly while it boiled. She threw instant-coffee granules into her thermos mug and dumped boiling water and milk on top, then went to grab her shoes. She'd left her socks upstairs, she realized. It wasn't the weather to do without, and she ran up to grab the thickest pair she could find. She was fully dressed and standing at the front door by 6:53, her blond hair pulled back into an untidy bun that would just have to do.

She paused with her hand on the bolt. She needed a moment

to prepare, mentally, for the few steps to her car. Climbing into the vehicle quickly meant having her keys ready. Her bag looped over her shoulder just right. Her movements planned out.

She was pretty sure there would be nobody out there today. Who would want to hang around her house before dawn on a freezing morning? But she was going to make sure anyway.

She'd developed a habit of pulling the door shut as she moved off the doorstep, letting the Yale lock click into place, and it was so practiced that she didn't even need to think about it today. She checked right and left as she approached the car, too, which she had reversed up as close to the porch as possible. There were no footsteps in the snow, she saw. No sign of anyone close by.

It took five paces to get to the driver's door, and she had the car unlocked on pace number two. By pace number three she was pretty sure she was alone, but she kept moving at speed anyway. She didn't pause until she was inside the car with the doors locked and the engine running.

She spent a moment, after that, doing nothing more than breathing in and out. She hated that she felt like this. She hated, too, that it was almost worse when he wasn't waiting in the shadows than when he was.

DCI Jonah Sheens was buzzing with curiosity as he pulled his Mondeo into Saints Close. He'd been sad to climb out of Jojo Magos's warm bed and to miss their one lazy morning together. He also felt a little grubby in yesterday's shirt and trousers. But overriding these considerations was keen interest. An unidentified man at a residential house. A death. All the questions that went with it.

Saints Close turned out to be a meandering little group of '60s houses off Belmont Road. Chunky detached buildings with decent-sized gardens out at the front. A place of solid salaries. But nothing particularly flashy. No million-pound piles. Volkswagens rather than Audis parked in driveways.

Jonah noticed that someone had added an apostrophe after the final *s* of "Saints" on the street sign, using some kind of sticker that was much larger than the rest of the typeface. He smiled slightly to himself. That kind of a street, then.

He hitched the car half up onto the sidewalk behind the scientific-support van. Three emergency vehicles in total, and Hanson's little Nissan parked farther up. The cluster stood out, the only vehicles that were clean and free of snow. He was glad to shrug on his thick padded jacket and pull on ski gloves before he climbed out.

The garden to Number 11 was bounded by trees. Snowy firs standing between leafless sycamore branches. At the front an overgrown hedge screened the ground floor from view. It looked like it would be gloomy in that front garden, even in daylight.

Approaching the gate, he struggled to make out much beyond the white forms of the forensics team and a nylon screen being manhandled into place halfway down the garden.

One of the overalled figures moved to meet him. Linda McCullough, forensic scientist for Southampton and the New Forest, and undisputed lead of the scene-of-crime team. He took a step forward onto the clear plastic sheeting that had been rolled out from the front door up to the pavement.

"Tell me," Jonah said.

"We've only just arrived," McCullough told him, lowering her mask to speak to him. "Victim's a young white male. The homeowner called it in. She told us she'd found him just before six-thirty."

Jonah saw that one of the figures was spooling a cable out of the front door, unwinding it toward a pair of wide-based portable floodlights. He couldn't see much within the house. A lighted hallway. Stairs to one side.

"Anyone else in the house?"

"Your constable's here, but nobody else."

The floodlights burst into brilliant life, dousing the garden with light. He squinted against the sudden brightness, and then followed McCullough behind the screen they'd now erected on the grass.

A young man lay a few feet behind it, his white dragon-motif T-shirt dominated by a large crimson bloom. As McCullough involved herself in angling the lights, Jonah crouched down over the body. He gazed first at the colorless face. A chiseled, high-cheekboned face. It had been handsome, he thought, up until today.

He took in the powerful shoulders and lean abdomen and a knife that lay close by, sticky with drying blood. Then his gaze traveled to the stained snow beneath the body.

"Not much blood," he muttered.

McCullough gave an audible sigh as she lifted her mask back into place. "Sheens . . ."

"All right, I know." He grinned at her and straightened up. "You do your job, and I'll go and make the coffee."

BEN LIGHTMAN ARRIVED after that, only just returned from annual leave and looking as perfectly unruffled and movie-star handsome as ever. He clearly wasn't dressed warmly enough to hang around outside but showed no signs of concern. It was as if the cold were something that affected other people.

He listened in stillness to the sparse information they had so far.

"I'd like witness statements from the surrounding houses," Jonah finished up. "You can have my coat and gloves. Juliette's with the homeowner so I'll go and check in with her."

Lightman nodded, taking the offered coat and beginning to put it on. "And presumably Domnall can come with me once he's here?"

"He can," Jonah agreed. "Give him a few."

Of the four of them, Domnall O'Malley actually lived the closest to the crime scene. But O'Malley had never been a man to hurry unless he had no other choice, and despite a previous career in the military he managed his life in a haphazard, seat-of-his-pants fashion. Jonah was well used to it and was happy to let him do things his way.

Jonah headed inside and found Hanson in a large, beautifully decorated sitting room just off the hall. She'd managed to dress herself formally in a navy suit and cream shirt, and looked respectable, if slightly thrown together.

The woman who sat near her looked unprepared for any of this. She was somewhere in her early thirties and was swathed in a thick dressing gown over pajamas. Her feet were bare, and she had the remains of makeup around her eyes. Her very dark hair looked damp and had been scraped back into an uneven ponytail. She shivered continuously, most likely because there was a dead man in her front garden, but just possibly also because of the blast of arctic air that was making its way through the two open doors.

"Ah," Hanson said, giving him a smile. "This is my DCI. This is Louise Reakes, sir. She found the body and called us in."

Hanson's hint of a Birmingham accent had stepped up this morning, and Jonah guessed it was deliberate. An unthreatening regional burr was reassuring.

"Let's get this door closed," Jonah said, pushing the sitting-room door shut. "We can at least stop the cold getting in here." And then, as he pulled up an upright chair opposite the woman on the sofa, he added, "I'm so sorry for all of this."

"It's all right," Louise said hoarsely. "Can't be helped. It's not like you put him there. . . ." Her mouth twisted slightly in wry humor. For a moment she looked like she might be about to apologize, and then she dropped her gaze to her hands.

"Did you know the victim?" Jonah asked, gently.

Louise shook her head. "No. I've never seen him before in my life. I'm sorry."

"Once we've identified him, we'll try to get some images

from social media," Hanson said. "Sometimes it's hard to recognize someone when . . ." She nodded instead of finishing the sentence.

"OK," Louise said. "But I'm pretty sure. I mean, he's big, isn't he? Tall and . . . and strong. I don't know anyone like that." Again that twist of the mouth. "And Niall's friends are all middle-aged GPs or lawyers."

"Is Niall your husband?" Jonah asked.

"Oh. Yes. He's away until later today. Conference in Geneva."

"Do you work too?" Hanson asked.

"God, yes. I'd never be a housewife. I'd go crazy." Louise laughed, slightly nervously. Her eyes traveled to Jonah again and back. "I'm a musician."

Hanson grinned. "That's great. Modern or . . . ?"

"I'm a harpist." Louise jerked her head toward the hall. "My music room's through there."

"Can you tell me how you found him?" This from Jonah. There was a clear change of expression. Louise retied her dressing gown over herself before saying, "Sure." It was a tight, constricted word. "I woke up just before six-thirty, really hungover. I had my friend April round last night, and she's a massive drinker." She smiled slightly. "Terrible influence. I always end up wrecked when we hang out."

"She didn't stay here?" Hanson asked.

"No." Louise shook her head. "She usually goes home."

"So it was just you last night," Hanson confirmed.

"Yes," Louise said. "Just me." She paused, finding her thread again. "So I woke up early feeling like shit. I wanted to make tea so I went to get the milk from outside. We have proper deliveries here. In bottles." She suddenly shook her head. "Sorry."

"It's OK," Hanson said. "There's no rush."

"So I saw this . . . shape on the lawn. And I couldn't quite process it at first. And then I went to see and . . . and I called the police."

"And you didn't see anyone else out there?" Jonah asked. "Anyone on the street?"

"No . . ." She shook her head, and then said, "But I thought . . . Maybe it's not much use, but I think I got woken up in the early hours by a loud car engine."

"What time was that?"

"I don't know. . . ." She looked off to one side. "I'm not sure if I checked. A while before. Could have been four A.M."

"The victim wasn't there when your friend left?"

"No, definitely not," she said, twisting her hands over each other. "Shit, I could never have gone to bed with . . ."

"What time was that?"

Louise gave him a slightly confused look, and then said hesitantly, "I'm not—I suppose midnight."

"And there's nothing else you can remember?"

"No," she said. "Sorry."

Jonah nodded and rose. "We'll see if anyone else heard anything. I might have a few more questions at some point, but I hope we won't be too long here."

"That's OK," Louise said.

Hanson got to her feet, too, and looked down at Louise's shivering form. "Let me make you a tea before I head out."

"Oh, thank you." Louise's expression was a little pained. "Are you sure you don't want me to . . . ? Everything's in particular places, you know." And then she made an obvious effort to smile. "But that would be nice. If you're sure."

THERE WERE PEOPLE, O'Malley had always found, who could obstruct justice without even trying to. The woman who lived in Number 9 Saints Close was one of those. A stubborn, slightly self-righteous fortysomething named Pamela, she stood on the doorstep, flatly refusing to wake her husband for questioning and yet simultaneously trying to tease out information on the events next door.

"Well, I suppose it's some kind of violence, then?" she said as an ambulance drew up slowly behind the paramedics' car.

"I'm afraid we really can't comment," Lightman said patiently, for what must have been the third time, while O'Malley leaned his substantial frame against the wall with a feeling of his life draining away. He was too old for this stuff, and it was too cold for it as well. "You said your husband was woken up a lot in the night . . . ?"

"Yes. So I'd appreciate it if you'd keep it down." She peered toward the road. "Was it Niall, then? Has he attacked his wife?"

"Do you have reason to expect that?" Lightman asked.

The neighbor—Pamela—fixed Lightman with a defensive look. "Well, it's generally what happens, isn't it?"

In the end, O'Malley stepped in. "Listen. You can see this is a serious crime. We need your help. If your husband heard anything, we need to know. It could make all the difference."

At his long, imploring look Pamela finally relented. "All right." She opened the door properly behind her. "But after that, you leave him in peace, all right?" And then she called, "Phil! Phil, the police need to see you. Sorry, love."

O'Malley was a little disappointed by the quiet, slightly overweight man in blue tartan pajamas who descended the stairs. He'd expected someone thuggish and intimidating.

Phil's account was fairly disappointing too. He'd been woken by a slammed door sometime after two. He thought it had come from Louise and Niall's house, but wasn't sure. He was pretty sure he'd stayed awake until five-thirty, and hadn't heard anything else.

"You can bet he wasn't really awake until five-thirty," O'Malley said to Lightman in a low voice as they left. "His window's at the front. Surely, if he'd been awake, he'd have heard someone being murdered in the next-door garden."

"Unless they did it awfully quietly," Lightman replied with a trace of a smile, "out of consideration for the neighbors."

. . .

"IT'S BEEN WIPED," McCullough said, her gloved finger hovering over the handle of the knife to show him the lack of blood over the patterned grip. It would have been a beautiful object without the brownish crust over the blade. A black grip patterned with elaborate silver detailing. A long, tapered blade curved to a hunting point.

There were three of them hunkered over the body of the young man. The pathologist had arrived and Jonah had been satisfied to note that it was Dr. Peter Shaw attending. Jonah had worked with him only once before, but his calm, measured approach had been a key part of achieving a murder conviction. He had turned out to be good on the witness stand too. Less flappable than Jonah had expected of a fairly young man.

"No prints, then," Jonah said, looking away from the perfectly crafted weapon. "But it's pretty distinctive, isn't it?"

"It is. There's a chance you could track down its owner," McCullough said, and then, to Shaw, "I'm interested in the smears. It looks like someone wiped the handle clean of prints and deposited it here."

"He wasn't stabbed here," Jonah said.

It wasn't a question. It had been clear to him from the lack of pooled blood below the body. He'd seen victims of knife crime before. The extraordinary spread of blood. The way it saturated everything. This looked to him like the end of a journey, one that must have involved a great deal of blood loss along the way.

"No, he wasn't." It was the pathologist who answered this time. He glanced toward the gate. "Has your team marked up the footprints yet?"

"Yes, done," McCullough said, and they made their way carefully out onto the road.

The team had now put a cordon up round the sidewalk and grass verge, and McCullough led the two of them to the edge of the road.

"Here," she said, gesturing to several pieces of plastic that had been skewered into the snowy grass. Alongside each, there was a depression in the snow, and in some places the snow was stained with what seemed to be blood. "They start at the curb."

Jonah turned to look at the road. "Are they definitely his?"

"They seem to match his shoes," McCullough replied, "and I think it would be difficult for someone to carry him."

"We should look up what time it snowed last night," Jonah said thoughtfully. "There's no snowfall on top of them." And then he looked toward the edge of the curb. "You think he arrived by car?"

"It looks fairly likely," McCullough said. "I would say a taxi, except I think they'd have noticed if he was bleeding to death in the back."

"So someone else dropped him," Jonah said. "That person might have carried the knife in some kind of cloth before leaving it next to him?"

"Well, it certainly wasn't pulled out of him in the garden," Shaw said. He frowned down at the footprints. "Interestingly, it doesn't look like he was running or staggering."

"The prints are quite flat-footed and steady," McCullough agreed. "So if he was escaping an attacker's vehicle, it doesn't look like he fled in terror."

"So he might not have known how badly injured he was?" Jonah asked.

"He might not," Shaw said. "Though people can exhibit a strange sort of calm when suffering severe blood loss."

Which was, Jonah decided, too depressing a line of thinking to pursue right now. "Let me know when I can ID the body," he said, and turned to take a little reconnaissance of Saints Close.

HANSON HAD BOILED the kettle, rooted out a mug and teabag from the cupboards, and poured the water before she looked in the fridge and found no milk. But of course, Louise wouldn't have brought it in. She wouldn't have remembered the milk when she'd seen a body on her doorstep.

Hanson headed outside, treading carefully over the cables that led into the garden, and saw that the milk crate beside the step was empty.

She leaned into the sitting room to say, "Sorry. I can't seem to find the milk. Did you put it somewhere . . . ?"

"Oh." There was a moment of pure blankness on Louise's face, and then she said, "No, I was being stupid. There is no milk on Saturdays." She gave a laugh. "What an idiot."

"Well, good work on being an idiot," Hanson said, smiling. "You wouldn't have found him so soon otherwise."

Louise nodded at her, and then said, "I can have it black. That's fine." Just as Hanson was turning away again, she asked, "How long will it be until you know who he is?"

"I'm sure it won't be long." Hanson tried to make it reassuring, instead of ominous.

"Will you tell me, when you find out?" Louise asked, her stare very fixed. "I really need to know."

It DIDN'T TAKE Jonah long to walk to the end of the close and back, and in an effort to keep moving he decided to go back up toward Belmont Road too. Dawn was approaching rapidly, though the temperature was still well below zero. The sky toward Holly Hill was a warm orange that somehow slid into washed-out blue, and many of the houses had lights on, some showing anxious faces through the window. A whole street, summoned to watch by the flickering blue lights of the squad cars.

"Has someone done her in?"

The voice rang out from a large whitewashed house with red-tiled eaves and a protruding porch. A gravel drive led up to it in a sweep, bordered by clipped shrubs, many of them tied with twine.

It was a much older house than any of the others, probably by a good hundred years. Jonah wondered if the land the street was built on had once belonged to this house. It had the look of a small manor about it, with its tall windows and high roof.

The voice came from a figure standing in the porch. He was a man of somewhere between sixty and eighty. Corduroy trousers and a V-neck sweater over a checked shirt were finished off by sheepskin slippers.

Jonah gave him a flat look. "Sorry?"

"I asked if someone had done her in." The slippers-wearer raised a slightly crooked finger to point toward the squad cars. "Wouldn't be such a surprise, with that one." He nodded in what looked like satisfaction.

"Why do you say that?" Jonah kept his voice neutral. However distasteful comments like that were, they were often useful. Jonah's was a world where every petty, mean-spirited remark was to be hoarded. To be treasured. To be written into his notebook and fed into the workings of the case in the hope that it might point them the right way.

"Well, I've been half expecting it," the older man said. "The number of times I've seen her stagger out of a cab in the early hours, barely able to stand. The kind of woman who ends up a victim, don't you think?"

Jonah nodded, almost but not quite as if he agreed. "Mrs. Reakes is fine, luckily, but I'd be interested to know if you saw or heard anything unusual last night."

"Me? No." The man in the slippers shook his head. "Nothing unusual. The standard Friday-night drag race went on, but I don't give them the time of day now."

"Drag race? You mean fast cars?"

"Yes. The lovely lads who like to tear along Portswood Road and then down past the end of the close."

"So you heard them last night? What time would this have been?"

"Oh, gone midnight," the gentleman said. And then he added,

"If something's happened, I'd say they were likely to have been involved."

"But you don't know who any of them are?"

The gentleman shook his head. "I'm afraid I'm not in the habit of strolling out at that hour of the night."

Jonah nodded, slowly. He might not be, but there were traffic cameras not far away. Louise Reakes had mentioned a loud engine, too, which made this account more interesting. "Just let us know if you think of anything else," he said. And then he made his way back to Number 11.

Shaw was done with his observations and was in the midst of discussing the removal of the body to the city mortuary. Lightman and O'Malley were hovering near the gate. Presumably they'd finished quizzing the nearest neighbors.

"Am I cleared to look for ID?" Jonah asked.

"Yes," Shaw agreed. "Be my guest."

McCullough pulled a pair of purple latex gloves from her pocket and handed them to Jonah. He slid them on and was immediately hit by their smell. A sex-and-death smell, McCullough had once said. Jonah had laughed, and then felt a little nauseated the next time he'd torn into a foil packet and recognized the scent.

O'Malley crouched next to Jonah as he maneuvered a wallet out of the victim's back pocket. He opened it carefully and slid out a credit card, touching it as little as possible.

"A. Plaskitt," he said, and then continued to look through the cards until he found a gym membership. "Alex. Alex Plaskitt."

McCullough held out a plastic bag for Jonah to slide the wallet into, and he shifted so he could reach into the man's right-hand pocket, which looked like it might have a phone in it. It was much harder to pull out. The victim's legs were drawn up so that the phone was wedged against his hip. But by pushing it up from the outside of the pocket, Jonah managed to lever it out.

An iPhone. Fairly new, he thought, and cased in a plastic protector with an elaborate dragon pattern over it that almost matched his T-shirt.

Jonah pushed the home button and it lit up, showing a series of messages from someone saved as "Sex Kitten Issa."

Alex's girlfriend, probably, Jonah thought as he scanned them. The last one was from half an hour ago and read:

Where the fuck are you?

2

LOUISE

Niall, there's so much I need to tell you. A whole messy story that surrounds and encompasses the morning I woke up next to a stranger and panicked like I've never panicked before.

I know it might well be too late for any of this. I'm sitting here without you, and I'm not even sure I want you to come back. But after so many stupid secrets, I think it's time to lay everything bare.

And I should probably say here that I'm sorry for my part in it. I really am sorry for what a mess this has turned out to be and for the actions I took that led us here.

But apologizing isn't an explanation, as you've told me before. So here's everything, and it starts a lot further back than you might think. With the night we met, which was obviously also the night I met April. Though, in fact, there were three of you I met that night, and all of you came to dominate my life in a way I could never have predicted.

As much as you might want to believe that *you* started our story, it's abundantly clear to me that it was April Dumont who started it. Even you can't deny the power she has. Everyone was watching her during the wedding, from the moment she stomped in late, with her dress that showed off her midriff (and the side of each breast, too, just in case that wasn't enough). They stared at her tattoos. At her high-heeled cowboy boots that were the coolest fucking thing I had ever seen.

I bet you winced at that, didn't you? I bet if you were reading this in front of me, you'd roll your eyes and ask me if that kind of language was necessary.

Well, I'm afraid it is, my darling. This is a *fuck* kind of a story from start to finish, though I honestly will try to spare you whenever I can. I want you to keep reading, Niall. I really do.

So, back to that wedding, when I was still a meek, anxious, painfully shy person. I've often wondered what I would have turned out like if my darling mum had lived a little longer. If I'd spent my teenage years with her, instead of with my increasingly neurotic, messily grieving father. If I'd had someone to tell me how great I was. I might have been a confident, talkative young woman. I might have been *sexy*.

But there's no point wondering about that, really. I wasn't confident, or talkative, or sexy. I was shy and awkward and frightened of attention.

At least I was before April. Before my life was picked up and turned luminous by the cowboy-booted girl who made her noisy way up the aisle, ignoring all the other free seats, and came to sit next to me. Next to mousy little me.

It was me she rolled her eyes at over the truly awful poem the maid of honor read out. It was me she showed her service sheet to, with the word "cock" circled in the name of some poor composer called "Peacock." I was the one who started laughing, to the point where everyone around us turned to look, which made us partners in crime. And to my surprise, I found that I didn't mind being looked at just then. Not when April was on my team.

"Thank Christ that's over," she said, once the service was done, and if I hadn't already been in love with her, that strident Tennessee drawl would have clinched it. I didn't quite keep up with everything she said to me for the rest of the night, which I'm sure you can imagine. The high tempo and volume of her speech. The sudden low-voiced asides. But it didn't really matter.

She walked with me to the reception, telling me about her baby sister back home and how I looked just like her. Dee, she said. Dolores, but always called Dee. It seemed to mean something to her, that resemblance.

I asked her, keenly curious, how she'd ended up in Southampton. She just seemed so exotic to me and so out of place.

"You wouldn't believe it, but I used to work for Big Pharma, like the groom," she said, and grinned at me. "My first husband and I got jobs over here, and then got sick of the sight of each other. He went back home; I stayed. Though I got the hell out of that job."

"What do you do now?"

She gave me a sidelong look. "I do a little consulting for some of the pharma firms still. Freelance, you know. So I can tell them where to shove it when I want. But mostly I spend my third husband's money. It's a tough job, but someone's gotta do it."

I couldn't help laughing. And then, two seconds later, I half tripped on my heels and had to grab hold of someone's garden fence to steady myself, which for some reason made me laugh even harder.

"You OK?" she asked, and looped her arm through mine. "It's the weirdest thing. You're so like Dee! Almost, if you just had the accent . . . you could be twins."

"I'll work on it," I said.

As far as I can tell, she decided right then and there that we were going to be best friends forever.

She put her arm round me the moment we arrived at the reception, and glanced around until she saw someone with a tray of champagne. "Thank God," she said, and plucked two glasses from it.

I didn't want to tell her that I wasn't a drinker. It's a difficult thing to admit to someone who clearly sees alcohol as a lubricant to their social interactions. Which is why I never told you, either, Niall. I've consciously hidden the fact that, until that wedding, I was essentially teetotal.

The strangest thing is that I don't think you would have believed me if I'd told you. I'm pretty sure you're struggling to believe it now. You can't even begin to imagine a Louise who doesn't get shitfaced and out of control.

The truth is, I was genuinely afraid of being drunk. Still more afraid of humiliating myself or losing my keys or phone or, I don't know, some part of myself. My sense of control, maybe. I found the idea of not being in command of everything daunting.

But here was April, handing me a glass and necking hers before I could even start. I wanted, so badly, for her to keep liking me. And so I drank. Quickly. I loved April's approval as she put the empties back and grabbed two more. I loved, even more, the way she smiled at the waiter with a look that thanked him and hinted at a promise of something. And I decided that I was going to be like April, whatever it took.

I felt none of the dizziness I'd expected as the alcohol kicked in. I felt warmth instead. A sense of everything suddenly mattering less. It became easier to act like my new friend. To laugh and even, for the first time ever, to flirt.

April introduced me to the groom's side of the family. They actually seemed to like me, and that told me I was doing the right thing. I didn't resist when April took me to the bar, or to the washrooms, to touch up my eyeshadow and restyle my hair. Little by little, she managed to erase the Louise I'd been, and replace her with someone shinier. Better.

And in response, everyone suddenly seemed to want to talk to me. The DJ. That sultry Italian friend of April's. The best man, who was definitely married. They actually wanted to flirt with me and be flirted with. At twenty-eight I finally felt desirable.

Somewhere along the line, I began to imagine that I really *was* a new person. A bubblier, sexier, *better* Louise. I started to feel like

I was watching this better person interact, and the loss of control wasn't terrifying, like I'd expected. It was liberating.

In short, Niall, it was the birth of Drunk Louise. She didn't crawl out of some terrible depth like you might imagine; she emerged, butterfly-like, out of the drab, wilted chrysalis of my previous life. And God, I loved her.

You've told me how you felt the first time you saw me. How you were drawn to me, magnetically. Well, when you looked over at me and kept looking, it was this shiny new version of me that you were seeing.

I remember your expression. How you looked a little dazzled. And when you demanded to be introduced, it didn't surprise me as it might have. *Of course* you would like this new Louise. She was so much fun.

Drunk Louise somehow knew what she was doing when she looked at you archly and asked if you were anyone important.

I loved how you laughed. And even more how you said, "I'm the second most important person in this room."

"Come on, at least third," I told you. "Me, April . . . you can be third." It wasn't the kind of thing I'd ever said to anyone. But that new me somehow knew that she could.

"I can deal with third," you told me, which made me feel a rush of warmth toward you. It only got better when we bantered on for a bit and then you asked, "Shall we do some shit dancing?"

You weren't lying. It really was awful. I remember shaking my head at you in mock disappointment, while I couldn't stop grinning.

In the middle of it I was summoned to perform. I hadn't told either of you that Hannah had asked me to play a harp piece at the reception. I could tell that it added something to your liking for me, the fact that I was a musician too.

I was getting on for being very drunk as I settled myself on the hard chair and started to flow into the Bach. But as I have come to know since then, there's a sweet spot that you hit with alcohol. Where it loosens you up and makes you feel like you're part of your instrument. When *you* get out of the way, and something else takes over. Someone else. *Her.*

And there was that other feeling too. Of the way your eyes were on me during every touch of every string. I felt beautiful just then. Genuinely beautiful.

WHEN YOU'D GONE to the bar later on, April told me all about you and Dina. About how she'd lasted two months of marriage with you before deciding on an upgrade. April pointed out glamorous, hard-looking Dina and her new man to me. She did it too loudly, though, so that Dina looked over, and I cringed. But of course April didn't care. She just called, "Hey, Dina! Looking great!" and then steered us both away.

The story about Dina made me feel for you. It also made me admire you for having the courage to turn up at that wedding, when you knew your ex-wife would be there with her rich new boyfriend. It must all have been so raw. And when you were alone for any time, I could see the way your gaze would slide over to her. Each time it happened, you looked troubled. Confused, maybe.

It's strange how I felt a surge of jealousy erupt in me, even then. Or at least how quickly it erupted in *her.* It made Drunk Louise burn with fury and a desire to win. She didn't like being ignored, Niall. She didn't like it at all.

I asked April if she thought you were a good choice. I was almost afraid of what she might say. I'd already started to think of you as someone in my life, and in spite of the alcohol, I could feel nerves rising as she hesitated before answering.

But in the end, she said, "You know, I think he's a great choice. He's a kind person. Sometimes too kind, you know? Like, I think he's been taken advantage of in the past, because he likes to take care of people." She gave a grimace. "And he's probably a little hung up on what watch he's wearing or what car he's driving, but honestly, I think a lot of that came from Dina. I think he could shake it off."

"He isn't still in love with her?" I asked.

April gave this some thought. "No, I don't think he is. I mean, I half worry that it's too soon for him to move on, but actually, I think you'll be the best possible thing for him. Somcone with a good soul, to make him realize how shallow their relationship was."

I didn't know quite what to say to her amazing faith in me. But I stored it away and, in the way of stupid people the world over, decided that I could save you.

It was later on that the other thing happened. The thing I've always wondered if I should have paid more attention to. It was an argument between you and my new best friend. One I probably shouldn't have overheard and that I always doubted I'd got right.

The two of you were outside, where April had gone for a smoke. I'd finally, belatedly, remembered to congratulate the bride, after realizing I hadn't spoken to her once all day. By that time Hannah was reeling, and spent some time hugging me and kissing me on top of the head and telling me how glad she was to know me. Once I'd finally escaped, I came to find one or the other of you, not expecting to find you both together.

April was standing facing the gardens, on that little raised graveled terrace at the back of the house. I don't know if you remember it that clearly, but I do. It was beautiful, that place. Part of a night that seemed universally beautiful.

There wasn't as much to see now that it was dark. Just a few solar lanterns scattered through the grounds. But April was looking out at the view anyway, twisting her lower lip to blow smoke into the air.

And I'm positive you were saying to her, "Whatever you're scheming, I want you to leave her out of it."

"Oh, please," April said dismissively. "I have a right to talk to anyone I want."

And I remember that you made a frustrated huffing noise. You said, "What about everyone else's rights? Don't they matter?"

For a moment April just inhaled and exhaled, and then she said, "No, not really."

"Please," you said next, in what I now know to be a very rare tone of voice for you. "Please don't."

And April turned toward you and said, very slowly and clearly, as if she'd been play-acting with her tumbling sentences all evening, "I'm going to do exactly what I want."

Then she started to walk inside. And in the fraction of a second I stood there—before pretending I'd just arrived and greeting you both with false enthusiasm—I saw your expression. You looked desolate. Like a man who had just lost something.

3

The team held a miniature briefing outside the front garden of Number 11, their breath billowing into the air. Jonah kept it as swift as possible in the bitter cold, for his own sake as much as theirs.

"I'll take Juliette to see Alex's girlfriend," he told O'Malley and Lightman. "Domnall, you take Louise Reakes to the station to give her statement. And make sure she mentions the car engine on the record. I'd like Ben to check with this friend of Louise's to find out if she saw anything strange when she left the house. Louise thinks that was at about midnight. And, Domnall, see if you can find out when it snowed last night. We have footsteps probably belonging to the victim that were made after the snow stopped. Hopefully some of that might narrow our window before we get on to traffic cameras. Currently we're looking at twelve until four, and we've so far got two references to loud engine sounds last night."

Lightman nodded. "The neighbor in Number Nine also says he was woken by a door slamming at two. He thinks it was at the Reakes house, but I wouldn't rule out it being a car door."

"As far as Louise has said, there were no exits or entrances from her house after midnight," Jonah said. "So that could be interesting."

They ran for their cars after that. Jonah started up the Mondeo and watched his two sergeants maneuver their way out of the close before he eased out into the road ahead of Hanson. Policing was, as Jojo frequently liked to tell him, a very carbon-intensive job.

THE TRAFFIC WAS on the verge of becoming busy by the time Jonah drew up outside Alex Plaskitt's house. It was on Alma Road, barely a mile from where Alex had died.

Jonah always found this part of the city disorienting. As in the Polygon, across town, most of the streets here looked basically the same, with identikit pairs of semidetached houses set close to the road, each of them redbrick and touched with white details.

They were definitely a step down the ladder of affluence from Saints Close, but Jonah infinitely preferred the effect of these older, more modest buildings. Many of the owners on this side of the road had filled their tiny walled front gardens with brightly colored garden furniture and pots. In today's snow they looked Christmas-card pretty.

Hanson followed him up to the front door, looking less nervous than he had expected. This was only the second time his detective constable had broken the news of a death. Assuming, of course, that Alex's girlfriend actually lived here. The messages seemed to suggest so.

Having to give the worst news possible was grueling, and it never really stopped being grueling. You just found ways of distancing yourself.

Hanson seemed to have clocked some of those quickly. She was looking methodically at each detail of the house and street, noting it all, and clearly keeping her mind off what was about to come.

Jonah rang the old-fashioned push-button bell, and immediately heard rapid sounds from within the house. The door opened with some difficulty. It made a sliding sound and jammed, and whoever was behind it apologized.

When the door finally opened, it revealed a fairly short, lightly built man of thirty or so, who was in the process of returning some car keys to the top of the hall table. He was dressed quite formally for this early on a Saturday, in an open white shirt with a subtle stripe and a pair of stone-washed jeans. Dark, tired eyes. Black hair gelled until it stood up. A bronze complexion.

He put his left hand up to the doorframe, and Jonah saw that there was a wedding band on his fourth finger.

Issa, Jonah thought, unsure why he had assumed Alex's partner would be a woman.

The dark gaze darted between him and Hanson, and Jonah said quietly, "I think this is Alex Plaskitt's house."

Jonah saw the almost non-reaction he had grown used to. The stillness of Issa's body and the very slight brightening of his eyes.

"Would you be Issa?" Jonah tried next.

"Yes. What is it?"

"Might we come in?" Jonah asked.

Like almost everyone in this situation, Issa already knew what Jonah was going to say. Jonah could see it from the sagging of his body against the doorframe and then the uncoordinated way he turned to lead them into the colorful sitting room.

Any doubt that they had the right person disappeared as Jonah sat on the cushion-laden futon. A chrome-framed photograph on the table beside it showed Issa and their victim in wedding garb. They were grinning at the camera, Alex's head a good six inches higher than Issa's. He had one arm over the smaller man's shoulder. Alex looked about twice as wide as his husband too.

Jonah focused on Issa and took a breath. "I'm very sorry to have to tell you that Alex was found dead earlier this morning."

Issa's brow creased and he put a hand up to his mouth. "How?"

"It looks like he was attacked," Jonah said. "The pathologist will conduct a full postmortem, but it seems clear that he was a victim of violence."

Issa took a large, unsteady breath. "Was it at a club?"

"We're unsure where the attack took place," Jonah said carefully. "He was found outside a residential address."

Issa gave him a strange, sharp look. "What residential address?"

Hanson said soothingly, "A house on Saints Close. Do you know it?"

Issa shook his head immediately, and then stood up and went rapidly over to a desk. He picked up his phone, his hand shaking badly.

"He was supposed to come home," he said. "I tried calling him."

And then he started to cry.

"YOU SETTLE YOURSELF here, so," O'Malley told Louise Reakes, who was now fully clothed in a jersey dress with a fur-lined parka over the top. He placed an oversized mug of tea down on the interview-room table. "We'll get your statement done as soon as Detective Sergeant Lightman is back."

"Thank you," Louise said to him. Her hand went to the mug, but then dropped to the table. She stared at the steam, unmoving.

"When will your husband be home?" O'Malley asked, thinking of her going back to her house alone after this and having to walk past the place where the young lad had died. She could do with some support, he thought.

She looked up at him slowly, and said, "I'm not quite sure. Sometime in the afternoon, I think."

"Where's he coming from?"

"Geneva."

"Ah, so a fair distance." O'Malley nodded. "He must be worried about you."

There was a moment where Louise just stared at him, in apparent incomprehension, and then she said, "He won't be worried. I haven't told him yet."

O'Malley found himself looking back at her with much the same expression. "Did you not send him a message or so?"

Louise shook her head, glancing down at the phone she'd placed on the table in front of her, and then, in an agitated movement, folded her arms over herself. "No. I wasn't sure I should."

"Well, I'd do that," O'Malley said quietly. "You'll feel better once you've talked about it."

She didn't look at his sympathetic smile but instead angled her head to look toward the floor.

"I'll leave you to it," he said.

Louise's face seemed to grow, if anything, paler as she nodded. By the time O'Malley left, she'd made no move to pick up her phone.

LIGHTMAN HAD TRIED calling Louise's friend April a few times with no joy. In the end he'd decided to drive over to her flat on Admirals Quay. It made up part of the very modern Ocean Village development on the dockside, and Lightman knew from having looked idly at the brochure once that the flats were well beyond his price range.

The ground floor was like a hotel. There was a bar, a concierge service, and a lift that you needed a key fob to operate. Lightman persuaded the concierge to rouse April Dumont and grant him access to the lift. The graying man leaned in and pressed the button for the top floor before inclining his head and turning away. The whole process made Lightman feel awkward.

It turned out that April's flat actually occupied the whole of the top floor. He stepped out of the lift into a hallway with a single door. The space was lit in gold colors and featured what Lightman thought of as show-home furniture. It didn't display many signs of anyone living there. This was an entirely different world from Louise Reakes's solid suburban semi, and Lightman wondered what April did for a living.

The door opened before he'd got there, and a messy-haired

blond woman wearing a very short negligee with a silk dressing gown slung over it asked hoarsely, "What's going on?"

"I'm so sorry to wake you," he said, coming to stand a little in front of her. He felt the inevitable discomfort of standing in front of a woman wearing very little. So he did what he generally did and reduced the experience to a cataloging one. He noted her accent, which had the drawl of an American from the Deep South or Midwest. He saw the makeup smudged below her eyes. The glazed expression. The tattoo visible just above the line of the negligee. "I just need to ask two or three very brief questions about yesterday evening."

"Yesterday?" April asked.

"A young man was found dead in the garden of a house on Saints Close this morning," Lightman told her. "I believe you were there last night."

"What the hell?" April asked. She stood back, suddenly, and said, "OK, come in for a second. It's just me. . . ."

He followed her into a huge, light living area with blocky modern chairs, floor-to-ceiling windows, and a view of the harbor on two sides. Like the hallway, it looked almost unlived-in. Only a pair of used tumblers, a pack of cigarettes, and a lighter on the coffee table spoiled the show-home effect.

April flung herself onto one of the sofas with a very quiet groan.

"OK. Better." She brushed some of her hair back out of her eyes. "Sorry. I may have overdone the tequila yesterday. Please speak slowly."

"Of course," Lightman said. "It shouldn't take long. We just wanted to confirm what time you left the house, and whether you saw or heard anything strange."

April continued to fiddle with her hair as she thought. "The cab must've arrived at eleven-fifteen. I booked it just before eleven, and there was a little wait."

"Was there anyone outside at that point?"

"Not that I saw," April said, and then she looked at him with more focus. "Hey, is Louise OK? You said this dead guy was in the front yard? Garden?"

"Yes. Louise seems all right, but finding him was obviously a bit of a shock."

"Jesus." April's expression was dark. "I'll drop her a line."

"Did you hear anyone driving around?" Lightman went on. "Any strange sounds?"

There was another pause, and April shook her head. "No. The cab was sitting there with its lights on and the engine off, so you'd think we would have heard anything. . . . Does Louise remember hearing something?"

"Nothing definitive," Lightman replied.

April nodded, very slowly. "Shit," she said. "This is the last damn thing Louise needs. The last."

4

LOUISE

So. You know now how Drunk Louise was first born. It may surprise you to know that I almost turned my back on her the next day. I'd never had a hangover before, and this one was so intense that I honestly thought I'd damaged myself irreparably. I was sick all day, right up until four P.M., and for all of that wretched time I could only look back on every single thing I'd done with nauseated regret.

But then April got in touch to arrange a coffee, telling me she needed me in her life. And you messaged me later on, as you'd promised. You told me how much fun I was and how much you'd like to see me again.

These were two sudden points in Drunk Louise's favor, and as the mild alcohol poisoning receded, I imagined that I might be able to drink again, if I was more careful.

It helped Drunk Louise's case that I was nervous about meeting you when I was sober. I had no idea how to flirt without her help. So having booked in a date, I decided that I'd let myself have a few glasses before we met.

It was such a relief to feel it happening again. To feel her take over. It was like putting on the warmest of coats. If you can imagine a warm coat that somehow also made me look smoking hot.

I still could have kept it under control, I think, even then. I wasn't inclined to drink most of the time. It was just a few drinks when I hung out with April, which I'd started to do twice a week. Though it was generally more than a few when I saw you.

I think you finally, belatedly, need to take a little responsibility for that, Niall. Drunk Louise didn't gain power and frequency without help. She bloomed under your encouragement as much as mine.

I want you to think back to those first dates of ours. To think back honestly, and to ask yourself how they must have been for me. How hard it was every time you told me about Dina, and about the raw anger you felt toward her. The hurt.

It's not the only thing I remember about those dates, of course. I remember learning things about you. Your hatred of ABBA. Your love of Miles Davis and Nat King Cole. Your secret obsession with *Star Wars*, which nobody from work was allowed to know about. Your equal love of food and your determination to eat organic.

I'm aware of your influence on me too. It was through you that I started to appreciate really good food. Beyond pizza, I mean, which I've always enjoyed heart and soul. The first time you cooked beef Wellington, it was a revelation. It was extraordinary to me that you could make something so good in an ordinary kitchen.

You laughed at me as I gorged myself on three helpings.

"There's a whole other course to come, you know," you told me.

I said I'd just have to borrow another stomach from somewhere, and you gave me the hugest grin. You told me how happy you were that I enjoyed food.

"It was so frustrating being with someone who was constantly dieting," you said. "Dina made food her enemy."

I honestly didn't know whether I felt good about that or awful. I washed away any more thought with another glass of Médoc.

I also learned in those early days that you were far more impulsive than I have ever been. Far more likely, too, to put everything off until tomorrow. I remember being fascinated and horrified when you said you'd leave the washing-up until the morning. How I itched to do it, because I knew I would lie awake worrying about it. Though, in fact, by the time we'd spent a good hour in extended lovemaking, I slept like a baby. It was a revelation.

You were far more comfortable in your own skin too. Watching you speak to waiters and waitresses with warmth and without worry made me feel safe for some reason. And witnessing the way you laughed when you dropped something or screwed up filled me with wonder. Where was the immediate self-loathing that plagued me? And why weren't you angry when I messed up too?

It occurred to me, for what was honestly the first time in my life, that I didn't actually need to be hard on myself. That there was a choice in this. And every time I broke a glass or lost something, as you rubbed my arm and helped me sort it out, I let a little bit of the dislike I'd long felt toward myself drift away.

In fact, Niall, if it hadn't been for Dina, you might have been nothing but good for me.

5

"We'd really appreciate any information you can give us on Alex's movements last night," Hanson said to Issa quietly, once his racking sobs had subsided into occasional juddering breaths. Jonah was happy to let her be the comforting presence in this conversation. He'd never been sure he was that good at it. "I know it's hard when you're trying to process this, but the more quickly we start looking for Alex's killer, the more likely we are to bring them to justice."

Issa nodded, drew in another breath, and then nodded again. "Yes. Yes, I want to—help." He turned his eyes up toward the ceiling, gathering himself together. "Alex was out with one of his—our friends." He looked at Hanson. "I was away. I didn't get back until one, and he was still out. I wasn't there to protect him."

Jonah gave him a nod. The idea of the diminutive Issa protecting the powerful Alex looked a little ridiculous on the face of it, but there were other forms of protection than the physical. There was, for example, the kind that involved persuading someone to stop drinking when they'd had enough. Or that talked them out of aggressive behavior.

"Do you know where they went?" he asked.

"Yes." He nodded. "A gig in the Porterhouse, and then they ended up staying out." He shook his head. "The last I heard from him—they were in Blue Underground, and he was quite drunk."

The tears gained the upper hand for a few moments, and then Jonah asked him, "Could we have the friend's name?"

He nodded, silently at first, before managing to say, "Step. Step Conti. He's Stefano, but he's only ever called Step."

"You know this friend well?"

"Yes," Issa said, swallowing. "He's a good friend to both of us. Alex likes to go out—with Step and a couple of others. I sometimes join them and sometimes leave them to it. I'm not quite such a hard drinker." He gave a watery smile.

"You don't think he could have . . . argued with Alex?"

"No, of course not," Issa said, his voice shaking. "He was his friend. I don't know how . . . If Step had been there, he would have helped. You don't know what happened to him?"

"I'm afraid not," Hanson said. "You presumably haven't spoken to Step this morning."

"No." Issa shook his head. "It didn't—occur to me, for some reason. I just thought Alex had got drunk and—and maybe was sleeping off his hangover there."

"So you can't be certain that Step wasn't involved?" she went on.

Issa's gaze flicked from Hanson to Jonah and then it rested back on Hanson.

"No," Alex's husband said in the end. "I just don't think he could be."

Hanson gave him a half-smile, one of those expressions that sat uniquely between solemn sympathy and warm support. It was a hard expression to pull off, and Hanson, Jonah thought, did it very well. "Of course. We'll need to talk to him."

"Yes. Yes." Issa picked up his phone from the side table and read out Step's number and then his address, both of which Jonah wrote down.

"Are there other family members we should inform?" Hanson asked gently, once that was done. "Parents? Siblings? Or would you prefer to call them?"

Issa's expression made Jonah's chest ache. He was so transparently a man unable to believe he really had to do this.

"His parents live in Surrey," he said inconsequentially. "I'd . . . rather you told them. We never got on all that well."

Once they had taken their contact details, Jonah told Issa as gently as possible that he would need to identify the body, either in person or over a video link. Alex's husband shook his head at the suggestion of a remote link.

"I have to see for myself."

"The coroner requested a postmortem," Jonah said. "I know it's a hard thing to have to deal with right now, but it will help us. It's standard practice with a sudden death like this. Once that's done, we'll call you in."

"What if—what if it isn't him?" Issa's eyes were large and dark, and full of a peculiar hope. "What if you've got it wrong?"

Jonah found himself momentarily unable to think of anything to say. He couldn't tell Issa that he had seen the body, and knew that it was Alex. It seemed unreasonably cruel. And yet to say anything else seemed even crueler.

"We'll make sure we get everything right," Hanson said after a moment. "We'll take every care. We owe it to you and the victim."

It seemed to be the right thing to say. Issa nodded, and then said quietly, "Thank you."

JONAH SENT A swift text to Jojo as they headed back to the car, explaining that his Saturday now looked to be a write-off. She was supposed to be taking him indoor climbing, his first proper introduction to her slightly obsessive hobby. He was sadder about not getting to see her than he was about dodging the session, but he knew she would happily head down there without him anyway. Jojo was never short of climbing buddies.

And then he called Alex's parents through the Mondeo's Bluetooth, with Hanson listening in from her own car via Skype. They needed to inform the family of the death now, before it reached them in another way. Although Jonah hated giving news like this over the phone, it was the only real option when the parents lived hundreds of miles away.

Issa had given them a landline number for the Plaskitts. Alex's father answered with that fantastically old-fashioned method of reciting his own phone number. His voice was the full upper-class Surrey gentleman, which was not quite what Jonah had been expecting.

"I believe you're Alex Plaskitt's father?" Jonah asked, having introduced himself quickly.

"Yes," the urbane voice said, and there was the sound of a door closing afterward, as if he'd decided the call needed privacy. Jonah expected him to give his name, but he went on, "Is there . . . has Alex . . . done something?"

"I'm very sorry to have to tell you that we have bad news. Alex was found dead this morning. It looks like he was attacked."

There was a silence, and then Alex's father said, "Are you—are you sure?"

"His husband is going to identify the body shortly, but the victim matches Alex's description and was carrying his ID. Alex didn't return home last night."

Another, longer pause followed, and then the father said, "That's . . . terribly sad news. Thank you for letting us know." There was an audible breath in. "Is there anything we need to do?"

"At present there's nothing pressing, but we will need to know anything you think might help us. Anybody who wished Alex harm. Any recent arguments. Any involvement with potentially violent groups."

"I'm . . . sorry, Chief Inspector," Mr. Plaskitt answered, "but I don't think we'll be able to help. We've hardly seen Alex since he moved to Southampton. Perhaps three or four times in five years.

He's drifted out of touch, and we don't really know anything about his life."

"Why might he have lost touch?"

"Well. I suppose he didn't really fit in at home. In staid old Surrey." There was a note of slightly cutting irony to the remark. "He changed when he went to school, and then more at university, in Brighton. He fell in with a . . . a group that wasn't what we really wanted. We felt that he'd been led astray. That they'd indoctrinated him." Alex's father sighed. "I suppose we let our disapproval be known a little too much, and Alex decided it was easier not to see us."

"I see," Jonah said, wondering at Mr. Plaskitt's calm. At his collected, unemotional speech, when his son had just been murdered. Everyone dealt with news of death differently, but Alex's father seemed to be barely affected by it. "So when was the last time you saw him?"

"It would have been . . . the Christmas before last. So a little over a year ago." There was a trace of emotion this time. Embarrassment, Jonah thought.

"And did anything in particular happen then? A . . . disagreement?" Jonah asked.

There was a pause once again, and then Mr. Plaskitt said, "No more than at any other family Christmas. Emotions ran high, and Alex got upset that we weren't being kind enough to his other half. Which was an unfair accusation. We have always welcomed him into our home, despite the personal pain we've felt."

Jonah could well imagine why they felt pain at Alex's marriage, and decided to shift the topic of conversation.

"I'm happy to come to Surrey to talk further, but it might be that you'd prefer to come here, to Southampton."

"Oh. Yes. Well, it doesn't sound like there's any need for that right now, does it?"

Jonah heard a very faint indrawn breath from Hanson.

"It might be more for your benefit, Mr. Plaskitt," he said gently. "To allow you to ask questions and talk to Alex's friends."

"Edward, please," Alex's father replied. He hesitated before saying, "I'll discuss it with my wife. It might be better anyway for you to see our daughter, Phoebe. She lives in Winchester, so she's much closer to you."

"Thank you," Jonah said. "Would you be able to text us her details?"

He recited the contact number and then said, "I'd like to send a police community support officer to see you in the interim."

"I . . . No, that won't . . ." Edward's voice sounded defensive. Almost angry. "I think we'd prefer to grieve in private, if you don't mind."

"Of course. I understand. Thank you for your help, Edward."

Jonah ended the call with Edward, and the moment it showed up as complete, Hanson said, "That was like a lesson in respectable homophobia. That poor lad, having a dad like that! Talking about how 'painful' it was, having to socialize with his husband . . .'"

"I hope it's more complex than that," Jonah said, "but I suspect you may be spot-on."

"Can we arrest him?" she asked. "Just to ruin his day?"

"If you can think of any reasonable charges," Jonah replied, grinning.

JONAH WAS KEEN to talk to Step Conti, but given he was out in the New Forest, it made no sense for Hanson to drive there separately. They both went via the station and Jonah hovered while Hanson parked. He fielded a brief reply from Jojo while he waited.

A major incident is a pretty long way to go to avoid getting shown up on a wall, Copper Sheens. But I suppose I'll let you get away with it this once. J xx

Jonah couldn't help laughing, as he so often did when communicating with Jojo. He sometimes caught himself in the middle of it all, wondering exactly how he had become so happy.

This wasn't how any of his previous relationships had gone. Particularly not the slow splintering of his six-year relationship with Michelle. And it was strange remembering that he'd jeopardized a future with Jojo only four months ago, before their relationship had even begun.

He'd known how he felt about Jojo by then. He'd only been waiting for her to come back from Africa before trying to pursue anything. It should have been enough to make him resist anything else. But he had bumped into his ex-fiancée while very drunk, and it had been like being hit over the head with past regret. Michelle had been rolling drunk, too, and the result had been pretty inevitable.

The morning after, he'd thought he actually wanted Michelle back. That was the strangest bit. He'd spent the day after their liaison depressed that his ex-fiancée seemed uninterested.

He could only feel profoundly grateful, in retrospect, that Michelle hadn't wanted to pick things up again. For once in his troubled romantic life, things had turned out for the best. And he knew enough to grab on to that lucky break with both hands and make the most of it.

HANSON TOOK A moment, once in the car, to message Jason. She knew he'd been planning on working today, which meant they would both end up in CID at some point. A slight compensation for a ruined weekend.

Jason, a detective inspector with one of Sheens's fellow DCIs, generally worked a lot more independently than Hanson did. He was happiest playing lone investigator. And though he was obsessive about his work to the point where he sometimes seemed flat-out moody, he was a kind soul underneath it all.

Their relationship was a strange one. Hanson had certainly

never intended to get involved with Jason, and wasn't aware that she'd ever flirted. A sudden invitation for a drink (which had come during the rather heightened emotions at the end of a case) had been accepted, and had turned into a series of drinks. She'd been very reluctant to let those drinks become something more, not least because she wasn't sure how she felt about anything at the time.

But sometimes, Hanson had learned, you ended up falling into things without consciously choosing them. The drinks had turned into dinners, and then, a month after the first one, into going home together for the first time. And it was all . . . nice. Simple, normal, and worlds apart from her abusive relationship with Damian.

The only downside to it all was that she and Ben Lightman no longer seemed to be friends. Things had got suddenly awkward, and it was hard to get her head around given that she and Ben had no history.

There had, it was true, been a weird long hug a few hours before she'd gone for that first drink with Jason, an event that still made her feel embarrassed and strangely sad to think about. But that wasn't really a reason for things to have turned sour, and she was at a loss to explain why everything had changed so quickly. Why she always resorted to false cheerfulness, and why he had become as distant and as detached from her as if they'd never been friends.

STEP CONTI LIVED not far from Jojo. He was on the edge of the New Forest in West Wellow, which was a little less picturesque than Furzley. There were more blocky '60s structures, retirement bungalows, and modern touches. The effects of lying just outside the boundary of the national park. Modernity had been allowed to creep in.

Step's house, however, was on a lane that ran southwest out of the village into an open area of heathland. Houses lined one side of the tarmac with unspoiled land on the other. Today, with a fall of snow over it all, it looked dazzling.

Jonah eased the Mondeo along the lane carefully, trying to stay on the road surface as he maneuvered around parked cars. There were deep, snowy tire tracks running down the side, and he had no desire to test out the car's four-wheel drive just now.

Step's house, at the far end, had a new-looking wooden gate and a thickly graveled drive. Someone had tied a pair of balloons to the gate, one pink and one blue. Jonah winced, thinking that a murdered friend was not the sort of news to be bringing to a kids' party.

The gravel driveway held only a metallic red Qashqai and a bike rack with one small pink bike in it. Which hopefully meant they had arrived before the party kicked off.

"Ready for another one?" Jonah asked Hanson, once they'd emerged from the car.

She gave him a wry expression. "Totally. Can't think of anything I'd rather be doing."

They approached the house, which bore signs of recent and extensive work. Jonah wondered whether this had once been a '70s bungalow, like a lot of the other homes in the village. Whatever the original building, the finished product was both large and elegant.

He rang the bell, and was rewarded by the sound of thundering feet on stairs. Hanson made an uncomfortable noise, and muttered, "They are definitely not expecting the police."

It was a relief when the door was opened by a sandy-haired young woman in a polo-necked sweater instead of any children. The young woman was in the midst of saying, "Probably the postman," when her eyes took them in properly, and she hesitated.

"I'm so sorry for coming unannounced," Jonah said, giving her a slight smile, "but might we speak to Step? I'm DCI Sheens, with the Hampshire Police."

He saw her give a shiver, and then nod. She turned to say, "Just someone for Daddy. Let's finish the banner."

As she let them in, Jonah had a glimpse of a small girl in a blue ballet outfit and a slightly older boy dressed as what looked like a witch before their small forms disappeared back upstairs.

"Step!" the woman called toward the back of the house. "For you!"

She hovered in the hallway watching them, before suddenly saying, "Karen," and holding out a hand. Jonah shook it. Karen looked as if she wanted to ask them something, but then decided against it.

A few moments later, a young dark-haired man appeared. He was something of a surprise. His name alone had made Jonah picture Italian flamboyance. Instead he had what Jonah would have described as slightly bland good looks. He was carrying a box full of brightly colored plastic balls, his expression patient. The whole impression was of a family man.

Step looked slightly puzzled. "Sorry, is it . . ."

"They're the police," his wife said in a falsely cheerful voice. She glanced at Jonah, and said, "Do you want me . . . ?"

"That's absolutely up to you," Jonah answered.

"You'd probably better stay with the kids," Step said, and gave her a nod. His accent was totally English. Jonah guessed he was at least a second-generation immigrant of Italian parents.

"We just need a quick conversation about Alex Plaskitt," Hanson said.

"Alex?" Step gave her a blank look. "Why . . ." He suddenly seemed to remember himself. "Sorry, why don't you . . . ?"

He turned as if to lead them into what looked like a sitting room, and then hesitated.

"Probably quieter in the kitchen," he said, and walked instead into a room with warm red flagstones on the floor and light-colored farmhouse furniture everywhere else.

He settled himself at the large wooden table, putting the box of balls down carefully on the floor. While Jonah and Hanson pulled out chairs, he looked on calmly. Patiently.

"I'm very sorry to have to break the news," Jonah said, "but Alex was found dead in the early hours of this morning."

There was a long moment while Step seemed to process this. And then he said, "Oh, Jesus." He looked away. "How did it happen? Was he robbed?"

"It seems not," Jonah told him. "As yet, it's unclear what happened. We wondered if you could help by telling us about yesterday evening."

"Sure," Step said. "I . . . God, it might all be my fault." There was little emotion in his expression, but Step paused again as if working this through internally. "I went home and left him. I knew he was a bit drunk, but I . . . maybe he was too drunk to look after himself."

"Can you tell me where the two of you went?"

"I'm sorry," Step said, lifting a hand toward his head and then letting it fall. "A gig. A friend's band was playing at the Porterhouse. And then we went to Blue Underground."

"That's a bar?"

"A club," Step told him. "On London Road. Farther up past the Wetherspoons?"

Jonah knew London Road well, at least as it had once been. He had spent months doing circuits of the pubs up there at seventeen, eighteen, nineteen. Back when his friends had been in feverish pursuit of university girls and had abandoned their traditional stomping ground around the quay in order to track them down. There had been clubs back then, too, each of them attempting to seduce those same university girls just as feverishly, because where the women went, the men would follow. And so the road had been awash with laminated boards from nine o'clock onward. Two Malibu and Cokes for a quid. Two-for-one Blue Lagoons. Free entry for ladies before eleven.

That part of it probably hadn't changed, even if the prices had.

"How long were you there?" he asked Step.

"We went at about ten-thirty, and I was there until . . . twelve? Maybe just before?" Step swallowed hard. "I had to get back. It's Lisa's birthday today. We had a lot of prep to do for the party."

"You weren't to know," Jonah said quietly. "What was Alex doing when you left?"

Step lifted his head. "He was dancing. In the—in the eighties room."

"With anyone?"

"No." Step shrugged. "He generally just dances by himself. He loves it. He's a great dancer." And then Step tailed off, halted by the inevitable clash between tenses; between someone who *is* and, quite suddenly, someone who *was*.

"He definitely wasn't talking to anyone else?"

Step thought for a while and then said, "No. No, he was definitely on his own."

"Had he . . . talked to anyone earlier in the evening?"

"Not at any length," Step said with a shrug. "Brief chats with the bar staff, that kind of thing. Nothing that would make me think . . . that implied he might have argued with anyone."

"There was nobody in the club who seemed to recognize him?" Hanson asked.

Step shook his head slowly. "No, I don't think so."

Jonah nodded, his eyes roaming the orderly kitchen before coming to rest on Step again.

"Can you tell me what Alex was like?" Jonah asked. "Was he patient? Boisterous?"

Step fixed him with a slightly bright-eyed gaze. "You mean do I think he brought it on himself?" Step shook his head. "He was a profoundly gentle person. And a kind one. Even when he was trashed, he was always a good guy."

"Did he get drunk a lot?" Hanson asked.

"Every so often." Step gave a shrug. "Like most guys in their late twenties. Probably less than most, really. He believed too much in his health."

Jonah gave him a nod. "How's his relationship with his husband been recently?"

"Good," Step said. "It's never been anything other than good. Issa and he were . . . They were close from the moment they met. They look after each other."

"There's nobody Alex has had any disagreements with recently?" Hanson tried. "No involvement with any groups that might have wanted him dead?"

"No," Step said, shaking his head more quickly. "He was likable, and definitely law-abiding."

"Thank you," Jonah said. "I'd really like to know anything else you think might help. People he might have met up with. Messages he sent. Anything."

"Of course," Step said. And then he leaned forward, so that his elbows rested on his knees, and asked, "You don't have any ideas, do you? Who it was?"

"We're doing our utmost to find out," Jonah said as soothingly as he could.

"OK. OK."

During the drive home, Jonah found himself wondering about that last question of Step's. Questions like that could come from wanting a loved one's killer brought to justice. But they also might come from a fear of being found out.

"It's a little weird," O'Malley muttered, as he and Jonah stood looking in at Louise Reakes from the observation room. "I don't know if she's called him now, but when I mentioned it she looked like the thought made her ill. It made me wonder about him. Maybe he did know the guy. Maybe Alex was a friend of his. Could be nothing, but could be some kind of criminal involvement, if she's scared of him. Ben's looking him up on the system to see if there's anything."

Jonah nodded, considering. "I guess criminals can live in suburban bliss too. I'll talk to her."

"I've told her you just wanted to drop in before she goes. We've got the statement. I didn't push her."

Jonah smiled. "I can do the pushing. Anything else?"

"I was looking at the weather for last night," O'Malley said. "It's tricky to be positive, but as far as I can make out from a number of sites, it snowed somewhere between one-thirty and four A.M. across most of the city. We'll probably know more if we get CCTV footage, though that won't be local to Saints Close."

"Potentially useful," Jonah said. "If we could at least rule out him dying after four A.M., that's a start." And then he let himself into the interview room and sat in front of Louise, who moved ever so slightly away from him.

"Thank you for giving your statement," Jonah said. "There are just a few things I wanted to check."

Louise fixed her eyes on him and nodded. "Sure."

"Going back, first, to this question of the victim's identity," he began. "It seems strange that the young man would have ended up in your front garden if he was unknown to you."

Louise lifted her hands, a helpless gesture. "I know. I have no idea why he'd come to us, unless it happened to be the nearest house, and he was desperate. If it were me, I suppose I could see myself aiming for the porch light, hoping for help." Her lips twisted. "Poor fucker. Bleeding out his life without . . . without anyone even knowing."

"Someone knew," Jonah said quietly.

The sharp look she gave him made him reassess her. Louise might be hungover and afraid, but she wasn't in any way stupid.

"Mrs. Reakes," he said in a harder tone, "I'm sure you're

aware that we'll need to speak to your husband directly. It would save us time if you could pass on his contact details."

There was a curious twist to Louise's face as she said, "But I haven't—been able to get through to him yet. Do you mind if I try again before you call? Just so he doesn't lose his shit?"

Jonah nodded, slowly, finding the occasional peppering of profanities a little disconcerting. They were a strange contrast to her otherwise meek manner.

"We'd appreciate it if you'd call him as soon as we're done here. Straight afterward."

"Yes," Louise said, and swallowed. "Of course."

Jonah watched her for a few seconds, happy to let her discomfort increase. He agreed wholeheartedly with O'Malley. Something about contacting her husband concerned her. Was it possible that he wasn't, in fact, away? That he had murdered a man at their property and then gone to ground?

"When did you last speak to him? Your husband?"

"Yesterday," Louise said. And then, when Jonah watched her without replying, she added, "Before April turned up. Probably . . . five?"

"Can I take your friend's full name?"

"It was just over the phone, though. My chat with Niall. Why do you want to know?"

Jonah allowed the silence to build, considering his options, and then he decided that pushing her now, while she was tired, hungover, and anxious, was probably his best option. "Is your husband really away, Louise?" he asked.

She gave him a genuinely startled look. "Of course he is. I wouldn't have got drunk with April if he . . . Niall's been in Geneva since Thursday."

"And this was a work trip?"

"Pharmaceuticals conference," she said. "He's a rep. He does this a lot. Takes GPs to nice places and spoils them." She suddenly gave a strange half-smile. "Look, he has nothing to do with what happened."

"Then why are you afraid of contacting him?" Jonah asked, his eyes fixed on her face.

He saw a blush creep up Louise's neck, and then she said quietly, "Because Niall is . . . he can be a tad self-righteous. He'll be angry with me for getting drunk. He'll think this is my fault."

Jonah gave a small, involuntary smile. "I think he'd be hard-pressed to make a dead man in your garden your fault."

Louise looked up at him, with that half-smile back on her lips. "You haven't met my husband."

6

LOUISE

The first night that really fucked things up for us was my birthday. Though it wasn't the night itself. It was, of course, Dina. Your gorgeous, hideous ex.

God, I hate remembering it. Dina suddenly *had* to meet you for lunch that day. And it was incredibly clear to me what she was going to say. I suspect it was to you too. You went along hoping she wanted you back.

And of course that was what she was going to say, whether it was true or not. It was my birthday. What better time to ruin things for both of us? I can imagine how she let delicate tears slide down her cheeks as she told you she'd made a mistake. That she missed you. It was deliberate and predictable and thoroughly, thoroughly cruel.

I've never quite been able to admit to you how much I hate Dina. How could I, when you cycled so regularly through fury at her and sudden loyalty? When it was OK for you to call her a horrible human being, but absolutely out of the question for me to do the same?

That day justified every thought I'd had about her. It was abundantly clear after you'd met her that you were halfway to being hers again, and my birthday party became a hollow, bitter experience when it should have been fun.

I drank more than I've ever drunk before. I started early on, with April. I had never valued more her freedom to sack off work and drink whenever she felt like it. And although I didn't tell her why I was so determined to get shitfaced, she drank with me through the afternoon anyway, and managed to make me laugh a few times in spite of everything.

I kept going once we all met up for cocktails. While you hunkered over your phone at the bar instead of mingling with my friends, I drank. I waited for Drunk Louise—*her*—to take over so I didn't have to feel. But that happy-go-lucky, irresponsible version of myself somehow stayed away, no matter how hard I chased. It was the first time she'd let me down.

So I kept chasing her. I chased Drunk Louise so hard that I eventually vomited into the toilet for twenty minutes.

When I emerged afterward, stumbling and probably smelling of vomit, you looked horrified. Appalled. Like you were wondering what you'd been thinking. I wasn't the wonderful, fun Drunk Louise: I was a mess. I was so ashamed, and so very much aware that April was now watching too.

I honestly thought I'd lost both of you.

But then my best friend took my hand and turned to face you. "What the hell are you doing, Niall?"

You looked genuinely taken aback. *"Me?"*

"Yeah, you," she said. "You have a girlfriend you don't deserve. She's gorgeous and talented and smart. And on her birthday you've been standing at the bar and messaging your ex-wife. I'm not surprised she wanted to get blind drunk. I'd have done the same, only I would have dumped your lousy ass first."

For a moment you just stood there looking at her with your mouth slightly open. And then you looked away, gathering together what I fully expected to be anger. I thought you were going to tell us both to get lost.

But when you turned back again, it was as if something had

given way in you instead. You looked so guilty, and so sad. I think that expression was what saved us just then. What let us carry on.

"I'm—I'm really sorry, Lou. She's just . . ." You shook your head. "It's all messing with my head, but I'll sort myself out."

"You need to know something about Dina," April added. "You need to realize that she would throw you under a bus without even thinking about it. She's actually tried to do it already, Niall. It's me who stood in the way."

And I saw the way your expression changed. How your mouth dropped slightly and your eyes fixed on her.

"What do you mean?" you asked.

"What the fuck do you think I mean, Niall?" she asked with a raised eyebrow.

I watched your expression as you looked down at your phone and then slowly put it away. And after that, when you folded me into a hug, and told me you were being an idiot, all my anger and distrust seemed unimportant. I let it all go, and let you look after me.

But the damage had already been done, I think. The slide had already started. I began to obsess over what you'd been saying to Dina and, unable to cope with those feelings, I drank. I couldn't think of any other way of dealing with them.

On top of that, my fear grew that you didn't really like my sober self. Everything you told me that you loved about me was really about Drunk Louise. The fun. The laughter. The way I made your life better. I knew it was Drunk Louise you'd fallen in love with.

So the more time we spent together, the more she bloomed. And although I'd got to know April better by then, in sober times as well as drunk, I developed a profound fear that she might decide I was boring too. Which meant that I never turned up sober to see either of you.

I was aware, though, of a growing disconnect between Drunk

Louise and me. I would occasionally be alarmed at things she'd done. Like the time she talked you into getting sexy in an office at your work Christmas party. Like when she and April stole a bottle of champagne from an unattended hotel bar in London. And there were increasing blanks in my memory too. Whole hours or parts of evenings where I didn't know what she'd done, and felt nervous about finding out.

I thought it was all OK, though. It was only later that I began to be afraid of her.

7

ightman was making good progress with checking up on the Reakes family. He had so far established that neither had a criminal record, and that Niall Reakes had a strong and respectable Internet presence through his drug-rep work. He'd worked with several of the bigger pharma companies, and was currently listed with Pollai as a clinical sales specialist in the field of arthritis.

His LinkedIn photo was a classic black-and-white headshot, with Niall coming off as both impressive and approachable, an effect helped by his slightly chubby face and beaming grin. There was nothing to suggest any criminal involvement: no articles in which he featured, and no apparent firings, though that didn't mean they hadn't happened. It wasn't the policy of big firms to broadcast bad hires.

Louise Reakes had her own slick-looking website. It advertised her services as a wedding, event, film, and TV harpist, with an impressive list of past work. It was a hugely visual site, with slowly fading images of spring sunshine and Louise herself playing while draped in long, floaty dresses.

He'd just about finished looking the site over when a call came in on the team's line. Hanson was immersed in something on-screen, headphones in and eyes following some video, so

Lightman picked up and found himself talking to the duty sergeant.

"I have a caller. He says he's the dead man's husband."

Issa Benhawy, Lightman remembered from Hanson's brief update.

"Put him through."

There was a click, and then a very precise voice asked, "DCI Sheens?"

"This is DS Lightman," he said. "I work with the DCI. He's just tied up, but perhaps I can help?"

"Oh, I see." There was a pause, and then Issa said, "I just wondered about Alex's things. I don't want them getting lost."

"I understand your concern." Lightman pulled his notebook closer and clicked his pen out. "We do label and store everything carefully during inquiries, so everything will be kept safely and returned to you as soon as possible. Was there something in particular . . . ?"

There was another pause, and Issa said, "There's a ring that I gave him. And—and his phone." When Lightman didn't immediately reply, he added, quickly, "It's full of photos. I don't want them getting lost."

"Of course," Lightman replied, writing carefully in the notebook. "With the phone, it's hard to say exactly when that will come back. Our tech team won't delete anything, but phones often reveal a lot about who's been in touch with the victim."

"I can help you with that," Issa said immediately.

"That's very good of you, but there might be people you weren't aware of."

There was another silence, and then Issa said, "All right. Just . . . be careful. With the photos. And please don't pry into our messages."

"It's never our intention to do that," Lightman said gently.

Once Issa was done, he wrote another sentence in his note-book.

Particularly anxious about the phone and their messages.

And then he underlined it.

ALEX PLASKITT'S LIFE turned out to be quite a public one. He had more than three hundred videos uploaded to YouTube, all of them dedicated to helping people achieve a healthier lifestyle. He had twelve thousand subscribers and clearly used the account to drum up business.

Hanson had started with the most recent video, from a week before. Alex appeared immediately, his head and shoulders visible on the camera and some kind of fitness-studio setup behind him.

"You should never feel embarrassed about the level of fitness you're starting from," he was saying, his blue eyes fixed on the camera. "Most of my clients start out struggling to run at all, and I don't worry about it. Fitness is for everyone, and it's my job to encourage and support you until you start to love it as much as I do. The trick isn't to go at it hard and feel like a failure. It's about making small gains. If that's running for a hundred meters without stopping for the first time in years, then that's a huge achievement, and I want to be there to celebrate that with you."

Hanson continued watching and then loaded up a few more. Alex's YouTube vlogging was miles from the narcissistic fitness clips she'd seen on her Facebook and Twitter feeds. He came across as warm, supportive, and one hundred percent genuine. With his Queen's English, big blue eyes, and chiseled cheekbones, he also came across as a little bit upper-class. Where in other people it might have seemed obnoxious, Alex's laughing apologies for his love of good wine and his trips to Lords were endearing.

She tried not to think about the fact that he would never upload another video, and scrolled down to look at what his viewers had written on some of the latest. She half expected to see tributes to him, but knew it was too soon. News of his death had not been officially announced.

Instead there were lots of profoundly grateful comments. Viewers told him how much weight they'd lost since starting his fitness plan. Others were clearly direct clients, referencing sessions with him and recipes he'd recommended.

And then, of course, this being the Internet, there were other comments too. The kind that made the person half of Hanson burn with anger, and the cop half sit up.

After fifteen minutes of scanning the abuse, Hanson felt in need of a gin. Or at least, she thought, a coffee. She slid her headphones off, but before she could move, the chief came over for an update. Lightman dived straight in.

"We've checked for criminal records for the victim, his husband, and Louise and Niall Reakes. Nothing for any of them, and the husband seems fairly high-powered."

"Nothing linking the Reakeses to Alex?" Sheens asked, looking between him and Hanson.

Hanson shook her head. "They aren't Facebook friends or following each other on anything, and it doesn't look like Louise was a client of Alex's. But his online presence is actually pretty interesting." She swung her screen around to face him square-on, showing a still of Alex Plaskitt's face from one of the videos. He was caught grinning at the camera, his mouth half-open as if he'd been in the middle of speaking. "Alex is a minor vlogging celebrity. Twelve thousand subscribers, so not huge. He seems to use it in part as a way of drumming up business, and in part to inspire people to become active."

"So he had a chance of being recognized while out," Sheens said thoughtfully.

"Yes, and some of these are interesting." She scrolled down to the comments on the video, letting her mouse rest on a comment from someone called S88*burger, whose comment was five homophobic slurs in a row.

"Are there more like this?" the DCI asked.

"Quite a few. There are a few other videos that feature Issa briefly, or where he talks about him. They attract quite a bit of attention. But most of the accounts seem to be throwaways."

The DCI's phone rang, a summons from the pathologist to attend the postmortem. There was a nervous twist to Hanson's stomach as Sheens glanced around at his team. She'd managed one postmortem in her career so far, and knew she would survive another if necessary. But that wasn't to say that she would ever feel positive about them.

Sheens's eye eventually fell on Lightman, and Hanson slid away to make coffee with a slightly shameful sense of relief. She was safe for today, free to dig into the murky world of Internet trolls.

LOUISE WAITED UNTIL the door to the interview room was shut before she opened up her contacts list. Her thumb hesitated over Niall's name. It was right at the top, with a star next to it. Her favorite. Her husband. God, she didn't want to do this.

But it was like pulling off a wax strip, she thought. It might sting at the time, but it was never as bad as you imagined.

Which was a shit analogy, she realized. Because this might turn out to be infinitely worse than she'd imagined. The stripping away might never stop.

As she hesitated, her phone buzzed. April, sending another message of support, and obeying her request to text instead of calling.

> I can't even imagine how awful that must be. I'm so sorry! I want to call so let me know as soon as you're out of there, OK?
> I have the mother of all hangovers but I'm here. Xx

It was a good message to read before dealing with her husband. Unquestioningly supportive. Kind. Normal.

Niall was none of those things. At least not now. And that thought made her feel even worse.

She sighed, minimized the text, and pressed the Call button. She rubbed at her right temple as the phone rang. She should have asked for Tylenol. No. Not for Tylenol. For codeine. Morphine. Something strong enough to knock her out until everything had somehow improved.

"Hey, sweetie! How's it going?" Niall asked, over background noises of people talking. Presumably he was still at the conference, and she'd caught him in a gap between meetings. She almost wished she hadn't.

"Fine," she said automatically, and then corrected herself. "Well . . . not really fine. There was . . . Someone was killed right outside the house. I found them this morning."

There was a silence, and then Niall asked, "Are you serious?"

"Yes. Sorry." Louise gave a short laugh. "I wish I wasn't."

"Killed how?"

"Stabbed," she said. "In the stomach."

"Who—what, a teenager?"

"A bit older, I think. He looked quite big."

There was another silence, and she felt her heart rate speed up as he asked, "So just . . . some stranger? Not someone you know?"

THE POSTMORTEM OF Alex Plaskitt was uncomplicated, but it left Jonah feeling somber. He and Lightman had watched Shaw's initial examination of the knife, and listened to his quiet voice describing the three-inch, slightly tapered blade. He'd noted that it had a decorated metallic grip. This was not a utensil but a weapon, and one that almost certainly had a sheath that had not yet been recovered.

"McCullough's putting us in touch with a weapons specialist she knows," Jonah told Shaw. "We may get something useful back from him."

The pathologist moved on to look at the hands, which showed bruising on the knuckles, but no abrasions.

"Would you still say they were defensive wounds?" Jonah asked.

"They could be, but they could equally well have happened a little earlier in the evening," Shaw said. "Slight swelling and visible bruising has begun to appear, which would have taken at least some minutes. But then he would have taken some minutes to die."

Shaw moved to look at the knife wound and surrounding tissue. Removing organs in turn, he explained the damage to the upper part of the large intestine and the splenic artery.

"The entry wound has cut the wall of the large intestine just below the stomach. However, it slid fairly neatly between the spleen and stomach above." He lifted an elastic pinkish-gray strand. "The damage to the splenic artery, which is what almost certainly caused his death, happened when the knife was removed."

"You're sure?" Jonah asked.

"Yes. You can see here that the back and underside of the artery have been damaged, while the upper and forward parts remain intact. The cause looks to be upward movement of the blade as it was pulled out. The rupture would have caused extensive bleeding, which would have resulted in death within fifteen or twenty minutes."

Jonah asked quietly, "Any indication of whether it was removed by his attacker?"

Shaw gave a slight shrug. "It's not clear, but if you're asking whether he might have pulled it out himself, then yes, it's entirely possible. I don't know how that ties in with it being wiped, though, unless the killer deposited it there later."

Jonah glanced at Lightman and nodded. They had both been part of investigations into knife attacks before, and both remembered a teenage boy who would probably have made it if he hadn't pulled a blade out of his chest before going to get medical help.

It was all odd and dissatisfying. If Alex had removed it, he must have done it elsewhere or there would have been more blood. If the killer had deposited it next to him, there should have been footprints. Whichever way he looked at it, the series of events was muddy and unclear.

"We could really do with some witnesses," he said to Lightman, once Shaw had finished with the other organs and taken blood samples. "I'm going to head over to that nightclub."

LOUISE REAKES WAS allowed to head home at twelve-fifteen, which felt to Hanson like at least six P.M. It looked like Louise's involvement in this inquiry was done. A quick follow-up call to the Reakeses' neighbors at Number 9 Saints Close had produced no suggestion of any arguments or strange behavior. Louise, they said, was generally free to do her own thing, and did so. They gave their opinion that the two would be fine if only Louise would stop drinking.

This filled Hanson with relief. The idea of having to delve into a case that involved an abusive partner had made her feel distinctly sick. It was too close to the past, and to the present too. Too close to everything she was trying so hard not to think about.

On top of that, it felt like a dangerous topic for her own relationship. She was four months into dating Jason, and she'd never quite got around to telling him about Damian, the abusive partner she'd tried to leave behind in Birmingham.

JONAH DROPPED LIGHTMAN back at the station and picked up O'Malley, who had printed out photos of the victim. His Irish sergeant was generally the preferred choice for casual meetings with witnesses, assuming he was actually somewhere to be found and not off pursuing his own leads. There was a warm humor to him that both disarmed the more obstructive folk and encouraged the more helpful ones to bend over backward.

"Are we headed to Blue Underground for some moody daytime drinking?" O'Malley asked, once he'd levered himself into the car.

"You know it?" Jonah asked, with interest.

"I met a witness there once." O'Malley shrugged. "It's OK. Cocktails and a pretentious DJ one floor down, and an eighties disco cheese-fest the floor below. But it's not drugged-up, and there's not a lot of brawling either."

Jonah nodded, remembering that it was the expensive, exclusive Midnight Bar that had been closed down a few years ago after a drugs bust. The most likely clientele for party drugs were, it turned out, wealthy men and women in their forties.

Twenty minutes later, Jonah pulled into a pay-and-display space a few yards down from the club. The doorway to Blue Underground lay between an estate agent's on one side and an oriental food shop on the other. The sign above it spelled out the name in cursive lettering on a midnight-blue background, and almost managed to look classy.

They made their way down the stairs and turned the corner to find the entrance barred by a security door. The sound of a vacuum cleaner came from just beyond it, and Jonah rapped sharply.

The vacuum cleaner grew louder and then ceased, and a middle-aged Latino man wearing a black polo shirt and matching trousers opened the door.

"DCI Sheens," Jonah told him. "I spoke to Charlie earlier."

He let them into a slightly featureless corridor and pointed them down to a bar at the far end. Bright overhead lights had turned what was presumably a dimly atmospheric nighttime grotto into a slightly tatty-looking cellar. The chairs were all up on the tabletops, and there were boxes of beer standing on the bar, where a tall thirtysomething man with a Mediterranean look was discussing stock with a diminutive girl in another black polo shirt.

"Would you be Charlie?" Jonah asked him.

The man turned, revealing a cheerful, tanned face marred by a bruise on his cheekbone.

"Yes. You're the police?" He moved to the end of the bar and walked around it. "Come and have a seat. We've got coffee if you want it?"

His accent was pure Sheffield, and the chirrupy manner was encouraging. He liked their chances of getting as much help as they needed out of Charlie.

"No coffee, thanks," Jonah said.

"Joanne, could you make me a cappuccino?"

The diminutive Joanne disappeared through an archway, and Charlie took three chairs down off a table with a "Here."

"We'd like a little help from you and your staff. We're looking for anyone who can remember this man," Jonah told him, handing over a photo. "He was here last night."

Charlie took the photo and studied it, and O'Malley added, "He's a big guy. Six-three and quite stacked."

"Yeah, he was definitely here," Charlie confirmed. "I sort of know him. He's been a few times. He had a friend with him. Also a regular."

"Do you remember any incidents involving him?"

The sound of a coffee grinder started up beyond the archway, ridiculously loud in the brick-walled space. Charlie spoke loudly over it. "Nothing major. He's a nice enough guy, I think. He got a bit tetchy with one of the bar staff, but that's pretty common."

"He didn't do that?" O'Malley said, nodding toward Charlie's cheek.

"Sorry? Oh." Charlie put a hand up to the bruise and gave a rueful laugh. "No, that was the arsehole who didn't like being told he'd had enough to drink, and went for one of the guys before I stepped in. Fortunately doesn't happen too often, and the bouncers were on it pretty quickly."

"Did he get kicked out?" Jonah asked, thinking that an aggressive and aggrieved man hanging around outside the club could well be involved in attacking Alex.

"Your guys picked him up," Charlie said. "He wouldn't stop lashing out, even when a squad car got here, so he ended up getting himself arrested."

That almost definitely put him out of the picture, Jonah thought, since anyone arrested for assault that late would probably have spent the night at the station. But he made a mental note to check last night's arrests.

"And there wasn't any brawling involving Alex at any time?" O'Malley asked.

"No, nothing like that," Charlie said, with a laugh. "Just some bitching about being ignored in the queue." Joanne reappeared from the archway carrying a coffee in a tall glass. "Jo, was it you or Mark who had the big guy being a bit of a twat to you?"

Joanne glanced up from her focus on the glass. "Mark, I think."

Charlie turned back to them with a shrug. "Like I said, not major."

"But he was quite drunk?" O'Malley pressed.

"Yeah, fairly."

"Did you see him talking to anyone else? Particularly late in the evening?"

Charlie gave an uncertain look. "I'm really not sure. I mean . . . I think he was chatting to a girl for a while, but I'm not . . ." He turned toward the bar, where Joanne was back to stacking shelves in the fridge. "Do you remember him chatting to someone, Joanne? I feel like it might have been that brunette who was all over the place."

She glanced up, and then paused to think. "I think that might be right. In the queue, and then for a bit afterward."

Charlie frowned and turned to them. "There was a girl who kept falling off her chair, or into people. She was absolutely shit-faced, and I was quite worried about her but she did take herself off home in the end. It's not . . . this isn't about her, is it?"

"We don't really know," Jonah admitted. "All we do know is that Alex Plaskitt ended up dead."

"Him?" Charlie looked shocked. "I figured this must be about something he'd *done*."

"I'm afraid not. So if there's anything more you can remember . . ." Jonah suggested gently.

Charlie looked at Alex's photo again, and then shook his head. "I don't think so. But I can ask the others if he had any arguments." He shivered. "Fucking hell. How did he end up dead?"

"It looks like he was attacked," O'Malley told him. "We'll know more soon."

"Could you give an estimate of what time he left?" Jonah added.

"Not really . . ." Charlie pulled a slightly helpless face. "You don't really clock-watch when it's busy, and people drift around. He could have headed downstairs and been here until closing, and I probably wouldn't have seen him."

"You mentioned CCTV . . ."

"Yeah, we've got one by the door. The data files go to my computer. I'll be heading home in an hour, so I can pick it up. It's a bit erratic, to be honest, but if there's anything at all, I'll send it over."

"Thanks," Jonah said. "That would be appreciated."

As he and O'Malley climbed into the car, his sergeant said, "I sort of see everyone's point, about Alex not being an obvious victim."

"Yes, though he could have been incapacitated by drink," Jonah commented. "Or —"

"Taken by surprise," O'Malley said, nodding. "Yeah. Which implies an attack that came from an unexpected quarter."

"Are you thinking of the apparently shitfaced brunette?" Jonah asked him.

"They wouldn't be the first to pull off a sting," O'Malley said. "There was a couple I helped arrest when I was a DC who had a whole routine worked out. They'd go to a bar, she would be all over some guy, apparently very drunk, and then at some point she'd either slip his wallet out or lead him outside, where the boyfriend would act drunk and aggressive and extort money." O'Malley shrugged. "Could be something there."

"Yes," Jonah said thoughtfully. "An extortion gone wrong is possible. But then anything is possible at this stage."

He just hoped that there was some working CCTV somewhere between the club and Saints Close. Something to explain how Alex Plaskitt had ended up dead in a suburban garden.

8

LOUISE

The fear began to kick in long before you noticed anything. At least, long before you started to question me about what Drunk Louise had got up to. Before your reaction to me changed.

We'd had eight increasingly happy months. Dina had receded into the background a little. Your work was going well, and so was mine. I'd finally succeeded in joining the Mother Pluckers after two of the members put me forward to audition, and although a couple of others were patronizing as hell toward me about not being a parent, it was generally a kind and talented bunch that I liked spending time with.

Then came the anniversary of the day you'd married Dina. Which was also the night we found out that Dina was now engaged to her new man.

I'd watched you descend into a foul mood the day before, already steeped in resurging resentment at how quickly Dina had left you. I'd started to understand, by then, that what other people thought of you was more important than you claimed. It was the real reason for the expensive clothes and the flashy car. In the way you liked to mention the specifics of the eye-wateringly pricey wine you bought.

It had taken me a while to really put my finger on it, though. I suppose the constant effort to hide my own insecurities made me blind to yours. Perhaps I'd seen you acting up a little around your posher friends. Suddenly booking tickets to the opera just before we met up with Patrick, and then talking at length about it. Insisting we had to have monkfish parcels and tuna carpaccio when he came for dinner.

But it didn't really hit home until the time you brought the wrong credit card to dinner and then couldn't pay at the end of the meal. I'd never seen you humiliated before, and I'd never have guessed that you could sink into seething self-laceration as bad as mine. My breezy statement that I was delighted to pay my way for once did nothing to lift you out of it.

I began to reinterpret what had happened with Dina, and to see it as a massive blow to your sense of self-worth. I tried to reassure myself that you felt nothing for her now. But it didn't really convince me that I was safe, and I woke up on the morning of your anniversary with the heaviest of depressions hanging over me.

Your morose silence that day did nothing to lift it. You didn't tell me about the engagement. You barely put a whole sentence together all day.

April clocked that something was up when we spoke on the phone that afternoon, and despite feeling profoundly humiliated by it all, I told her what was going on.

She responded with a frustrated sigh. "He needs to let it go, and realize she's just a waste of space." Being April, she then moved straight on to, "Let's go out. You and me. Let him sit and wallow and miss you, and we'll have some fun. Forget all about it."

It seemed like the perfect plan. Instead of sitting around and being the stressed-out girlfriend, I was going to get dressed up and have girl time. Laugh about it all and maybe flirt harmlessly with a waiter or two.

You were happy enough for me to go. From your slumped position at the kitchen table you managed to stir up a small smile as I kissed you goodbye.

"I'll see Drunk Louise later," you said. Do you remember that? You found it cute, still, that whole Drunk Me/Sober Me thing.

I gave you a grin I didn't really feel. "You'd better have water and Nutella ready."

The night started out all right. April was her usual hilarious self, and it made everything feel better. But then she showed me Dina's engagement announcement on Facebook, and asked me what I thought.

It was a nauseatingly perfect picture, one that had, in all probability, been filtered to within an inch of its life. Dina was cuddled up to her handsome, clean-cut new man, her left hand displayed on his chest, with a frankly ridiculous diamond on the fourth finger.

"Look at the background," April said. "That's Florence. They've been back almost a week. She's saved it up just for today."

"Oh my God." I felt, for some reason, more sickened than I had on my birthday. It felt so calculated. Evidence of such a long game, and one I was certain I would lose.

I knew, right then, that I was going to get drunk. So drunk that I had no recollection of anything, and felt nothing. Drunk Louise would handle the night from here on in.

It must have been late when I suddenly snapped back into myself. I guess I'd had a gap in the drinking, and sobered up just enough to surface.

And it was the worst awakening. I found myself pressed up against a man I didn't recognize, with his hands moving up the back of my thighs toward my backside and his face close to mine.

It took me a second to retreat. And then, when he came with me instead of letting go, another few seconds to push at him.

"Hey!" I could hear him say, over the music. "What the fuck?"

And then I was screaming at him and lashing out, my hands connecting with his upper arms and chest. I was telling him to get off me. To let go. And eventually he did, with an angry shove that sent me reeling backward.

For a moment I thought about hurting him. I had a crazy, offbeat idea that I could smash a glass over his head. But it ran through me in an instant and vanished, leaving me shaking.

I had no idea where I was going. It was sheer good luck that I stumbled on April, who was chatting to a couple of guys in the queue for the bar. I was so worried she would think badly of me for wanting to go home, but she responded with concern. She gathered me up and took me to get my handbag and coat, then climbed into a taxi with me. She waited, patiently, for half the ride without saying anything. By that time I'd got myself together enough to tell her what had happened.

"I must have led him on," I told her, tears starting to work their way out. "I must have made it happen."

"I don't think you can assume that," April said gently. "There are a lot of assholes out there. And even if you did . . . Well, I don't think anyone could blame you." She put a hand out to my arm and rubbed it.

"But I feel like . . . like a shitty cheat."

I regretted saying it immediately. I'd been with April while she'd kissed other men, and while her second marriage fell apart as a result. Now on to her third, and only one year in, she was just as willing to be unfaithful.

"Sorry. I'm being a twat," I said.

"You're just being a human being who's had a rough time," she argued. "There's only room for one twat around here, and that's going to be me."

I felt a little better about it all after that, but then fell back into awful guilt the moment I walked through the front door and found you half-asleep on the sofa.

"Hey, Lou-Lou," you said, sitting up and taking my hand. You drew me to sit next to you, your eyes and body drowsy. I was shaking hard now, from the alcohol withdrawal and the guilt of it all. "Come here."

Wrapped up in your hug, I felt even more profoundly stupid for having risked this. Us. All of it.

But it was you who apologized.

"I'm so sorry for being an idiot," you murmured into the top of my head. "It really, honestly isn't that I miss Dina. It's that I—I feel stupid for having ever thought she was a good person. She's just announced that she's engaged. Today. And she knows what bloody day it is. I'm sure she does. It's all designed to hurt, and I . . . I just feel like such a dickhead for falling for her." You sighed, and I loved being able to feel the movement of your chest underneath me. There was something soft and all-encompassing in it. "And the last thing I should have done was get grumpy with you. You're so different from her. So wonderful. I love you."

"I love you too," I said, and I didn't tell you that the tears that oozed out onto your shirt were nothing to do with Dina, and all to do with a man in a nightclub.

9

Hanson was trying to get a response from YouTube about two of Alex Plaskitt's most persistent trolls when Jason appeared in CID. He gave a resigned shrug that very clearly asked why they were spending their Saturdays here. She shook her head wryly in return, but found herself smiling.

Jason winked at her as he settled himself at his desk, and then gestured with his hands to make the letter *T*, then held up five fingers. Hanson gave him a thumbs-up. Tea in five minutes, and an opportunity to tell him about the murder inquiry, sounded good to her. He was always great to talk policing with. He loved his job as much as she did hers.

Her phone buzzed a few minutes later. The DCI messaging to say that Alex Plaskitt's sister was free to talk this afternoon. He suggested that she and Ben should head over there.

The idea made her stomach drop slightly. The address was up near Winchester, a good forty-five minutes away. She wasn't sure she felt equal to three-quarters of an hour in a car with Ben Lightman just now.

She glanced across at Ben, who seemed to be very much involved with something. She'd leave it a little while, she thought. They could go after she'd had a cuppa and a chat with Jason.

She put her phone back on the desk, and found that there was an email waiting from one of the YouTube technical team. He'd come back with an email address for another part of the company, and then added that, while they might be able to help, anonymous accounts could be very difficult to trace.

Hanson sighed and briefly replied to say she was aware of that, and then thanked him for his help. She'd been to a talk just before Christmas on how digital footprints were making the detection of criminals easier and easier. She wondered when that might actually start to influence her day-to-day work for the better.

LIGHTMAN FINISHED HIS phone call to the duty sergeant and typed up his findings in the database. After that, he rang the DCI back to confirm that they could rule out any involvement from the aggressive drunk at the nightclub.

"He was picked up before one and kept in until seven this morning," Lightman confirmed.

"Thanks," Sheens said. "Are you and Juliette on the road to Phoebe Plaskitt's?"

He glanced over at Hanson, who gave him a thumbs-up.

"About to leave, I think."

"I'd particularly like to know what she thinks of Alex's husband," the DCI told him. "Any issues between them. How she thinks they were doing."

"Sure," Lightman agreed.

He hung up, and decided he could do with a coffee before their journey. He was about to suggest making one when Hanson rose, gave him a vague smile, and headed toward the kitchen. He glanced across at Jason Walker's empty desk, and nodded to himself. He'd wait a few minutes.

JASON WAS ALREADY waiting in the kitchen with two mugs of fully made tea on the counter. He was leaning against a cupboard, one arm folded over his stomach and his phone out.

It was a note of disappointment that he'd already made the tea. Hanson hadn't yet had the heart to tell him that she liked it brewed for about twice as long as he ever gave it.

"How goes it?" she asked, touching his shoulder lightly.

"Not too bad." He smiled and squeezed her hand, putting his phone back into his pocket. The two of them had their office-level displays of affection worked out precisely. It was all about brief, non-intimate touching. "I've been looking for more of this stolen sound gear on eBay," he went on. "You'd be amazed how many of the exact model of amp are for sale on there."

"I thought you'd already found all of them?" Hanson said, picking up the slightly less anemic of the two mugs of tea.

Jason had spent some weeks digging into a network of house-breakers. It had taken time. The group had been extremely careful, and they had sold their stolen items carefully. They'd listed them individually, through numerous different eBay and Gum-tree accounts.

"I thought so too," Jason said. "But the audio theft at the uni and all those bikes at the sports center weren't sold on any of the accounts we've identified."

"Oh, that's a bugger."

"It's OK." Jason gave a brief shrug. "I'll get there. Even if it means no arrests today." He straightened up and reached for his mug of tea. "How about you? Murder?"

"Yup." She gulped some of the weak brew. "Stabbing."

"How's it going?"

"Slow so far." She shrugged. "Not a lot of people hanging around residential areas in the early hours of the morning."

She suddenly found herself thinking of Damian sitting in his car outside her house, watching her through the kitchen window, and she could feel a cold sweat sweeping over her. She tried to take another sip of tea, but the mug banged into her teeth, painfully.

"Are you OK?" Jason asked, reaching out to squeeze her arm. She glanced at him, seeing his concern. It occurred to her that she really could just tell him about all of this. Share it.

She couldn't even explain why she'd resisted telling him in the first place. She justified it to herself that it was to avoid overshadowing their relationship. Though she knew it was more complicated than that, and tied up with shame for what she'd put up with. And the more she'd put off actually telling him, the harder it had become, until it seemed like a huge thing that she was hiding from him.

She teetered on the edge of just telling him everything, but it seemed the wrong time and place. So she put the tea down, quickly, and tried to smile.

"Just a young guy," she said, "dying like that . . . He seemed really nice, from his YouTube account. Murders are shit, aren't they?"

VISITING A SUSPECT. That was all Hanson needed to think about. Not about the forty-five-minute journey to Winchester with Ben Lightman. Not about the awkwardness, or her confusion over their lost friendship. And definitely, definitely not about the night before she'd started seeing Jason, when she and Ben had gone to a bar. When he'd seemed for a very intense moment like he might tell her what was going on under the unruffled facade, and then had suddenly shut her out and left.

The first five minutes of the drive went past in absolute silence. There was nobody on a par with Ben for keeping quiet. In contrast, Hanson felt an increasing sense of pressure to say something.

She sighed without meaning to, and then tried to turn it into a yawn. And then, barely a minute later and with her gaze firmly fixed out of the window, she said, "I meant to ask about . . . your dad. Ages ago. I'm sorry for being rubbish."

"Oh." She thought she caught a good-natured shrug out of

the corner of her eye. "You aren't rubbish. There's not much to say. He's been in and out of hospital, and it's been a bit . . . shit. There isn't a lot anyone can do."

"I could be a better friend," Hanson countered, glancing at him and then away again. "A bit more supportive."

Lightman seemed to think for a moment, and then replied, "It's difficult. I don't always find it easy to take offers of support. I hate thinking about my dad, so I avoid talking about it, too, and it always feels . . . awkward."

Which wasn't entirely unlike how she felt when it came to telling Jason about Damian, she thought, surprised both at finding some point of similarity with Ben's reticence and at his willingness to volunteer that much information about himself.

"Makes sense," she said, and then she added, with a slight grin, "I mean, you being awkward."

She heard Ben's slight laugh, and it made her smile properly. It had been months since she'd made him laugh. It always felt like a victory, with Ben. And not just, she thought, because he looked like the school heartthrob she'd grown up trying to impress.

"But what about you?" he asked her. "How are things?"

"Oh, they're all right," she said, feeling the beginnings of heat in her cheeks. "I'm overdue spending time with my mum, and I seem to be incapable of doing laundry at the moment. Other than that, fine."

Ben nodded, glancing over to her and then back at the road. She was poised for him to ask about Jason, but instead he said, "What about the awful ex? Has he been making life difficult?"

"Oh . . ." Hanson found herself lost for anything to say. How had he known to ask that question? Hanson hadn't mentioned Damian since late last year, and she hadn't told anyone about the way her life seemed to have imploded. Not anyone.

She was still framing an answer when her phone buzzed, and she grabbed it like a lifeline.

"Just Domnall," she said, opening her messages with a forced laugh. "He wonders whether we'd like to get some Krispy Kremes for tomorrow on the way home."

Ben shook his head. "Not unless there's pizza waiting for us when we get back."

"Yeah, good point." Hanson took her time typing out the reply, and then, once finished, she turned away from Ben to look out of the window, as if they'd never begun a conversation about Damian. As if things were absolutely fine.

JONAH SAT IN one of the comfortable beige chairs in the entrance hall to the mortuary, wondering about Issa. There was grief there, and it currently took the form of denial. Six or seven times on the drive over, Issa had begun a sentence with, "If it's not him . . ." and Jonah had struggled to find the right words in reply.

He would have been more comfortable asking formal questions. There was a lot to ask him at a better time. It was difficult to ignore that Issa had sent at least two extremely angry messages to Alex.

Anger at one's partner was clearly not always a motivation to commit murder. Men were also murdered by their partners less often than women were, though it happened more frequently in same-sex partnerships. Added to that, Issa's messages had seemed to suggest that he hadn't known where Alex was.

But Jonah wondered whether there were more messages from Issa, and exactly what they said. Following proper procedure, he hadn't made any attempt to unlock or look at the phone itself. That was a job for the tech team. So the only messages he'd seen were the ones on the lock screen.

He'd already made a request through Detective Chief Superintendent Wilkinson for the technical team's work to be fast-tracked. The DCS had agreed that would be appropriate, and Jonah hoped they would have data about Alex's whereabouts and communications later in the afternoon.

With that thought, Jonah's phone buzzed. He'd switched it to vibrate while they were in the mortuary, but he felt that he needed to be in contact with his team. When he checked the screen, it turned out to be not his team but his significant ex, Michelle.

He felt an uncomfortable squeeze in his stomach at the sight of her name. An unwelcome reminder of the last time he'd seen her, and the guilt he'd felt about it all since.

Her message was brief and apparently casual.

Hi. Would you be free for a quick call today at some point? I could use some advice.

He let out a sigh, strongly suspecting that it was an excuse to make contact again. If he had to guess, he'd say that Michelle had just gone through a breakup and was feeling vulnerable. She was reaching out to him because he'd shown himself to be interested, even after a year apart.

He wondered whether he should reply at all, and if so, what the hell he should say, but before he could decide anything, his phone buzzed again with the insistent vibration of a call.

He glanced toward the door into the rear part of the building. There was no sign of Issa returning from IDing the body, so he made his way to the front door to take the call.

"This is Charlie," he heard, in the nightclub owner's unmistakable Sheffield accent. "We spoke earlier at the club? I've looked through the footage at the door, and your victim left at one-thirteen."

Jonah nodded to himself. "That's great, thank you. Is he with anyone?"

"No," Charlie said, "but you know I mentioned the brunette? The really drunk one? She left just before he did. It looks like he may have been following her."

Jonah glanced toward the rear room of the mortuary, where there were sounds of movement. "Can you send me a still of the girl? We'll need the video, too, but if you could get that straight over, I'll see if anyone recognizes her."

"Sure," Charlie said. "I'll do it now. Is your email . . . ?"

"On the card I gave you," Jonah said. But he told him what it was anyway.

As he hung up, Issa was being led to one of the chairs by the manager of the mortuary, a woman Jonah had unbelievable respect for. Issa's face was white, pinched, and terrible, and Jonah felt an awful lurch of vicarious grief.

"Take a few minutes to rest," the manager said as Issa sat heavily. He looked close to vomiting, and Jonah wondered whether it was the physical sight of Alex that had done it, or the sudden and complete loss of his desperate illusions. It was no longer possible to ask if it might not be Alex; Issa had seen his husband's body with his own eyes.

Jonah wondered, too, whether denial had been Issa's way of escaping what he had done. He wouldn't be the first killer to convince himself he hadn't hurt anyone.

"I . . ." Issa turned his head, and stood again. "I need . . . some air."

"Sure." Jonah watched Issa leave by the main door, and went to fetch him water. As he was filling a paper cup from the cooler in the corner, an email arrived from Charlie. It had two large video attachments, which he knew his phone would take a while to download. But there was also a still, presumably of the drunk brunette.

It was clearly too soon to show Issa an image of someone Alex may have known, but Jonah was curious anyway. He opened it, his left hand pressing the button awkwardly and his right hand on the cup.

He came close to dropping his phone as he opened the attached image. The girl leaving the club was, unquestionably, Louise Reakes.

10

LOUISE

You probably want to know why I didn't stop drinking straightaway. Right after I realized there was a strange man pawing at me and that I had no idea how it had happened.

I did actually stop, for a while. I managed a week. But it was torture. Every time you and I saw each other, I felt stilted and awkward and dull. After the third time you'd looked at me strangely and asked if I was feeling OK, I told you I'd been under the weather, and then I sank three glasses of gin.

I decided I'd have to wean myself off the sauce more slowly and learn to behave the same way around you once I was sober. But I didn't really believe I could.

I did, at least, cut down on drinking the rest of the time. I explained to April that I couldn't get blind drunk ever again because the guy in the club had scared me. It was easier, I told her, just not to start drinking in the first place. She genuinely seemed to understand, and not to think I was boring. She told me she'd look out for me better in future, but that she respected my decision.

That didn't mean she didn't keep tempting me, though. Every time it was her round, she'd arch an eyebrow at me before paying, as if to ask if I wanted a shot in that nonalcoholic cocktail. The shameful truth was that I did. I really did. But I didn't trust myself.

It's possible that I didn't quite trust April either. I knew some of her behavior was bad for me. The way she would sometimes arrive to meet me in what she liked to call Predator Mode, which I've never once told you about. I didn't think you'd want me to spend so much time with a serial cheat who would periodically home in on some guy while we were out and leave me to get a cab home.

But I didn't worry all that much about it. I was more responsible now. I didn't need her to stay the whole night and keep an eye on me. I wasn't drinking, and I was in control. There would be no more guys with their hands all over me.

It all seemed manageable until, three weeks after Dina got engaged, you proposed to me.

I'm not blaming you for proposing. I'm really, truly not. My first rush of unbelievable happiness on that Iceland trip, when you dropped down in front of me in the shadow of Gljúfrabúi (I had to look up how to spell that again) was one hundred percent real. You looked beyond handsome, more so because you were clearly nervous. You cared so much that I accepted you.

And that ring you chose. God, it was wonderful, Niall. It was like you'd somehow been there every time I'd sighed over someone else's sparkles and understood that I would want something slim enough and small enough to wear when I played. You hadn't gone for some great big, flashy stone like the one Dina was waving around, but for something I would genuinely love.

I've never told you quite how grateful I was for that, Niall. It was that, as much as anything else, that made me cry as I said yes.

That night was without doubt the most wonderful one I've ever spent. Discussing where we would hold the wedding and what we would do with decor; who the bridesmaids would be and who you'd like as your best man. And, beyond that, talking about kids for the first time. About having the child I'd craved for more years than I'd like to admit.

You told me, that night, that I'd make a wonderful mother.

That you could see me already, teaching them music and juggling my part of the childcare with work. I loved how you added that you'd take paternity leave too. That you wanted to be part of it all.

When we wandered out into the cold night and stood wrapped around each other, I felt as if everything was perfect. Everything.

It was only later that panic started to set in.

It actually started a little while after you'd dozed off half on top of me. I felt a sudden rush of sadness at not having my mum around to tell, and then I imagined how she'd react if she were still alive. And for some reason, in my head, my wonderful, deeply missed mum asked a terrible thing. She asked if you'd thought of proposing before Dina got engaged. Whether you were just doing it to make a point.

My real mum would never have been so cruel. This was purely my subconscious talking. Or perhaps it was *Her,* because I'd certainly had enough champagne that night for my drunk persona to make something of an appearance.

It only took that thought to drive me straight from contented joy to total paranoia. I started imagining that these two proposals were really just some kind of conversation between you and Dina. A dialogue that I had no part in. You were toying with each other, I thought. And her new fiancé and I were just collateral damage.

By the time I arrived back in the UK I was a wreck. I think you put a lot of it down to the overexcitement of our engagement. I was grateful that you did. There was no way I could talk to you about this. I knew you would be furious with me, and I was more than afraid that you might call the whole thing off.

All this was in my mind the night Drunk Louise did something truly terrible. Something that might still, to this day, turn out to be worse than I thought.

And I knew none of it at first. I knew only that April and I had gone out, and that I had woken up in pieces, with what must have been the worst hangover I've ever had. Worse even than that first one.

You spent the morning laughing at me and making me tea. You weren't angry, even then. You were happy with my explanation that April had bought us a lot of champagne to celebrate, that I just hadn't eaten enough to cope with it. You were cheerfully accepting of it all, until we were curled up on the sofa watching *Lawrence of Arabia*, and my phone buzzed.

I saw the message flash up on my home screen at the same time you did.

> Hi Louise, it's Matt. It was so great to meet you last night. Let me know if your free to hang out later. I'd love to see you again.

However bad you felt right then, Niall, I can guarantee that I felt worse. It felt like my whole world was falling apart. I couldn't help looking at you, and I saw when your cheerful face became hard. Cold. Furious.

"What the actual fuck, Louise?"

It must have been bad for you to swear like that. I mean, even with your slightly gendered view of the appropriateness of swearing, I've almost never heard you do it.

I was silent for a long time, and then I shook my head. "I don't know. I don't know who that is."

The silence was terrifying. And when you said "Give me your phone," it didn't sound like you.

I was actually too frightened of you to argue. Even though I knew it might make everything worse.

I was shaking as you opened my messages, and something awful happened to my heart as I saw that I'd messaged this guy first, with the word hello.

I watched your face, and I cringed away from you. There was nothing in your expression except rage. It twisted your face into something else, and for the first time I thought you might do something violent. Did you teeter on the edge of it, Niall? Because it looked like you wanted to put your hands round my throat. I'd like to know if I'm right.

It was words you lashed out with in the end. Asking if I was a drunken whore. Asking why the hell I'd said I wanted to marry you when I really just wanted to screw around. And on, and on, until eventually, crying so hard I could barely say it, I told you to ask April what had happened.

I was terrified when you called her, but I also desperately needed you to stop. To pause.

April reported what she'd said later on. She told you to stop being stupid, apparently. That obviously it was just some asshole taking my phone. No, of course I hadn't given anyone my number. No, I hadn't flirted with anyone. There had just been some guy who was keen on me and he had clearly crossed some lines.

I know it helped, what she said. But nothing was ever quite the same after that. Not for you, and not for me. Because April admitted to me, privately, that she had no idea whether I'd given him my number. She'd been too busy with his friend. That's something I never told you, either, and I feel like it stands against me now, a terrible judgment on my character. Or at least on *her* character. On Drunk Louise's.

That message from a strange man was the beginning of your interrogations. My alter ego suddenly lost her charm in your eyes, and my hungover, sober self lost all your sympathy. You waited for me to overdrink and you attacked me for it, though I tried so hard to stay on the sober side of the line and almost always succeeded. I really did try, Niall. But I couldn't cope without it. I was so afraid you would see through me and leave me. And simultaneously afraid that you'd never wanted me, and that everything was still about Dina.

And, of course, the more you criticized, or gave me the silent treatment, the more anxious I became, and the more I needed the alcohol.

I say anxious, but what I really felt was a combination of fear and profound sadness. My life started to look hopeless.

The worst part was when we talked about kids again, two weeks after that incident. You were so cool. Unemotional. You said we obviously weren't going to be ready for that for a while.

I could see in your expression that you didn't trust me to have your children anymore, Niall. And it felt like you'd driven a knife into me.

11

The DCI's phone call came half an hour into the journey, and Hanson felt nothing but relief. She wondered whether Ben, who had driven in silence for the last twenty minutes, felt the same. There was nothing in his expression to suggest that he was uncomfortable. But then there never was.

"Chief," Lightman said.

"It looks like Louise Reakes may not be as unconnected as we first thought," the DCI told them in a slightly muffled voice. "She was in the same club as Alex Plaskitt last night, and he left shortly after her."

"Interesting," Ben said, at the same time that Hanson said, "Wow, OK."

"I'll be asking O'Malley to bring her in," the DCI went on. "Where are you two now?"

"Still fifteen minutes from Phoebe Plaskitt's house," Hanson said with a sudden lift in her spirits. "Do you want us to come back?"

"No, you carry on," Jonah said. "She's expecting you, and whatever happens with Louise Reakes, I want to know more about Alex."

"Right," Hanson said, her brief hope shattered. "Can do."

The silence felt worse once the phone call was done, and,

after a minute, Hanson leaned forward and pressed the button for the radio. "Are you OK with Radio Four?"

"Sure," Lightman said equably. "Whatever you like."

Louise Reakes's manner was a little defiant. She seemed genuinely outraged to be back in the station. But Jonah was certain he detected a note of panic beneath the affront.

"I don't understand why I'm here," she said to Jonah, as soon as the tape was running. O'Malley, alongside him, was tapping on a laptop, and Louise gave him a look of irritation before she gazed back at Jonah.

"You're here because we think you lied to us," Jonah told her.

"I've told you nothing but the truth," she said. And yet Louise looked close to breaking. It was clear that she was hiding something.

"What about when you told us you didn't know the victim?"

Louise gave him a look that seemed genuinely confused. She glanced toward O'Malley, who gave her his warmest smile.

"I didn't know him," she said after a beat. "There's nothing untrue in that."

"My sergeant is going to show you a video clip taken from the entrance to a club called Blue Underground," Jonah said. He could see the sudden step up in tension in Louise's body.

He turned toward the side wall, where the ceiling-mounted data projector shone its image. As a bright rectangle lit up across the wall, O'Malley rose and dimmed the lights.

The CCTV footage began, a moving version of what Jonah had seen once before, but just as silent. Just as grayscale. Just as stark.

Louise Reakes appeared, with the fixed gaze and wavering gait of the very drunk.

"This is you leaving Blue Underground at just before one-twelve A.M.," O'Malley said, his voice still affable. It jarred with the starkness of the image.

Even in the dim light it was obvious that this had hit Louise hard.

"Oh my God, I'm . . ." She gave Jonah a slightly desperate look. "I don't remember leaving the house. She—we must have decided to go out. I'm so sorry. . . ."

Jonah looked back at the screen and asked O'Malley to rewind it and play it again.

"I can't see any sign of April Dumont in this image."

There was a brief silence, and then Louise said, "No."

"When did April go home?"

"I don't know," Louise said unsteadily. "I don't remember any of it. I thought I'd stayed at home. Like I told you."

O'Malley paused the image as Louise was about to vanish off-screen and they both waited, looking at Louise instead of the projection.

"Maybe I felt too drunk, and left," she said. "Or . . . I guess she could have been . . . with a guy."

Neither Jonah nor O'Malley said anything.

"I'm sorry," she said, looking at the screen and then back at them. She squeezed her hands together, and Jonah could see that they were shaking. "But I really wasn't trying to hide anything. And it doesn't mean anything. I wasn't out with some gang or with the victim or anything."

O'Malley and Jonah remained silent, but O'Malley pressed the Play button.

There was a short pause, while all that showed on-screen was the bouncer shuffling closer to the desk to say something to the woman who was manning it. All they could see of the latter was the top of her head, her part a bright-white line in her dark hair.

And then another figure appeared. Taller than the bouncer and slightly wider across the shoulders, though he was definitely a great deal slimmer around the waist. He slid his feet a little, a sign of drunkenness perhaps less severe than Louise's.

When Jonah glanced at Louise, she looked dumbstruck. Horrified.

"What . . . ?"

"This is Alex Plaskitt, leaving at just after one-thirteen. He was only a minute and a half behind you."

There was absolute silence as O'Malley let the video play for a short while longer, and then paused it once again.

Louise eventually turned toward Jonah. "But I didn't know him." She put one of her shaking hands flat out on the table between them. "When I saw him in—the garden, I didn't recognize him. I can't have met him. Please believe me."

"But you claim not to remember major details of the night," O'Malley said. "How can you be sure?"

"Because I'd surely have felt some . . . hint of recognition," she said, her eyes very wide.

"You didn't talk to him earlier in the evening?" O'Malley went on.

"Please listen to me." Louise sounded close to crying, but she took a deep breath and went on. "It's the world's worst coincidence, him being there and us being there too. But I promise you, I didn't know him."

"So please enlighten us as to how he ended up dead in your front garden," Jonah said, his voice dripping with acid.

"I don't know," Louise said with something between frustration and earnestness. "It's so fucking mad, and—and horrible." She shook her head. "Maybe . . . maybe he followed me for some reason. Maybe he was attacked outside the club, and he stumbled after me. I don't know if that's even possible, but I'm telling you I don't remember him at all." She balled her hands into fists. "April will tell you. She'll remember more."

"You left without her," Jonah reminded her. "You could well have met up with Alex Plaskitt without her knowing."

"But I'm not like that," Louise said loudly. She suddenly sat back, put her hands up to her head, and tucked a strand of hair behind her ear on each side, then folded her hands together in front of her. Jonah wasn't sure if it might be calculated, but the effect was somehow more respectable. The tucked-back hair and the folded hands. Age-old signals of self-containment. Of virtue. "I'm a married woman, and I don't go flirting with men I don't know."

Jonah considered this in light of what she had said about her husband. About his ability to make everything her fault. He thought that a married woman who felt criticized might well try to flirt. And the flip side was that Niall Reakes might have had reason not to trust his wife.

Louise was holding his gaze, that earnestness still there. *Believe me,* she was saying silently. *You have to believe me.*

Jonah broke the gaze. He looked toward the wall, which still showed the last frame of the projected video.

"Detective Sergeant O'Malley is now going to show you an image. I'd like to know if you recognize this knife."

Louise's head dropped in exasperation. But she looked at the screen, where O'Malley had put up a photo of the bloodied knife with its elaborate ornamental handle.

"No," Louise said firmly. "I don't. Except from when I saw it next to . . . to Alex, on the ground." And then she shuddered and looked away.

"It's fairly distinctive," Jonah said.

"I can see that," Louise said, slightly more quietly, her gaze on the table. "And that makes me one hundred percent certain that I'd never seen it before." She gave a long breath out, and then lifted her chin a little. "Look, I want to help you. I want to know who killed him. It was right—right where I live. I want them to be caught." Her jaw trembled slightly. "But I can't, because it wasn't me. I don't know him, and I'm sorry that I can't help."

Jonah watched her. Read her expression, and wasn't quite sure what he was seeing there.

. . .

PHOEBE PLASKITT'S HOUSE, out in much snowier Winchester, was named the Dovecote. It had clearly started out as its name implied, before someone had decided to turn it into a dwelling. As a result, it had been extended in a style that was basically in keeping but that had left it looking off-center. The cote itself was to the far right, with the front door at the other end.

The young woman who opened the door to them was probably twenty-five, Hanson thought. She was a lot shorter than Alex, and lacked his muscle. But the cheekbones, eyebrows, and chin were almost identical to their victim's.

"I'm DS Lightman," Ben said. "And this is DC Hanson. I wonder if we could come in?"

The young woman seemed dazed, though they knew she'd been expecting them. The raw redness of the skin under her eyes looked like a sign of recent crying. Perhaps someone in Alex's family had cared about him.

Phoebe nodded slowly and backed away. She tucked her hands into the ends of her overlong cardigan sleeves as she waited for them to enter and then shut the door behind them.

"Do you need tea? Anything?"

"I'm OK, thanks," Hanson said, and Ben shook his head too. "We stopped off on the way."

"Sitting room, then," Phoebe said.

"Are your parents coping all right?" Hanson asked as they were led along the varnished wooden floor to one end of the house. It was hopefully an easier question to answer than one about Phoebe's own grief.

"I think so," Alex's sister said, pausing very briefly with her hand on the last door. She turned the handle and opened it, letting them into a bright room that had a view of the garden through tall windows. It was all pale colors and long, low sofas. All of it looked, Hanson thought, expensive.

There were a few photos scattered around. Hanson's eye was

caught by a formal family portrait of the Plaskitt family propped up on a bookshelf. It was probably close to twenty years old. Alex was recognizable even as a boy in trousers, shirt, and tie. He looked the perfect little heir. Phoebe was starchily dressed and probably somewhere between four and six.

Of particular interest to Hanson was the vision of Alex's father in what must have been his mid-thirties. He looked so very like Alex looked in his training videos, except with all the warmth taken away. He was unsmiling, and the hand resting on his wife's shoulder looked heavy.

The wife was very pretty, Hanson thought. Dark-haired and brown-eyed, with skin a lot more tanned than her husband's. Perhaps of Mediterranean heritage.

Hanson dragged herself away from the photo and found a seat. Phoebe looked even smaller as she folded herself into an armchair. She must have been a good foot shorter than her brother.

Lightman began as soon as they were seated. "We'd really like to know what Alex was like."

"Well . . ." Phoebe's eyes moved sideways and it was clear that she was trying not to cry. "He was . . . very kind. Very patient. Hugely into sports, but always . . . a great sportsman."

"So not particularly competitive?" Hanson said.

"He . . . no," Phoebe said. "Well . . . he was fairly competitive. He wanted to be good, and he was very driven to improve himself." Her mouth twisted slightly. "When Alex was very young, he was a bit of a mummy's boy. At least that's what Daddy used to think. Sport became Alex's way of proving himself to him. So he's always been quite . . . fierce about it."

"Did they end up bonding, then?" Lightman asked. "Your father and Alex?"

Phoebe shrugged. "I suppose so. They were quite close for a few years. But Daddy's struggled with . . . a few things." She shrugged. "I wish he could get over it all, but I don't think he's programmed that way."

"With Alex's sexuality?" Lightman queried gently.

"Yes, and . . . some of the boys he's fallen for."

"Like his husband, you mean?" Hanson asked.

Phoebe grimaced, and looked down at her sleeves. "I think he was the last straw, really. A very unmanly Muslim. The last in a long line of people Daddy felt to be inappropriate . . . He kept asking him why he hadn't settled for any of the women he'd dated. Why he couldn't try harder to make things work with someone female."

"So Alex had dated women too?"

"Not for any length of time," Phoebe replied. "The only people he'd ever loved were men."

"How did you feel about Issa?"

Phoebe looked slightly surprised. "Totally different. I was relieved. Issa isn't drugged-up or violent or anything."

Lightman glanced over at Hanson, clearly as interested in this as she was. "Alex had violent ex-boyfriends?"

"Not violent like hurting anyone," Phoebe said quickly. "Not murderous. And only the one, really. Most of them were just no-hopers. But at school he fell for a troublemaker called Danny, who was—who was sweet, really, but riddled with issues. He would do destructive things because he was unhappy. He took a lot of drugs, and he sort of took Alex with him. They got into constant trouble, and Alex and Daddy really fell out."

It was surprising, Hanson thought, that Phoebe was willing to talk so openly about all of this. Particularly with such an emotionally closed-off father.

"Has Alex been in contact with this Danny recently?" she asked.

"Oh no, Danny's—Danny died." She looked at Hanson with an expression that seemed genuinely regretful. "He overdosed while they were at uni. It was pretty shit for Alex. Maybe it was good for him, in the long run, but it was horrendous too." She shook her head. "Poor Danny."

Hanson nodded, feeling a dip in her spirits at the closing off of this obvious line of inquiry. "Did Alex and Danny have any mutual friends who might be on the scene?"

Phoebe thought for a moment, and then shook her head again. "Alex pretty much started over after Danny's death. It broke him, and then he had to put himself back together. He stopped seeing that whole crowd, found a new group, and ultimately met Issa. He's been a lot healthier and happier since." Phoebe gave a small, humorless smile. "My parents don't know that we still see each other. Saw each other. He messaged me sometimes too."

"It's OK, we're not about to tell them," Lightman said, smiling. "Have any of his recent messages contained anything strange?"

"No," Phoebe said definitively, and then asked, "Was it not—random, then? That's where all this is going, isn't it? You think someone singled him out. Someone he knew."

"I'm afraid we have no theories as yet," Lightman said gently. "We need to cover everything."

Alex's sister took a long breath in and then let it out. "OK. I don't know much. He just sent occasional updates. We last talked on the phone a couple of weeks ago. . . ." There was a pause, as Alex's sister once again tried to swallow down rising tears. "He seemed—fine. Normal. Whatever happened wasn't—I don't think he was in any weird trouble."

"And he didn't mention meeting up with anyone new?" Hanson asked, thinking of Louise Reakes. That she had been at the nightclub, and might be hiding the fact that she knew Alex. "A female friend?"

Phoebe focused on her. "He's never really had female friends." She shrugged. "I know it flies in the face of the stereotype, but he's always been more comfortable around other men. I'm the one exception, really." Her eyes narrowed slightly. "When you say 'friend,' are you . . . ? You think he was seeing someone? A woman?"

"We really don't know," Hanson admitted. "We're just trying to work out who the people at the club with him were and if there were any connections."

"Well, I don't think he was having an affair, if that's what you mean," Phoebe said. "He loves Issa."

"Are you close to Issa too?" Ben asked.

There was a brief pause, and Phoebe said, "We're all right. We used to be closer, but then we argued. Issa wanted Alex to do less social-media stuff and I told him to stop interfering."

Hanson sat forward slightly. Issa had completely failed to mention Alex's sister. Could this be the reason? "He doesn't like him doing it?" she asked.

"No, not after the trolling started." Phoebe pulled a face. "It's been predictably awful for both of them. Alex is open about having a husband. He's put clips of Issa on there too. Some people are totally hideous. I'm sure you know this. But anyway, Issa got to the point where he couldn't stand seeing himself and his husband abused and threatened, and he told Alex to stop. Which really upset him. It's his job, and the trolls are in the vast minority."

"Which you thought too?" Ben asked quietly.

"Yes," Phoebe said. "He—Issa—came round and tried to tell me I had to weigh in on his side. I told him I wouldn't, because it would damage Alex's business. So he got angry and read out some of the comments, and said I was heartless when I wouldn't budge. I thought he'd get over it, but he's stayed angry with me."

"Do you think any of those trolls could have really wanted to harm your brother?" Hanson asked.

Phoebe gave her a bleak look. "I didn't think so. And I don't really . . . I mean, it's just people with no lives. Nothing better to do. They do it online because they're too cowardly to do it for real, don't they? I read about it."

"That's generally true," Hanson agreed. "But we obviously need to check every possibility."

Phoebe looked away, her face screwing up. "God. How much will—will he hate me, if it's—if it was one of them who killed him and I could have stopped it?"

12

LOUISE

It sometimes surprises me, looking back, that we ever made it to our wedding day. There was so much resentment building, and so little trust.

Though, of course, that isn't to say that there weren't good patches. After those shaky weeks where you looked at me as if I were some kind of criminal, things gradually returned to an easier state, if not to a blissful one.

There was a good month where we managed to talk more about wedding plans than suspicions. But I can remember, clearly, how hard I tried to suffocate all the rising doubts. The number of times I turned away from you with a feeling of desolation.

So many people told me how happy I looked in the weeks before our wedding. I suppose I must have done a good job of pretending. As time went on, I even started to believe the facade. At the dinner with our families the night before, when you kept putting your arm round me and kissing me, I remember clearly thinking that everything was perfect, and would be wonderful from then on.

And the day itself, which is a little hazier in my memory, seemed to be a long-awaited prize. Some kind of confirmation that you did love me and hadn't got engaged to piss off your exwife. I felt fierce love for you. Pride too. You were so charming and gentle with my friends. And I think I actually loved you still more when I saw your obvious embarrassment in your very ordinary family, and the way you'd schemed to keep them away from your middle-class friends. I saw it all through a haze of adoration, where every part of you now belonged to me.

But I also remember the next day. When I asked you how it felt, and you said you couldn't remember that much of it, but you were glad we'd done it.

Glad we'd done it.

I remember laughing at your unromantic ways while inwardly I felt like I was being crushed. I knew you had a capacity for romance. It had been clear from the little things you'd done early on and from your proposal. I had somehow just stopped stirring it in you.

I was glad when the subject moved on to April and what she'd said at the wedding reception. How she'd drawn you to one side and said, unusually slowly, that I was the best person she knew, and she'd kill you if you ever hurt me. I remember the sheen of sweat on your brow as you told me about it, even a day later. I could see it had shaken you more than you wanted to admit. But you were angry about it too.

Who does she think she is, saying that to the man who loves you?

I remember feeling for you when you said that. I would have been angry, too, I thought. But now I think not. I think I would have assumed April just cared about her best friend. I would probably have forgiven it.

Maybe your anger came from somewhere else. From guilt.

Those are the only really strong memories I have of our wedding. The photos seem to be of some fantastical dream I once had.

I sometimes wonder whether I would have gone through with it if I'd known everything I do now. In particular, if I'd known about the money.

I'm being honest when I say that I never even suspected it. The truth only hit home three months after our wedding, during that strange, rather disappointing time when the ceremony and the party were all done, when the gifts were all opened and had been used a few times or put away, when life had returned to normal and I'd really understood that marriage was never going to make me feel secure.

I remember trying to move things on. To think about the next thing. To bring up the subject of children again. And it was only on the fourth of these occasions, a Wednesday evening when we were eating a Greek salad and flatbreads that I'd thrown together in the hope of pleasing you, that you finally seemed to grow angry.

I remember the expression on your face as you put your fork down and said, "I don't think you're responsible enough to have a child, do you?"

I shouldn't have asked what you meant. I already knew.

"Come on. Anyone who gets blind drunk and can't remember what they've done isn't responsible." Your voice was loud. Full of outrage. "You lost your handbag and keys a week ago, Louise. At a nice restaurant. God knows what you're like when I'm out of the country. How would you look after a kid?"

I felt breathless with hurt. We'd got drunk *together*. You'd been just as shitfaced as I'd been. And I'd been so, so well behaved the rest of the time. With April. When I was on my own.

"But I don't do anything when you're away," I told you, my voice tight. Choking. "Not anymore. Not after that—that horrible man . . ."

You got to your feet at that point, pushing your kitchen chair back so hard that it made a screeching sound on the linoleum.

"Look, I don't want to talk about this right now. OK? I'm tired. It's been a long week."

And it had, of course. It had been like every other week. You'd been away for three days, and I'd been either performing or rehearsing around that. This was the one night we'd had together, and I suddenly felt awful for having ruined it. So I let it go. I swallowed the hurt, and I cleared up the remains of our dinner in silence.

But I didn't forget it. I dwelled on it for the next four days, until the morning I opened your bank statement instead of mine. There are probably a lot of truths discovered about spouses this way, though I imagine that some husbands or wives are clever enough to open them on purpose.

I'm happy to admit that I wasn't clever at all. I assumed that your lavish gifts and lifestyle were based on a serious salary and savings. I thought I could sit back and enjoy it. That the amount we spent on our wedding had been entirely justified given how much you earned. I really did think this, Niall. It was never willful ignorance on my part.

And then I read that statement, with its fully used overdraft of thirty thousand, and it filled me with horror.

It pulled the rug right out from under me. You were so *together*. So *grown-up*. How could you possibly have let this happen?

But as I looked at the payments in and out, I started to have some idea. The clothes you wear so well are all designer, aren't they? And those company nights out where you lavish free drinks on everyone are costing you thousands per year. And then there's your car, which I right then discovered wasn't "a really good deal." I know now that it costs you nine hundred a month. It costs a mortgage, Niall. A *mortgage*. And I find it incomprehensible that not long after this, you mentioned swapping it for a newer model when you are so deep in debt that it's terrifying.

The money coming in was almost as worrying. It was clear that you were taking out loans. The sums were too big and too round to be anything else. And I know what those kinds of loans cost in interest.

The more I saw, the more I started to doubt everything you'd ever told me. More than anything, I doubted that you actually liked yourself. How could anyone who felt comfortable in their skin be so desperate to have so many symbols of status? Because there was status written all over every single payment you'd made.

I went pretty quickly from being frightened of those numbers to being searingly angry. Four nights earlier, you'd held up my erratic behavior as a sign of inadequacy. As definitive proof that I couldn't cope with having a child. And while you were punishing me for that, you were busy being as irresponsible as it was possible to be.

I know you'll wonder why I said nothing. I could so easily have confronted you.

But as I sat there with that statement in front of me, and I thought about having an open conversation, I felt everything in me protest. I wasn't strong enough. Not just then. And part of me worried that you would react defensively, and tell me off for snooping. I don't know even now if that was unfair of me.

So I took that statement, envelope and all, and I hid it in a copy of Handel's *Messiah,* which I slid back onto the shelf in my music room. It was somewhere you would never look. We were three months married, and you had already lost interest in my music. It had become, if anything, an irritation to you when I played. I'm pretty sure it was before this that you first came and shut the music-room door while I was practicing, so you could continue your evening uninterrupted.

It took three glasses of wine to stop me worrying about that bank statement. And then another three to make me calm enough to be normal when you got home. To make you dinner and to listen with a smile as you told me about the rheumatologist you'd converted into a champion for your drugs. I did my job well, I think, because you came over to me as I was clearing away, and smoothed my hair back out of my face. Your eyes studied me, and you said "Love you, Lou" for the first time since our honeymoon.

And then, instead of having a difficult conversation, we made love, then put crap comedy on the upstairs TV and lay next to each other. It felt like a dangerous corner that I'd managed to swing into and out of. It felt like I'd made the right decision.

Perhaps I was wrong to hide it. Perhaps you had actually been waiting for a chance to talk about it. It might have been a massive relief for you, and it would have become *our* problem instead of *yours*. You might have thanked me for forcing it out into the open, instead of telling me I shouldn't have been looking at your mail.

But I feel that your behavior since Alex Plaskitt's death has proved all my fears justified. Don't you?

13

O'Malley agreed to take April Dumont's information over the phone. What the DCI wanted from her now was a simple account of what Louise Reakes had done the night before.

"Ask me anything you want," she said firmly. "I can tell you she has no earthly thing to do with some poor guy's death."

Anyone, O'Malley thought, who described Southern U.S. accents as soft or lilting needed to talk to April Dumont. This Tennessee twang was all hard edges and rapid rhythms. There was nothing remotely lilting about it.

"What makes you say that? Has Louise told you she feels under suspicion?"

"She messaged to say you'd dragged her into the station again," April said. "So I guess there's something going on."

"Not so much that," O'Malley said in a soothing tone. "We just need to check things. That's all. Due diligence and all that. Could you tell me if you'd arranged to meet someone at the club?"

"No, we didn't," she said. There was a momentary pause and a murmur. O'Malley caught the words "whisky sour," and realized she must be in a bar somewhere. "That's never what we do. It's always just the two of us. And Louise wasn't even that keen at first. I insisted we had to go out. I thought she needed cheering up, and, to be honest, I did too."

"Why would Louise need cheering up?"

"Because her life's been increasingly depressing." April made another impatient sound. "Look, I don't want . . . This is Louise's business. But . . . it's hard when you want kids and don't seem to be making any progress with having them. OK?"

"Sure, OK," O'Malley answered. "And I know it seems intrusive, but all this stuff is useful so we can stop looking at someone who wasn't involved."

"I guess I get that," April said, sounding a little less combative.

"Louise's husband was away, so you felt free to go out? Is that right?"

"Darn right. Niall's not too fond of his wife drinking anything these days." April gave a short laugh. "And he thinks I'm a bad influence too."

"So he'd be angry with her if he knew?"

"He'd be preachy," April corrected. "And that's enough of a pain in the ass. Look, I've got about ten minutes before a meeting and I thought you wanted to know about last night."

"That's fine," O'Malley said easily. "Can you tell me when you arrived at the club?"

"I guess . . . eleven-thirty or something?"

"And you were with Louise the whole time?"

"Well, I went to the bar and the ladies' a few times," April said. "And then I—sorta hit it off with this guy. . . ."

"And you didn't see Louise talking to a young man?" O'Malley asked. "He was tall and obviously athletic. He probably would have stood out."

"No, I didn't," April insisted. "I didn't see her talking to anyone except the bar staff all evening."

"And while you were with this fella . . ."

"Louise went to get drinks."

"And then?"

"And then I guess . . . I'm not sure after that," April admitted. "She would have waited awhile. You always do somewhere that serves cocktails."

"When was the last time you saw her?"

"On her way over there. So I guess . . . around midnight."

O'Malley paused slightly. "So you left with this . . . guy? You didn't say goodbye to Louise?"

"I know I should have," April said with a touch of defensiveness, "but I was rolling drunk by that time. And sometimes you don't make great decisions in those circumstances."

O'Malley waited a moment, certain that April would feel compelled to say more. He wasn't disappointed.

"Look. Whatever Louise did after that, she didn't end up killing some guy," she said, sounding frustrated. "She's this warm, loving, kind person. I felt bad this morning because I worried something could have happened to her, understand? I would never in a million years worry she'd hurt someone else. So you need to send Louise home so she can sleep and recover. She probably feels like a heap of shit right now, and she should be in bed, not being grilled by some drama-hungry cops."

"I'm sure she'll be heading home soon."

JONAH TRIED TO fill some time while waiting for his team to update him. As much as he valued the space to think during investigations, there were too many gaps in his knowledge to get to grips with it all, and the two other cases on their books from the week before were at similar stages, without the sense of urgency of a murder.

He decided to look at some of the earlier video footage sent over by Charlie as a starting point. It was all filmed from the same spot close to the door, and caught everyone entering and exiting. It was largely uninteresting, except for a brief brawl at 11:50. Then, at 12:10, Step Conti appeared. He was markedly more sober than anyone except the staff. Jonah noted the time down and switched the video off a few minutes later.

At three he decided to chase up the technical team about Alex's phone. He suspected that they would now be waiting another day. Getting the civilian parts of the force to come in on days off and work swiftly was a constant challenge. Only Linda McCullough would generally show willing, thanks to her obsessive attitude toward her work.

"We're nearly done," a begrudging Intelligence officer told him. "I'll send it to you as soon as it's ready."

Jonah hung up with a rare feeling of satisfaction. DCS Wilkinson must have done a good job of leaning on them.

He spent a few minutes writing up his notes on Louise's interview, and headed back out to CID. Lightman was back at his desk, and Hanson was making her way over with Jason Walker, who had presumably met up with her outside rather than going along for the ride.

Jonah arrived at Lightman's desk at the same time Hanson did, and watched in some amusement as Jason melted away and Hanson blushed very slightly.

"How was the sister?" he asked them both.

"She had a few things to say," Lightman said thoughtfully. "She's not on great terms with the victim's husband because Issa apparently wanted Alex to stop doing his fitness videos. He disliked the trolling. Phoebe Plaskitt refused to take Issa's side."

"She described her brother much as Step Conti did," Hanson added. "Alex was a patient, protective person who generally defused fights rather than getting into them."

Jonah nodded again, digesting this, and then asked O'Malley for an update on April Dumont.

"Everything matched what Louise Reakes said most recently," O'Malley told him. "April copped off with a guy she'd met there. She then left with him. She's positive she didn't see Louise talking to anyone who looked like Alex Plaskitt. She's also pretty keen that we let Louise go immediately. A concerned, mildly threatening friend."

"Well," Jonah said, getting to his feet, "she gets what she wants. Louise is going to have to be released while we work out if we want to arrest her."

"I'll drive her home," Hanson said, swinging her chair around. "She's tired and hungover, and it's possible she might say something she shouldn't."

"Good," Jonah said. "Was there any update on CCTV on London Road?"

"Sod-all," O'Malley said. "I'll ring them again."

"Thanks," Jonah said. "I'd like to chase the traffic cameras up too."

He collected Louise from the interview room, glancing at her sweat-sheened face. She'd put her coat on now, and the white fur lining made her look both younger and even more off-color. But she'd been out drinking last night, so there wasn't necessarily anything suspicious in looking nauseous. He'd been there himself on other occasions.

"Detective Constable Hanson has offered to give you a lift home," he said, once they were close to his team.

Louise faltered. "Oh. That's OK. I can get a cab."

Hanson grinned at her. "It's no problem. I want to grab a sandwich anyway."

Louise's expression was clearly unenthusiastic, but she let Hanson walk her out. Jonah, watching Hanson's very slight smile, felt almost guilty for handing Louise over to her. Almost.

"I'm so sorry about this," Hanson said quietly, once they were out of CID. Up close Louise looked, if anything, worse than she had from a distance. There was a heavy look to her eyes that spoke of barely being able to keep awake and she was gleaming with perspiration. "I know it's not much consolation, but it's just the DCI doing his job."

Louise gave her a doubtful look. She said nothing.

"I've got some ibuprofen and co-codamol," Hanson tried, once they'd climbed into the ice-cold Nissan. "Would you like some . . . ?"

"God, I'd love some," Louise said with sudden feeling. Hanson grinned and rifled through her handbag until she'd found them. Louise held out a hand and let Hanson squeeze four tablets onto it, two sugar-coated and two chalky. "Oh, do you have any water . . . ?"

Hanson reached around to the backseat and retrieved a half-full bottle of Evian.

"It's only from yesterday," she said, "and I promise I don't have the plague."

Louise seemed unconcerned by the idea of germs. She tipped all four tablets into her mouth and then drank all of the remaining water as she swallowed them down.

"Such awful timing, having to deal with this on a hangover," Hanson commented as she started the ignition and began maneuvering the little car. The steering wheel was painfully cold. She wished the heating worked better. If she turned it on now, it would blow cold air at them and then never really get hot. The only answer was to leave it for a good ten minutes with the engine running and then put it on full-blast.

"It's horrible," Louise agreed in a low voice, and then added in a rush, "I don't know where the hangover ends and the shock starts. I wish he'd, you know . . . gone somewhere else."

"I'm sorry," Hanson said. "It must feel completely unreal, him turning up like that with no warning."

Louise nodded, but said nothing else. A short while later, she made a sniffing sound, and when Hanson looked over at her, there were tears tracking down her cheeks.

Saints Close was back to its quiet state, free of ambulances, squad cars, and forensic vehicles. In fact, it was quieter than it had been before the flashing blues had arrived. Many of the other cars were now missing. Louise's neighbors had presumably gone to spend their Saturday afternoon in pilgrimages to the shops or kids' sports clubs.

Hanson pulled up outside Number 11. There was little to show what had happened here aside from the craze of footprints and trampled snow left by so many crime-scene investigators.

"Thanks for the lift," Louise said, and started to lever herself out of the car hurriedly. As she stood, her eyes went to her front gate and she faltered.

Hanson could well guess what she was imagining. The dead man lying on the grass. Perhaps the screens that had been set up, and the white overalls moving around it all.

Hanson undid her seatbelt. "I'll walk to the door with you. It can't be easy, after . . ." She gave a shrug.

Louise paused for a moment, and then said, "Thank you."

Hanson climbed out onto the sidewalk. She let Louise through the gate first, and then, as she followed, moved to block any view of where Alex Plaskitt had been lying a few hours ago.

Louise kept her gaze fixed ahead and unlocked the front door hurriedly. As she pulled the keys back out, she fumbled and dropped them onto the doorstep with a noisy jangle.

"Do you need anything?" Hanson asked as she picked up the keys and moved to step into the house. "Tea? Company?"

"I'm . . . I'm fine," Louise said, her face pallid and sick-looking. And then she suddenly lunged forward, dropping her bag and running for the stairs.

Hanson heard her climb to the first floor and trip. She instinctively stepped forward to help, but Louise seemed to have recovered and rushed farther into the house. "Louise?" she called.

The sounds of Louise vomiting were loud enough that Hanson could hear them from the foot of the stairs. Hanson hesitated for a moment, and then went to the kitchen and pulled open the cupboards until she'd found a pint glass. She ran the tap cold, filled it, and then quietly moved upstairs.

There were still isolated noises of retching, but it sounded as though there was little coming up now. Hanson followed the sounds into a large double bedroom at the front of the house, where she had a view through into an en-suite bathroom. She could just see Louise's feet, her soft gray boots resting on the tiles. She was clearly kneeling over the toilet.

The human side of Hanson was both sympathetic and hesitant. She wasn't entirely sure Louise would want a police officer intruding while she was being ill, but she wanted to offer help in case it was needed.

And then there was the copper in her, which was alert to everything else. It was taking in the details of how Louise lived, from the perfectly made-up bed to the spotless surfaces. From the severe Scandinavian colors to the obvious high quality of everything she was looking at.

It was the copper in her that picked up on the one small imperfection. The tiniest spot of dark red on a pale gray carpet, just under the edge of the large double bed.

Hanson paused momentarily between one step and the next. Her mind went through the options. It might be nail varnish. Coffee. Some flaw in the carpet.

But Hanson had learned enough of Louise to doubt it. She was clearly obsessive about tidiness and order, and it seemed impossible that she would have let a mark spoil that carpet.

Hanson could see more of Louise now. She was facing almost entirely away from Hanson, slumped on her arms, which were folded across the toilet seat. The picture of misery.

Hanson was only too happy to use that misery to her advantage. She moved over to the bed, and then crouched. Close up, the spot on the carpet was rusty red, and Hanson felt a shiver run through her. It looked very much like dried blood.

She ran her eyes along the bottom edge of the bed, which was a pale gray velvet. And then, glancing toward the bathroom again, she put a hand out to a point just above the stain on the carpet and lifted the very edge of the sheet.

It took one glance to tell her everything she needed to know, and she felt dizzy as she tucked it in again and got back to her feet.

She took another two steps toward the bathroom, and Louise turned, her eyes bloodshot and her expression stricken.

"Have some of this," Hanson said gently, and handed her the water.

She stayed with Louise for ten more minutes, helping her to her feet and back down to the kitchen, where she made her another cup of tea without milk and talked cheerfully about how much better Louise would feel after a nap on the sofa.

And then she climbed back into the car and called the chief as she maneuvered back onto the main road.

"We need a search warrant," she told him. "As quickly as you can."

14

LOUISE

There are a few events that I look back on now and see as turning points for us. The crossroads that sent us down this crappy path. There was a darkness to realizing how much money you owed, and how easily you had lied to me. It made me more willing to believe that you'd lied about other things too. But that wasn't what did it for us. There were still signs of hope afterward.

One of those was your reaction the first time I slipped up and got really drunk again with April. I hadn't meant for it to happen, but I'd had a mortifying experience at rehearsals with the Mother Pluckers. Helen, whose smiling viciousness I'd already experienced in the past, had asked me why I looked so tired.

"You aren't pregnant at last, are you?" she'd said in a low voice while we were getting set up.

"No," I told her, blushing. "No. I'm pretty sure not. We've not had any accidents. . . ."

I saw the way her eyes narrowed. The next bit was said much more loudly. "But I thought you said you were trying? Has something changed? Niall got cold feet?"

It was clear that the others had all heard. Their conversations tailed off into silence.

I've never felt so mortified. I had no reply, because that *was* what had happened. I could feel myself going scarlet until kind-hearted Lyn joked that Niall was sensible. That she'd just spent a morning with a vomiting toddler and wouldn't wish it on anyone.

Things then moved on, but for the whole rehearsal I felt their gazes on me. The one non-mother of the group, who perhaps had only been allowed in because they all thought I'd have kids soon.

I pretty much launched myself at the wine when April and I met up. She soothed me and told me they were all pathetic, but none of it helped. The only thing that made me feel all right was sitting back and letting Drunk Louise take over until late, late into the night.

I remember how you looked at me the following morning, with none of the anger I was expecting. You seemed concerned for me. Caring.

"Do you think you should go and see someone?" you asked, having come to sit on the bed next to me.

It knocked me back, that suggestion. Even then, I didn't really think of alcohol as a problem. If anything, it seemed like a solution I was no longer allowed to take.

I shuffled up in the bed until I was sitting, trying to turn this into a conversation between equals.

"I hardly drink at all now," I told you. And it was true. Even when I was with you, I'd cut down. I wanted so badly to prove to you that I had everything under control. That I could be a fantastic mother. "I go days and days. I drink less than you most of the time too. I'm really all right. I just didn't eat enough last night, that's all."

I saw your reaction. Your expression changed to something between exasperation and desolation. You nodded and gave a strange half-smile. Then you rubbed my shoulder and got up. It looked like I'd damaged you somehow, and thinking of the hurt I might be inflicting did more to wake me up than anything else.

I went out a few days later. It was the Sunday afternoon after the big concert, when the Pluckers had agreed to meet for lunch. I'd promised myself that I'd only have a couple of glasses. But somewhere along the line, beaten down by more snide remarks from Helen, I'd had a few more, and let Drunk Louise take the reins again. I have a hazy memory of being hilarious, and of the nicer Pluckers telling me how great I was.

But then I remember it being six P.M., and it being me, the other Louise, who was at the helm. I remember that my hand was firmly round a glass of Pinot Noir, and I had no idea how it had happened. It was like I'd been pinched awake again.

It was your heartbroken expression that I thought of just then, Niall. I suddenly saw the wine as the cause of it, and I put it down. I took a breath, and then I went to the bar for water and a few packets of crisps.

For three hours I drank nothing but water and juice. I ordered myself a plate of pasta, and I sat and waited for sobriety to return. I felt strangely proud of myself. And determined to turn this all around.

At nine I smiled at all of them and said I was going home for crap TV and cuddles with my husband. I left imagining you telling me how well I'd done. I ached to hear you say it.

I let myself in at nine-fifteen, and felt an immediate dip as I realized that the house was empty. I was pretty sure you'd said you were at home, and it puzzled me. But then I doubted myself and sent you a message. I asked you what you were up to. That was all.

I got myself another glass of water and put my coat and handbag away, and while I was doing that you messaged back cheerfully to say you were on the sofa watching *Game of Thrones* and accidentally fell asleep.

And, you know, I think that was the first time I'd ever known you to outright lie to me. I mean, there was the money thing, it was true, but you'd never actually told me that you were solvent. You'd just let me assume. And you hadn't hidden what Dina had said to you, either, even if you hadn't been quite open about how you felt.

But now here you were, telling me a stark untruth. And, in this case, I was certain it was for a really, really bad reason.

I desperately wanted to know where you were, but I had no way of knowing without alerting you to the fact that I was home. And for some reason that was the scariest thing of all.

So I did a crazy thing instead. I went back out there, in another rip-off cab ride, and I started stalking your favorite bars and restaurants. At first I told myself I'd just check a couple. I figured you might be at La Mejican or the Pitcher and Piano. When you weren't there, I thought of a few more. And a few more.

I was out there for three hours, and when I finally gave up because the blisters on my heels were too bad for me to walk any farther, it was after midnight. You still hadn't messaged me to tell me you were going to bed. You'd only sent a query at eleven, asking if I was still having fun, which I replied to with a thumbs-up, because I had to reply somehow.

I was so sure you were still out there by the time I gave up. I was certain you were meeting up with someone. Cheating on me. I cried all the way home in the cab.

The house was still empty when I got in, and I couldn't face being in the sitting room or in bed when you returned. I just couldn't. So I went to the music room and huddled on the sofa in the dark.

You actually didn't get back that long after I did. An hour at most. But it felt like years had passed. I'd been unable to sit still.

I heard you arrive home, then make yourself tea before you went up to bed. I had all my things with me, so there was no reason for you to know I was there. I listened, hardly breathing, to the sounds of running water. You showered for a long while. Were you washing off traces of whichever woman you'd been with, Niall? Is that what you were doing?

I stayed where I was that night, unable to face curling up next to you. So when you woke me, you thought I'd stumbled in and slept right there on the music-room sofa.

The fact that you were angry with me about it was the unfairest part. You gave me a cold look when you woke me and asked if I wanted breakfast, as if I'd been the one who'd done wrong.

God, I wanted to throw it in your face. But I was too scared to find out that we were over. Isn't that pathetic?

So I said nothing when you got at me. I didn't apologize. I didn't argue. I ate the breakfast you gave me and said nothing at all, and I think something in that eventually got to you, didn't it? Because after I'd gone to shower and got myself dressed and told you I was going out, you suddenly turned to me and wrapped me in a hug and apologized. You said that you loved me and it was concern that made you act like an arsehole sometimes.

Later on, you saw the blisters on my heels and bandaged them up. You kissed me gently and told me you'd fix me up somehow.

I guess you remember that bit, and how we had two weeks after that which felt like the old us. Two weeks where we were fine. Happy. The best of friends who told each other everything (except not quite everything).

But it was all false. I was sure that your good behavior was nothing but guilt. I wanted desperately to look at your communications but was too frightened, and so, as a coping strategy, I became increasingly obsessed with tidiness and order. I would sometimes catch you watching me clean, an expression on your face like you wondered what on earth you were doing with me.

And, as the two of us fell apart, the other me returned too. It was just one night at first. A single night off while I let myself enjoy Drunk Louise taking over.

But the thing I've now learned about her is that it's never just one night. Once Drunk Louise has me again, she doesn't like to let go.

15

Damian punched the steering wheel again, letting fury seep into him. Reveling in the rage.

Everything about his relationship with Juliette had made him feel worse about himself. He could see that now. That was why he'd needed to spend so much to feel better. And it was why he'd been messaging other women.

Juliette was poison. That was what it came down to. Her apparent sympathy for him had quickly been revealed as cold judgment. Every decision he'd made had been resisted, bloody-mindedly. And she'd belittled him in public, too, by flirting with other men.

The trouble with that kind of poison was that it was addictive. It wasn't his fault he'd been unable to get her out of his system. Two girlfriends had already walked out on him for still trying to contact her, and earlier today a girl he'd only been on three dates with had told him she didn't feel comfortable about his attitude toward his ex.

He'd told her to go fuck herself and climbed into the car. It was inevitable that he'd ended up driving toward Southampton and that bitch Juliette.

He'd made the trip several times recently. He'd been trying to work out whether Juliette was shagging someone. She'd changed phones, so he could no longer check her messages using the apps he'd installed on the old one. He had to be there in person to find out.

She'd definitely stayed away overnight multiple times in the last few months. His immediate assumption had been that she'd got together with the perfume-model cop she worked with. But having followed him home, he'd seen no sign of Juliette visiting.

It was only today that he'd put everything together and realized that the moody-looking bloke she'd sometimes walked to the pub with was now her boyfriend. It had sent a strange, sick electricity through him watching her turn to give him a peck on the lips in the station car park.

God, she was a bitch. She'd clearly never cared about him at all.

What she needed to learn was that she couldn't do whatever she felt like and get away with it. He was going to get even.

And the thought made him smile.

LOUISE REAKES'S ARREST ended up being quite a public event. The forensic team arrived at a little after five-thirty, just as the sun was setting. Numerous families were at home, and others were able to gawp on their way out for the evening. Jonah had been aware of at least ten people stopping to watch as the squad car and scientific-support van had pulled up behind him.

It had taken an hour and twenty-five minutes to procure a warrant for the search of the house. Which was, in fact, terrifically fast, while also feeling infuriatingly slow.

He was profoundly grateful that Hanson had acted so carefully. She must have been tempted to arrest Louise Reakes. She could have used it as a justification for searching the house immediately. The power to search on arrest was a gray area that had certainly been exploited that way in the past. But whole cases had sometimes collapsed in the courts as a result. A good barrister could argue that such searches had not been carried out legally, and some judges were inclined to agree.

Hanson had played it perfectly, however. She'd requested the search, and been calm and collected giving her evidence to the magistrate via video link. She hadn't even mentioned the blood. Instead she had explained that Louise had previously lied about her whereabouts that night. She had then expressed concern over Louise's reaction on arriving back at the house. Vomiting, she felt, was likely to have been the result of guilt or anxiety.

The magistrate had agreed.

Hanson had asked to be there while the search took place, and Jonah had been more than happy to bring her along. If they ended up making an arrest, he wanted Hanson to have the satisfaction of doing it.

It was hard not to feel a little sorry for Louise as they converged on her front door, however. Her neighbors were unlikely to forget this particular scene. Though at least the front of the house was fairly well screened. Louise herself wouldn't be on full display.

Jonah knocked loudly, reverting to the loud rapping they'd been taught when he'd first become a constable. Knocking that was too loud to ignore. Too loud for "I didn't hear you." The kind of knock used only by police officers or bailiffs.

Louise's eyes were very wide as she opened the door. She said nothing as Jonah showed her the warrant and told her that they had the right to search the property. She did no more than nod, and then move slowly aside.

Linda McCullough had already been primed to search the bedroom. She left three of her overall-covered team downstairs and headed upward with just one of them. Jonah gestured for Hanson to follow them while he prowled around downstairs. Louise retreated to the far end of the house and Jonah left her to it for the time being.

What was to follow was both thorough forensic work and a little playacting. They had to let a reasonable amount of time pass for it to look like the blood had been discovered organically. So Jonah drifted in and out of rooms, asking the three forensic staff to look at a few things. A faint mark on the wall next to the stairs. The laundry hanging on a rack in the tiny utility room.

McCullough left it fifteen minutes before she called him upstairs. Jonah was in the music room at that point, where Louise was sitting with her legs pulled up on a futon. In that position she was largely hidden behind her harp, but he could still see the side of her face through the strings.

It was clear from her expression that she knew what McCullough had found. Her legs moved instinctively, as if she were about to get up, then froze in the act and tried to sit back naturally.

Jonah left her there. He climbed the stairs and entered Louise and Niall's bedroom. McCullough and her assistant had stripped the sheets back from the bed, exposing a tide mark of brownish red. Hanson was standing to one side, a satisfied expression on her face.

Despite having been prepared for this, Jonah found himself a little nauseated at the extent of the blood. It had soaked through most of the mattress. The only white details remaining were the little plastic buttons dented into its top.

"I'm confident we'll be able to get DNA," McCullough said. "The underneath hasn't entirely dried yet."

"Good," Jonah said. "And quantity . . . You'd say it looks enough for him to have died here?"

"I'll get you a volumetric estimate," McCullough said, "but on a visual reckoning it looks more than enough."

Jonah gave her a small smile. McCullough was renowned for being difficult to pin down. She hated committing herself to theories, and tended to offer stark fact with no interpretation. For her to give him that much meant she had no doubt at all.

Hanson went back downstairs with him. He let her walk into

the music room first. Louise's expression looked hopeless. Her fear was stark and obvious, even viewed through the strings of her harp.

"Louise Reakes, I'm arresting you for the murder of Alex Plaskitt, and for perverting the course of justice," Hanson began.

"I'm sorry for lying," Louise said, before she could go on. "I'm really sorry."

"Did she say anything else?" Lightman asked an hour later. His eyes were on the pale, sick-looking face of Louise Reakes.

He, Jonah, and Hanson had gathered briefly in the observation room. Louise's solicitor was on his way over. Jonah had gone into the interview room to tell her, but Louise had said nothing. Done nothing. He wondered whether she had really understood him.

"Not a word," Hanson murmured. "We both tried asking her why she'd lied, but we only got head shakes."

"Any news on the husband?" Jonah asked.

"No reply from his mobile," Lightman told him. "Presumably in flight."

Jonah nodded. He didn't go on to say anything more yet. About the significance of the blood being in Louise and Niall Reakes's marital bed. About the fact that Alex Plaskitt had been married to a man and yet had almost certainly died in bed with a woman. There were too many questions that needed answering, and no way of making sense of any of it without a lot of strange assumptions.

"Juliette, I want you and Domnall to go and see April Dumont. And we should talk to Alex's husband again as soon as we can. It's high time we found out whether Alex and Louise actually knew each other before that night, and I doubt Louise will tell us."

The pressure was now on to pin this thing down, and soon. They might have only twenty-four hours to charge Louise Reakes with murder. But Jonah had already applied to the superintendent for an extension to the standard twenty-four-hour limit. He was asking for an initial thirty-six hours, but fully intended to apply to the magistrates' court for the maximum after that, which was ninety-six. Given the seriousness of the crime, with the added charge of perverting the course of justice, it was highly likely they'd be granted their request.

If, in the next ninety-six hours, they could prove that the blood on the bed was Alex's—which was the only reasonable explanation—then they would almost certainly have passed the threshold for Louise to be prosecuted. They could charge her knowing that the prosecutor would be happy to work with them to obtain further proof. Which was satisfying, but it wasn't enough.

As far as Jonah was concerned, within those ninety-six hours they needed to know whether she really had killed him and why. Because although the circumstances and her actions pointed that way, there were an awful lot of unanswered questions.

"I've got something for you," Lightman said quietly, a few minutes after he and Hanson had returned to their desks.

Hanson looked at him in surprise as he smiled at her. Was this banter? With the exception of their car journey, Ben hadn't offered anything like that in months.

Recovering, she asked, mock-seriously, "Is it a cake? Please let it be a cake."

Ben smiled more widely and shook his head. "Sadly not. But it is great." He leaned across the desk. "As well as being a solo harpist, Louise Reakes is a member of a harp ensemble. They're called, get this, the Mother Pluckers."

Hanson gave a delighted laugh, in part at the name and in part because he really was bantering again. "All right, that is genuinely almost as good as cake. Are they all mums or something?"

"Looks like it," he agreed. "There are loads of cheerful and not-at-all-posed pictures of them with their children. Louise seems to be the odd one out."

"I have to look at this," Hanson said, and was in the process of typing it into Google when the DCI emerged.

"Louise Reakes's solicitor's just arrived downstairs," Sheens told them. "I'll give them a quarter of an hour to get their ducks in a row and then we can head in, Ben."

Hanson watched him return to his office, still a little disappointed at missing out on Louise's grilling. Not that she didn't have plenty to be getting on with. She needed to put together a new social-media post asking for information on Louise Reakes, and ask her colleagues in Intelligence to circulate it to the public in case someone had seen her on her way home. It would also be up to her, as the team's constable, to appear in front of the magistrates tomorrow to ask for their custody extension. But before doing any of that, she finished loading up the Mother Pluckers' website. She shook her head as she flicked through their pictures.

"Oh my God, look at this one," she said, turning her screen so that Ben could see. It was an aggressively arty black-and-white image of the group posing in leather jackets. "It looks like a poorly thought-through eighties album cover. I love it."

Ben nodded. "Fo sho, motherplucker."

Hanson laughed so loudly that Jason looked over from the far side of CID with a frown. She mouthed at him, *I'll tell you later*, a little guiltily, and then, still grinning, started to get their case against Louise Reakes moving.

PATRICK ARRIVED A little over an hour after Louise had called him, and her feelings as the dashing, ever so slightly chubby solicitor was let into the interview room were entirely mixed. Relief made up a big part. She had someone to fight her corner now. But on top of all that, she felt a nauseous, squirming sense of shame. Patrick was the last person she wanted to be going into all this with. She wished, helplessly, that he could have been simply her lawyer and not Niall's best friend.

Patrick's smile was warm and confident, and she tried to return it. She wondered how he would look at her once she'd explained everything. Once he knew.

He settled himself into a chair opposite her, and placed his dark-brown leather case, which looked like it cost about the same as Niall's car, on top of the table. Then he drew out a notebook and a silver fountain pen as though they were his weapons.

"How are you holding up?" he asked her, all brown-eyed charm.

"All right," she said. And then she added, wanting to make sure he really did like her before the shit hit the fan, "Better now that you're here."

"Good. Good. I've managed to get through to Niall. He's at the airport. He won't be long."

It was supposed to be comforting, Louise knew. Instead, the threat of Niall arriving drove her anxiety up to a critical level. She'd thought she'd have more time.

Patrick unscrewed the lid of his fountain pen. "So. Tell me."

"OK," she said, and then without meaning to she gave what was almost a laugh. "Please brace yourself because it sounds—it sounds fucking awful, and I'm a little afraid you're going to think exactly the same as the police."

"Of course I won't," he said soothingly.

"Well, I went out drinking last night." She swallowed. "I remember almost none of the later part of the evening. Nothing about how I got home. When I woke up early this morning, there was a dead man lying next to me."

Patrick's writing hand went absolutely still, and he fixed his gaze on her. "Cause of death?"

"He was stabbed," she said, feeling heat in her eyes and then wetness tracking down her cheeks. "And they think—they think I did it. But you have to believe me, Patrick. I don't know who the hell he was, or how he got there. And I'm—I'm sure I could never have stabbed anyone. I'm so very sure."

SOMETIMES YOU HAD to attack. To be relentless and without mercy. It was clear to Jonah that this was what he had to do today, to get in there and shake Louise up in the seconds before her solicitor could intervene and distract or calm or deflect. And so he took Lightman with him, told him to play it cold and clinical, and began as he meant to go on.

"Alex Plaskitt died in your bed," he said harshly. "Not in the front garden, as you tried to lead us to assume. In your bed. This man that you apparently didn't know."

"My client's statement that she didn't know this man stands," Patrick Moorcroft said easily and loudly. "Did you have an actual question, or just a series of statements to make?"

Jonah had dealt with Mr. Moorcroft once before. Only the once. He was too expensive for most of the people Jonah interviewed. And he was expensive because he was bloody good. Or, to put it from Jonah's perspective, bloody infuriating. But Jonah couldn't help feeling a grudging respect for him, however frustrating it was to have an interview essentially dictated by a solicitor.

"How did a man you don't recognize end up in your bed?" Jonah tried instead.

"I'm afraid I don't know," Louise said with a glance at her solicitor. And that was all she said. Louise seemed collected now. Focused, in a grim sort of way, and less afraid. Presumably because her expensive solicitor was now there.

Patrick gave him the smallest of smiles, and Jonah shared a momentary glance with Lightman, both exasperated and amused in spite of himself. Lightman's expression in return was, of course, unreadable. Jonah turned back to Louise.

"I'd like to know how Alex Plaskitt died."

She glanced at Patrick Moorcroft, and then said, "I want to be able to help. I wish I could, because what happened to him was awful. But I don't remember anything about the later stages of last night." She looked down. "I've tried. I've tried over and over again. But there's nothing. All I know is that I've never done anything violent, and I don't believe I would have harmed Alex Plaskitt or anyone else."

Jonah kept his gaze on her. "Why would he have been in your bed?"

Louise's expression changed slightly. A note of discomfort crept in.

"I can't think of any reason at all. In five years there's been nobody in that bed except me, my husband, or, on a few occasions, his parents." Her mouth twisted slightly. "I wasn't out on the pull, if that's what you might be thinking. I've never cheated on my husband and in the memories I have of yesterday night I was talking to April, not to any men."

"And yet Alex ended up there," Jonah said. "In your bed."

Patrick leaned over to murmur to her, and Louise said simply, "I've told you already that I can't explain it."

"You claim never to have met him before," Lightman commented.

"I hadn't."

"It seems unlikely that you would have invited an unknown man back to your house, to sleep in your bed, unless you had a sexual motivation," the sergeant went on.

"Who says I invited him?" Louise asked coldly. "For all I know he took advantage of me."

"Was there any sign of that?" Jonah asked.

Louise's face flushed a deep red. "I don't—I don't know."

Jonah expected another murmur from her solicitor, but Patrick, surprisingly, said nothing. He kept his gaze on his papers.

"If you need an examination," Jonah said, more gently, "we can get you one. If that's what happened, then it's important for us to know, as well as for you."

Louise shook her head rapidly, and then said, "I don't want an examination."

Jonah nodded, not without frustration. It wasn't uncommon for possible victims to panic at the idea of an examination. But Louise could equally well know that she hadn't been assaulted, and still want to keep the possibility open.

"Do you often experience complete blackouts after nights out drinking?" Jonah asked, changing tack.

"What relevance does that have?" Patrick Moorcroft asked.

"It gives us an idea of whether her apparent failure of memory stands up," Jonah replied, giving him a level stare. "In addition, Mrs. Reakes has suggested that Alex Plaskitt might have sexually assaulted her. If she makes a habit of going out and becoming incapacitated through alcohol, it's possible that she and Mr. Plaskitt had met on another occasion, without her remembering it."

The solicitor leaned over to mutter to Louise, and she said in a quiet voice, "I do lose . . . time, sometimes. Some events. Not normally quite so much, but . . ."

"Do you often drink alone?" Jonah asked.

"No," Louise said. "I don't."

Jonah signaled to Lightman, who brought up the slide containing the photo of the knife.

"I'd like to ask you once again whether you recognize this weapon."

"No," Louise said. "I told you that before."

"Then how did it end up in your garden, alongside the body of Alex Plaskitt?"

"I don't *know!*" Louise said, suddenly half shouting. "It isn't mine, and I didn't stab him!"

"Then who did?"

Louise dropped her head to her hands and let out a growl, but Patrick stepped in smoothly to say, "It is the duty of the investigating officers to suggest other suspects. It isn't my client's responsibility."

Jonah had to smile slightly. He gave Patrick a nod.

"Well, at the moment, our theories are fairly limited," Jonah said. "We have a man who clearly died in your bed, a murder weapon found in your garden, and a frantic attempt to cover up the crime scene."

"It wasn't how you're trying to make it sound," Louise said angrily, before her solicitor could say anything more.

Jonah nodded again, in satisfaction this time. He was getting to her, and if he kept on prodding her into speech, then her solicitor wouldn't be able to help her. "So how did he wind up in your front garden when he died upstairs?"

Louise took a deep breath, as though she'd realized that she needed to calm down. To keep to the script. Her voice was much more measured as she said, "When I woke up this morning, I was still very much under the influence of alcohol. I was terrified when I found a bleeding man in my bed. At that point I wasn't certain that he was dead."

"It wasn't obvious from the quantity of blood?"

"I'm not a doctor," Louise said with a slight spikiness back in her voice. "I don't know how much blood loss would kill someone."

"So your reaction would have been to call for help," Jonah said. "To call an ambulance."

"It might have been if I'd been in a more rational frame of mind," Louise countered, "but unfortunately I panicked. I think it was a combination of the alcohol clouding my judgment and sheer fear. I thought I needed to get him to someone. A neighbor. Anyone. So I dragged him outside, telling him it would be all right, and not understanding that it really wasn't all right until he was lying on the ground. I realized—I realized . . ." She waved a hand in what looked like frustration, her eyes filling with tears.

Jonah sat back, watching her for a moment, absolutely certain that this was an account her solicitor had rehearsed with her. They might even have rehearsed the tears. The problem for him, and the prosecutor, would be that it *could* just about be true, and therefore was difficult to disprove. Despite its unlikeliness. Despite all the obvious doubts that her actions raised.

"I'll admit that I'm finding that hard to believe," he said, after a deliberate pause for consideration. "Particularly given the care you took to clear up any traces of Alex being in your house."

"However hard it is to believe, you need to start trying," Louise said thickly. She drew in a slightly ragged breath. "I didn't kill him, and somebody else did. I want to know how he ended up there too. I really, really want to know, so I can prove to my husband that I wasn't shagging someone else."

She descended quite suddenly into actual sobs, and dropped her head into her hands, the heels of her palms squeezing into each eye socket.

Jonah glanced toward Lightman, whose face was as neutral as ever as he sat up to ask, "Do you know a man called Issa Benhawy?"

Louise raised her head slightly, and her mouth twisted, as if she hadn't expected any kindness and was almost satisfied to have it confirmed. "No," she said from behind her hands. "I don't think so."

"What about Step Conti?"

"No," she said, pulling the hands away and scrabbling in her handbag until she found a tissue. Her eyes looked raw and red. Perhaps the tears had been real this time. "Definitely not." She looked toward Patrick, and then asked, "Why? Who are they?"

"Alex Plaskitt's husband and his best friend."

There was a profound silence for a moment while Louise stared at Jonah, her mouth ever so slightly ajar. And then she said,

"His *husband*?" at the same moment that her solicitor said, "Are you serious?"

"Indeed," Jonah said, answering both of them with a very small smile.

"Let me just clarify this," Patrick said. "You are attempting to suggest that my client was involved in some sort of one-night stand with a gay man, and . . . what? I'm not quite clear. Decided to stab him? Without motive?"

"What your client and Alex Plaskitt were doing in her marital bed remains unclear," Jonah said, his voice and expression hard. "The outcome is, however, exceptionally clear."

There was a slight pause, and then Louise said, "Do you think . . . he might have been trying—to rob me?"

Jonah glanced at her in surprise. The theft angle was on his list of possibilities, but he hadn't expected Louise Reakes to think of it. Unless, perhaps, Louise remembered more than she was letting on.

"What makes you ask that?"

"I suppose we have money and . . . the only thing I remember about the later part of the night is that at some point I was afraid. I have this . . . fragment of a memory, and there's a man's voice in it, hushing me." Her eyes took on a slight sheen. "It might have been him."

Jonah looked at her expression, which seemed halfway between eager and agonized. As if Louise both wanted to believe this and desperately didn't all at once.

THE HIGHLY ANTICIPATED data from Alex's phone arrived just after they'd left Louise to eat sandwiches with her solicitor. Jonah forwarded it to Lightman and, before leaving to speak to Issa, asked his sergeant to run a quick check for Louise Reakes's phone number.

"Nothing," Lightman said after running a search. "And no Louise listed in his contacts."

"OK. Any messages sent last night?"

Lightman scrolled through the records. "Quite a few to and from his husband, plus one two-minute phone call at a bit before midnight. A couple between him and Step Conti, but that's it."

"OK." Jonah put a hand on his shoulder. "I'd like a full report, if you're OK to wade through."

"Sure."

Of course he was OK. Ben Lightman was always OK with the kind of in-depth, laborious work that would have driven most people mad. There was a reason two of the new Intelligence staff had now nicknamed him the Cyborg. Though there was another related reason too. One of them had been infatuated with him and had made a move on him at a retirement party a couple of months ago, but Ben hadn't been interested. He never was.

Jonah turned to Hanson and nodded toward the door. His constable rose readily, grabbing her jacket and handbag.

"Issa is at home and ready to talk. I'm stopping at Costa on the way," he added. "In case you need anything."

"God, yes," Hanson replied. "I could murder a ham-and-cheese melt."

The traffic was still heavy. Traveling back and forth across the city was a time-consuming element that Jonah could have done without, but he specifically wanted to talk to Issa at home. He wanted access to any recent videos Alex had made and to his email accounts, if possible. Anything that might contain some form of contact between him and Louise.

"What went on with Louise Reakes in the interview room?" Hanson asked between mouthfuls, once they were back on the road and attempting to eat hot sandwiches without letting any cheese ooze anywhere.

"She's not admitting to anything except moving the body," Jonah replied. "And even then, she says she thought he was alive and was dragging him to the neighbors' for help."

Hanson gave a slight laugh. "I'm sure we'd all immediately try to lift a ninety-kilo man down the stairs."

"My thoughts entirely," Jonah agreed.

"Has she told us anything about last night?"

"She claims she remembers nothing at all beyond talking to her friend April." Jonah tried to squeeze the rest of his sandwich farther up the cardboard pack and then swore as one of the pieces of bread slid up and out, landing in his lap.

"I've got baby wipes," Hanson said. "You can have some once we get there."

"Thanks," Jonah said with a wry grin. "I clearly need some kind of nanny."

"Oh, don't worry about it," Hanson answered cheerfully. "I'm the same. You'd be amazed how much a baby wipe will clean off. I actually sometimes worry about what they put in them." She took another mouthful, chewed thoughtfully, and said, "She remembers nothing? As in, there's a complete blank?"

"Yes. From when she was at the club with April, who snogged some other guy, until the morning, or so she says." Jonah shook his head. "There's clearly a lot she's hiding. I need to find some way of pushing her, but it's going to be hard getting anything past her solicitor."

There was a brief silence from Hanson, and then she said, "But maybe she really can't remember anything."

Jonah glanced at her. "Because of how drunk she was?"

"Yes, or because her drink was spiked." She was gazing somewhere toward the dashboard, obviously thinking this over. "What if it was nothing to do with Alex, and he just walked her home? Then somewhere down the line she freaked out and thought he was trying to attack her."

Jonah considered. "There's some point to that." He nodded. "Let's get a blood test."

He put a call through to Lightman, asking him to get Louise Reakes's consent to blood testing.

"Sure," Lightman replied. "And while you're on the line, you might want to ask Issa Benhawy about the messages he sent his husband in the early hours of the morning."

"Are they aggressive?"

"I'd say so," Lightman replied. "And one of them strongly implies that Alex had form for going home with other people. I'll send Juliette some screenshots. I'm not surprised he was keen to get Alex's phone back untouched."

He heard a quiet "Wow" from Hanson a few moments later as the screenshots arrived on her phone.

"Interesting stuff?"

She read out three messages in turn, the last Issa's vicious threat to end it if Alex had gone home with a "slut."

Jonah took this in, lining it up with everything else they had so far. Alex had died in Louise's bed. That much was certain. Issa had accused his husband of sleeping with somebody else. In isolation Jonah would have assumed he meant another man. But the term "slut" could be applied to someone of either gender.

Was it worth seriously considering Alex's husband as a suspect? They couldn't be certain that Louise had been the one to kill Alex, even taking into account her frantic efforts to cover things up. As Hanson had suggested, Alex could have walked Louise home, an action that was open to misinterpretation. Or he could, in fact, have gone home with Louise for sex. There was no reason to assume that Alex was only interested in men.

The question was whether his jealous husband could have made his way to Saints Close. Could he have tracked Alex through his phone? Or gone to the club to confront his husband, and then followed them to Louise's house? Killed him, assuming he was being unfaithful, and then . . . what? Left him in her bed to punish her?

It was one solution to the bizarre discovery, but it was still all a bit of a stretch, Jonah thought. And proving any of that theory to be true was highly unlikely to be easy.

. . .

LIGHTMAN WAS ALONE in CID when the team's phone rang. The duty sergeant, whose voice Lightman didn't recognize, sounded a little harassed as he explained, "I've got a Niall Reakes here. I believe you're interviewing his wife. He'd like to see the senior investigating officer immediately."

"I'll come and get him," Lightman said, then added, "but he's going to have to make do with me for the moment. The chief's out on an interview."

There was a pause, and Lightman could imagine the sergeant asking why, exactly, a DCI felt it necessary to go out and interview people. But after the pause he just said, "OK. Not sure that's going to go down well."

Lightman made his way down to reception quickly, fully expecting a tirade from Niall Reakes once he got there. But Mr. Reakes looked stressed-out rather than angry. He was pacing the waiting area with clear agitation, looking strangely like a fair haired, neurotic version of his wife's lawyer. Niall, too, had boyish good looks, and was slightly running to fat. He was also impeccably dressed in a blue-gray suit and a white shirt. Despite the fact that he'd been traveling all afternoon, they showed very few creases.

He shook Lightman by the hand when he introduced himself, and said, "Sorry for blazing in here, but this has all really . . . It's knocked me back. You know?" He looked over at the duty sergeant. "I've not been able to talk to Louise and my—her solicitor says there might be a murder charge."

"It's clearly a very stressful situation," Lightman said. "I'll do what I can to help. Do you want to come on up to CID?"

"I . . . guess so."

Once they were in the stairwell and out of earshot of the duty sergeant, Niall asked in a quiet voice, "Why has she been arrested?"

"You're aware that a young man was found dead in the garden

of your home," Lightman said, sticking to the rule of giving away as little as possible at any given moment.

"Yeah, but she said it was a stranger," Niall said as he waited for Lightman to use his swipe card on the door of CID. "Nobody she knew."

Lightman glanced at him, able to divine that this was as much a question as it was a statement. Niall Reakes was looking for reassurance, and Lightman would not be giving it to him.

"We need to clear up a few things with both of you," he said evenly, keeping his expression absolutely neutral. "I'm sure the DCI can tell you more as soon as he's back."

He opened the door, and was surprised to feel Niall's hand on his upper arm in a clumsy grab.

"Please," Louise's husband said in a desperate voice, "please tell me if she was screwing someone else. I need to know."

A NARROW GARDEN with a high fence ran from the back door of Alex Plaskitt's terraced house down to a blue-painted single-story building at the far end. The green-brown skeletons of climbing plants and a few rhododendrons gave the only signs of life. The rest of the garden looked bleak in the spotlight over the back door. Half-melted snow lay over patches of grass and mud, and the rest showed no sign of disappearing.

"It's a lot nicer in daylight, and in summer," Issa said with a note of apology. "Alex spent half of last summer out here, either filming or doing . . . workouts." He faltered, his eyes fixed on the widest part of the grass, as if seeing Alex there. His expression was desolate.

"So that was his studio?" Jonah asked, gently, nodding toward the building at the end.

"Yes." Issa looked up at it. "His gym. I've got the key. . . ."

He led Jonah and Hanson to the side of the building, planting his feet carefully on each of the slippery, moss-covered stepping-stones that meandered down toward it. The door was locked by a simple padlock through a ring with a metal flap. "It's not a real building," Issa said, apparently still feeling the need to apologize. "We just bought a really big summerhouse for a grand and a half and assembled it. Alex did most of it on his own."

Issa leaned in to flick a light switch. Jonah stepped in first, and said, "It's impressive," in part to make Issa feel better. But also in part because it was. Along one wall were racks containing stacks of free weights. At the rear were a rowing machine, treadmill, and spinning bike. The center of the space was covered in rubberized matting, and sported two exercise balls of different sizes.

The desk occupied the wall nearest the house, and had windows on two sides that presumably gave quite a bit of light during the day. Perched on top were a desktop computer and a freestanding webcam with a tripod. It was pointed toward the center of the shed.

"Did he edit his videos in here too?" Jonah asked, glancing at the desktop. It was cold enough in the studio that his breath fogged in the air, strikingly lit by the two overhead lights.

"Yes," Issa said.

"Would you be happy for us to look through the hard drive?" Hanson asked with a sympathetic smile.

"I don't . . . mind." Issa gave a tearful shrug. "But why do you want to?"

"His YouTube videos often include mentions of what he's been doing that day, or is planning on doing later," she explained. "They also show some of his clients. Though the ones with them in are normally filmed at a public gym, I think?"

"It's the SimpleGym," Issa told her. "When he goes, he takes the camera with him and plugs in his laptop. You might need to look on there for anything recent." His gaze wandered, and then came to rest on Hanson again. "Do you think this wasn't random, then? That it was someone he knew?"

Jonah nodded to Hanson, a sign that he would take over again. It was only fair that he should be the one to break the news to Alex's husband.

"It seems that Alex didn't die in the garden, as we at first thought," he said. "He was inside when he died, and his body was removed to the garden to mislead our team."

Issa's mouth moved, an involuntary twitch. "What was he doing there?"

"We don't know, but it's clear that he died in bed. The woman who lived there with her husband was with him, though we don't know in what capacity."

Issa turned his head away, and the twitching of his mouth became a chewing on his lip that looked hard enough to hurt.

"Would you have any reason to expect Alex to have been in bed with a woman?"

Issa's voice was half-choked as he said, "He's done it before."

16

LOUISE

I hid my gradual slide down the slope of alcoholism for some while. I would save it for when you were away. I'd get obliterated, and then set alarms for myself that went off at seven in the morning, just so I could send you a cheery message proving I was up and at 'em. The irony being that you, in most cases, were hungover as anything following conference dinners or client pissups. That didn't count, did it? You didn't have previous form for terrible drunken behavior.

I would also delete every message that might have incriminated me, and scour my phone for new contacts or apps each morning. There was always something that needed deleting. A harsh message about you to April. A mortifying website I'd visited. A really grim meme I'd shared. I began to feel like Drunk Louise was working as hard as she could to fuck up my life.

I have a video somewhere of the two of us, me and April, on one of our nights out. Except of course it's not me. It's Her. Anyway, I found it on my phone the next day and it's just April and Drunk Louise with the phone held overhead in what I think is Drunk Louise's hand, shouting, "We hate you, Sober Louise!" And watching it made me feel ill, like I was seeing my friend and my worst enemy united. Stabbing me in the back.

And then there was the time I found the Tinder app on my phone one morning, which felt like a trap laid especially for me by Her. There's a chance she downloaded it for innocent reasons. It might have been so April could show me some guy she was sleeping with. It might even have been a bizarre moment of curiosity, just a way of understanding what so many people talked about. But it might also have been for a much worse reason. I deleted it, googled whether it might show up in my phone's history, and then deleted my searches too.

But you grew wise to me in the end. When you walked in late in the afternoon after a trip and found me looking drawn and fragile, I could see that you knew. It was during this time that you started to make cutting remarks about April, or to grow angry whenever she was brought up. I knew you'd never really liked her, but the animosity stepped up and up, until I stopped mentioning her at all. But your silent, icy disapproval spread to encompass everything I did after that. It became, in fact, the one constant in our marriage.

The neurotic side to my personality got completely out of control during this time too. I became unable to stop cleaning. Tidying. Perfecting. And I could see that you hated this just as much. You saw it as another character flaw, one that you'd failed to fix.

And so we come, inevitably, to Friday. To the night when every one of my worst nightmares came true.

I thought it would be safe enough. I'd talked April into coming over to the house, because I was tired and hadn't quite shaken off the cold that had been lingering since Valentine's Day. The other thing that had lingered was depression. Another festival of romance had come and gone with the two of us barely talking. It had felt, for most of our dinner out, like you would have preferred to be elsewhere.

April arrived all made up, caffeine-psyched, and chewing on bubblegum. The bubblegum was a surprise, even for April. When she hey-sistered me at the front door in full-on Tennessee drawl, with the candy-pink gum rolling over her tongue, I wondered for a moment how she was going to fit in the talking and the chewing at once. But of course she managed it.

She talked, and I lined up wineglasses and bowls of nuts and olives while I laughed at her. I'm sure you can imagine the swiftness with which the plastic cork came out of the grim Rioja she'd brought with her. God knows why she can't spend some of her streams of alimony on something nice to drink. But for some reason that's just not her style.

I remember her asking about you.

"He behaving, that old Niall?"

She was leaning on the breakfast bar across from me. Her gauzy black top drooped low enough to show a line of hot-pink bra and the scrawled tattoo across her left breast. I didn't bother telling her she was flashing. She always knows exactly how much tit she's got on show. She must have got dressed up to meet someone for lunch.

She'd asked if you were behaving. I tipped back some of the cheap crap and shrugged at her. "Niall's fine. Back tomorrow." She fixed me with a very gray stare. "And do you miss him these days? When he's away?"

"We're married," I told her. "We don't do missing each other anymore." And it was so deliberate, that comment. It was one of those things I say to pretend. To make out that I'm in the kind of relationship where we can joke about our marriage and not mean it.

And then, in my memory, it was later. We were no longer in the house, but in a club I didn't remember going to. It didn't worry me, because I was no longer me. I was Her. I could tell because of the warmth in me. Because of the satisfaction I felt with myself and my life.

For some reason Drunk Louise was telling April that she'd made a decision. That she was just going to get goddamn pregnant, whatever it took, and you, Niall, would have to deal with the consequences.

"We still have sex," I was telling her. "I'll just manufacture an accident. Once it's done, he can't force me to get rid of it, and then he'll realize it was all I needed to motivate me to stop drinking."

It seemed like the best plan I'd ever had. I was so convinced it was going to sort my life out for good. I felt fantastic. Powerful.

Which all vanished when April leaned toward me and said, "Honey, I saw Niall with his ex-wife."

I don't know how I would have reacted if I hadn't been fairly merry already. As it was, even with the shield of a few glasses of wine between me and this truth—even with Drunk Louise ready in the wings—I wanted to be sick.

"What do you mean, *saw*?" I was wondering if she could have walked in on the two of you having sex, and at the same time I was thinking she must have made a mistake. The power of denial is strong, isn't it?

"I saw them drinking wine at Domo and they were . . . It was obvious something was going on." She gave a long, frustrated sigh and jabbed at her drink with her straw. "Look, I've had suspicions for a while. But I do actually like Niall and I wanted to give him the benefit of the doubt. I know they work in the same field, and it's good if they can get along, but this is clearly not right. If you're genuinely going to have a child together . . . You can't go into that blind. It's too important." She gave me a very serious look. "Did he tell you they were meeting up?"

I actually hated her a little bit in that moment for making me admit that you hadn't told me anything. Isn't that the worst? That the person I hated was not the person who'd been lying to me?

I couldn't admit to her, either, that I'd long, long suspected that you were seeing Dina again. Worse, that I was certain you'd been seeing someone, and I'd just put my head in the sand and hoped your affair had died.

"When was this?" I asked her.

"Last Saturday," she said.

I'd been away all weekend, at a concert in Edinburgh. One of those rare occasions when I'd traveled and you'd stayed at home. You'd gone to meet Dina while I was away overnight, when you must have thought you were safe.

"You said it looked wrong. . . . Wrong how?" I could hear how tight and stupid my voice had suddenly become. How *shrill* I sounded. I hate that word, but it's still the best description for it.

"They looked like a couple," she said simply. "I came in and stood at the far side of the bar, and I could see them across from me. They had a table by the wall, one of the high-up ones, and she was all coiled round this high stool, wearing a jumpsuit that was slit real low down the front. She was laughing a lot and touching his arm all the time. You know."

I remember that shivers started to run through me. And fucking Drunk Louise, whom I needed so badly right then, was nowhere to be found. She'd clearly scampered away to the bar and left me to deal with this shit.

I didn't want to know any more, but I felt unable to stop asking questions.

"How did he look?"

April shrugged. "I don't know. I guess like he was enjoying it."

"Did they . . . kiss?"

"Not that I saw, but it was all there in the body language." April gave me a look that was full of sympathy and anger in equal measures. "What you need to know is that he's a fucking idiot, OK? You deserve so much more, and he deserves hell. She's the vainest person I've ever met."

I nodded, and folded my arms round myself. "Do you think she wants him back? You know . . . properly?"

"For now," April said, "yes. But only so she can *win*. She feels like she lost."

"How?" I asked. I could feel myself getting tearful, and I decided to swallow it down with vodka, which was what we seemed to be drinking now. "How did she lose? She left him."

"She lost because he moved on," April told me. "She lost because her fantasy of him pining after her for years got overturned in a few months, and she didn't like it."

"She got *married*," I said.

"That doesn't matter a damn," April said. And actually, April's pretty good at weighing people up, something I think even you would admit. I trust her on Dina. "Winning is everything. She didn't want to actually *be with* her new guy. He was a rich married man, and she wanted to prove she could break apart his marriage. And now she wants to prove she can break yours apart too."

All of it chimed with everything I'd always thought about your ex-wife, Niall. The stuff I'd never wanted to let on to you. If you've ever doubted why April has always meant so much to me, you could put a lot of it down to her taking my side. *Mine.* She sees through your ex-wife like she's transparent.

Something bubbled up in me then. A huge feeling of resentment, all of it directed at you, not her.

"She didn't force him to go for a drink and—and whatever else. . . ." I shook my head. "He's a fucking arsehole too."

April lifted her glass. "I'll drink to that."

After that, I tried not to think about you, or the fantasy of our happy family that had well and truly died. I tried so very hard. But there was a burning feeling in my stomach, and I spent the next hour or so checking my phone constantly, to see if you'd looked at WhatsApp recently. Whether you might be messaging her instead of me.

And I drank. I drank to dampen that feeling, and to welcome my drunk self back. To let her take over and stop me from feeling anything.

So this time, it wasn't actually an accident that I ended up obliterated. I did it with a sense of grim purpose. I wanted to destroy myself with drink and turn into Her. And then I wanted, actively wanted, to become that pathetic wreck you always get so angry with, as a huge *fuck-you*. I even thought about finding some guy and screwing him in the toilets. About finally, totally ending our marriage. Not by waiting for you to leave me, but by doing something unforgivable and then telling you all about it.

I half remember a little more, from later on. I remember the moment I realized April was gone. It was definitely Sober Louise who realized, and not the other one. I know because of how frightened I suddenly felt. So afraid of being alone that I thought about calling you. I really thought about it, despite how drunk I was and how much worse I'd feel about myself.

I remember pulling out my phone and finding your name. I remember staring at it and wanting so much to have you there with me. Caring about me instead of Dina. Taking me home and looking after me.

And then nothing.

Well, nothing I'm certain about. There is a memory that hit me while I was trying not to doze in a chair between interviews.

It began with me walking through a tiny garden. But that garden turned quickly into an endless, awful forest, and there was someone behind me. I knew for a long time that there was. I kept turning round to look at him, but every time I did, he was smiling at me like he was innocent and trustworthy. And every time I turned away and then looked back again, he was closer, without ever seeming to move. His smiling face seemed to float somewhere in front of his body, which horrified me.

I tried to run, but my legs felt limp. Out of my control. I kept tripping over. Time after time, I found myself on the grass or the frozen earth, and he caught up more quickly each time, until he was right behind me. I was screaming and trying to run, and then falling again.

And I don't know why I didn't wake up at that point, because that's what should have happened. I should have woken up when I fell and he'd got me, but I didn't. I couldn't. I could only lie there, and feel him on top of me. Then he was pressing something sharp into my back, farther and farther, until I knew I was dying.

I had to wake up, because if I didn't, I would die in that dream. I knew that. I would die for real.

And somehow I dragged myself back. I woke up.

I'm glad I'd been left on my own for a while. It took me a long time to stop crying. I could still feel that pain in my back, and I remembered suddenly that it had stung when I showered that morning, along with all the other grazes I couldn't identify. So I stumbled to the reflective glass at the side of the interview room, feeling like I might be sick. I pulled my top up a few inches and turned my back, craning my head to see my reflection.

And there it was, on my back, right where I'd felt it in the dream. A scab where a cut had been, and around it dark purplish bruising.

I felt like I was falling.

17

The conversation with Issa was, from Hanson's perspective, hard going. He had sobbed his way through an angry, hurt, grief-filled account of Alex's past infidelity, while she and the DCI had begun to shiver in the unheated studio.

"She was one of his clients," he told them. "The daughter of a baronet who'd grown up in all-girls' schools riding ponies. She was a Plaskitt family sort of person, and it felt like—like the worst kind of betrayal. I couldn't believe *that* was the kind of woman he would go for."

"Was Alex bisexual?" the DCI asked.

Issa had nodded. "Essentially, yes. But he told me he'd only ever fallen hard for men. Just me and a boyfriend at school. It would have been easier for him to have married a woman, and I know it got to him sometimes. If he'd just decided on a nice young girl, it would have meant reconciliation with his parents. Grandkids for them to dote on. Seeing his sister more often. Mummy and Daddy would have approved and come to visit, and probably bought them a nice big house. Who knows?" He made a lunge for a drawer of the desk, and after some rifling pulled out a packet of tissues. He blew his nose into one before saying, "I knew that part of him was there, and it drove me mad. He wasn't the one whose family hasn't spoken to him in eight years. He wasn't told he was an abomination."

"Is that what your family did?" Hanson asked, quietly. "Cut you off?"

"You bet they did." Issa's mouth set into an angrier line. "I was raised an Ahmadiyya Muslim, with all the preaching of how forgiveness is everything. That we must be tolerant and seek peace, because those are the true teachings of Islam." He gave a bitter smile. "It turned out that there are exceptions, according to my parents. Tolerance is only for those of other faiths, not those of other sexualities."

Hanson winced. "I'm so sorry. That's a terrible thing to go through."

Issa gave another one of those not-quite-smiles. "It goes on being pretty rough, but I've made my peace with it." He gave a very long sigh. "I suppose it was hard to feel sympathy toward Alex for what was a much easier situation."

Hanson nodded and let the DCI take over again to ask, "When he cheated, was it a one-off? Or a . . . relationship?"

"He said it was a one-off," Issa said, a note of doubt in his voice, "and I didn't have any reason to think . . . They hadn't been working together that long, and he seemed devastated by it. He really did."

"Do you recall her name?"

"Yes." He gave her a defiant look. "I sometimes look her up, just to make sure she's really, you know . . . moved on. She's called Sarah Lang. But she lives in Monaco now. I doubt she's going to be of any interest to you."

Hanson pulled her notebook out and scribbled the name down anyway.

"Did you ever get the impression he might be pursuing other young women?" the DCI threw in.

Issa gave a strange shrug. "I got angry with him a few times for staying out later than he'd said he would. I didn't—I didn't like him hanging around with Step."

"You felt he was a bad influence?" Jonah asked.

"Maybe." He looked upward, the expression of a man trying to stop himself from crying. "Whenever they went out together, Alex seemed to want to party for longer. I had this—this feeling that he was flirting with girls."

Sheens took out a glossily printed photo of Louise Reakes from his pocket. It had been taken after her arrest. She looked pale and slightly sick. The lighting wasn't exactly flattering, but she looked like someone who knew she was in big trouble.

"Do you recognize this woman?" the DCI asked.

Issa took the photo and glanced at it before shaking his head. Hanson caught a twist at his mouth and asked, instinctively, "Does she look anything like the woman he slept with?"

"Yes," Issa said, in what was almost a whisper. He looked up at her. "There's quite a similarity."

Sheens pulled out another photograph. It was the murder weapon in all its gleaming glory.

"What about this? Might this have been Alex's?"

Issa's face grew visibly paler. It wasn't something Hanson had seen very often, a draining-away of blood. One of those often-described but rarely experienced occurrences.

"No, it's not his." He swallowed. "Why are you showing me this? Was this what killed him? Of course it wasn't his. Of course it wasn't. Why would he have a knife?"

"It's surprisingly common for people who carry knives to end up killed by them," the chief said in a sympathetic tone.

"He's never carried a knife in his life," Issa said. "He was a hardcore pacifist."

"He wouldn't have bought it just for the look of it?" Sheens asked. "It's a beautifully made piece."

"That isn't beautiful," Issa said, his eyes gleaming and his jaw set. "That's a monstrosity."

. . .

LIGHTMAN MANAGED TO get through to the DCI some fifteen minutes after leaving Niall Reakes in a relatives' room with a cup of black coffee. The call was picked up quickly this time, and he could hear background engine noises. He explained that Mr. Reakes was demanding to see both his wife's solicitor and the DCI.

"Let him talk to Patrick Moorcroft," the chief said after a moment of thought. "But inform him that any conversation between them will not be protected under client-solicitor confidentiality, as the solicitor is not, in fact, representing Mr. Reakes."

"And presumably you'd like me in the observation room while they talk?"

"You bet I would," Sheens confirmed. "We'll be back in twenty or so minutes and I'll probably talk to him then. And keep me posted if the super calls through to the office. I want to know if we have our thirty-six hours. Thanks, Ben."

LOUISE REAKES AND her solicitor were sitting in what seemed to be a strained silence. The solicitor was reading something that presumably pertained to her case, while Louise was brushing a strand of hair back and forth across her mouth, her eyes wide and unfocused.

"Mr. Reakes has arrived," Lightman said, and Louise immediately stood, her chair making a loud, low-pitched screech across the linoleum floor. "He's asked to see you, Mr. Moorcroft."

Patrick looked up at Lightman, his brow creased. He glanced briefly at his client, and then said, "In what capacity?"

"An unofficial one."

Louise stared at her solicitor while he reflected. As he moved to rise, she said, "I need to see him. I'm the one who needs to talk to him."

"I can explain the details of your case to him," Patrick said soothingly. He lifted his briefcase onto his chair and began methodically sliding his papers back into it.

"That's not the same," Louise countered. "He'll think . . . I need to explain it all to him."

The solicitor looked up at her for a moment and then said gently, "It would be extremely unusual for contact to be allowed between you while you were in custody on such a serious charge. I know how concerned you are about his reaction, but I really will put forward everything you've said, and I'm sure he'll understand that you are as bemused as the rest of us."

Lightman listened to this in faint surprise. He hadn't expected sympathy from the hotshot lawyer. He might have anticipated a cheerful dismissal of her concerns, but the quiet, soothing voice was unexpected.

It seemed unexpected to Louise, too, who gazed at him blankly and then said, "All right. Thank you—so much—Patrick." And then she turned away, her hand over her eyes.

The lawyer said nothing as Lightman took him to the relatives' room. His expression looked pensive, and Lightman wondered what he was working through in his mind.

There were still traces of tears in Niall Reakes's eyes as they entered. His reaction to the solicitor was somewhere between relieved and angry.

"The chief has agreed to let you speak to Mr. Moorcroft," Lightman said. "But he remains your wife's solicitor."

Niall Reakes, who had been in the process of getting up, looked sharply at Lightman. "What's that supposed to mean?"

"It means that we can speak, but without the privilege of solicitor-client confidentiality," Patrick Moorcroft explained.

"I'll leave you to it," Lightman said. He caught the solicitor's wry look. He was clearly aware that their conversation would be listened to.

By the time Lightman had shut himself into the observation room, Niall Reakes was saying heatedly, ". . . why in the hell she called you. You're my friend, not hers."

"I'm also the only solicitor you both know," Patrick said in a measured tone. He placed his briefcase upright on the table. "She probably didn't know who else to call."

"Well, she'll have to find someone else," Mr. Reakes said, his voice high-pitched and unsteady.

"She's asked me to represent her, Niall," Patrick said, slightly more firmly. "I'm her solicitor."

"You're joking," Niall said, half laughing in disbelief. "They've arrested her. They think—they must have a reason. Why are they holding her if she hasn't done something?"

Patrick looked, momentarily, almost awkward. And then he said, "The question over what she may have done rests on where the young man died. He was found to have died in your home, rather than outside it."

"Oh my God," Niall said, putting his hands up to his face. "I knew it. I knew she was . . ." He suddenly turned to Patrick. "She was sleeping with him, wasn't she?"

"That remains unclear," Patrick said. "He died in—in the bed alongside her."

"For God's sake!" He shook his head violently. "You can't represent her. There's no way."

"Niall . . ."

"There was another man in our bed!" He leaned forward to point somewhere toward the door, as if the bed lay in that direction. "Some stranger who's now dead!"

"It's clearly a horrible thing to find out," Patrick said. "I'm so sorry, Niall. But from the moment she hired me, I became her legal counsel as well as your friend."

"She doesn't effing deserve legal counsel," Niall Reakes said through gritted teeth.

Lightman found himself smiling slightly at Niall's non-swearing. His wife seemed to be much happier with colorful language.

"Everyone deserves it, Niall," Patrick said quietly. "Everyone."

"Well, I'm going to hire you instead," Niall said in sudden

triumph. "You won't be able to represent her, because it'll be a conflict of interest."

Patrick sighed. "I'm afraid the way it works is that I wouldn't be able to represent *you*. But then you aren't in current need of counsel, are you?"

"Yes, I am," Niall said. "I need counsel to explain to me what the hell happened."

"I can help you with that, up to a point."

Niall turned away, waving a hand in clear frustration, before he asked, "Did she take some—some—some bastard home and then find out too late he was violent?"

"Your wife can't remember a lot of the evening," the solicitor said. "She went out with her friend April. The two of them ended up drunk. April left with a man she'd picked up, and Louise was left alone, and has a large memory blackout covering the later part of the evening."

"Oh, really?" Niall almost laughed again.

"It may be worth knowing," Patrick Moorcroft said evenly, "that the young man who died was married. To another young man."

There was absolute silence. Niall moved his head, opened his mouth, and then seemed to falter. "What?"

"The details of the case are clearly complex. However easy it is to jump to conclusions, I think you need to be patient and let the truth come out. Louise has assured me that she doesn't recognize the man in question, and is certain she couldn't have been violent toward him or anyone else."

"And do you believe her?" Niall asked. He came to stand close to Patrick, his hands in his pockets and his body leaning slightly forward once again. "Do you think that's true? Do you?" There was a brief pause, and then Niall said, much more quietly, "Please, Patrick. Please tell me. I'm losing my mind."

"I know, Niall," the solicitor said quietly. "And I do believe her. She's clearly been through an awful day as well."

Niall shook his head, for some reason unwilling to accept this. "Of course she has. She tried to hide some—some kind of murder."

"Niall," Patrick said, his voice suddenly sharp, "I've told you everything I know. Perhaps it's worth you considering what you know of your wife's character, and whether she is capable of this action, before you damage her defense."

Niall's expression went momentarily slack. He looked, just then, like a chastened child. "I'm not . . . I'm . . . I'm sorry." He looked down, toward the floor. "I didn't mean to—I'm not accusing her of anything."

"Good," Patrick said, nodding. "I'm glad."

Another silence grew between them, and then Niall asked, "So what's next? What do I do?"

"Perhaps you should go home," the solicitor said.

Niall shook his head. "I want—I need to see the police. I want to talk to them. Myself." He looked up at the solicitor. "I found out that—that she'd been arrested from the bloody news."

"I called you as soon as I could, and I think the police have been trying to reach you—"

"Yeah, I know," Niall snapped. And then he added, in a quieter voice, "I'm sorry, Patrick. I should be . . . grateful to you. It just feels suddenly like there are sides. My side and hers."

"There are no sides as far as I'm concerned," Patrick told him, reaching out to put a hand on his friend's shoulder. He gave a small smile. "In my official position as your best friend, I'm here for both of you. All right?"

HANSON SPENT THE remainder of the journey back mulling over what Issa had told them. It seemed possible that Alex and Louise had gone home together for sex, but they had no proof that a liaison had occurred at the club. Nothing on any of the cameras. Nothing from the bar staff or Louise's friend. And the two of them had technically left separately.

She was still thinking it all over as they drew back into the car park at the rear of Southampton Central. As she climbed out of the chief's Mondeo, she found herself looking at a black BMW 3 Series that was hovering up near the entrance to the station. She felt her heart squeeze in immediate response.

It's not him, she told herself as she removed the laptop from the car and closed the door. But she couldn't look away from the car. She thought she could make out the driver's shape in the light from the streetlamps, and in her mind he became Damian, sitting at the steering wheel and watching her.

He'd still been driving the BMW the last time she'd seen him. The car that she'd paid the deposit on, stupidly believing that he would pay her back. A car that was far, far too expensive for Damian's modest salary and immodest debts. But of course Damian had to have it. He had to have the best of everything, always, as if the world owed him luxury.

She lowered her head and started to follow the DCI, refusing to look toward the car. It probably wasn't even him.

Lots of people have black BMWs, she told herself.

But she was still shaking as she stepped into the rear lobby.

She wished they hadn't built the place with so much glass. She could feel her skin crawling until she'd closed the door of CID behind her.

JONAH'S CALL FROM the superintendent came as he was halfway to his office. He deposited the desktop computer he was carrying on O'Malley's untidy desk in order to answer it.

It was a mercifully quick call. The superintendent agreed that a custody extension was warranted, and approved a further application to the magistrates' court for longer if needed. Technically, this meant that only Hanson, as the team's constable, would be required to take Louise Reakes to the court the next day. But Jonah would go too. It was useful to have a senior officer there to answer any difficult questions, and kinder to support his junior officer.

"Right," Jonah said, with the call done. "We have our thirty-six hours, and we'll plan for a court application. Can I get a download on what Niall Reakes said to his solicitor, Ben?"

Lightman told him in his measured, precise way about the conversation. He outlined Niall Reakes's doubts over his wife and his demand for Patrick Moorcroft to represent him instead.

"They are clearly friends rather than solicitor and client, and Mr. Reakes seems to feel betrayed by his friend's decision to represent his wife. He implied that it pits her against him somehow, though exactly how that works isn't clear. It was a fairly heated conversation," he added, in such a cool voice that it was slightly comic.

"So he found it easy to imagine his wife cheating, and even killing," Jonah said.

"Yes," Lightman agreed. "That's a good summary. He's now demanding to see you. His wife, meanwhile, is demanding to see him."

Jonah gave a wry grin. "Well, I'm demanding coffee. Let's see which one of us gets what we want first."

O'MALLEY TOOK A thermos and went to do a Costa run. "You don't need a crappy disposable cup, so," he said, waving the thermos at Jonah. "Those things last for centuries before rotting down."

It made Jonah grin. This was clearly a new concern for O'Malley, who was well on the way to being a takeaway coffee addict. He noted that O'Malley's hectic desk had three disposable cups sitting on it, their contents in various stages of molding over.

He took a few minutes to retreat to his office and mull things over before he spoke to Niall Reakes. Though, in fact, when he sat down and woke his desktop, he found a note in O'Malley's sloping scrawl asking him to call Linda McCullough. The call had clearly slipped his sergeant's mind.

Their forensic scientist answered swiftly, and with clear enthusiasm.

"I've talked to my guy about this knife of yours," she said. "And it's actually pretty good news. Unless it's a copy, which he doesn't think it is, it's a Ukrainian import. At the moment there's only one firm in the UK that sells them."

"Wow, great work," Jonah said, not really surprised that McCullough had contacted him herself instead of just putting them in touch. It was very much her style to go beyond her brief. "Can you give me the name?"

"It's Steel and Silver, and they're an online retailer with shops in Newcastle and London," McCullough told him. "Let's hope they don't sell so very many of them."

"Let's hope they don't," Jonah agreed.

18

LOUISE

You won't want to read about this next part. I know you won't. But it's vital that you know. If I don't explain the sheer, heart-twisting panic I felt when I woke up on Saturday morning, then you'll never understand why I did what I did. Even now, I hate that the picture you have of me in your head is all wrong. All distorted.

I've told you how it was when I found him there next to me. But I need you to understand now the awful, awful things I began to think. I imagined that Drunk Louise had seduced and then killed him, and that she'd done everything she could to make sure I suffered for it.

You're probably thoroughly sick of all this talk of Her, aren't you? By this point you must be railing against it, wanting to shout that it's all *me,* and this artificial distancing of myself from Her is both childish and pathological.

But to say that is to misunderstand the nature of me and Her. It is to trivialize the dissociation that happens each and every time. I can see now that there is something more profound at work in my psychology than simple alcoholism. And, in part, I can see it more clearly because of another version of me that I met that morning.

It was the anxiety that triggered it. Fear like I have never known before. It reached an unbearable crescendo, and then something snapped. I vanished, and another me came into being. She was—well, she was unstoppable.

That new Louise knew more than I did. She knew she had to get the body of this man out of the house. She could see herself being jailed for something she had no way of defending herself against. She had to stop it happening.

And, as a side point, isn't this refreshing? An alter ego who is actually looking out for Sober Louise. One who clears up the mess instead of making it. I can't help liking her.

It felt very much like watching someone else as she set to work. She knew she had to do it while it was still dark, and that it would be better to do it naked, so she stripped off and put my going-out clothes into the wash. She noted as she did it that I was missing a diamanté earring but dismissed it. It didn't matter if it turned up somewhere on the streets if the crime scene was going to be in my front garden.

She put on a pair of disposable cleaning gloves and heaved him out of bed. He was unbelievably fucking heavy but she did it anyway.

Did you wince again just there? Did you feel more revolted by the swearing than you did by this vision of your wife dragging a well-muscled dead man out of our marital bed? I almost want to know.

Anyway, she was a determined person, this newly born Louise. After a good twenty minutes, she'd made it outside with the body, and five minutes later had finished smoothing out the snow to remove the marks of having dragged him there. Having disinfected the knife in case she'd touched it at some point, she put it down next to him and stood back to take a look.

There wasn't enough blood, she realized. Nobody would believe he'd been attacked there. She needed to make it look like he'd come from somewhere else.

So she took his shoes off him, soaked them in blood off the mattress, slipped them on to her own feet (over some thick socks), and left a fake trail from the pavement to where he lay, making sure on her way back to step only on the marks she'd already left.

Doing it, she thought about dead men's shoes, and it made her laugh. She actually laughed, out there in the bitter cold in stocking feet, with the threat of discovery hanging over her. And that isn't the black mark against her character you might think. There is a great, terrible absurdity in having to handle a dead body, and I defy most people not to be hit by it at some point.

After she'd put his shoes back onto his feet, she started to clean everything up. And I bet at this point you're laughing a little bitterly and thinking, *Of course she cleaned*. But it was absolutely needed. It turns out both versions of me were born for this.

Cleaning everything took us until twenty to six. Getting up early is clearly the first habit of successful justice perverters.

The final and biggest problem we both had was the mattress, which was still steeped in blood. She was equal to this, though. She used my hair dryer on a cool setting to blow-dry it. By the time she'd finished, it left a smudge on her hand only if she pressed it hard. None of it showed once she'd got the spare duvet and pillows out and made it up again. Though I guess we both must have missed the drop of blood that made its way out onto the carpet.

That other version of me stayed right up until the police arrived. She was there with me, telling me what to say. Guiding me. Stopping me from messing everything up.

And I know you're going to be certain now that there's something wrong with me. That this constant dissociation from myself shows that I'm deeply damaged. But I'm starting to understand that these parts of me come into being out of necessity. That life, and the people in it, sometimes just push me too hard.

So whatever you think of my other personas, I'll tell you this: I miss them intensely now that they've left me. Each of them did, in their way, what I so badly wanted you to do, Niall. They made me feel like everything would be OK.

19

With Lightman volunteering to check up on Niall Reakes's trip to Geneva and O'Malley on coffee duty, Hanson was free to investigate what she chose. She needed to take her mind off that black car in the car park and, more particularly, off her own adrenaline-filled reaction to it. Off the way it was all getting to her.

Alex Plaskitt's tower computer was still on O'Malley's desk, sitting at an angle on top of some paperwork. She had his laptop case perched on her own. Between the two machines, they had all of Alex's videos to work through, and she might as well get on with them.

She hesitated over which to start with and chose the laptop. This was presumably where any more recent unedited footage would be found. She knew finding something significant was a long shot, but at the very least she hoped to understand more about the man and his frame of mind. Something to tell her whether he might have wanted to sleep with Louise Reakes, and whether he could ever have been violent.

She loaded up the laptop, half listening to Ben in the background. He was now talking to a second person at Niall Reakes's pharmaceutical firm to ask them about the conference. She had the strong suspicion that they were being difficult from the way he was repeating his requests extremely politely. She'd never known him to get angry with anyone. Not a witness, or a suspect, or a colleague. Though she often wondered whether he felt more underneath it all.

She pulled her headphones out of her desktop and plugged them into the laptop, hoping that she wasn't about to get a telling-off from the cyber team for accessing the files before they'd had a look.

It took her a few tries to locate Alex's personal videos. There was nothing in his documents, but eventually she thought to look for online storage folders and found a batch of them sitting in Dropbox. Ben had finished his call and started another by the time she'd loaded up the most recent one.

This video had been recorded the day he died, and Hanson took a long, steadying breath before pressing the Play button.

Alex appeared in excessive close-up, having clearly just pressed the Record button on the camera. His expression, even in that unplanned moment, was warm. Excited. Open.

Alex backed away until he was standing in the middle of his studio, and then, after a brief pause, he launched himself into a greeting.

"This is Alex Plaskitt, your health and fitness coach, and today I'm looking at how to do a really great core-workout session. Now, a lot of people will use plank holds as their core training, without movement. What I want to show you today is taking that position and turning it dynamic, because your core will always be trained better when you move."

He hunkered down onto the ground and put himself into an easy plank position, his feet on the floor and his body supported with enviably straight forearms.

"Now, trying to hold a static plank for longer and longer to try and get a better core is like weight training by holding a car over your head. It's likely to cause injury, and it doesn't really help. Like with weights, we need movement."

Alex began to demonstrate a series of moves, all based on

forward and side plank, and Hanson found herself taking mental notes. This was good stuff, which made her think again of what a stupid waste his death had been.

The clip ran smoothly for five minutes, and then Alex got up to turn off the camera. There was nothing in there about his life. Nothing to suggest why he might have ended up dead.

She tried the previous four videos, which were much shorter, and it turned out that these were all outtakes of the same short segment. In the first one, Alex fell over his words, made a burbling sound, laughed, and went to turn the video off. In the second one, he made it through the intro, and then tripped trying to move into the plank. He collapsed into a fit of giggles that was infectious and, for Hanson, achingly sad.

The fifth clip was less engaging. Alex was filming himself doing 2k on the Concept 2 rowing machine. He gave a brief introduction, saying he was filming it for posterity, and then he turned some pounding music on and started.

Hanson skipped ahead twice, seeing nothing much of interest. And then, at five minutes in, Alex suddenly faltered and came to a stop. He let go of the handle, breathing heavily, and then he let out a roar. He undid his foot straps with a furious rush and staggered to his feet, swinging close to the camera.

"For fuck's sake, you fucking pussy!"

Hanson actually flinched as he shouted. It didn't seem possible that it was the same voice as those cheerful, encouraging comments on the other videos.

His movements were no less aggressive. He started to kick the wheel of the Concept 2, lending a rhythm to his shouts of "What—the—fuck—is—wrong—with—you?"

The anger went on for a good minute, and then Alex collapsed onto the floor and began to cry, still half raging between the tears. Calling himself a useless twat. A pathetic fag.

Hanson paused it, wondering for a moment where the rage

had come from. Then she remembered what Phoebe had told them.

He was a bit of a mummy's boy. At least, that's what Daddy used to think. . . .

She felt slightly sick as she moved on to look at the other videos.

"NIALL REAKES'S ALIBI seems to hold up," Lightman told Jonah, after tapping on the door to his office. "His firm has sent over a few social-media photos of the conference and forwarded on his flight bookings. He was on the fifteen-forty home today."

"OK, thanks," Jonah said, reflecting that this would make things simpler. If Niall had been abroad, Louise alone had been responsible for moving Alex Plaskitt's body, and quite possibly for killing him too. But that didn't mean that speaking to her husband was any less important.

Jonah braced himself for something of a confrontation, given Niall's earlier blustering, but in fact the interview went smoothly. It was clear that Niall had burned off a lot of energy while he'd been waiting. By the time Jonah entered the relatives' room, he was sitting meekly at the table, his expression mild and eager to please.

Jonah explained to him, briefly, why they needed to hold Louise. About the terms of custody and their application to the magistrate.

"You can make this a lot easier, however," Jonah went on. "If, for example, there's any previous behavior of this kind you can tell us about. . . ."

Niall gave a slightly helpless expression. "Behavior like—like being involved with a dead man and then . . ." He gave a short laugh, and then shook his head. "She's never been in trouble with the law before. I don't know if that's what you want to hear."

"And she's never brought anyone else home?"

"I don't think so," Niall said a little hoarsely. Niall looked a lot like his friend Patrick, but as he spoke, Jonah could hear differences. Where Patrick was clearly public school–educated, Niall's accent was neutral southeast England. He seemed more open too. Less in control of his emotions. Easier, Jonah thought, to provoke.

There was a brief silence, and Jonah raised an inquiring eyebrow.

Niall looked uncomfortable, and added, "When I'm away, I guess . . . I wouldn't know if she was . . ."

"You've never had reason to suspect?"

Niall hesitated, then shook his head.

"But the drinking?"

"I guess . . ." He sighed, briefly and sharply. "Yeah, it's a bit of a habit. I mean, not often. A couple of times a month. But it's always a mess."

Jonah nodded. "Is that to imply that you've had to step in at times?"

"I usually just have to pick up the pieces," Niall said. "Although these days she mostly waits until I'm abroad, so all I get to see is the terrible hangover. And she's—she's a nightmare, hungover." He shook his head. "Just deeply self-pitying and guilty."

"Has she had things to really regret?"

Niall gave a tight laugh. "Nothing most people would worry about. She can beat herself up over having said something a bit impatiently, or having lost her keys. Just not . . . you know. Terrible."

"You didn't get the sense she was hiding worse things? Thinking back to the last few times this has happened?"

Niall paused for a moment and then shook his head. "It's hard to say, but . . . I don't think so."

"Has she often been unable to recall much of the night before?" Jonah tried.

Niall gave him a long, considering look before he said, "I honestly don't know. She normally remembers some things, at least.

I'm not sure she'd tell me if she had huge blackouts. She said she had once, but . . ."

Jonah watched him, briefly, and then said, "Your wife would like to see you. It's not standard practice to allow suspects to see family while in custody, but I'm prepared to make an exception, given that you've been away from her for several days."

He saw Niall stiffen slightly. And then, to Jonah's surprise, he said, "I don't want to see her."

JASON AMBLED OVER to Hanson's desk while she was writing up her notes on the video footage.

"I'm done. They're screening the game at the Hammer and Tongs so I'm going to head over there. See if I can catch the end and then eat something unhealthy." He gave her a slightly ironic look. "Your perfect evening."

Hanson laughed. She had admitted to Jason early on that the Hammer and Tongs was her least favorite pub. It was devoted to sports Hanson had no interest in, had a generally sticky floor, and served only one type of cheap gin alongside the countless lagers. But Jason was a huge rugby fan and part of a group of detectives and uniforms who used it as their local. They went there three or four days of the week and often watched obscure matches streamed off a PC. Hanson had dutifully gone along with Jason a few times, but avoided it when she could.

"Thanks," she told him. "I'll be here awhile, and then I might find myself just too tired for such a fantastic event. You can come to mine afterward if you like, though. I may have beer."

"I'll see how I go," he said, throwing his car keys up and catching them. "Don't work too hard."

JONAH DUCKED BACK into Interview Room 1, where Louise and her solicitor were still waiting. Louise was gazing at nothing, her whole pose defeated. Patrick Moorcroft rose from his chair the moment Jonah was inside the room.

"I need to get back home to my family," the solicitor said. "I assume there's nothing more for me this evening."

"No," Jonah agreed. "We'll continue tomorrow."

The solicitor collected his coat and briefcase, and spoke to his client quietly. "I'll check in tomorrow morning. I'll work out what time I need to be here." Louise nodded without looking at him. Patrick glanced at Jonah. "I assume you're pushing for a magistrates' court hearing."

"Yes. We should know by midmorning."

"We'll discuss that tomorrow," Patrick told Louise, looking at her with an expression that might have been slight concern. "You'll be here for the night, but it should be relatively comfortable."

Louise nodded again and then looked up at Jonah. "Has Niall gone?"

"Yes," Jonah said quietly. "I'm afraid he wasn't feeling equal to seeing you."

Louise's mouth twisted and she looked down at her hands. "Poor Niall."

"There's a constable on the way to take you to a cell. She'll get you sorted with some food too." Faced with her desolate expression, he added, "They aren't bad, the cells. They have TVs, and the beds are OK."

It was always an odd thing, holding a suspect in custody. They were at once the enemy and within your care. The fact that Louise Reakes may have killed a man and then tried to hide it made Jonah feel no less concerned for her welfare than if she had done nothing wrong. She would clearly be having a hard time for the next few days, whatever happened.

He left the interview suite along with Patrick Moorcroft, allowing the solicitor to walk ahead of him. Neither of them spoke as they made their way across CID, but as Jonah held the door open for him, the solicitor turned briefly and said, "Niall may well regret his decision not to speak to her. If he does, would you be willing to grant him access?"

Jonah studied his expression, wondering if his question was down to his friendship with Niall, or reflected concern that Louise's husband might undermine her defense.

"I'd certainly be willing to consider it."

"Thank you," the solicitor said, and left.

Jojo GAVE JONAH her version of the third degree while they drove to dinner at Roy's house. He'd had to push the timing back by an hour and a half, and felt lucky to be making it at all. Fortunately Roy and Sophie were unshakably relaxed about that kind of thing, and Roy had even said cheerfully that it might mean the house ended up tidy before they arrived.

Jojo's form of interrogation always started with "Did you manage to arrest anyone today?"

"No," Jonah replied. "Massive fail." He grinned at her. He'd stolen one of Jojo's current favorite phrases, which she'd stolen from the younger climbers and a good portion of the people she followed on Twitter.

"God. It's a wonder they pay you at all, Copper Sheens." She shook her head, and started scrolling through radio stations out of a general disgust with his allegiance to Radio 2. "You said it was a murder?"

"Yes. A stabbing."

"Young person or old?"

"Young."

"That's cruddy," Jojo said, more seriously.

"It is," he agreed. "And it's definitely more complex than a random on-street attack. The body was moved, by someone who may or may not have killed him." Which was as much as he could say to her about it, however greatly he trusted Jojo's discretion.

She gave him a sidelong look. "Sounds like just your cup of tea."

"You may be right," he agreed.

They arrived a few minutes later in Lyndhurst, where Roy and Sophie had bought themselves a fairly substantial marital home. The parking was alongside grass on an unlined, very rural-looking road. He took care not to let the tire dip down off the tarmac. He'd made that mistake last time and then spent ten minutes getting it unstuck again.

He cut the engine and turned to look at her. "I like that dress," he told her, reaching out to tug the material farther off her shoulder. "Particularly the way you can see the strap of your bra. It's got a kind of . . . rebellious-chic thing going on."

"Oh, really?" she asked, moving in on him. "That's interesting, because I'd say you've got a sort of slutty-authoritative vibe."

"I always have that vibe," he said. "It's what they say about me after my press appearances."

"Yeah." She kissed him, and then sighed. "They're all over you. It's so hard dating eye candy."

He pulled her toward him for another, longer kiss, before releasing her. Four months in, he was still hugely proud of taking her out to see his friends. But that didn't mean he wasn't equally impatient to get her home at the end of the evening.

HANSON CHECKED THE car park several times before heading to her car. There was, luckily, no further sign of Damian or of any idling cars. Her Nissan was only ten feet from the door, and she climbed into it thankfully. It may have been freezing in there, but it was a safe space.

She set the engine running before doing anything else. She found herself looking across the road toward the Hammer and Tongs, wondering whether she should go and find Jason. She knew he'd appreciate it, for all his facade of independence. And maybe afterward they could go home and have a proper talk, and she could tell him about Damian at long last.

But the idea seemed too much just then. With her mind half on the murder inquiry and having worked six long days this week, she was tired and fragile. She could also feel a headache coming on and knew that a loud pub would be the worst thing for it. It would be better to find time when things had calmed down a bit.

Decided, she plugged her phone in, hit the Play button on some of her running tracks, and pulled out onto Southern Road. By the time she'd got most of the way home, the music had worked out some of the tension in her head.

She backed the Nissan into its customary position as close to the front door as she could manage and killed the engine. The silence left by the music seemed worse than usual. And then she realized that it wasn't the quiet that had hit her; it was the darkness.

She turned her head to look back at the house, where the security light usually came on when anyone came up the driveway. She could see its outline, faintly, but it was in darkness.

She felt a rush of unease, and thought about driving away again.

But this was her house. She needed to go home. To shower and change. To sleep.

She hesitated and then picked up her baton. There was no point being unprepared. Hefting it, she climbed out of the car slowly. She tried to look everywhere as she walked, letting nothing escape her notice. But it was hard to make anything out in the tiny front garden. She was suddenly aware that it was riddled with hiding places. Behind the conifer. Round the corner of the house. By the side gate . . .

God, she hated this. Hated how rattled she felt at a simple light not working.

But as she trod toward it, her feet encountered the unmistakable crunch of broken glass. She looked up at the light, her heart jumping. It had been resoundingly smashed, in what looked like a frenzied attack. The light itself was hanging off at a sad angle, trailing wires behind it.

There was a sound up by the gate, and she spun wildly, her baton held out in front of her. But the shape crossing her view turned out to be a Chihuahua. It paused at the far gatepost to lift its leg, and then her neighbor appeared after it, his eyes on the illuminated screen of his mobile.

She lowered the baton in case he turned and saw her, though she needn't have worried. He was too engrossed in the screen and must have been totally night-blind.

Trying to force herself to breathe steadily, she reached into the car and picked up her bag and coat. Her hands were shaking as she let herself into the house, and they kept shaking as she shut the door and checked every room.

There was no broken glass. No forced entry. Nothing to be afraid of. And a quick glance outside showed her that the big fake but realistic security cameras higher up the wall were still intact.

She moved back into the hall and finally put her bag down. But she kept the truncheon in her hand and used it to hit the carpeted stairs as hard as she could. The sound was loud and satisfying, but not as satisfying as when she yelled "Bastard!" at the top of her voice.

The Hammer and Tongs was, predictably, crowded. There weren't many places that screened club matches, and this had been Southampton playing. They'd played well too. As a result, a lot of groups had stayed after the match and there had been a long wait for food.

Jason had caught some of the second half of the game and was feeling as cheerful as most of the other punters. Queuing for the bar when it was finally his round turned out to be a slog, but one that had become strangely companionable. Everyone was either enthusing about Southampton's performance or talking about the upcoming Six Nations.

He eventually made it to the front and found himself squeezed in a little uncomfortably next to a strapping bloke in a Hackett shirt. He made an involuntary noise and the guy said, "Sorry," and shuffled away a bit. "I'm fatter than I think."

"You're all right," Jason said with a nod.

A barman came over to him and he managed to get his order in before anyone else. Once he was done, the bloke next to him asked, "Are you guys coppers?"

He turned to look at this man a little more carefully, trying to work out why he was being asked. The guy didn't seem to be angry. Just cheerfully curious.

"Yeah," Jason answered. "We are. But off-duty."

"Oh yeah, obviously." The guy shrugged. "You have to have time off. I used to tell my ex that. She was always on the job. Though actually"—he gave a laugh—"it turned out it was bullshit, and she was on a different job."

"Ah, I'm sorry," Jason said, his eyes on the first almost-poured pint. "That's tough."

Jason had never known why he gave off such a strong aura of "tell me your problems." He was tempted to blame the psychology degree, though it had happened to him as a teenager too. Somehow people found him approachable whenever he didn't actively give them fuck-off vibes. And sometimes even then.

"I was pretty cut up at first," the guy said in a lower voice. "But actually it was the best thing for me. I was tired of the games. And oh my God, Juliette loves to play games. She got me to move here, and then was stringing some poor bastard in her team along too."

Jason found his pulse quickening. It was no different from the feeling when a witness said something incriminating.

He glanced at the big bloke, who was holding on to the bar with one hand now, bouncing his other fist off the surface. He was clearly in his late twenties. Quite expensively dressed. Attractive. And his accent was decidedly Brummie. He was from Birmingham, like Hanson.

"Your ex was called Juliette?" Jason asked, as the two pints arrived in front of him.

"Yeah," the guy said, glancing at him and then away. "I'd worry she might come in here, but this isn't Juliette's kind of place."

"What kind of an officer is she?" Jason asked, lifting one of the drinks with a hand that felt cold. "Uniform?"

"No, a detective," the guy said. "She came here to become one."

Jason took a long, steadying breath in through his nose, and then said, "Let me buy you a drink. What was your name?"

"Damian," the strapping bloke said, looking a little taken aback. "You really don't have to. . . ."

Jason cut across him, with a very determined smile. "I'd like to hear more about your ex, if that's OK with you."

20

LOUISE

owe you something of an apology, Niall. In all of this, I haven't been quite honest about a few things. Though it's not that I've actively lied, really. It's more that I've failed to tell you significant details.

I don't even know why I care what you think anymore, but for some reason it's still hard to admit a few things to you. Perhaps because it's hard to admit them to myself. It could be that. But I'm starting to realize that the only way I'm going to feel better is to blast every secret out of the water, and leave the truth standing bare. Probably dripping onto our spotless fucking carpets.

So, the first untruth by omission. It's a long-standing one, and I know that you're going to hate it.

You were not the first man I kissed at Hannah's wedding. More than that, I almost ended up going home with someone else entirely.

I told you that April's Italian friend had flirted with me. I don't remember anything he said to me. Or much else about him. Just that he was tall, attractive, and didn't really sound all that Italian.

And in fact, I don't really know how it happened. One minute I was talking to the bride, and the next I was in a corridor, pressed up against a wall while this handsome man slid his tongue into my mouth and his hand round my back.

I'd never done anything like that before. I've already told you how hard I used to find it to attract attention. Alpha men, in particular, used to look straight past me. So it was extraordinary to me. Wonderful. I was a willing participant as he drew me into an empty bathroom and locked the door behind us.

A more experienced, more self-possessed woman might have taken it further. There might be another reality where I am that person, and where you and I never got together because I decided pushy Italian men were my thing. Maybe it's an inverted reality, where Drunk Louise is the real person and Sober Me is the sniveling creature who only comes out after I forget to drink enough.

But that isn't how it was. As he pinned me against the counter and started to lift my dress, Sober Louise made a comeback. I suddenly felt like it was too much. Too fast. Like I shouldn't be doing this with a man I didn't know, and particularly not with one who was so very much in control.

I went from desire to panic. I found myself fighting to be free of him. He was asking me what was wrong, and then someone started banging on the door. They must have seen us go in there.

We separated and straightened our clothes. When my almost-lover opened the door, he pretended I was ill. That he'd had to look after me. The middle-aged man outside looked like he didn't believe a word of it. I was almost grateful that he was there, though. It meant I could hurry away from the hot Italian without looking at him. It meant I could pretend not to have been frightened.

So when I came to find the two of you outside, you and April, I wasn't walking out fresh from a nice conversation with Hannah. I was doing it with the taste of that man still on my tongue, and with a feeling between relief and regret that I'd run from him.

Does that make you reevaluate everything about us, Niall? Does it make you look back and ask how you'd been so blind?

I really hope it does, darling, because I'm beginning to want nothing more than to hurt you.

21

The magistrates agreed to their request for a custody extension early on Sunday morning, which meant it was now up to the team to build enough evidence for a prosecution within a total of ninety-six hours. Jonah shut himself away in his office on his return from the court, equipped with supplies of coffee and three caramel biscuits from O'Malley's rapidly diminishing supplies.

Sundays were often a frustrating grind of a day, when businesses were closed to inquiries, Intelligence staff were largely at home, and labs did not process results. The unique value of being at CID on such a deadbeat day was that it allowed him downtime to reflect.

In this case, he had a strange collection of hard facts and large questions. The fact of Alex dying at the Reakes house, compared with the question of how and why. The fact of Louise Reakes moving the body outside, placed alongside uncertainty as to exactly what she had been covering up, and for whom.

He spent a while looking at a map of the area between Louise Reakes's house and Blue Underground. Then he pulled out the printed photo of the knife. After a few minutes looking at it, he rose and asked his team to make their way into one of the meeting rooms.

He got his laptop set up and connected to the data projector, and then settled himself on the edge of the central table while the team trooped in. He waited until Hanson had closed the door behind them all before he said, "There seem to be three things all this hangs on, at the moment."

He clicked on a Google Maps tab on his laptop, bringing up the London Road area. He zoomed out and maneuvered it until they had Louise Reakes's street visible at the top right.

"The first," he went on, "is how—and why—Alex Plaskitt ended up at Eleven Saints Close. What happened on the way could tell us everything we need to know about how he died. Was there someone else who made their way to the house with Louise and Alex? Did Louise wait somewhere for him? Did he stumble after her in confusion? There might have been an altercation on the way. They also might have been seen together at some point, though we've not had anything useful back from our appeals to the public."

He paused for a moment, letting the three of them finish writing all of that down, and then went on, "Related to that is point two: whether we believe that Louise Reakes suffered a total blackout or she's hiding a crime. We probably want to approach both of these questions in the same way." He highlighted the bottom of London Road with the laser pointer. "We still haven't had CCTV back from the Wetherspoons to the south of London Road or the kebab shop farther north. I want to prioritize getting footage from those two places, and anywhere else between the nightclub and Louise's house. Either Louise or Alex or both might have gone south to pick up a cab from the taxi rank on the corner of Cumberland Place. Alternatively, they might have gone north, and then either continued up London Road or headed east along Bellevue."

"If they did cut through Bellevue, they probably would have gone up Onslow Road afterward," Hanson said. "There are loads of places along there that'll have CCTV. I'll get on it. I can chase up the other ones too."

"Thanks, Juliette. The third thing," he went on, "is the knife." He brought up an image of it on the screen, and then glanced at Lightman. "Do we have any updates from the makers, before I go on?"

"I've left messages with Steel and Silver," Lightman said. "Emails, voicemails, and web contact form. No reply as yet. Head office is in Newcastle, so hopefully they'll get back to us before we end up having to visit."

"OK, thanks," Jonah replied. "So, my thinking. That knife isn't something you'd happen to have with you. It's a weapon, and it was presumably being carried for a reason."

O'Malley gave him a speculative look. "Criminal involvement?"

"Of one sort or another, possibly," Jonah replied. "If Louise Reakes is telling the truth and had never seen the knife before, it could be Alex's. But if he brought it out with him, that implies premeditation. Do we think Alex Plaskitt went out that night with the intention of threatening, raping, or hurting a young woman?"

There was a momentary silence, and Hanson said, "If he had predatory intentions, why didn't he leave with her? She was drunk enough. Do we even know she was still in sight once he'd left?"

Jonah gave a wry smile. "You think the predatory male idea doesn't fit?"

"Not really," Hanson replied. "And to be honest, no kind of violence seems to fit with what we know of his character. It's hard to even imagine him fighting to defend someone. I mean . . . I've seen him throw a tantrum on-camera at his own uselessness, but I just don't see him attacking Louise."

"There's also the high quality and high price tag of the knife to consider," Jonah added. "Those features point to something."

"Someone who owns it because they get a kick out of it," O'Malley said immediately. "They enjoy using it."

"Or at least someone who enjoys the idea of using it," Lightman offered. "A gang member might own a weapon like that to up his power to intimidate."

Jonah nodded again. The city's gang culture was depressingly strong, and it was generally an angle they considered in most cases.

"Can we match any of that up with our suspects?" Jonah asked.

There was a long silence, and Jonah knew they were mulling over Louise Reakes, Step Conti, Niall Reakes, and Issa Benhawy with the same lack of conviction that he was. None of them seemed likely to be criminals of any kind.

"What about April Dumont?" Lightman asked thoughtfully.

"As a gang member?" O'Malley asked. "I mean . . . maybe, but I'd doubt it." He paused, and then went on, "She is awfully protective of her friend, though. She might have thought Alex was threatening her."

"But then," Hanson replied, "if she killed him to protect her, why would she leave Louise to deal with the body?"

"Fair point," O'Malley said with a shrug. "But it would make sense of Louise trying to cover it all up."

"So," Jonah said, "that basically leaves us needing to know a lot more about our group of involved people. But it also means we should keep the possibility of an unknown attacker in mind. If Alex Plaskitt really was stabbed by someone with a fetish for knives, it could have happened while Louise Reakes was unconscious. She might only have left the door unlocked and suffered the consequences."

Jonah could feel his team's reaction to this idea. Or at least O'Malley's and Hanson's reaction. It would be a huge blow if Louise turned out to be uninvolved when they'd worked hard both to bring her in and to win as much custody time as possible.

"Ben," he went on, "I'd like you to see Step Conti and April Dumont again. I want to know what sort of a person Step is. And

I'd like you to press April on whether she really left with another man."

"Sure," Lightman agreed.

"Domnall," he added, "I want you back on those traffic cameras. Make sure we have license plates for Niall Reakes, Step Conti, and April Dumont. Docs Louise Reakes have her own car?"

"I'll check it out," O'Malley replied.

"OK. Let's go to it."

"So we're not viewing Louise Reakes as prime suspect?" Hanson queried as she got to her feet.

"I feel we should be viewing her as the first option of many," Jonah said. He gave her a slightly wicked smile. "Business as usual."

Hanson went to pick up her coat, keys, and phone, relieved to be getting out of the station again. The sun was out in force today, and yesterday's snow was almost gone. It was bright and pretty out there, even if it was still freezing, and she wanted to be out in it.

She checked her phone before putting it away. She had an eBay notification on a jacket she'd bid on, but no messages. Nothing from Jason.

And actually, now that she thought of it, she hadn't heard anything from him last night. She hadn't genuinely expected him to come round after the rugby. He generally got stuck into the beers and ended up going for a late-night curry. He was too considerate to roll in drunk only to pass out on her bed. But it was a little odd that he hadn't messaged her to say so. Or to check in this morning.

She took a moment to send him a quick greeting, asking how he was doing. She might be too busy to reply until later if he did get back in touch, but she'd like to know that he was alive and well.

She grabbed the big square wool scarf that she'd looped over the back of her chair and nodded to Lightman, who was putting down the phone without having spoken. She felt a need to keep the amicable conversation going. To keep things friendly with him.

"No response from April Dumont?" she asked.

"No," Lightman agreed. "And nothing from Step Conti either. Though I've got stuff to be getting on with until one of them replies. The company that sells those knives finally emailed. Apparently one of the managers should be in from two."

"On a Sunday?" Hanson asked, winding the scarf round her neck.

"I suppose if they have orders in, they can ship them with a courier," Lightman said with a shrug. "I'm guessing it's a pretty small enterprise."

"I hope they keep proper records."

"Yeah, I was thinking the same." Lightman gave a very short sigh. "It's so rare to have a weapon that might be traceable. It'd be supremely shit if it came to nothing."

"Supremely," Hanson agreed, and left the building feeling a little better about everything for some reason.

AFTER SOME TIME spent banging on the door, Hanson had at last been shown into the cluttered office at the kebab shop and let loose on its old desktop computer. The hard drive had all the shop's CCTV footage, broken down into three-hour chunks.

She sat on the battered foam of the chair and loaded up the file from twelve A.M., wondering what sort of view they were going to get. The answer was, unfortunately, not a great one. The camera was placed at the door and pointed downward fairly steeply to catch the faces of everyone coming in. The view of the pavement was limited to a distance of about twenty feet along and to the near side of London Road. Anyone walking on the other side wouldn't be caught at all.

She scrolled through to 1:13 and then hit Play. To her relief,

Louise Reakes entered the frame after two minutes. Hanson noted the time and added a comment that Louise looked as drunk as she had on the nightclub footage. She had the unmistakable straight-legged gait of someone who was having trouble balancing, and in the few seconds of footage they had she veered sharply from left to right.

Hanson wondered if Louise might have been so out of it that she could have gone too far in defending herself. Though whether she could have been coordinated enough in that state to take a knife off someone and stab them was less clear.

Hanson started the video again, guessing that Alex wouldn't be far behind Louise. He'd been less drunk. He was probably walking in straight lines.

And there he was, coming onto the screen seventeen seconds after her. Hanson immediately froze the clip, and wrote the time down with a suddenly accelerated pulse. On the still she had, he was moving aside to let someone out of the kebab-shop door, but his gaze was fixed down the street. As if he were looking at Louise.

Hanson breathed out, and then pressed Play. Alex began to move again, and then unexpectedly faltered. His hand went to his pocket.

Hanson found herself fixated. Were they about to see the knife, and end all speculation over whose it had been?

His hand emerged, but it was holding something smaller. Something concealed easily by his palm. Hanson refroze the image, trying to tell what it was, but it wasn't clear enough. It was definitely too small to be his phone.

Frustrated, she pressed the Play button once again. She watched as Alex turned, and then, in a move she really hadn't expected, walked into the kebab shop. He disappeared from view, and as time ticked onward, the truth dawned on her. Alex had been looking to see if he had his bank card. He'd gone to buy himself food.

Seven minutes later, Alex emerged clutching an open kebab in a wrapper. Although Louise Reakes wasn't in sight at this point, it was clear she would be long gone by now. Alex and Louise hadn't met up outside the club, and it didn't look like he could possibly have followed her.

So how, Hanson thought, *did he end up dying in her bed?*

PATRICK MOORCROFT MADE it to Southampton Central just after midday. He was wearing a different but equally expensive-looking suit-and-watch combination, and to Jonah's thanks for coming in he responded with a terse "Let's get on with it, shall we?"

Louise's expression was more resigned today, though Jonah suspected that part of that was tiredness. Few people slept well during their first night in the cells.

With the preamble done and Lightman ready next to him, Jonah began the interview.

"In your account of Friday night, you insisted that you remembered nothing from the later part of the evening."

"That's right," Louise said, her voice lifeless.

"Louise," Jonah said in a low, urgent voice. "I want to be clear on this. We aren't interested in condemning you for your behavior. We want to know what resulted in the death of a young man. Whatever happened, it is vital that you tell us the truth."

"I have," she said, her eyes gleaming slightly.

"My client has expressed no wish to alter her statement," Patrick Moorcroft said. "She has also explained her lack of memory to you."

"Understood," Jonah said without looking away from Louise. "But there may be confused, hazy memories that you haven't told us about. Perhaps things that make no sense to you."

Jonah saw clearly the way Louise reacted. It was the expression of someone who has been seen through.

"I don't think I . . ." Louise shook her head. "There's only been a dream. And . . . and a few . . ."

"We need to know."

Louise turned to Patrick. Her solicitor looked torn, as well he might. It was unclear whether anything Louise said was likely to incriminate or exonerate her. But it was important to show that his client was cooperating where she could. He glanced at Jonah, weighing things up, and then nodded.

Louise gave a long sigh. "I think I remember someone chasing me. Not him. Not Alex. But it's a dream, so maybe it was meant to be him. I knew they were a threat, and they kept coming, and I kept falling." She gave a sudden, loud sniff, and then continued with an unsteady voice. "I fell, and they were suddenly on top of me, hurting me. There was—there was a pain in my back, and when I woke up and looked in the mirror, there was a bruise where—where I remembered it."

"OK," Jonah said with some satisfaction. He felt instinctively that she was telling them the truth. "It's important that a female officer photographs any bruising. Any injuries at all."

"I know." Louise's cheeks were wet with tears again.

He watched her, briefly, as she rubbed at one of her cheeks. "You said you fell onto the grass. Was there anything else in your surroundings?"

"Trees," she said indistinctly. "I thought there were trees. But I don't—I don't think I was in the woods, after a night out. I don't think that's right."

Jonah glanced at Lightman, who was writing notes with unusual energy. He suspected that Lightman's thoughts mirrored his own. That with a large blank in her memory it was possible she'd ended up almost anywhere.

"Was there anyone else in the dream?"

Louise's expression grew distant. She tried to speak, swallowed, and then said, "I don't know. There could have been someone else. At some point in the evening someone was angry. Maybe with me, or maybe—maybe I just saw a fight. But I don't—I don't know. None of it's clear."

Jonah nodded. "That's all right. And what else was there? You said you remembered a few fragments?"

Louise paused for quite some time, her eyes on her hands, before she said, "I think I talked to the victim. In the club. I don't know how long for. I just have this memory of his face as he's saying something and I have no idea what it was." She gave Jonah an anguished look. "I only remembered that this morning. I'm sorry."

Lightman glanced at Jonah, and then asked, "You think this was after your friend April had left?"

"I suppose so."

"And what else?"

"Nothing else." She sounded dejected rather than combative. "I'm sorry."

Jonah waited a moment before he asked, "You mentioned that Alex Plaskitt might have tried to rob you."

"I wouldn't have hurt him," Louise said immediately.

"And yet you tried to hide his death," Jonah argued. "That was not the action of an innocent person."

"I told you—"

"Who were you covering up for, Louise?" he asked, cutting across her, his voice steely.

Louise looked upward, as if trying to find strength somewhere. "I didn't know what I was covering up. I panicked."

"Why were you so afraid of telling your husband what had happened?"

"I wasn't—" Louise gave a short, strange laugh. "I already told you." Patrick leaned over to murmur something, but she shook her head, impatiently. "He hates it when I drink, and I thought he'd think it was my fault somehow. That's all."

"That's a strange idea," Lightman said, interjecting. "That the death of a young man was somehow your fault."

"I didn't—what I meant was, he'd say I shouldn't have been that drunk, or maybe I would have seen something. Stopped it."

Louise looked close to the fine edge between coping and not coping at all.

"I would caution you against overanalyzing comments made by my client in a state of shock," her solicitor said.

"Did he have some reason for thinking that you were having an affair?" Lightman pressed, not acknowledging the solicitor.

"No!" Louise's protest was a gasp of outrage. "Why would he? I'm bloody devoted to him."

"What did he say when you told him what had happened?" Lightman went on, with an untouched coldness that was impressive.

Patrick Moorcroft shifted in his chair, his gaze moving from Lightman to Jonah. "How are these questions related to your inquiry into Alex Plaskitt's death?"

"That will become evident," Jonah said firmly, his gaze fixed on Louise. "Please carry on, Sergeant."

"Would you tell us what he said, please?" Lightman said evenly.

Louise shook her head in small, quick jerks. "I don't know. He just asked—what had happened."

"I'm sure you can be more specific," Jonah said, his voice a great deal less measured than Lightman's. Where his sergeant did a wonderful line in being relentlessly unemotional, Jonah's real skill had always lain in attack. In suddenly bringing out such harsh, scathing tones that it broke suspects down. The deep marks left by his father's abuse would always have their uses. "You claim not to be able to remember Friday night, but yesterday morning, when you called your husband, you were stone-cold sober. So what, *exactly*, did he say?"

"He asked—if it was someone I knew . . ." Louise said, and then she stopped, and he saw one of those rare, intensely telling expressions. She wasn't looking at Jonah, though. She was looking toward the wall, with her face a mask of shock.

22

LOUISE

I realize that telling you about the Italian man at the wedding was something of a sidetrack. If we're going to continue chronologically, then the next thing to address is the revelation that hit me like a bus earlier today.

I'm not sure quite how it took me so long to realize. I've thought back to the phone conversation we had so many times. I've thought how heartbreaking it was that you were so ready to believe this was my fault, before there was anything to point in my direction.

It occurs to me, having written this all out, that I understand you better tonight than I have ever understood you. I understand why you've been so angry with me for so long, and that it hasn't really been about my drinking, or my desperation for a child. It's had nothing to do with the times I couldn't help tidying when you just wanted to relax.

It explains not only your anger but also your swift belief that I'd cheated. That I'd killed. Because if you could be angry with me, it exonerated you, didn't it, Niall? Nothing that you'd done could ever be as bad as that, and that left you free from guilt.

But anyway, back to that phone call. The bit I kept forgetting about was the start of it, when I waited for five rings for you to pick up. Waited with a ringtone in my ear that was not the long, irritating beep of an international call but instead the standard double-chirrup of a bloody UK one. Long before you should have even boarded a plane home, you were back in this country, and had probably been back before any of this shit even happened.

You lied, and it took a police interrogation to make me realize the truth. I wonder how I can have been so slow.

23

Louise hadn't even tried to hold out on them. When Jonah asked her, sharply, what it was that she'd realized, she had looked at him, her eyes large and unfocused, and said flatly, "Niall wasn't in Geneva."

They'd got a few more words out of her before Patrick Moorcroft had intervened and demanded a private conversation with his client. But they had heard enough.

"We need to get confirmation from the airline," Jonah said to Lightman as they walked rapidly back to CID. "Find out when he did actually arrive back, and see if we can trace him to Southampton on Friday night. Get O'Malley onto it."

"Of course," Lightman answered, a little awkwardly. "Sorry. I've dropped the ball. I should have pushed the airline earlier. . . ."

"Hindsight is a wonderful thing," Jonah said. "We'd already taken steps to prove he was at the conference and it seemed to tie in. He went to great efforts to cover his tracks. The big question is why."

"Given his immediate assumption of an affair," Lightman commented, "could he have been trying to catch Louise out?"

"It is possible," Jonah agreed. "An attempted trap that went wrong. I think she was telling the truth about someone attacking her, and I want to find out where it happened. Louise remembers falling face-first onto grass, and trees around her. If the ANPR cameras haven't picked up any of our suspects' cars in the area, then our search radius is fairly small. As far as a drunk woman could stumble." He paused outside his office door. "Do we know when Juliette's going to be back?"

"I'll find out," Lightman replied.

"I want the two of you to work out any likely places for an attack. And when you have any, get Linda McCullough to meet you there."

As Lightman wrote himself a note, Jonah briefly updated O'Malley and asked if he'd had any joy with the traffic cameras.

"Louise Reakes's car wasn't on the road," the older sergeant answered. "April Dumont I've only picked up much earlier in the day. She must have got a cab to Saints Close, which means any movements later would have been in a cab too. I'm checking Step Conti now."

"When you're done with the airline, I want to look for Niall Reakes on those cameras," Jonah said tersely. "Someone attacked her, and Niall wasn't where he said he was. We need to know where he went, and what happened to his wife." And then, realizing that this was a little sharper and more melodramatic than his usual style, he added, "Please."

"I'M SO SORRY," Louise said quietly, as soon as the officers had left the interview room. She couldn't bring herself to look at Patrick. "I didn't . . . I'm too tired to think. I'm not trying to get Niall in trouble."

There was a moment of silence, and then Patrick said, "Of course not, and I'm sure he isn't in trouble. It's sensible for you to explain everything that casts doubt on this idea of you as perpetrator."

There was another pause, and then Louise said, "I think it'll be OK for Niall. I'm pretty sure I know what he was doing. And who he was doing it with. It isn't what they're thinking."

After another moment, Patrick said, "Perhaps you should tell the police what you think. But I'll be sorry if it's that too."

JONAH PICKED UP the phone to Hanson twenty minutes after leaving the interview room.

"So we definitely have no sign of a meet-up between Alex Plaskitt and Louise Reakes on London Road," she summarized. "And he was too far behind to be following her. So either they met at the house by prearrangement, or something else went on."

"That's very interesting," Jonah said, not sure how to fit this into everything else. He briefly imagined Louise letting Alex into her home, and Niall arriving back to find them there together. Had Louise been lying about the attack? Or had something else happened on her way home?

"I've also traveled along her most likely route home," Hanson went on. "If she was attacked, I think it must have been on Asylum Green. It's bang on the way, it's the only real green space, and once she was under the trees, she'd be pretty much invisible from the road. Can we get someone out there?"

"I'll send Linda's team," Jonah told her. "Are you on your way back?"

"Yes, almost there," Hanson confirmed.

"Good. Pick Ben up and meet Linda at the scene."

O'Malley leaned in through the door of Jonah's office. "Niall Reakes is on his way in. And I've tracked down his movements. He ditched the doctors and came back late on Friday night, from Zurich instead of Geneva. He landed at Gatwick at ten-twenty, and could easily have been back here by twelve-thirty. Time enough to work out the house was empty and go out and find his wife."

Jonah gave him a grin. "That's excellent news."

As O'Malley let himself out, though, Jonah became thoughtful. If Niall had found Alex and Louise in bed together, he might well have killed them. But how did Louise being attacked on the grass fit? Had Alex stumbled on an attack and thwarted it? Or was

Louise Reakes, who had proven adept at hiding the truth, still sending them on a merry dance in order to protect her husband?

Even that made little sense, though, Jonah thought. Why would she protect the man who had killed her lover and left her to deal with it? Unless Niall had threatened her. Or unless Louise had been involved from the start.

HANSON DECIDED TO park at the magistrates' court, which was right by Asylum Green. It limited the amount of walking they'd have to do in the freezing wind, even if they did end up standing around in it.

Driving into the car park gave her a strange feeling of déjà vu. It had only been a few hours ago that she'd come here to ask for a custody extension.

She'd been in a very different frame of mind then, her anxiety limited to the tiny flicker of nerves at having to speak in front of the magistrates. There had been no constant panic like a siren somewhere in the background. No feeling of everything having gone wrong. She knew it could be nothing, even now. Jason could have read her message and forgotten to reply. She did that sometimes, only to be told off for it later. But this was Jason. The man who always messaged back, and dropped her a line at bedtime. Which meant something was really wrong.

Ben seemed to be oblivious to her mood, thankfully. He climbed equably out of the car, stretched his shoulders slightly, and began to amble back up the road toward the green. As Hanson caught up with him, pulling her scarf up as high as it would go to protect herself from the wind, he said, "I wonder if she walked this way often during daylight hours. Louise Reakes, I mean. You'd probably avoid going across a deserted area at one A.M. in the normal run of things. But if it was a frequently used route and she was drunk, she might default to it."

"Yes," Hanson said. Then she added, "She looks like someone who runs. Could be a route she uses for that."

Lightman gave her a sidelong look. "Do I look like someone who runs?"

"Probably." She glanced at him. "Do you not run?"

"Only under duress," he said. "If there are no pools open anywhere, or tennis courts or anything."

Hanson shook her head, trying to bring some kind of banter to mind now that it seemed to be back on the menu. But she felt as though it had been drained out of her, and she wondered suddenly whether this feeling really had anything to do with Jason, or whether it was just the long-term effect of Damian's persistent presence in her life. Whether she'd actually just reached some kind of breaking point.

They crossed the Avenue, the two-lane road that described a long, thin loop like a racing circuit. Asylum Green sat in its center, a narrow strip of parkland that bulged at its southern tip. Linda McCullough's scientific support vehicle was parked up at the bottom, near the green's widest point. She emerged from the driver's door, white-clad and ready for business. A male assistant climbed out of the other side and gave them a nod.

"What are we looking at?" McCullough asked.

Lightman glanced at Hanson, and she realized he was letting her do the talking.

"Thanks for coming so quickly," she said, grateful that her voice seemed to sound normal in spite of everything. "We're looking for evidence of some kind of attack on our suspect. I've been looking at routes. If she crossed the green, it's likely to have been at this end. She would have emerged from London Road, and it's likely she'd cut across the diagonal path to get onto the far side of the Avenue."

"OK," McCullough said, pulling a set of latex gloves out of her pocket and handing them to Hanson. "You two may as well look too. Any scuff marks, dropped items, signs of discoloration of the soil, or obvious blood on the grass or paving, call me over."

So Hanson and Lightman began treading the snowy grass,

stepping slowly and carefully. They moved in and out of the sun-light between the trees. It was strange how quickly they got into a soothing rhythm, despite the freezing air. There was nothing to do except look at their feet and make occasional remarks.

When she glanced over at Ben a few times, she realized that he looked less neutral than usual. There was an aura of brooding about him.

"You aren't beating yourself up about Niall Reakes's flights, are you?" she asked him, quietly. "If you are, you're being an idiot."

There was a note of surprise in his expression as he looked at her, and then he gave a very small smile. "I've never denied being an idiot."

"You spoke to the conference organizers," Hanson said. "You spoke to the airline. It's not your fault they hadn't bothered checking properly."

"But I always work on the assumption that people don't bother," he said with a shrug. "It's how I make sure of things. And I should have chased them up."

"It didn't make any difference," Hanson told him. "Niall Reakes is still going to have to explain himself. So cut yourself a bit of slack. Otherwise it makes the rest of us feel worse."

Ben's smile turned into a laugh, and she was pleased to note that he seemed a little less morose as they trod onward. It made her feel incrementally more useful and in control of things, and that was important right now.

After ten minutes, Lightman found an empty cigarette packet in a patch of remaining snow. Linda came over and bagged it up, despite the low chance of it meaning anything. Five minutes later, Linda's team found a single glove that looked like it might belong to a woman. It was navy fleece, the cheap kind you got in petrol stations, and it was sodden with melted snow. It got bagged up too.

A few minutes later, at a midpoint in the green, Hanson

caught a glint of reflected light. Crouching down, she saw an earring nestled into the grass. Its triple rows of hanging diamantés were set into silver squares. It looked, to Hanson, like the sort of thing Louise Reakes might well have worn on her night out, and she tried to remember whether earrings had shown up on the CCTV.

Lightman stepped carefully past her where she crouched, and then stopped.

"There's blood," he said.

JONAH'S WORKING OF Niall Reakes began the moment he walked through the door of CID. Assuming a mantle of full-blown officialness, he dispensed with any conversation at all as he took the drugs rep quickly and angrily through to the interview suite. O'Malley was already waiting for them by the door, and Jonah almost felt tempted to laugh at the pitying expression his sergeant gave their suspect.

If Niall had looked anxious on arrival, he was actually shaking by the time Jonah introduced them all for the tape. Jonah gave him nothing but a piercing stare once the introductions were done, and Niall caved within seconds.

"I need to tell you something," he said, putting a hand out to the table as if to steady himself. "It isn't—it's got nothing to do with the death of that guy, but I know you're going to think it does."

"Would this be about your whereabouts on Friday night?" Jonah asked, whip-sharp.

"Yeah." Niall swallowed. "Yeah, it is. I flew home early from the conference. I told Jessie, my assistant, that my wife was really ill, and she said she'd cover the final night and morning."

Niall's accent seemed to have slid a whole step less middle-class, making it clear that he spent much of his life acting. Trying to be more than he was. It elicited a surge of sympathy in Jonah.

"And yet you didn't go to look after your wife," he said.

"No. I lied." There was an ugly-looking sheen to his face, and Jonah focused on that instead of his sympathy. On how distasteful this man was. It made it easier to go on the attack in the short window they had before Niall requested a solicitor. "I flew back to meet up with my ex-wife."

Jonah glanced over at Lightman and said, "I find that difficult to believe."

"It's—true." Niall looked desperate. Sick-looking. "It isn't the first time, and Dina can back me up."

"You're telling us you were having an affair?"

"Not even an affair," Niall said, clasping his hands together. They were trembling uncontrollably. "Though I—she's been pushing for one."

Jonah gave a short laugh. "You're asking us to believe that you lied to your employers and your wife, and then spent a great deal of money flying home early to meet up with your ex-wife, all purely for a platonic chat?"

"She's getting me a job," he said, just before Jonah had finished. "A VP role at Glaxo. A friend of hers there is on the board. She told me about it back in June and I—I really wanted it. It's where I've wanted to work forever."

"Why not simply tell your wife about it?" O'Malley asked. "If a perfect job was being offered."

"Because . . . Look, Dina obviously seems like a threat to her," Niall said, trying for some sort of boys-together tone and not achieving it. "I knew Louise would tell me to stay away from her, which would have meant no job."

"So let me understand this," Jonah said. "You've been carrying on what might as well be an affair with a woman who has promised you a job on the basis that, what, you sleep with her after it's all sorted? Is that it?"

"No," Niall said, his expression pained. He clearly thought this unfair. "There's never been any agreement of any kind. I never would."

"How did your marriage to your ex-wife end?" Jonah asked.

"I . . . She left me. For someone else." Niall Reakes looked, for some reason, more awkward admitting this than he had at any point so far.

"Why would she now want you back so desperately that she's found a way of offering you your dream job?"

"She misses me. She realized it was a mistake breaking things off the moment I got married to Louise. But . . . but I love my wife. Very much."

"Despite the ease with which you believed she was having an affair," Jonah countered. "Despite your swift assumption that she is guilty of murder."

"I never assumed that!" Niall said, looking angry. "I was effing furious with her because—because all of this is probably going to screw everything up." There was a pause, and he said in a more measured voice, "I lied to my company, and now I probably don't have a new job to go to. It's all been forced out into the open because—because Louise got pissed again."

Jonah felt overwhelmingly tempted to ask whether Niall thought that might be karma, but instead he asked, "Where did you stay on Friday night?"

"At the Gatwick Hilton."

"And you met Dina in your room?"

"No. In the bar."

"Until what time?"

Niall considered for a moment, and then said, "A bit after twelve, I guess."

"What car do you drive?"

Niall looked wrong-footed. He sounded a little defensive as he said, "A Jaguar. An F-Type."

"That's a nice sporty car," Jonah commented. "So you could easily have driven back home by, say, quarter to two. Probably even earlier if you'd floored it."

"I didn't," Niall protested.

"You didn't arrive back and find your wife in bed with another man?" Jonah asked. "You didn't decide to do away with him and leave her comatose to wonder if she'd done it? I mean, it would be a pretty effective form of revenge, wouldn't it?"

There was a silence for several seconds, and then Niall said, "I want my solicitor now."

"So I'LL CALL the ex-wife now?" O'Malley asked, following Jonah back into CID.

"Yes," Jonah said. "Though I strongly suspect that he's made some sort of arrangement with her."

"You don't believe him?"

Jonah glanced at his sergeant. "There's a small chance that it's true. But looked at rationally, he went to a hell of a lot of trouble just to meet up about a job offer."

"Agreed," O'Malley said. "And I'm interested in why he flew from Zurich. He must have driven for two or three hours to get there. I'm going to look up whether there were other flights he could have taken without the long drive."

"Yes," Jonah said, trying and failing to picture where the two cities were on a map. "That's probably the weirdest part of it." He paused for a moment, thinking of the distinctive murder weapon. "It might also be worth checking whether there's a retailer who sells those knives in Zurich."

"I'll get on it," O'Malley answered.

"The blood tests from Louise Reakes are sitting with the lab, aren't they?" Jonah went on, thoughtfully.

"Yup," O'Malley said. "Also useless until tomorrow."

"Unless we work on the good nature of our colleagues," Jonah said. He pulled his phone out and dialed Linda McCullough's number.

There were traffic noises in the background as she picked up.

"We're on-site at Asylum Green," she said immediately. "And we have blood."

"Blood?" Jonah asked dumbly.

"Yes, Sheens. You'll know it as the red stuff that runs through most people's veins."

Jonah half smiled as he replied, "I'll look it up."

"There isn't a lot of it. Did your female show any signs of injury?" McCullough asked.

"Nothing she showed us," Jonah said thoughtfully, "but she mentioned pain in her back, which we're going to get photographed." He glanced up at O'Malley, who nodded. Presumably that was already being sorted by one of the female PCSOs.

"We've got a few personal belongings bagged up too," McCullough went on. "They may or may not have anything to do with an attack."

"Thanks," Jonah said. "How long do you think you'll be there?"

"Why do I suspect that this question isn't about my mental health?" McCullough asked.

"I have no idea," Jonah countered. "But we've got a blood test for Rohypnol I badly want back, and a nonfunctioning lab."

True to form, McCullough complained loudly, and then agreed. "I'm still waiting for all those pints you owe me, Sheens," she added.

"Just say the word," Jonah replied.

THE TEMPERATURE WAS now just above freezing, and Hanson was suffering. Even with her coat zipped up to her chin and her hands shoved in her pockets, she was shaking with cold.

"Should have brought another four or five layers," she said to Lightman, as the two of them huddled beneath one of the trees on Asylum Green. Or at least as Hanson huddled. Lightman looked as unaffected by everything as usual.

"Do you want to wait in the car?" he asked her. "There's no reason for us both to hang around here."

"That's extremely kind," Hanson said, meaning it, "but my pride would never recover."

McCullough came over a few minutes later to announce that they were packing up, and Hanson sighed with relief.

"We've got blood and soil samples and we've taken cuttings of the grass," she said.

"Can you tell how much there was?" Hanson asked. "Like whether it was a serious injury or just, I don't know, a nosebleed?"

"It's not a lot," Linda said. "A splash only."

"And I suppose we don't even know if it was connected," Hanson went on, more quietly.

"No, we don't," McCullough said cheerfully. "Welcome to my world."

Lightman and Hanson walked briskly back to the car after that, and Hanson turned the engine on immediately in the hope that it might warm up. She pulled her bag off over her head and felt her phone buzz as she did so. Pulling it out, she saw a message from Jason. It began with the words I don't quite know what to say to you. . . .

She opened it up with an unreal feeling. She read his words, feeling as though she was slipping sideways out of the car as she did.

"Everything all right?" Lightman asked from beside her after a moment.

And to Hanson's absolute humiliation, when she tried to answer, nothing but a ragged sob came out.

O'MALLEY HAD BOTH a mobile and landline for Dina Weyman and managed to reach her on the latter. The call was originally answered by a disgruntled-sounding man who was presumably Dina's husband.

"Why do you want to talk to her?" he asked gracelessly when O'Malley explained who he was.

"We want to corroborate a story given by a witness," O'Malley told him. "We're told your wife can help."

There were movements on the other end, and a ferocious-sounding muttered conversation followed by the slam of a door. O'Malley wondered whether he'd called in the middle of some sort of domestic dispute.

Eventually, Dina said, "Hello?" in a voice as cheerful and unconcerned as a child's.

"Is that Dina Weyman?"

"Yes," she said. "I understand you're with the police." There was a slight sigh to her voice, as if talking to the police were immeasurably boring.

"Detective Sergeant O'Malley," he told her. "I want to ask you about Friday night."

"What about it?" The question could have been rude, but she managed to inject just enough lightness into it to save herself.

"Niall Reakes tells us that you met up with him at a hotel," O'Malley said. "We just wanted to confirm the details."

There was a pause, and Dina said, "I'm sorry, Niall said I met up with him?"

"Yes." O'Malley found himself sitting up very straight. "On Friday night."

There was another pause, and then Dina said, in a much less light tone, "I'm very sorry, but we didn't end up meeting. Niall asked to see me, and then he stood me up."

24

LOUISE

I want to tell you about the one other memory I have, one I'm not even sure is real. But I need to tell you because it scares me every time I think of it.

In my memory, or my dream, because I'm no longer clear on which it was, I remember crying. Lying on my side on what feels like cold ground with my hands in my hair. I'm sobbing and sobbing, and somebody is shushing me.

It's the thing that makes me panic more than anything else, remembering that gentle hushing noise. It sends blades of fear running through me, and I don't understand why.

25

Jonah found it hard not to laugh as O'Malley summed up his conversation with Dina Weyman. It was partly a laugh borne out of victory, and partly a reflection of the absurdity of it all.

"Did it sound like she was expecting us to ask about Niall Reakes?" Jonah asked, once O'Malley was done with his brief summary.

"No," O'Malley said, "but then I got the impression she'd be good on the stage. Very much in control of how she comes across, you know?"

"So there might have been some kind of an agreement," Jonah said thoughtfully. "One she then went back on. OK. Well, we have a new prime suspect. Any news on Niall's solicitor?"

"Nothing yet."

"I'd like to have more to throw at him before going in there anyway," Jonah went on, thinking as he spoke. "The guy up the road talked about being subjected to boy racers gunning their engines late on Friday. Niall Reakes drives an F-Type. That's a good audible, racy-sounding engine."

"But we didn't find him on any of the ANPRs," O'Malley pointed out.

"Can we check farther afield?" Jonah asked. "He might have gone home by an unexpected route."

"I'm pretty sure I've got all the routes to Saints Close covered," O'Malley said doubtfully, "but I'll check. We've got to check up on those knives too," he added. "Which may take a while . . ."

"Let's get Ben on that as soon as he's back," Jonah suggested.

"Ah, he'll like that," O'Malley agreed with a grin. "A good bit of careful checking."

Jonah glanced at his watch. It was gone half past five. They needed to make some real progress before heading home for the day. They couldn't hold Niall Reakes overnight without arresting him, and Jonah wasn't going to arrest a second suspect without strong evidence.

He felt slightly frustrated, too, that he had no clear picture of how all this might hang together. Louise's attack might tie in with Alex being stabbed somewhere other than Saints Close. But if Niall Reakes had attacked them, how had they both ended up at the house?

He felt an urge to get out of the station. To do some active investigation. But there was nothing specific for him to follow up on.

The phone on O'Malley's desk rang and Jonah was still trying to work out his own next move while O'Malley answered it. He saw his sergeant wince slightly at what was obviously a tirade. Though as Jonah watched, his expression changed from long-suffering to alert.

"I'm very sorry to hear that, Mr. Derbyshire," he said after a few moments. "We'll get someone out to take a look."

He hung up and said to Jonah, "That was one of the residents of Saints Close. He wants to know when someone's going to come and clear up all the blood."

"The blood?" Jonah said blankly.

"Apparently, now the snow's melted, you can see pools of it all the way down the road."

. . .

"I'M SO SORRY."

It must have been the tenth time Hanson had said it. Each time she intended for it to be the end of the tears. But they kept on oozing out, as Ben gently persuaded her to swap seats so he could drive and then pulled the car in at the drive-up Starbucks so he could pick up tea. He let her sit in the passenger seat to try to compose herself while he went to buy it, but nothing had changed by the time he got back. And it was still the same after several scalding mouthfuls of Earl Grey.

"There's nothing to be sorry about," he told her again. And then he said, "You don't have to tell me anything, but it might genuinely help."

She would have kept on resisting if everything hadn't felt so terrible.

She handed Lightman the phone and let him read for himself all the horrendous things Jason now thought about her.

> I bumped into your ex, a man I didn't even know about. A man you were still seeing up until last week . . .

She tried to swallow the tears along with another mouthful of tea while he read. It took Lightman a good thirty seconds to finish reading. She wondered if Ben would take it all at face value, too, and it made her feel desolate.

Damian had even woven Ben into his lies, a fact that added its own extra turn of total humiliation.

> He told me that you'd been making moves on another colleague, too, and bragging about it to your female friends because he was good eye candy. I assume he meant Ben Lightman, and I only hope he realizes what he's letting himself in for.

And the real clincher, of course, was the way Damian's lies had used truths and then twisted them to make them work against her. That had always been the way it worked with him. Genuine, incontrovertible facts that he grossly, hideously misrepresented.

Jason had been putty in his hands.

I might have questioned it if it hadn't explained so much. The fact that you claim to be busy so often in the evenings, and to like your own space. The fact that you've never introduced me to any friends, or suggested a visit to your hometown. It must be exhausting keeping all the lies going, Juliette, and I feel sorry for you.

The sad fact was that Juliette *had* no real friends in Southampton. And Damian was the prime reason she now avoided going home to Birmingham. But her ex knew exactly how to retell it all.

And if Jason believed it, what was to stop Ben believing the rest of it too?

But once he'd finished reading, Lightman lowered the phone and said, "Jesus. That's . . . what a total manipulative bastard."

She felt such a rush of gratitude that it made the tears worse, not better. But she managed to smile at him, shakily, and say, "Oh, he's a real keeper."

"Which one?" Lightman asked, with a raised eyebrow, and Hanson actually laughed slightly.

"I can definitely pick 'em, can't I?"

Ben took a gulp of tea, the phone held loosely in his other hand, and then said, "I take it this isn't the first time Damian's tried to wreck your life."

Hanson shook her head, feeling the truth rush to make its way out. "He's been messaging me. Constantly. All from anonymous accounts." She swallowed, feeling strangely all right about saying it now that she'd begun. "And turning up at my house. Sometimes watching me from his car. Never quite often enough to constitute harassment, and not always—not always close enough for me to be certain it's him before he leaves." She gave another humorless smile. "He's a clever bastard like that."

Lightman nodded again, slowly. "Have you written it all down?"

Hanson started to nod, and then shrugged. "I started doing. More recently I've been—I've been a bit lax. It's been getting to me." She took a large, steadying breath. "I wrote down some of the worst times, though. Like when I got outside and found all my tires slashed. And the—the mutilated Barbie doll he left on the doorstep. And the smashed security light last night."

Lightman shook his head. "The man has problems. You reported all of those?"

Hanson nodded. "Not the security light. Not yet. But the other two. I couldn't prove it was him, though. I did put up two big, noticeable, completely fake CCTV cameras off Amazon, but he still took out the light. Looks like he stood at the end of the drive and threw rocks at it until it went."

"I'd say the odds are definitely in favor of it being him," Lightman said dryly. "You don't generally go around pissing people off that much."

"Hey," she protested. "I work pretty hard at being annoying."

"Granted." He hesitated for a moment. "I should probably say that this isn't the first defamatory bullshit I've read from your ex."

Hanson's shaky sense of certainty took another dip. "What do you mean?"

"A month after you joined, I got an email," he said. "An anonymous one. It tried to claim that you'd been dismissed from your last role for gross malpractice, but that Birmingham had hushed it up."

"Oh my God."

"I thought I should take it to the chief, and it turned out he'd had an email too."

Hanson turned away from him, a reflexive instinct based on defense. She hadn't thought she could feel any more humiliated by her ex-boyfriend. But of course, Damian could always sink lower. Could twist the knife in that little bit further. She'd never met anyone with such a gift for hurting people.

"I would have told you," Ben said with a note of apology, "but the chief was convinced it would just stress you out, even if you knew he didn't believe a bloody word of it. And I thought he was probably right."

"You're sure he didn't believe it?" she asked. The thought of it made her cringe. This must have been, what, a week or two after she'd had a showdown with the DCI over his own behavior in an investigation? What must he have thought of her?

"Come on," Lightman said with a grin. "He's too smart for that. What he actually did was have a quiet word with our IT department, asking them to filter out any similar content and report it to him. He was hoping to catch the perpetrator out. And by the way, his immediate guess was a disgruntled ex, which was what I thought too."

There was a short pause, and then Ben said, "I guess the question is what we do about all this."

The word "we" made Hanson feel indescribably better.

"You aren't starting to wonder if Damian's actually telling the truth?" she asked, trying to keep her voice light. "Whether I am actually a deeply manipulative, deceptive psychopath who's been stringing everyone along?"

Lightman out and out laughed at this. "Don't give yourself airs, Constable."

"Yes, Sarge." Hanson found herself grinning, a genuine grin that almost broke into real laughter.

"So we're going to sort this." Ben gave a nod.

"Do you think so?" she asked, a little less cheerfully. "I mean, I've seen how this stuff goes. Women being stalked and harassed. The full weight of the law means nothing in so many cases."

"Agreed," Lightman said. "But there might be better ways than the law itself to stop him."

"Maybe you're right," she answered thoughtfully. She'd thought that herself, early on, before it had all seemed to pile up on top of her.

"I can explain things to Jason," Lightman said after a moment. "If it comes from me, he's not going to end up dismissing it."

Hanson felt her face growing hot. "You don't need to do that."

"I honestly think it would help."

"It's OK," she said. And then she swallowed. "The speed with which he chose to believe it is . . . well, I think it tells me something. I mean, he's the one with the bloody degree in criminal psychology. He's the one who's supposed to know what to look out for."

"I assume your ex-boyfriend played on his feelings," Ben said quietly. "I wouldn't blame him too much."

"And yet here you are," Hanson countered, "not in a relationship with me, and refusing to believe a word of it."

"Well," Lightman said, "as you'll know, I don't have any feelings to play on, so . . ."

Hanson gave a real throaty laugh at that. "Fair point."

"And can you turn to your right?"

The female officer was softly spoken. She sounded like she came from Swansea, and she seemed sympathetic. Kind, even.

Louise turned as directed, feeling strangely like she was back at her engagement photo shoot with Niall. Though they'd been in the grounds of a National Trust property that day. Not in a small bare room in a police station. She'd been wearing a brand-new wool sweater and jeans too. Not just her bra and leggings.

And it had only been her constantly smiling mouth that had ached on that day. Not her back. Her head. And somewhere difficult to pinpoint in her chest.

The soft flash of the camera came three times, and the officer asked her to extend her left arm out to the side. Louise twisted, trying to see the arm herself. There must be bruising that she hadn't discovered yet.

"If you could just look forwards . . ."

Louise straightened her head, having caught sight of nothing more than a purplish-yellow tinge on the back of her arm. The camera flashed again.

And then suddenly Louise was not in that room, but face-down on icy grass, the taste of mud and leaves in her mouth. She was fighting to move. To breathe. There was pain in her back, and in her left arm, where his hand was pushing her down.

That's a knife, sweetheart, he was saying. *You feel it? I'm going to squeeze down on it every time you move. So you'd better keep fucking still, hadn't you?*

And then she was crouching on the floor of a brightly lit room, her breathing rapid and shallow, begging them to let her have some air.

With Hanson and Lightman back in CID, Jonah called a briefing in the big meeting room before doing anything else. The one advantage of being in on a Sunday night was that they had their choice of rooms, which meant they were back in the much-coveted conference room, complete with big windows and comfortable chairs.

He gave them all a moment to settle, his gaze resting briefly on Hanson. It looked as though she'd been crying, and very recently. She now had the hesitant, careful air of someone just holding it together. He needed to check in with her again. It was frustrating that it might have to wait, though. They had two people in custody, both potentially to be charged, and a limited time frame to do something about it.

He loaded the map up on to the projector again and began.

"Having established that Alex Plaskitt died in Louise Reakes's bed, it now looks fairly certain that he wasn't actually attacked there. There are significant splashes of blood down Saints Close, none of which were visible until the snow melted."

There was a brief silence. Then O'Malley said, "It might scupper our theory about Niall Reakes finding them in bed together and going mad."

"It might," Jonah agreed. "Though it still remains possible that he went out hunting for his wife, found something going on, and went on the attack."

"We have blood found at Asylum Green," Lightman said. "It could be Alex Plaskitt's. We also have an earring and a glove. If Louise identifies either as hers, we can pin down some kind of event happening there. Possibly an attack."

"If it was Louise's husband," O'Malley commented, "is it possible she's still covering for him? Out of a sense of guilt for having cheated?"

"Would he really have risked refusing to see her if so?" Hanson asked doubtfully. "Surely he'd want to keep her sweet."

"Unless refusing to see her is just an act," O'Malley countered with a shrug. "They're pretending to have argued when they were both in on it."

"We'll have a clearer idea once those bloods are back," Jonah said, aware that he was, as usual, slightly damping down the general enthusiasm. "We need to work out whether Niall really was in Southampton. I want to check public transport. Trains. Buses. Taxis."

"I'll get on it," Hanson offered.

"And then there's Niall's strange trip to Zurich," Jonah went on. He switched tabs to bring up a zoomed-out version of the route from Geneva to Zurich. "We've got the receipt for the new flight he booked, and it cost him a small fortune. Zurich is also a three-hour drive from Geneva. O'Malley's looking to see if he went there to purchase the murder weapon."

"And I've confirmed there were spaces on flights from Geneva," O'Malley commented. "For less money, generally. He could have flown straight home."

Hanson glanced up. "But if he went to buy the knife, then the attack was premeditated. That doesn't tie in with him finding her with another man."

"It could, if he was already convinced his wife was cheating," O'Malley countered. "He may not have known Alex Plaskitt, but he might have had reason to think there was infidelity going on. He could have been planning this for months."

Lightman shifted slightly, and Jonah asked, "Thoughts, Ben?"

Lightman breathed out for a moment. "It's . . . strange behavior. If it really was all planned, then it seems unlikely that he would have left the ticket purchase until the last minute. He was running a big risk that he might not get one."

"Yes," Jonah said thoughtfully. "He was."

"Doesn't it read," Hanson asked slowly, "more like a sudden crisis? That ex-wife of his . . ."

"Dina Weyman," Jonah said.

"Are we positive she isn't lying?" She glanced at Lightman. "Maybe she did summon him for an urgent conversation."

"It's hard to say," Jonah told her. "Perhaps we need to see her in person. But Niall Reakes's story about a job offer is more than a little farfetched. As you say, his actions sound more like a crisis."

"So our hypothetical situation would be that Dina needed to see him in a hurry," Lightman said slowly, "for some reason requiring him to get to Zurich first. He was doing something for her, maybe. And then, once they'd met, Dina denied it."

There was a brief pause, and then Jonah said, "Talk to her. And to anyone who knows her." He glanced at O'Malley. "Didn't you say April Dumont knows the ex-wife too?"

"Yeah, she does," O'Malley said, and gave a grin. "And she doesn't seem much of a fan either."

"Talk to her, as soon as you can," Jonah said.

"I've arranged to see Step Conti again shortly," Lightman commented. "Should I keep that appointment or bunk it?"

Jonah hesitated. Their priority seemed clear: Dig into everything to do with Niall Reakes. But the possibility of Niall having planned his attack shifted things. It made him wonder whether they were missing a link between him and Alex Plaskitt.

"I think see him," he said in the end. "Show him photos of the Reakeses and see what he says. O'Malley, let's go and talk to Niall Reakes. Juliette, see if you can book us in to see Dina Weyman later this evening." He gave her an apologetic smile. "Happy crap weekend."

"Ah, I have nothing to do except watch shit TV," Hanson said with strange cheerfulness. "It's all good with me!"

HANSON WAS GLAD that their investigation seemed to be going somewhere, and not just for its own sake. It meant she could get her head down and work, and not think about Jason and how awkward it was going to be seeing him every day from now on. This, she thought, was why you should never date someone at work.

And also, she added to herself, *why you should get yourself an actual social life.*

She woke up her desktop, and her eyes drifted over to where Jason sat on a normal working day. She thought of Louise and her husband, who had been so quick to condemn her. And she thought how, in a way, Jason had done exactly the same.

She suddenly found herself coming to a decision. Pulling out her phone, she typed him a brief message.

> Thank you for that essay. I have nothing to say in reply except that I want your things gone from my house before I get home later.

And with that done, she was ready to work.

. . .

JONAH HID HIMSELF away to prep for the interview with Niall Reakes. He knew he needed to be on form. Niall had ended up being represented by Daniella Hart, who was with the same firm as Patrick Moorcroft. Like him, she was expensive, and Jonah's one encounter with her had been exhausting.

He'd dropped in on the solicitor and her client to give them warning and found the atmosphere a little tense. It was clear that having someone who wasn't Patrick was galling for Niall. It was equally clear that Daniella Hart didn't like being second choice. He couldn't help smiling as he left them again.

Midway through getting his notes together, Jonah's landline rang. McCullough, with the blood results.

"Her blood tests are negative for Rohypnol," McCullough said, her voice slightly raised to speak over music she had on in the background. "There was still alcohol present, indicating that she'd drunk more than twenty-four units that night. Enough to explain serious memory loss. But perhaps more interestingly, she's showing traces of Viagra."

"That's . . . slightly odd . . ."

"They do say it's the modern man's drug of choice," Linda commented dryly. "There are lots of rumors online that it can be used to make women aroused. If true, that would be a score for any potential rapist. It's pretty easy to defend rape if the victim was clearly horny as hell in the earlier part of the evening."

"And is it true?" Jonah asked with interest.

McCullough gave a derisive laugh. "I'd say it's pretty unlikely to do anything at all. Viagra works by increasing blood supply to the groin. Men who take it don't need it because they can't get horny. It's because they can't get an erection."

"Right," Jonah said, not sure quite why he'd thought this conversation a good idea. "So it's more than a little odd that Louise Reakes had it in her system."

He thought of Niall and decided that this was a strong sign

against his involvement. Unless he'd somehow spiked something that he knew Louise would drink. Viagra tablets could presumably be crushed and added to most things. But that would be a bizarre move. Could he really have got himself into such a twisted state that he'd *wanted* his wife to cheat so he could take revenge?

"I've also taken prints from the articles we found at the park," McCullough said. "Obviously no analysis will be run until tomorrow, but if you need to show them to your suspects, they're now yours."

"I'll get one of the team to pick them up, thank you."

Jonah ended the call feeling as though nothing quite added up. The only theories he currently had to explain everything seemed more than outlandish.

Which meant they had to go for hard facts, however small, he thought. There were things they could pin down.

He ducked back out into CID and told O'Malley he'd be ready in a minute, then asked Hanson if she'd had any response from Dina Weyman.

"She's going to call back," Hanson replied. "She's supposed to be at some important meeting but will see what she can do."

"OK, great. I'd like you to show Louise the items you picked up at the park. They're ready to collect from Linda."

Hanson nodded and rose, her expression still distant, but not bleak or on edge, he thought. Whatever was going on, she seemed to be holding it together.

"Is everyone hanging in there OK?" he asked O'Malley once she'd left, trying to say it lightly.

"Ah, sure, I think so," O'Malley said with a shrug. "I mean, sure, it's Sunday night and we'd all rather be at home, and I think Juliette got hypothermia at the park, but, you know."

Jonah nodded and glanced over at Lightman, who was on the phone.

"Is Ben on the line to Step Conti?"

"Yup," O'Malley agreed. "Just started the call. Do you need something from him?"

"Nothing that can't wait until we've seen Niall Reakes," he said. "Let's go."

"SORRY ABOUT THIS," Lightman told Step, once his wife had fetched him to the phone. "I know Sunday evenings aren't the best time."

"Are you kidding?" Step said. "You got me out of the world's longest *Peppa Pig* marathon." He added, more seriously, "And I'm happy to do anything I can to help. Alex was the closest thing I ever had to a best friend."

Lightman thanked him. "There are a few things we need to ask you. The first is whether you saw Alex with a woman on Friday."

There was a long pause, and then Step said, "I'm sorry. I should have said before. Karen—my wife—was angry with me for not telling you about it. I just . . . Yes, I did see Alex with someone." There was an audible swallowing noise down the line. "There was a woman who was—well, she was hitting on him quite hard. And—he ended up kissing her."

"Why didn't you mention this before?"

"Because it happened much earlier on," Step said. "A long time before I left. And he clearly immediately regretted it. He backed off, and she was angry about it. I actually had to get involved, to try and calm things down."

There was a note of defensiveness in his voice, one that was possibly understandable in the circumstances.

"She felt rejected?" Lightman asked.

"Yes."

"How did she react after you talked to her?"

"She calmed down after a few minutes," Step said. "I think she was just drunk, you know? Anyway, she left him alone after that.

I saw her talking to another couple of guys before I left, and she looked like she was having fun."

"I'm going to share a photo with you," Lightman said. "If that's OK. A woman we know to have been at the club. Do you have your mobile on you?"

"Yes, I can look now," Step offered.

He waited in silence as Lightman forwarded both the arrest photograph of Louise Reakes and another image of her captured from the CCTV. He heard a faint chime in the background as they arrived on Step's phone.

"Can you let me know if that's the woman Alex kissed?"

There was a brief silence, and then Step said, "No, it wasn't her. Sorry."

Lightman found himself momentarily at a loss. Given everything that happened later that night, how could it possibly have been anyone other than Louise Reakes?

"That's fine," he said, as smoothly as he could. "Could you describe the woman you saw him with, perhaps?"

"Sure," he said. "She was pretty noticeable. Blond. Really tall in her heels. She had tattoos. One across her chest and another one on the small of her back." He looked away for a moment. "Oh, and she was American. Southern. Really, really hard to understand."

"Thank you," Lightman said. "I think we know who that is."

NIALL REAKES SEEMED a lot less panicked than he had during their last interview. It seemed to Jonah that he was expecting Dina to have backed him up. That this would all be cleared up shortly. He even smiled when Jonah apologized for the delay.

Daniella Hart, next to him, was all cool self-possession. She watched him with a faint hint of a smile, and Jonah returned it. He remembered this from the last time he'd met her. This slightly mocking air. He felt tempted to tell her he was immune to it now.

He'd spent the last four months dating someone who mocked him incessantly.

Jonah decided to keep things friendly during the preamble, allowing Niall to remain confident that everything was running smoothly. And then, once the interview had officially started, he said very calmly, "So, we've now spoken to your ex-wife about the meeting at Gatwick on Friday night. Dina denies having met you at any time in the last few months."

There was a momentary pause, and then Niall gave a short, almost explosive laugh. "Sorry?"

"Dina Weyman has denied that you were with her on Friday night," Jonah repeated. "She said you asked to meet, and then stood her up."

"We'd like to know where you really were," O'Malley said.

Niall shot a glance of desperation toward his solicitor, who leaned to murmur rapidly in his ear. But Niall shook his head, violently.

"I did meet her! What the hell is she . . . ? Look." Niall leaned forward and clenched his fist on the tabletop. "I don't know what she's trying to do, but I bloody met her."

"Why would she tell us you didn't?" O'Malley asked conversationally. "It seems like a strange thing to do."

Niall looked between them, his jaw visibly tightening. "You can't . . . This is what she does." He shook his head, and Jonah could see a shake running through him now. "She plays games. I don't even know why she's saying it, but . . ." He trailed off, and Jonah watched, in satisfaction, as some thought occurred to Niall.

"I think you know exactly why she'd do that," Jonah said.

"Asking my client to speculate on the motivations of his ex-wife seems counterproductive when you are able to ask her these questions yourself," Daniella Hart said.

"It's never counterproductive to respond to someone's expression," Jonah replied, smiling. "That's just good police work."

Niall started to shake his head and then laid his hands flat on the table, as if trying to control the situation and himself.

"What about your little jaunt over to Zurich?" O'Malley asked. "Why didn't you fly home from Geneva? There were flights available, and they were a lot cheaper. You could have been home for dinner."

Jonah watched Niall carefully, and was fairly sure that he lost a little color just then.

"Were you on your way to buy something?" Jonah asked.

"I'm not . . . going to say any more," Niall said with difficulty. "Just talk to Dina again. Please. And tell her . . ." Niall paused, almost as though the act of speaking had become difficult. "Tell her you know we've been meeting up for months. Maybe it'll help jog her memory."

"WE HAVE TWO items we'd like you to look at," Hanson said, glad of the presence of the female PCSO. Louise Reakes looked a fraction closer to falling apart every time she met her. Her nervous movements and darting gaze were unsettling.

Hanson handed the first evidence bag over to Louise. It contained the woman's glove they'd found on Asylum Green. There was condensation on the inside of the bag, presumably because the glove was still damp. But the shape was relatively easy to make out even so.

Louise took it, and examined it for a moment, before shaking her head. "It's not mine, and I don't recognize it."

"OK," Hanson said, and then passed the earring over. This time, Louise's reaction was immediate. She nodded and ran her thumb over the length of the earring through the plastic.

"It's mine," she said. "I was wearing them on Friday. Where did you find it?"

"On the route we think you took home," Hanson replied.

Louise nodded, and put a hand up toward her left ear, her gaze distant. Something changed in her expression. And then she said in a dull voice, "It got caught on his sleeve. When he pinned me down."

JONAH LEFT THE interview room with the conviction that there was a lot more going on between Niall Reakes and Dina Weyman than he yet understood.

"Can you run a check for Dina's license plate too?" he asked O'Malley. "If Niall Reakes didn't drive himself to Southampton, maybe she gave him a lift."

He took himself back to his office, wondering how this was connected to Alex Plaskitt's death, if at all, and why Niall had looked so sick when they'd mentioned his journey to Zurich. And, on top of that, why he was so set on them talking to Dina again.

Lightman tapped on his door, and Jonah nodded him in.

"Ben. How's it going?" he asked.

"Interestingly," Lightman told him. "Alex Plaskitt did, in fact, have a romantic liaison in the club, but not with Louise Reakes. It was with April Dumont."

Jonah gave a slight, shocked laugh. "You're kidding."

"Conti's description didn't leave much doubt," Lightman said.

"OK," Jonah said, growing more serious. "I want her here, as soon as possible."

"She's unfortunately now in Leeds until late tonight so I told her nine o'clock tomorrow. Sorry, Chief."

"Nine tomorrow will have to do. Did Step have anything to say about Niall Reakes?"

"No, nothing," Lightman said. "He didn't recognize photographs of either Niall or Louise when I sent them over either."

"That's useful. Thanks, Ben."

Ben let himself out again, and Jonah's thoughts bounced between Louise Reakes, her husband, and the sudden introduction of April to the proceedings. He mentally balanced up the time they still had in which to charge Louise Reakes, and his determination not to arrest her husband until they absolutely had to. If they were going to mount an entire new case, against him, Jonah didn't want to be rushing to make another custody deadline.

He approached O'Malley again, where he was still working at his desk, his eyes bloodshot.

"You've definitely drawn a blank on Niall Reakes's car?"

O'Malley nodded. "He's not on any cameras until Saturday morning. Dina Weyman likewise."

"Louise has identified the earring as hers," Hanson chipped in. "And she's added to her statement. She says she remembers a man holding her facedown on the ground and pressing what he said was a knife into her back. She remembers the pain of her earring catching on his sleeve as he adjusted his grip, and it coming free."

"Anything direct about an assault?"

Hanson nodded, her face a little grim. "He pulled her dress up and dragged her underwear down. That's all she has, but assuming her account is true, it sounds highly likely that she was raped. She's accepted an examination this time."

Jonah tried to fit in this idea of rape. Could Niall have raped her after finding her with Alex Plaskitt? Had he stabbed Alex and raped his wife? What, then, had happened to Alex while the rape was happening? And was it really nothing more than coincidence that Alex had kissed Louise's best friend only an hour or so before?

"Have we managed to raise Dina Weyman yet?"

O'Malley shook his head. "Sorry. I've tried both numbers. Want me to send a uniform round there?"

Jonah looked at his watch and let out a long sigh. "It's seven forty-five. That might have to be one for the morning. We can't keep Niall much longer without arresting him." He nodded to himself. "OK. I want to get Louise Reakes released on bail as soon as the examination is done. I'll tell her husband he's free to go, too, and ask him back in here tomorrow. The house has been thoroughly searched, so there's no evidence there to destroy or dispose of. I suspect we may have more to gain by letting some kind of confrontation happen between them. And we're going to be there to see it."

O'Malley grimaced. "And there was I thinking you might be about to send us home."

"I don't mind being on stakeout," Hanson said. "In case that helps."

Jonah nodded. "I'll see whether Ben can back you up later. If you can manage until one between you, that'll probably cover it. We'll get some uniforms to do the night shift. Domnall, perhaps you can take over in the morning. In place by eight?"

"Thanks, Chief," O'Malley said. "Very kind of you."

"Boss of the year, me," Jonah agreed.

HANSON HAD ANOTHER message from Jason as she was getting herself ready to leave and felt impatient with it. There was paperwork involved in getting Louise Reakes out of the station, and Hanson needed to be in the car park by the time she and her husband left, ready to ease out into the traffic after them. Assuming, of course, that Niall drove his wife home.

She thought about ignoring whatever Jason had sent. She didn't want to read anything more from him. Right now, she didn't want to lay eyes on him again.

But she wasn't going to get her wish. She had to sit in the same room with him tomorrow, and on all the upcoming tomorrows. And so, once she had her coat and scarf on and her bag looped over her head, she opened up the message.

> So you don't want to tell me your side? To actually discuss this like adults?

It was a good thing Jason wasn't here in person. The anger she felt toward him then was a fierce, blistering thing. She felt her thumbs punching at her phone screen as she messaged back.

I don't have anything to discuss with someone who's willing to take a conversation with some guy he's met at the pub as absolute truth when it is so very much at odds with the person you claim to know I am. There has clearly been no point to the time we've spent together. If there had been, you wouldn't have been so ready to believe the incredible manipulations of a man I have been trying to block from my life for a very long time.

Her eyes were teary again, but the tears were angry ones. She was so very, very done with feeling betrayed.

LOUISE STOOD SILENTLY as they handed back her personal effects. They weren't returning her earring. She supposed that was still some kind of evidence. But her handbag, keys, and phone were there. She signed for them and slid everything into its slot in the bag, taking comfort in organizing it. It was good to think of that, and not the probing examination that had happened a while before.

Niall was a wordless, looming presence over her shoulder. He seemed unable to bring himself to say anything to her. Which suited her just fine. She couldn't bear to talk to him. The thought of being trapped in his stupid flashy car was horrible and she was considering telling him to leave. That she would prefer to pay for a cab.

But then she realized how it would look to the police. She was being judged on everything. She knew that. From the clothes she wore to the way she spoke; the way she treated her husband to the way he treated her in return. And so she walked out alongside him without speaking, and climbed awkwardly into the low passenger seat of the Jaguar, her body feeling stiff and underused.

She needed some exercise, she thought as she closed the door. A run. A swim. And then she needed to play something. God, she needed that. To let her hands move over her harp strings and blot out the last nightmarish forty-eight hours.

They were halfway home when Niall broke the silence, and he did so hesitantly.

"We need to talk about—things," he said.

"Do we?"

She saw the way he grimaced before he said, "Yes. We do. I think we both owe each other some kind of an explanation."

"I tried to give you one yesterday," she said coldly. "But you wouldn't see me."

"I know," he said. "I wasn't quite . . . You need to understand what a shock it was."

She found herself looking at him in dumb shock. "You want me to understand how shocking it all is for you? To find out that your wife had woken up next to a dead man? You want me to sympathize with that?"

"How do I even know that's true?" Niall countered loudly. "I have no idea what happened."

"And neither do I," Louise told him, wondering why she didn't feel more as she said it. "And we should both have faced it, together. We should have been a team. But we haven't been a team for a long time, Niall. And I'm so sad that I've wasted so much worry over us when we were dead in the water months ago."

He stopped trying to talk after that, and Louise turned sideways to lean against the door. There were so many things she should have been asking him, really. Whether he was in love with Dina. Whether they'd agreed to get back together. And what the police had asked him about too. But she felt too tired for all of it.

TAILING A VEHICLE was both easier and more challenging than people thought. It was easier because most people were so poor at checking the rearview mirror. You could be behind someone for miles without them even noticing, and even when they did notice, they didn't necessarily think anything of it. Cars generally followed major routes, and if you peeled off at some point before their destination, you were usually forgotten pretty quickly. Assuming, of course, that they weren't looking out for you.

The difficult bit was keeping them in sight. At each junction there was a chance of missing them, and the one thing that would bring attention to you was to hustle through a set of lights on their tail when they were already changing.

Luckily, there were only a few cars around, so it was easy enough for Hanson to keep behind Niall's Jaguar. To him and Louise, she was probably nothing more than an anonymous set of headlights.

It was going well enough that she was able to spare some thought for the traffic around her. She noticed that the car behind had one badly adjusted headlight. It was much brighter than the other and occasionally struck dazzling reflections off her wing mirror. It was irritating, and she waited impatiently for it to turn off onto another route.

But it stayed where it was, resolutely following her every move. And after a few miles, it occurred to her that she might not be the only person following.

And she thought again of Damian, who had taken unreasonable steps to wreck her life, and who loved nothing more than to frighten her. And she wondered whether she actually ought to be growing frightened.

26

LOUISE

All of this has brought us, inevitably, to tonight. To our silent, unhappy return from the police station. To a home that feels like it's made of nothing but paper. As if it's about to float away.

I keep imagining I can hear you moving around upstairs, even though the door shut behind you hours ago. The fact that you've gone makes me rage and hurt even while I wanted you out of my life. I'm a mess of conflict, and I wonder if you are, too, or whether that silence of yours was the mark of someone who's already moved on.

I spent almost an hour cleaning rooms that were already clean, and then I suddenly just ran dry. Poised with a cloth in my hand, I felt the urge to move drain away, and I felt really, truly bereft.

It was you I was thinking about. You and Dina. I found myself finally wanting to know everything. Every detail of what's been going on between the two of you.

And so, for the first time, I loaded up the desktop computer in your study, grateful that it had been inconvenient to take to a hotel with you. I'd always been afraid of looking at it, despite how many times it had occurred to me.

There turned out to be a mine of information on there, thanks to it syncing with your phone. Hidden amid innocuous photos of us and of your work events and of scenery you'd enjoyed, there were photos of Dina. Images she'd clearly taken of herself and then sent you. They spanned years, these images. Terrible, painful little points scattered through stills of our everyday lives.

There was only one of the two of you together. It had clearly been taken by Dina, evident from the edge of her bronze forearm in the frame. She'd lifted the phone over her head and snapped the two of you next to each other, your head close to hers and a slightly dazed expression on your face. The two of you were illuminated by the camera flash, in sharp contrast with the dim lighting of what looked like a nightclub scene behind you.

I looked at the date and location on it and felt a slight tremor of unease. It had been taken last summer, in Southampton. And I remembered being in a club like this. With April. And how I'd gone to find her with a couple of drinks and been absolutely positive that you were standing next to her when I caught sight of her.

I was so sure it was you. You, who were supposed to be in Birmingham but were for some reason in the same club we were, talking to April.

You were out of sight by the time I made it over, and when I handed April her drink and said, "Was that Niall?" she gave me a strange look.

"Niall? No." She glanced around, considering. "I guess he looked slightly like him. Which makes me feel weird for flirting with him." She laughed and took a long sip of her drink. "But definitely not your husband. Jesus, can you imagine what he'd say if he saw us here?"

I remember my certainty that I'd recognized you evaporating, chased away by relief that you hadn't caught me out drinking. And I suppose, after that, the drink did a good job of making me doubt it had ever happened.

But it did happen, Niall. I've saved the photo that proved it. You were there, with Dina. And April . . . lied about it.

It left me feeling like you've poisoned everything, that realization. I couldn't even trust my best friend, could I? She hid your affair from me, when I thought she'd always been honest. Particularly about Dina and all of her bullshit. Particularly about that.

I felt lost and furious. And desperate to call you up and yell at you. There was so much I wanted to say, but my pride wouldn't let me even think of it. I'd told you to get out, and I was going to stand by that if it killed me.

But then the idea of writing to you came to me, and it seemed like the answer. I could pour all of it out on paper, and then decide whether to send it to you or burn it. So for an hour, that's what I did. Right up until now.

I expected it to be cathartic, but I feel as angry and as empty at the end of it as I did at the start. Perhaps because you haven't read it, and may never do so. Perhaps because what I really want is answers.

You've explained nothing. And although part of that might be my fault, because in my seething sense of betrayal I shut you down, you should have tried. You should have bloody tried. After five years, I think I deserve it, Niall.

27

Hanson was now certain that the car was following her. The little three-car procession had turned down too many side roads for there to be any doubt about it. They were all weaving whatever complex route Niall Reakes had decided was the quickest. Hanson had been keeping well back on the almost deserted streets.

The car behind, however, had done no such thing. It had stayed close on her tail, as if willing her to notice it, and that had started to make Hanson angry.

Half a mile from Saints Close, she signaled left and pulled suddenly into a single parking space, forcing them to go past. She was confident that she could keep track of the Reakeses from here, even with a car in between.

She turned her head to watch the vehicle, expecting to see the sleek black form of the BMW. But the silhouette was all wrong. This was a smaller, older car. A Vauxhall Corsa, she thought. Or something like it. And it didn't slow down as it passed either. It accelerated.

Hanson let out a long breath, and moved back out onto the road. Sometimes coincidences happened, she thought. It looked as though this had been one of them. A car that just happened to be making its way along the same route.

She could just see the lights of the two cars up ahead as they turned in to Saints Close. And that made her feel slightly doubtful again. Was it really likely that both drivers happened to live on one tiny street?

She slowed down as she pulled onto Saints Close. She could see the bright-red illumination thrown by Niall Reakes's Jaguar, which he'd pulled up half on the pavement outside Number 11. Farther up the road, there were headlights in the act of maneuvering. The Corsa must have driven past.

Hanson pulled in a little way from the house, close enough to give her a good view, and switched off her headlights. She watched as the Corsa completed its turn and pulled up against the curb. Its lights died at the same time the Jaguar's did.

Niall and Louise emerged from their car, and Hanson tried to pay attention to their manner with each other while half her attention was still on the Corsa. Nobody got out of that second car, and the lights remained off while the couple moved silently to the door.

From what she could see, things were not rosy between Louise and Niall Reakes. By the time she lost sight of them past the trees, they had neither looked at nor spoken to each other.

And then, finally, it occurred to her that she'd got that car wrong: that it had been following them, and not her, from the moment they'd left the station.

Jojo messaged at eight twenty-five to ask whether Jonah would like takeaway at his house, and his response was the largest thumbs-up he could get his phone to send. His team had stakeout duty covered, with a couple of Heerden's uniforms covering the graveyard shift.

That left Jonah free to see his girlfriend, which inevitably made him feel guilty, but was sometimes how things went. He messaged to say he'd be there in twenty minutes, and then sent Hanson a quick text to tell her he was heading home but would have his mobile on at all times.

O'Malley had already left, and Lightman was filling a thermos to take with him. Jonah was waving to him when Hanson messaged back to say that there was another car there, and that the driver appeared to be watching the house. She asked if he wanted her to go and talk to them.

Jonah sighed and messaged back quickly to tell her to stay where she was.

"Do we know anyone involved with Alex Plaskitt or the Reakeses who drives a Corsa?" Jonah asked Lightman, as he returned from the kitchen.

"O'Malley might know," Ben said, picking up his coat. "Or I can look it up. Why?"

"Juliette's got another car parked up on Saints Close watching the house."

"Tell her I'll be there in fifteen," he said, transferring his keys to his coat pocket. "We can go and see who it is once I'm there."

"It should really be me," Jonah argued.

"Well, you're currently the only one of us with a girlfriend waiting, so I think you should leave it be. You can pay me back once I've sorted out my love life."

"Thanks, Ben," Jonah said with relief. He doubted Jojo would give him a hard time if he canceled on her, but letting her down again would have made him feel crap. "Keep me posted."

"Will do."

HANSON WAS FIXATED on the other car. The Corsa was perhaps twenty feet from her, its lights out, but without doubt still occupied. She could just make out a dark shape behind the wheel, an ominously still, unsettling unknown.

Ben had messaged her to say that he was on his way, too, and asked as an afterthought whether her psycho ex drove a Corsa. She'd grinned at that.

He wouldn't be seen dead in anything less than a Merc.

Ben's reply had been a thumbs-up, and then a comment about her amazing taste in men. And although she didn't feel she needed him here to watch out for her, she was glad that he was on his way.

The first sign of any movement from the Reakes house was the sudden bright-red illumination of the Jaguar's taillights. It was followed by the throaty growl of the engine, and the car began to maneuver. Niall must have left the house while she'd been focused on the other car. Was he alone?

Hanson picked up her phone and called Ben.

"We've got movement," she told him. "The Jaguar again."

"I'm just about to turn in to the close," Ben answered, his voice a little distant over his car's Bluetooth.

"You might want to hold off and tail him," Hanson said.

"Are you definitely OK there with the mystery driver?" he asked.

"I've got my baton and my stab vest," she said, only half-joking. "I should be fine."

The Jaguar had finished its turn out onto the road, and as it came level with Hanson she was granted a clear view of the driver. It was Niall Reakes, and he was alone.

"Looks like you've just got Niall," she told Ben. "Which means Louise is still in the house, with our mystery driver still at large. I'd definitely better stay put."

"OK," Ben said. "I'll let you know where he goes. Keep me posted on events there."

LOUISE HAD THOUGHT that she needed music. At every other low point in her life she had played. When her mother had died. When her father had suddenly flipped from neurotic overprotection and moved to the other side of the world, as if determined never to see his daughter again. Louise had got through it all with music.

As the door had finally closed behind Niall, she'd made her

way to the music room and gone to her chair. She'd drawn her harp toward her and leaned its reassuring weight onto her shoulder. Her hands had found their positions for the start of the Donizetti.

And then she'd thought once again of the first time she'd played for Niall, and she faltered. She found herself replaying conversations with him. And seamlessly, those thoughts turned into words she might have exchanged with Alex Plaskitt. Whole conversations she might have had with him at the bar of Blue Underground.

Minutes later, she was still sitting where she had been, a heavy feeling in her chest and her hands equally heavy on her lap. The only music she could hear in her head was the pounding beat of a dance track, drumming its way into her memory two days later.

She felt hopeless as she returned the harp to its place and left the room. How could she deal with this if she couldn't play?

She found herself in the kitchen, switching on the kettle. There were a few crumbs on the top of the stove, and she went to find a cloth. And then she saw that some of them had ended up around the kettle itself and behind the bread bin. Niall had always had an expressive way of cutting bread, one that littered the kitchen with detritus.

She started to move things onto the table so the surfaces were clear enough to wipe properly, and, once she started, it became difficult to stop. She took out sprays and gloves and cloths, and began to clean away every trace of dirt. She moved from the surfaces to the floor to the fridge. The oven. The utility room.

Her thoughts narrowed themselves down to finding the next imperfection and removing it. And, in spite of half hating herself for it, she began to feel comforted at last.

HANSON WAS NOW very much on edge. With the Jaguar gone, she felt as though something else had to happen. She'd expected the other driver to either follow or move again. But the car remained motionless. A full hour passed, and then most of another.

The lack of action was excruciating, not just because her car was now freezing cold. She was at the point of going to see who was in the bloody Corsa when there was movement at last. The driver's door opened, flooding the interior with blue-white light, and a figure stepped out. One who was huddled in a scarf, hat, and high-necked coat, and was frustratingly hard to make out. She couldn't even guess their gender.

Hanson picked up her phone and started to take photographs, willing them to turn toward her. The figure made its way over to Number 11, and Hanson climbed out of her car as quietly as she could to follow. Her breath fogged in the freezing air as she trod carefully along the pavement. She paused at the end of the drive, in sight of the Reakeses' front door.

The figure was now on the doorstep, and she could hear the bell chiming from where she was. She could also see Louise Reakes's face clearly as she opened the door.

"You know who I am," Hanson heard.

28

You know who I am.

Five words that fed into all the mass of uncertainty and fear Louise had been feeling, and sent her heart rate into overdrive. She didn't want to know what he had to say, this crumpled man on her doorstep. She didn't want to know anything more about the awful things she'd done.

"I'm so sorry," she said. "I don't. I need to go to bed. Please . . ."

And she started trying to close the door, but he was pushing against it.

"I spoke to you," he said. "I spoke to you. Don't you remember?"

"No," she said. "I don't."

But that didn't mean it hadn't happened.

"I need to talk to you," the man said, and then suddenly he was crying in an awful, ugly way. She was revolted by him. Repulsed. And yet she also felt for him. She'd cried a lot over the last two days, and she didn't want him to feel as bad as she'd felt.

And then she realized who he must be, and she stopped trying to push the door closed. "You're Alex's—Alex's husband."

He nodded, and Louise let out a long breath. As hard as it was going to be, she knew that she owed him a conversation. She opened the door and let him walk inside.

. . .

"He's still there," Hanson told the DCI. "I saw her making tea while he stood there, and now they're in the sitting room, where we spoke to her yesterday. Unfortunately, the curtains are shut, so there's not a lot I can see."

"Did they seem to know each other?" Sheens asked.

"I was supposing so," Hanson said. "But they spoke for a minute and then he walked in. So I suppose it could have been an introduction."

"And you think he was following you from the station?" Jonah said.

"Yeah, I do. So he might not previously have known where she lived."

There was a brief silence from the other end of the line. She could almost hear the DCI thinking.

"If you can get the car close enough and a window down, I'd like you to listen out for any raised voices. Beyond that, if he leaves, stay with Louise. It looks like her husband is checking in to a hotel, so I've sent a couple of uniforms to take over. Ben is coming back your way. He can go after Issa if needed."

"Roger that."

Hanson started the engine and began to maneuver her car, not relishing the idea of sitting with her window down in subzero temperatures. But she relished even less the idea of missing something important, and so she pulled the car up and dragged her stab vest and a jumper from the backseat.

Issa took the tea from her, his hand closing round the hot mug instead of the handle without any apparent reaction. He seemed to be too distracted to feel it. His eyes were darting everywhere around the room. They took in the furniture. The paintings. The photos of her and Niall. His scrutiny made her feel exposed.

She settled herself on the sofa, experiencing the same sense of unreality that had gripped her in the police station and then again in the car on the way home. How could she be sitting in front of a dead man's husband?

"I wish I could tell you more about that night," she said quietly. "I know you must want to know."

His eyes focused on her, slowly. "Did you meet him at the bar?" he asked. "Or was it before that?"

Louise shook her head. "I didn't know him. I only remember speaking to him briefly. I can't remember anything else at all."

"Do you remember talking to me?" he asked.

She shook her head again. "Were you there?"

"On the phone," he said, and she detected anger in his voice. "You must remember. I tried to call him, and you answered instead."

Louise could feel her forehead creasing with anxiety. It threatened to bring back the headache that had only recently abated after two whole days.

"I don't remember that," she said, and then, suddenly badly needing to know, "What did I say?"

Alex's husband's mouth pursed in distaste. "Nothing that can help me. That it was Alex's phone, but he was tied up right now. And then he got it off you and apologized. You sounded drunk. He did too."

Louise felt a swelling of shame. She could imagine Drunk Louise doing that. Drunk Louise always wanted to have fun, no matter who it hurt.

"I'm so sorry," she said. "I don't think I was myself on Friday. I was . . . upset. And I got really drunk."

But Alex's husband seemed not to be listening to her. He was looking at her belongings again, his brow wrinkling in what looked like frustration. Perhaps confusion.

"I expected you to be . . . richer," he said.

Louise almost laughed. "Richer?"

"That's what he liked," he said, his gaze flicking to her and then away. "The rich country girls. The ones his dad would have loved."

"Look," Louise said, feeling an increasing sense of unease, "I don't know . . . I don't think that's what happened. I don't think he was chasing me."

But then she listened to herself and thought of the man who had pursued her in her dream. Of the pain in her back and the dirt in her mouth. And she felt ill.

"Any kids?" he asked.

And Louise shook her head, and said, "No," wondering why he would ask that. "Sorry, I . . . what's your name?"

"Issa," he said, his voice quiet. Slightly childlike. And then he suddenly asked, "What is it you have?"

"I don't . . . understand," Louise said. He was staring at her as though she had personally betrayed him and it made her feel that she must have done it somehow. Must have been a traitor.

Alex's husband continued, his voice low with hatred. "What is it you have that made him want to risk everything? Just so he could fuck you?"

"I don't . . . I don't have anything."

Issa surged to his feet, and as he stood over her, she felt a return of her earlier fear. There was something not right about the way he was looking at her, and the heavy mug in his hand became a possible weapon.

"Whatever you tempted him with, it destroyed everything."

Louise flinched away from him and then said, her voice as firm as she could make it, "I think you need to leave."

IT WAS TEN-FORTY by the time Ben arrived back at Saints Close. Once Issa had left the house and she'd seen Louise Reakes moving around in her kitchen, Hanson had closed the car window again. But it was still freezing in the little Nissan and she was beyond grateful to see that Lightman had brought fast food and hot coffee with him.

"Oh my God," she said as he climbed into the passenger seat and passed it to her. "This might be the best thing you've ever done."

Ben smiled, lifting his coffee to his mouth. And then he paused and said, "There was that thing a few months ago where I took a knife off a psychotic woman. . . ."

Hanson took a large bite of cheeseburger and swallowed it before she replied. "Nope. This is much better."

"Well, that's good to know. For future reference." He chewed for a few moments. "What did you think of Issa, when you met him?"

"By the time we turned up on Saturday morning, I'm pretty sure he hadn't slept at all," Hanson said, considering. "And I don't think his mental state has improved with news of Alex's death. I'm not sure I'd trust him to be rational right now."

"Yeah, I'm not sure sitting in a freezing car outside someone's house for hours is rational behavior," Ben said. "Not if somebody isn't making you do it, obviously."

"Obviously," Hanson said, and then sighed. "I really want to know what they were talking about. Half of me thinks there's some kind of conspiracy going on, and the other half thinks Louise Reakes might actually be in danger."

FROM HIS POSITION on the sofa, with Jojo's legs wrapped round his and her head resting on his shoulder, Jonah felt a momentary resurgence of guilt. Ben and Juliette would be sitting in a cold car right now.

He stretched out to grab his phone, dislodging Jojo slightly, and she gave a quiet growl of protest.

"I was comfortable, Sheens."

"Last message of the night, I promise," he said, getting hold of the phone and typing out All OK? to Hanson.

"Last message unless something kicks off," Jojo countered as he sent it.

"Er, well, I was sort of hoping something else might kick off here. . . ."

Jojo shifted around until she was lying directly on top of him. She gave him a narrow-eyed look, her mouth twisting in humor.

"That can probably be arranged," she said, and ran a hand down his chest until she found the waistband of his trousers.

LOUISE COULDN'T STOP shaking. She felt so angry with every man on the planet. With Issa for his horrible, piercingly painful remarks. With that bloody DCI for not believing her, and not finding out what had really happened either. With Niall, for fucking *everything*.

And it was only now that the truth of her situation really hit home. That she was never going to feel safe. Even if she somehow avoided jail, Issa would still be out there, thinking she'd done it. Possibly trying to get revenge. And what if it hadn't been Alex who attacked her? What if it was someone else, who was still out there, faceless and awful?

She put a hand into her hair and squeezed it until it hurt. She felt as though she'd worked herself into a place she couldn't get out of. She should have told Issa about the rape, or attempted rape, or whatever it had been. God, and she should have got them to test her earlier.

After the awfulness of that truth came another one. It came more slowly, in a cold creeping sensation down her spine.

They thought it was her. Not her husband, who she was now sure had lied to hide an affair with his ex. He'd probably admitted it all to the police. They might even have brought Dina in to back him up, a thought that only made her feel more sick.

So they didn't suspect Niall anymore. They thought it was her, the woman who had slept next to a dead man and then tried to hide it. Of course they thought that.

Which meant they weren't looking for whoever had attacked her. They weren't even looking.

. . .

THE EARLY PART of the night had passed uneventfully for Hanson and Lightman, hunched in the freezing-cold car. The two of them had spent much of it in companionable silence, though they'd played a few pointless word games too.

They had spoken only briefly about Damian, after Ben had suddenly commented, in a voice full of humor, that this must be how her ex-boyfriend felt half the time.

"Just imagine how many hours he must have spent sitting waiting in his car, just for a few seconds of making you feel uncomfortable." He'd shaken his head. "The man seriously needs to get a life."

Laughing at Damian had been a very good thing. As soon as she started thinking about him as a sad individual, she felt enormously better.

It was only at twenty to twelve that they'd seen a taxi draw up slowly outside Number 11. Louise had emerged a minute later, her hair twisted up into a bun and her dress and leggings exchanged for jeans and high heels. With a sigh, Hanson had asked, "Any wagers on where she's going?"

29

LOUISE

I didn't think I'd be writing anymore, at least not yet. But more has happened. I *made* it happen. I suddenly found myself unable to sit alone and let this all just build and build beyond my control.

With the awful realization that nobody was looking for whoever had attacked me, I felt like I needed to do something. With no other obvious paths open to me, I tracked Alex Plaskitt down online and discovered a treasure trove. A YouTube channel full of fitness videos.

I found myself watching video after video, watching obsessively for signs of his character. What I hadn't really been prepared for was the reality of him. For how much of a punch to the gut it would be to see him alive, and animated, and likable. He seemed less and less like a predator and more and more like a victim whose death I had helped to cause.

And as I watched, a suspicion that's been creeping up on me for the last two days crystallized into certainty.

What I finally faced up to was that I did spend time with Alex Plaskitt that night. Every time I denied having met him, I was lying, and I think some part of me knew it. *She* knew it.

I don't think I just talked to him. I think I flirted, and I think it was entirely deliberate. Not just something that Drunk Louise wanted to do, something *all* of me wanted to do.

At some point on Friday night I sat beside him at the bar. I have a fleeting memory of imagining I was Dina. I remember consciously imitating what April had told me. I remember putting my hand on his arm as I laughed at something he'd said.

But that was all I could remember. Everything else was still a yawning void and it was driving me to agitation. I couldn't calm myself, even with more cleaning. I felt certain that I'd done something awful.

I knew I needed to know what I'd said to him. Whether I'd agreed to meet up with him at our house. I needed to know how much of this shit I'd brought on myself.

It was a momentous thing, leaving here alone, just before midnight, with a destination in mind that intimidated the hell out of me. But I did it. I had to.

You know what the worst part of it was? That I had to do it basically sober, because I needed to remember everything. I couldn't leave it all up to Drunk Louise and go along for the ride. I had a one-and-a-half-strength gin and tonic while I waited for my cab, and I walked up to the door of Blue Underground feeling basically myself.

I almost got turned back right then. The bouncer asked for my ID, and I looked all through my handbag without being able to find it. I came dangerously close to crying. Why had I been IDed tonight, of all nights? It only happened once in a while, when I somehow gave off the effect of being a teenager instead of an adult.

"I didn't think to bring it," I told him, with a note of desperation. "I'm thirty-three."

The bouncer sighed, and after another, more careful inspection of me, waved me into the club. I gave him a smile and hurried past.

The inside of Blue Underground looked vastly different in reality from every memory I had. A combination of it being only one-quarter full tonight, and Sober Louise now being the one to see it. The clientele were different too. Most of them looked like students or postgrads. Lots of them were non-English. And the music was more poppy. Less *club*.

I didn't really care about the music or about anyone else who was in there, though. I was looking at the staff, searching for someone I recognized.

It didn't take me long. A guy of probably twenty, down at the far end of the bar from me, one with curling hair and an eyebrow piercing, turned to give a customer his drink. He'd been there on Friday. I knew he had. I'd spoken to him.

It turns out that it's surprisingly easy to get served quickly by a particular person when you don't care what anyone thinks of you. I shoved my way in and got his attention with a smile and a lift of my credit card. He came straight over, overlooking three or four people who'd been there first.

"Kronenbourg, please," I said, choosing something that would keep him standing still in front of me while he poured. As he flipped a glass up and into place under the tap, I added, in a voice that sounded strangled to my ears, "And I need some help. I was in here on Friday. Do you remember?"

The guy glanced at me, and then I saw something change in his expression. He looked uncomfortable. Worried.

"I don't know. . . ."

"I was with a loud, blond American woman," I went on, trying to pretend I was confident Drunk Louise instead of myself, "with lots of tattoos. And after I left, something terrible happened. The police must have been here asking questions. They were here, weren't they?"

The barman glanced around, and then gave a slow nod. He'd almost finished pouring the drink.

"Sorry, that should have been two Kronenbourgs," I said.

I could see from his face that he didn't like that. He stayed still while someone squeezed in next to me, and then he grabbed another glass with bad grace.

"Please just tell me what I was doing," I begged him. "I need to know. I was so drunk, I don't really remember." I swallowed, feeling a flickering, sick beat to my heart. I was so afraid of what he was going to say. "Was I talking with a guy? A . . . tall, athletic sort of guy?"

The barman started to pour the second pint and gave a slight sigh. I could see it from the way his body moved, even though I couldn't hear it over the music.

"Yes," he said in the end. "You were sitting just along there with him."

"Over there?"

He nodded to the end of the bar that was farthest from the door. There were a few stools down at that end, but nobody serving.

"Was I . . . flirting?"

The guy shrugged. "I'd say so. But . . . you didn't go home with him or anything. He was a bit pissed off that you left in a hurry."

I felt another twist of my heart. "He was? Did he say anything?"

"No," he said. "But you notice this stuff, you know." He looked toward a barmaid working farther down. "Look, you need to pay, and I need to get on with work. You didn't do anything while you were here that might have . . . I heard about what happened, but I can't help. I'm sorry."

And then he was placing my two unwanted beers on the bar and holding his hand out for my card. And no matter what I asked, he said nothing more.

30

"So, what do we make of her?" the DCI asked as Hanson wrapped up her brief report on their stakeout. It was eight forty-five in the morning. Sheens had just returned from his early caseload meeting and, with the weekend done, CID was busy once again, though their team was down on numbers. O'Malley was on stakeout at the Reakes house, and Lightman had been sent to see April Dumont again.

"Of Louise?" she asked. "It's hard to say. Ben couldn't catch much of her conversation in the club, but if she really was doing her own investigating, it strongly implies that she's been telling the truth about not remembering anything."

"Agreed," Sheens said. "Though whether she was involved in Alex's death is still, frustratingly, up in the air."

"I want to look more at the knife," Hanson told him. "Surely that's still our firmest piece of evidence. If I can link it to any one of our suspects, we'll know who to press."

"I think you may be right," he said, nodding slowly. "See if you can work out what Ben's done on that so far."

Hanson found Ben's work to be as meticulously logged as she'd been anticipating. It took her no time at all to continue what he'd started, and she quickly immersed herself in cross-checking delivery addresses with their suspects. It was perfect work to avoid thinking about anything. Lots of facts and attention to detail.

It took her a while to notice someone loitering next to her desk. And when she looked up, she tried not to grimace. She'd momentarily forgotten that Jason would be here today.

But she was prepared for this even so. She'd decided how to play it.

She gave him a bright smile and said, "How can I help, sir?"

Jason visibly flinched at the deliberate use of rank. "Juliette, could we—could we please talk?"

Hanson glanced at her screen. "I've got quite a lot to do."

"So have I," Jason said with slight frustration, "but it's going to get done a lot more quickly if we can clear this up. I can't think like this."

Hanson was sorely tempted to ask whose fault it was that he couldn't concentrate. But this was still Jason, the man she'd cared about up until yesterday. The man she'd spent a great deal of time with. Even if there had been little passion in their relationship, she'd at least felt she could trust him. It was hard not to want him to think well of her on some level.

"All right," she said, standing. "I may as well do a coffee run."

She left a note on Lightman's desk, picked up her coat, and walked out just ahead of him. She didn't volunteer anything. She might be willing to talk, but there was no way she was going to kick things off. It was up to Jason to say his piece, or apologize, or whatever it was he wanted to do.

They were crossing the car park before he said, "So. Your ex. Damian."

"Yes," she said. "My ex." She stressed the word slightly, but that was all she was giving him.

"When did you stop seeing him?"

"Several months before I moved here. Would you like to know why I stopped seeing him?"

"Yes."

"Because he was an abusive narcissist," she said with as little emotion as she could. "The humiliating thing is how long it took me to see it."

There was a pause, and then Jason asked, "Abusive how?"

Hanson let out a sigh. "In every possible way. As soon as he'd moved in with me, he stopped paying rent. He claimed he was having a temporary money problem thanks to a previous girl-friend who'd run up bills in his name. Then he borrowed off me on top of that. Thousands in total. I had to borrow off my mum to cover it and he kept claiming he had a bonus coming up at work that would sort it out, only it never came."

Jason said nothing, but he nodded when she glanced at him.

"He tried to tell me what to wear. He told me my clothes made me look like a whore. He also accused me of *being* a whore because I'd once told him, when he asked me, that I'd tried an open relationship." She took a breath. "He resented every good thing that happened in my life and tried to undermine it. Roughly every two days he would say something so unbelievably nasty to me that I cried. As it progressed, I increasingly ended up scream-ing at him in rage too. But in the end, he always broke me down. Anger turning into misery."

They came to a stop at the pedestrian lights and Jason pressed the button. Hanson looked away from him before she went on.

"And then he would apologize. He would tell me he was try-ing to get help. That he had trauma, and it got the better of him sometimes. It should have been clearer earlier on that he apolo-gized because he'd got exactly what he wanted, which was to know how much he could hurt me. He got his kick out of break-ing me down, and then he needed to reel me back in to stop me actually leaving. So it was all 'my trauma, my trauma, poor me.'" Hanson gave a small snort of laughter. The lights changed and they started to cross. "The irony being that he dealt out trauma like nobody else. Oh, and he cheated on me with multiple women, which I damn well knew but couldn't prove because he deleted every message between them. One of them was a good friend of mine and I lost her because of it."

"When you say he deleted his messages . . ." Jason said carefully.

"I saw him delete them in front of me," Hanson snapped, knowing what Jason meant. Asking her if she'd been checking up on Damian all the time, as he'd probably told Jason that she had. "If I asked to see any messages, he got angry and told me I should trust him, whereas my own messages were continually hacked. He sometimes got my phone and said terrible things to my friends, while they thought it was me. I caught him a few times and I can only imagine what he said that I didn't see. That he deleted."

"How long were you with him?" Jason asked.

"A year and a half."

"Why did you stay with him?" The question was asked with such disbelief that Hanson almost laughed.

"Do you really need me to tell you how abuse works?" she asked him. "How they turn on the full force of their charm every time they apologize, and make you feel like it's all right now? How when you do break up with them, they find ways of making you feel guilty? They point out all this stuff they are doing 'for you.' The therapy sessions that, coincidentally, you are paying for. Do I need to tell you how you defend their behavior to all your concerned friends and family so many times that you become complicit in it?"

"But you're smart," he argued, stopping, and turning toward her. "Surely you could see through him."

"Like you did?" Hanson asked.

There was a very long silence, as Jason looked into the distance somewhere. "I'm sorry. It's just . . . I didn't see any reason not to believe him when he said it."

"Except for four months of getting to know me better than anyone else," she said quietly, and turned to continue walking.

. . .

O'MALLEY HAD STOCKED up well on breakfast materials. He liked to complain bitterly about stakeout duty whenever it cropped up, but he generally used it as an excuse to treat himself to unhealthy food. As a result, he almost looked forward to it.

Today's haul had come courtesy of the shop in the petrol station, which had the good sense to be open from seven. He'd arrived at Saints Close just before his clocking-on time, equipped with everything he needed for a long stint. The blinds and curtains in the Reakes house were still drawn.

Having eaten one sausage roll and a chocolate croissant, it was clear that he was going to have to vacuum the car later on. But it had been well and truly worth it.

There was still no sign of movement by nine. O'Malley guessed that musicians weren't required to be up all that early. He was quite happy with that situation, as it meant he got to drink coffee and mull pleasantly on his upcoming holiday to Morocco. He was holding out for that week of sunshine.

The daydreaming was rudely interrupted at ten past nine by the arrival of a metallic blue Corsa. So Issa was back. O'Malley wondered what his business was, and whether it was by arrangement.

Issa parked right outside Number 11, seemingly unaware of O'Malley's Astra perched on the curbside opposite. He climbed out with the look of a man on a mission and strode up to the door.

O'Malley watched him ring the bell, and then, after a minute, ring it again. After that, when there was no sign of life, he started to move around the side of the house, peering into the windows. O'Malley was on the verge of going to intercept him when Issa turned and walked back to his car. Instead of driving away, however, he let himself in and then sat in the driver's seat, his head turned toward the house.

"Who does he think he is?" O'Malley muttered to himself. "A fecking copper?"

. . .

Louise was barely functioning today. Another night of terrible sleep and ceaseless worry seemed to have finished off her ability to perform even the simplest of tasks efficiently.

She'd thought she'd be exhausted enough to sleep. But it hadn't come, and she'd found herself, at three, switching on her laptop and returning to Alex Plaskitt's YouTube channel.

The urge came out of an equal blend of guilt and determination to know more. Here was a man whose death she might have caused, but also one who might have pinned her down and raped her. She needed to work him out, and this was all she had.

She'd eventually dozed off sometime after five, only to dream of Alex. In her dreams, she had tried to save him, and then realized that he was a predator who was doing nothing more than tricking her. And later, at some confused point, she was pregnant with his child and about to marry him.

She woke again at eight feeling as though she'd been scoured out by emotion. She was so tired of being haunted. By Alex in the fullness of life, and then by his lifeless form. By memories of the club. Of attack.

And now, this morning, by Alex's husband, who had returned to lay siege to her.

She'd watched him from the upstairs hall window as he'd walked toward the house. She was glad of the muslin she'd hung there, despite Niall's complaint that it was as bad as a net curtain. She was able to see him without being seen, to watch him, with her heart in her throat, as he got tired of ringing on the bell and began to move around to the side gate.

What was she supposed to do if he tried to get in? Call the police? Call Niall?

But she couldn't call Niall. She could never call Niall again. And she felt as though the police wouldn't believe her. Why would they believe a suspect? They thought she was a killer.

Issa had eventually retreated again, and she felt a sag in her shoulders as he went back to his car. He climbed in, but the car stayed where it was. She couldn't see him from up here, but she felt certain that he was watching the house.

And then, of course, the obvious answer came to her. She could call the one person who always took her side.

Except, she thought, with a sudden drop in her stomach. Except that April had lied to her, and she needed to know why.

THE WALK BACK to the station had felt painfully long. Hanson had to hold herself aloof for all of it, and even ten minutes of it had been draining.

Jason had asked her, while they'd stood waiting for the coffee to be made, whether things could be all right between them. Whether she could look past the things he'd said in that message. She supposed that meant that he believed her. A small victory.

But she'd said no.

"How can I be in a relationship with someone who doesn't trust me?" she'd asked. "How would I feel confident and comfortable knowing how easily he talked you round? What if he came back more persuasively?" He shook his head, but she went on, "And all of those little frustrations he played on. That you don't like it when I go back home after seeing you. That I don't message often enough. That I still want to do Friday pub trips with my own team. They'd all still be there, and what Damian has done is to make it blindingly obvious that I don't make you happy."

Jason had had no answer, and she'd felt a heavy certainty as she had turned to begin walking back. He'd come to walk next to her, his own tray of coffee the match of hers, and the silence had lasted all the way to the station.

It was only when they reached the bottom of the stairs to CID that he suddenly seemed to wake up.

"Juliette," he said, and his voice had been so . . . so *sad* that she'd felt she had to look at him. "I know you think this was all based on lack of trust, or dissatisfaction with you, but it wasn't. It really, really wasn't. I was taken in by him, and I know you were too. Can you not understand that he can be as charming to a man as he can be to a woman?"

He gave her a long, beseeching look, and it was deeply uncomfortable because she knew that he was, on some level, right. And yet other people hadn't fallen for it. The DCI hadn't. Ben hadn't. They'd known her for less than a month, as a new colleague, when Damian had first tried to twist their view of her. And they'd dismissed it out of hand.

Jason took a step toward her suddenly, bringing his beseeching gaze that little bit closer.

"Just take a while to think about it. Please. I don't want to lose you. I probably haven't made it clear enough how much I care about you. Or how much it hurt when I thought all this shit was true." He squeezed her free hand briefly. "I'm sorry for being so stupid, but that's all it is. Stupidity."

As he let go of her hand, Hanson felt as though her defenses were being burrowed under. And it made her feel a sick, dizzy sense of déjà vu. This was what Damian had done to her, over and over.

She'd never thought of Jason as being anything like him. How had he managed to poison this so completely?

"Of course I'll think about it," she said as he gave her a questioning look. "I've always cared about you too. But I need to work now."

She entered CID ahead of him, and although she held the door for him, she didn't walk alongside him as she returned to her desk.

LIGHTMAN RETURNED TO the flat on Admirals Quay and parked up in the underground car park of April Dumont's building. The rigmarole with being allowed up in the lift was repeated with a new concierge, and he was deposited once again on the top floor.

April emerged into the hallway, dressed in a loose white top over a very visible black bra, and distressed silver and black leggings with biker boots. She looked unashamedly out of place in the ultra-sleek apartment.

"Dan's at work," April told him as she sprawled on one of the sofas.

"Right," Lightman said. "Dan is . . . ?"

"My husband," April said, and then laughed at the surprise on his face. "Oh, you thought I was footloose and fancy free? No. Some marriages run better on a little spice, if you want the truth."

Lightman nodded and decided not to write this down at present.

"You want a drink or something?" April asked with a slow smile.

"I'm fine, thanks," he said. "I need to ask you a few things about Friday night."

"I want to ask some things first," April said, sitting up. "Why did you arrest Louise? She isn't the kind of person to hurt anyone."

"I can understand your worry," Lightman said, nodding. "There were various circumstances around the finding of the body that are of some concern. But we are investigating—"

"I know Louise," April said, cutting across him. "She's not going to go home with some man she's never met. That is not her MO. Not her MO at all."

"You're saying that Louise . . . had nothing to do with anyone at the club?"

"Damn right I am," April said. "She was drunk and hurting and the most I saw her do was talk to a couple guys nicely."

"Could you tell us who you went home with?" Lightman asked.

April gave a short laugh. "Not really, honey. Except that his name was Adam, I don't have much."

"You went back to his house?"

"Yeah, I did. It was just a little fun. Dan and I've been having troubles. Like some others."

"Do you have an address for the house?"

"Hell no," April said. "I got a cab there with him, and I made him call me a cab after too." She shrugged. "It was somewhere this side of town is all I know. Kind of a nice place."

Lightman gave a vague smile, thinking that this meant no provable alibi for the time of Alex Plaskitt's death. And regardless of what Niall Reakes was hiding, April Dumont was still a suspect.

Lightman watched her for a moment, and then said, "I'm a little confused, if I have to be honest, about your behavior." He let her turn around and face him before he went on. "You clearly feel protective toward Louise. And yet you apparently left her while she was extremely drunk." He tipped his head slightly to one side. "It seems out of character that you simply abandoned her."

April's expression dropped. She looked deeply uncomfortable, and slightly angry. "I didn't just abandon her. I was—I was drunker than I should have been. I'd been there for her, helping her, you know." She looked at him with eyes that were slightly reflective, even in that bright light. "I got her water and I hugged her when she looked like she might cry. And I tried to help look for her driver's license. I did all the things a good friend does, up until I got too drunk and forgot I was supposed to be looking after her."

Lightman studied her for a moment. "She lost her driving license? In the club?"

"Yeah," April said. "She not tell you? She'd had it out ready, because she looks awful young when she's dressed up, and then later she realized she didn't have it anymore."

"And did you ever find it?" he asked.

"No," April said, shaking her head. "No, it stayed lost."

"OK," Lightman said, writing that down. He wondered, briefly, whether Alex Plaskitt had found it.

"So tell me what motivated you to leave with this man."

"Because fuck Dan if he was going to be an asshole."

"I believe that this Adam wasn't the first man you'd had some kind of romantic liaison with that evening," Lightman said quietly.

He had expected an expression of surprise or anger, but April gave an immediate smile of amusement. "Romantic liaison? Who in the hell talks like that?"

"Just us," Lightman replied, smiling slightly in return. "As far as we know, you kissed someone else that night."

April shook her head, still grinning. "Yeah, I did. Tall, upper-class kind of a guy with a six-pack. Who wouldn't have?"

"But you moved on pretty quickly?"

"Yeah," she said, the smile fading slightly. "Turned out he was married, and had a guilty conscience about it." She gave a shrug. "Which I guess is up to him."

"You weren't angry about it?"

April rolled her eyes. "Not really. I mean, I was a little pissed off for a second. He'd been so obviously keen. And his friend was all interfering too. I was more annoyed with the friend."

"You didn't try to follow this man?" Lightman asked. "Or meet up with him later?"

"I can take no for an answer," April said, beginning to look offended by his questions.

"Did you find out who he was, this other guy?" Lightman asked.

"No," April said, "I didn't. Why would I? And why are you so obsessed with it?"

"Because that man was Alex Plaskitt," Lightman told her. "The man who died in Louise Reakes's bed."

There was a long beat. "Shit. Seriously?" she said.

"I'm afraid so," Lightman replied.

April turned away from him, looking out of the picture windows toward the sea. "That's a hell of a shame," she said. "He was quite something. Even if he was a prude."

"You didn't see anything later on that evening?" he asked. "Anything to suggest why he might have been killed?"

April shook her head slowly. "No, I don't think . . . I guess the only thing I thought was how weirdly possessive his friend was." Lightman realized that April must mean Step Conti, and it gave him pause for thought. "When I kissed Alex," April went on, "it was almost like he was jealous."

31

LOUISE

It's morning now. I left my account where it was last night, wondering if I'd actually write any more, or if I was done. I felt like there was nothing more for me to tell you. There were, instead, a lot of unanswered questions.

But I hate leaving anything unfinished, as you know. And after talking to April, I felt an itch to write more of it down.

I called her this morning, in spite of my sudden doubts. This is the first time I've ever distrusted her. Perhaps that sounds ridiculous, when she's so willing to sack me off in order to chase the man of the minute, and when she clearly has her own secrets. She's perpetually vague about her job, and who's paying her, and even more so about life back in Tennessee. But she's always essentially been there, a strong, dependable rock for me to grab on to.

It was a vast relief to hear her voice. It was like an instant return to normality. She spoke, and the earth righted itself.

It didn't matter if I was still under investigation for murder, or that you'd left, probably for good, or that she'd lied a while back, or that I felt like I might never be able to sleep again without dreaming of a smiling man following me. The moment she said, "Lou, honey, I'm just the gladdest to speak to you," I felt like I was back in my own skin.

"You too," I told her. "Everything's been such a fuck-up."

"I hear you, honey," she said. "I've just spoken to that insanely handsome cop. Who is completely, one hundred percent immune to any kind of flirtation and it's heartbreaking."

I couldn't help smiling. "The older one or the younger one?"

"Well, he's a sergeant, I think he said," she tried. "Probably thirtysomething and with cheekbones like knives and the most incredible blue eyes." She sighed. "But nothing there, you know? Not a hint of sexuality."

"I know the one."

And God, the relief of talking about the police like that. Of not thinking of them as terrifying figures of authority.

"So," April said, "are you OK? I've been going crazy with worry."

"I know," I told her. There had been fourteen missed calls and eight messages from her on my phone by the time I got it back. Which was a lot, even for April. "I wanted so badly to talk to you. I'm back home now. Feeling like shit but on the up."

"Where's Niall?"

I flinched slightly. "I—I asked him to go."

"You did?"

April sounded genuinely surprised, and I rushed to defend my actions. "If you'd been there . . . in that fucking cell . . ." I swallowed, trying to be angry and not tearful. "He let me down so badly, April. He jumped to the immediate conclusion that I must have slept with someone else and then killed him, and he refused to see me to even ask about it." I used my thumb to wipe each eye, frustrated that I was once again tearful. I wanted to be stronger when I talked about you, Niall. To be the kind of woman who stands up to her awful husband and walks away with no regrets. "Even Patrick believed in me more than Niall did. And do you know what he was actually doing on Friday night? He was with Dina."

April hissed between her teeth. "So there really was something going on with those two."

"Yes," I said. "I've had zero other explanation. He couldn't even look me in the eye when we were released. How fucking dare he stand there and judge me after that? And I should just be angry but I'm so fucking sad."

"Honey," April said warmly, "I am positive he will come to his senses and realize what he's ruined. But that doesn't mean you have to take him back. Anyone who can do that to you—well, I'd be wondering if he was the right man to spend the rest of my life with."

"Too right." I said it so rebelliously, but I was still feeling lacerated by what you'd done, Niall. Whatever you felt when Dina abandoned you, what you've put me through has been infinitely worse. Trust me.

April sighed. "He's not the only man out there, you know. Hey, you remember that Italian bambino from Hannah's wedding? My friend Chez? He's still single."

"Oh . . . I think it might be a little soon, but thanks." I didn't tell her that the idea of seeing any other man was crazy right then, when I could close my eyes and remember someone pressing down on me. And beyond that, when I might be about to go to jail for a crime I was certain I hadn't committed.

And then, just after that, I remembered that I needed to talk seriously to April. About that other time in the club. And I felt my stomach drop further.

"Why don't I come over?" she offered. She sounded enthusiastic. As if there were nothing better she could think of doing than cheering me up.

I couldn't ask her about that lie right then. I just couldn't.

32

The DCI was on a call when Hanson returned to the office, so she parked her tray of Costa coffee and settled herself at her desk. She began looking through the spreadsheet once again. She identified another address that might be of interest a few moments later. A knife identical to their murder weapon had been sent to a firm of mortgage advisers based in Winchester. The addressee was a Mr. Marc Ruskin. She started looking to see if any of their suspects had anything to do with this firm, and the careful, methodical work was the perfect antidote to everything else she was feeling.

She'd only meant to fill a little time, but ended up so absorbed that she didn't notice the DCI coming to find her until he said her name from a few feet away.

"Sorry," he said, as she started. "Didn't mean to break your concentration. How's it going?"

"It's going OK, I think," she said. "There are a couple of addresses on the list from Steel and Silver that look promising. I'm just wading through any connections to the first one. And I got you coffee." She gestured to a cardboard tray from Costa. "I hope it's still warm. Flat white. Is that all right?"

"Oh, thanks. That's actually perfect." Sheens maneuvered the cup out of the cardboard holder. "So. If it's not a bad time, I wanted to bounce a few thoughts off you."

Hanson sat back from her computer. "Fire away."

"There's no way I buy Niall Reakes and Dina Weyman meeting about a job," he said. "But equally, if it was simply an affair, it seems bizarre that he wouldn't just admit it to us, as it provides a perfect alibi."

"Particularly since his fake alibi relies on his ex-wife anyway," Hanson added.

"Exactly. I doubt his wife would believe him about the job idea in any case, so there's no benefit to it. Unless both he and Dina are covering up for something else that's been going on."

Hanson looked away, toward her screen. Her mind was grinding through this, slowly. "He seemed quite sure that Dina would cover for him. But then she clearly decided it was better to scapegoat him instead."

"Which suggests something criminal," the DCI agreed.

"Niall Reakes drove to Zurich before he flew home. He booked the ticket at the last minute. As if he'd suddenly been summoned . . ."

The DCI gave her an odd look. "And he's a drug rep."

"His ex-wife," Hanson said quickly, "manages a whole team of reps at another big pharma." The DCI met her gaze. "Could it be that simple?"

The chief stood, his face in a half-smile. "If it is, it may have nothing to do with Alex Plaskitt. Let's bring Mr. Reakes back in."

O'MALLEY HAD FINISHED most of his food and was feeling over-sugared, in need of a comfort break, and a little nauseous. Neither Issa nor Louise Reakes had gone anywhere, and the inside of the car was now bitterly cold. Which made it about standard for a stakeout, in O'Malley's experience.

On the better side of things, he was now three and a half hours through his five-hour stint, and he had identified a petrol station around the corner that had a customer toilet. Naturally, he was within moments of taking a brief break when a Lotus came noisily down the road and hesitated outside Number 11. O'Malley had his camera phone out and ready, and had a clear view of April Dumont as she looked around for a space.

He took three photos and then waited as she found a spot farther up the already crowded close. She left the car half on the pavement and half hanging out diagonally into the road as she strode toward Louise Reakes's house. But instead of going toward the door, she moved across the road. For a moment her gaze swept over his car, and he thought he'd been seen. But she walked on past him, heading for the Corsa.

O'Malley hastily switched on the ignition and put the window down far enough to be able to hear any conversation, though the first sound was just a sharp rapping as April knocked on Issa's window. O'Malley couldn't see Issa himself, just April, her hair swinging down over her face as she leaned toward him.

"Hey," she said, her drawl loud and piercing. It seemed that Issa had not opened the window to listen to her. "So I know that you're grieving and all, but you need to leave. Louise has been through enough shit, and this is not reasonable behavior, OK?"

O'Malley found himself holding his breath slightly. He wasn't too clear on how Issa was going to respond. He imagined him erupting out of the car and trying to injure her. But there was silence until April said, "Hey! You getting this?"

And then the engine started up, and April backed away as Issa drove his car down onto the road. She stood and watched the car disappear from sight, and then she turned and walked toward Number 11.

O'Malley grinned to himself, deciding it was time for that comfort break.

NIALL REAKES NO longer looked anxious. He looked defeated. He moved slowly and without apparent care into the interview room and sat heavily. There was none of the self-righteousness that had characterized his first interview in this room, and Jonah was caught between satisfaction at his fall from grace and genuine empathy at his situation.

Daniella Hart, here as Niall's solicitor again, looked rather more cheerful. She threw a slightly combative smile in Jonah and Hanson's direction as they ran the tape. Jonah smiled back, guessing that Niall hadn't told his solicitor what he'd really been doing with Dina Weyman.

"Thank you for coming in again, Mr. Reakes," Jonah began. "I'm afraid we have yet to communicate with your ex-wife." He saw Niall's expression tighten very slightly, but it was almost as though he'd expected this. As though he had come prepared for betrayal. "There are, however, a few more questions that need some answers in the interim."

Niall did nothing more than nod, and Jonah glanced over at Hanson, who was primed to take the questioning from here.

"We've arranged to liaise with the Swiss police in order to trace your movements during Friday afternoon," she said with perfect coldness. "Before we pin down exactly where you went in Zurich, and prove what you were picking up, we want to give you the opportunity to cooperate fully with our investigation."

Niall's eyes were on the table, his jaw working. Daniella Hart's eyes were fixed on Jonah now, her pen poised over her notebook. The silence went on for a good few seconds and felt a lot longer.

And then Niall said, "Shit."

Hanson adjusted her pose and spoke more quietly. "This doesn't have to be an unmitigated disaster, Niall. You aren't the kingpin in this."

"I'd like to speak with my client alone," the solicitor said.

"I didn't want to get involved," Niall said, lifting his head and ignoring her. "They entrapped me."

"As serious an offense as drug smuggling is," Jonah said, "we're only interested in whether it relates to Alex Plaskitt's death."

"Of course it doesn't!" Niall said immediately. "There's a big difference between shipping stuff around and killing someone. I wasn't even in Southampton on Friday."

"Mr. Reakes," Daniella said sharply, "we need to have a conversation."

And this time, Niall nodded silently. Jonah switched off the tape.

IT TOOK THE solicitor and her client fifteen minutes to establish that Niall was going to cooperate fully. When Jonah and Hanson returned and ran the tape again, he told them, in great detail, about the new friends he'd met at a conference in Dallas eight years ago. Two wonderful new people who had turned out not to be who he thought they were.

"They were a GP and his dermatologist wife, they said. They struck up a conversation in the hotel, and they were just so . . . cool. The kind of people you immediately want as your friends."

Niall had met up with them again late on the second night of the conference, and they'd fed him a story about her having stage-two breast cancer. "The one experimental drug that looked like it was going to work wasn't on the market in the UK yet, which was why they grabbed any opportunity to come to the States. They said they'd been buying it for a fortune and shipping it to the UK, and had ended up with massive debts. They had to find a solution, or they were going to have to sell their house, they said." He sighed. "Somewhere down the line, I admitted I had debt problems too. And that I hadn't told anyone, least of all Dina, who was my fiancée back then."

It was clear how much Niall hated talking about this, and his shame added to Jonah's conviction that this was the truth. He signaled for Niall to continue.

"The wine was flowing and it felt really . . . natural to talk about it all. They seemed like they were being so open. . . ."

Jonah nodded. He could imagine it well. Successful hustlers

often had a particular ability to connect with people. Or to fake it, at least.

"The next night," Niall went on, "they told me they thought they'd found a solution to the cancer-drug issue. A way of making it affordable. They looked so ecstatic that I actually felt happy for them. They went off to bed, and we agreed to see each other on the last night. We partied late after the conference and rolled to bed. I didn't think I'd see much of them after that, but she—the wife—turned up at my room before breakfast on the last morning, freaking out, apparently."

"Their scheme with the drugs had gone wrong somehow?" Jonah asked.

"Of course it had," Niall said bitterly.

He explained, tightly, everything she'd told him. That their flight had been canceled and their airline was rerouting them via Boston, an airport where they used sniffer dogs. They'd picked up a large batch of her cancer drugs at a much cheaper price here, not actually legally. They knew they couldn't risk taking them through U.S. customs in Boston.

"She said, 'We can't afford to jettison them,' and she looked so . . ." He sighed. "So desperate. I didn't even stop to think about it all properly. When she asked what they should do, I just—I just said to give them to me. I was taking drug samples myself so it wasn't a problem to take theirs home too."

"And these drugs . . ." Jonah said.

"They weren't cancer drugs," Niall said flatly. "They told me later that they were MDMA. And no, I didn't check before I shipped them. I went to their hotel room with my case, and I let them thank me over and over as they gave them to me. They hugged me and cried a little, both of them, and I never even stopped to wonder if the bag sitting on the bed had a concealed camera in it. I guess I just don't think in the right way for that stuff."

"So what happened when you arrived home?"

"They came to get the drugs, and they said, 'Come on, Niall. You know they weren't cancer drugs.' Then they played me the little video they'd taken of me putting the drugs in my suitcase and pointing out my fake paperwork. They'd obviously edited out the rest. And I felt just so . . ." Niall's body sagged as he sighed. "I thought I'd made some lifelong friends. When all they'd done was recruit me."

"Did they pay you?"

"Yes," Niall said. "They paid me a lot. And they told me not to worry, because their organization would keep on paying me. They said they really were going to be friends to me. I was going to get right out of debt, they said." He glanced up at Jonah, and then added tightly, "I wish I could give you their real names, or some way of contacting them, but I can't. They became just the collection people, and the numbers they gave me were never answered by them. Always by someone else."

"Another team here will need to ask you about all of that," Jonah replied, not without a little sympathy. Jonah knew that the National Crime Agency would have a lot of questions for Niall about his contacts, but Jonah's interest was a lot narrower. "What we need to know about now is Friday. Is Dina involved in all this somehow?"

"Of course she is," Niall said, his mouth twisting. "I'd stupidly let slip in those early conversations about my fiancée, who worked in pharma too. They didn't touch her while we were together, but then I turned up at a drop-off and it was Dina instead of the couple. She became . . . They used her to recruit reps. She's risen up the ranks crazy fast. I guess she was in an ideal position to manage a whole group of runners. And she's ruthless enough to help dig dirt on her employees and then force them into it. The part that got to me the most was that she was suddenly above me in this scheme. I've spent the last four and a half years being answerable to my ex, and having to walk this constant line. Avoiding sleeping with her but keeping her sweet."

"But you kept doing it," Jonah said.

"What choice did I have?" Niall asked. "They had the video, and I had money troubles. They seemed to know exactly how to keep me tied in. There was never enough money to get me totally out of debt, and a lot of their deals meant going to expensive hotels or bars, which made it worse."

Jonah nodded. "So tell us what happened on Friday."

Niall's mouth twisted into a slight smile. "That was a massive balls-up. But it wasn't actually mine. One of Dina's reps in Zurich was supposed to take a shipment and got himself arrested." He shook his head, his hand coming up to rub his face as he thought about it. "I don't even know who he was, but you could probably find out. He got picked up in a bar for sniffing coke in the middle of the effing afternoon. He rang one of our group, who told me they were extracting his stuff from his hotel room, but I needed to get my ass over there or their buyer was going to be seriously pissed off."

"So you changed flights and collected it?"

"Yes," Niall said. "And it was bloody stressful. I could see everything crumbling, which it did. Just . . . for a different reason."

"Where did you go once you were back in the UK?" Hanson asked him.

"Oh, I met Dina at Gatwick Airport, like I said." He looked between them. "I wasn't lying about that. The stuff was supposed to go to her. . . . She could have just bloody lied for me, and this would all have been fine." Niall made a slightly disgusted sound. "You know, I don't even think they told her to throw me to the wolves. I've been thinking about it, and it's much more dangerous to have me questioned under pressure. I think denying it was all her idea. A way of making me know that she had power over me. She probably thought she could leave me to sweat for a few hours and then admit that she saw me."

"So you met her at Gatwick," Jonah said. "And the handover went as planned?"

"Yes."

"And then?"

Niall looked disconcerted. "Well, I stayed at the hotel, so Louise wouldn't find out I was back early, and I hung around there on Saturday morning. Went to the gym, had coffee, and read the papers . . . I was just killing time. And then . . . and then Louise called and told me what had happened." He shook his head, his expression angry. Even after everything he'd done, he still seemed aggrieved at his wife's actions.

"So you weren't in Southampton on Friday night?" Jonah asked, his voice hard. "You didn't make your way home, thinking to catch Louise out for drinking?"

Niall shook his head very definitely. "Why the hell would I do that? I was trying not to get caught out myself." He shook his head slowly. "I'm sorry, but I don't have a clue what happened to that guy. It had nothing to do with me."

"Do you believe him?" Hanson asked as they returned to CID. She wasn't quite sure why she was asking. Perhaps because she wasn't sure what she thought about it all.

"Not necessarily," the DCI said. "The people Niall works for are exactly the kind of people who might stab someone using a custom-made weapon. It's possible that Alex saw something he shouldn't have, and Niall ended up reacting violently out of desperation. But it does seem unlikely that he'd then leave the body in his own house. Or frame his wife, for that matter. It's too close to home."

"But he still could have had a knife like that and flipped out because he found Alex with his wife," Hanson countered. "I still want to try and link Niall Reakes to that weapon. Possibly his ex-wife too."

"Good," Sheens said. "I agree that we shouldn't rule him out."

They came to a stop next to Lightman's desk. Ben was typing up a report, presumably of his interview with April.

"What did April Dumont have to say?" Hanson asked.

"A few things," Lightman said thoughtfully. "She agrees that she kissed Alex Plaskitt, but had no idea he was the victim. She doesn't think Louise would have gone home with Alex either. She says it's not what she does. Interesting observations on Step Conti, though."

The DCI raised an eyebrow.

"He was apparently very upset when Alex and April kissed. April thought he might actually be jealous that Alex had kissed someone else. She saw some intense conversations going on between the two of them afterward."

Hanson cast her mind back to Alex's self-contained friend. He had seemed genuinely upset at Alex's death. Surprised too. Or at least good at pretending to be.

"He did seem close to Alex," she said thoughtfully. "Might he have been secretly obsessed with him? Or even seeing him behind Issa's back?"

"Nothing has pointed in that direction so far," Sheens said. "But it's worth looking at."

"I suppose," Hanson went on, "if he was obsessed, then if he'd seen Alex get together with yet another woman, that might have driven him to do something stupid."

"I wouldn't mind getting other views on Step Conti," the DCI agreed. "Let's try Alex's sister." He turned to Ben. "Anything else from April?"

"Yes. A small but potentially interesting other thing," Lightman said. "Louise lost her driving license in the club. I wondered if Alex might have tried to return it to her."

"Interesting," the chief agreed. His expression was thoughtful. "I need some more coffee and some time to think. Anyone want anything from Costa?"

"As many chocolate twists as they have," Hanson said. And then she added, "God, and I'd better do some exercise later. I've done nothing for days."

She didn't add that she'd largely stopped running because of Damian. It had lost a lot of its charm once she'd started looking over her shoulder for him. She'd ended up running in the gym instead, and she didn't enjoy it in the same way. Getting there was also needlessly time-consuming, so she inevitably went less often.

But as she settled herself at her desk, she decided that a run would be a good idea. She was going to face up to being alone, in darkness, and enjoy it. The threat of her ex had become less real. More ridiculous. She wished she'd told Ben about it earlier.

She loaded up the spreadsheet of knife orders again and spent a good half hour trying to link either Niall Reakes or Dina Weyman to the address in Winchester where the knife had been sent. And then, in the end, as she finished up one of the DCI's newly bought chocolate twists and threw the bag in the bin, she realized that the obvious route would be to call the firm and ask to talk to this Marc Ruskin, who had apparently taken the delivery.

It didn't take long to raise him.

"This is Marc Ruskin." His voice was brittle, his cheerful, Northern-accented speech not quite steady. "Is this . . . about Alex?"

Hanson had a momentary floating sensation. "Sorry, you mean . . . ?"

"My—friend? Who was murdered?"

Hanson tried to make sense of this. "Yes, I . . . Could you tell me how you knew him?"

"Through my cousin," Marc said. "Through Step. We were a group. Me, Step, Alex. Occasionally my brother, when he wasn't working."

"You used to go out together?"

"Yeah, we did." He gave a slightly emotional-sounding laugh. "I know we seem like a weird bunch. From finance people to personal trainers and everything in between. But we were pretty close."

Hanson made an effort to get mentally back on her feet. To take control of this interview. "When did you meet Alex?"

"A little while after he met Issa," Marc said.

"Were Alex and Step particularly close?" she asked next, April's comments about him very much in mind.

"Yes, I'd say so," Marc agreed. "The two of them meet up a lot more often."

"There's never been any . . . jealousy issue, has there?" she tried. "Between Step and Issa?"

There was a brief silence from Marc, and then he said, "I don't know. I think Issa can be a little bit resentful of Step sometimes."

"And the other way?" Hanson went on. "Does Step resent Issa?"

"Oh, I don't think so," Marc said. "Not really. Only when he tells Alex not to see him."

There was a silence as Hanson wondered how to move the conversation around to the knife. She decided there was no gentle way of doing it, so she went on, "Can I ask about a package that was sent to you, a while back?"

"Uhh . . . a package?"

"Yes," Hanson said. "From a company called Steel and Silver. This was in January last year."

There was a brief pause, and then Marc said, "Oh, you mean that Alex sent over? Yes, the knife for Step's birthday."

Hanson paused, very much aware of her heart beating in her throat. "It was a present for Step Conti?"

"Yes," Marc said. "Beautiful thing that Alex had found. It was just Step's kind of thing."

"So . . ." she said as her brain attempted to catch up with this. "So why didn't Alex have it delivered to his house?"

"Oh, because Issa would have lost his shit," Marc said with a laugh. "He's an absolute pacifist. I mean, Alex is, too, but . . . you know. He wanted to get Step something he would love."

"Is . . . Step into weapons?" Hanson asked.

"Well, he likes anything with workmanship, but he's got a particular thing for hunting knives and ceremonial swords, that kind of thing. Has a huge display in his house." There was a brief pause, and then Marc said, "Was there a particular reason . . . ?"

"We were just wondering what was in it," she said as calmly as she could. "Did Step like it?"

"Yes," Marc said, more slowly. "He loved it."

"Perhaps you could describe the knife, just so . . . ?"

"Well, it had a long, tapered blade," Marc said. "And lots of . . . of black scrollwork round the handle."

"That's great," Hanson said with a breezy, final note. "Thanks so much for all your help. We'll probably need to talk to you again later, but that's all for now."

"OK," Marc said. "Thanks."

There was something in his voice that told her he'd started wondering about that knife. She lost no time in heading to the DCI's office.

"A knife that matches our murder weapon was delivered to the workplace of Marc Ruskin," she told him, before he'd had a chance to say anything, "who turns out to be Step Conti's cousin. Alex ordered it himself, as a gift for Step Conti. He gave it to him for his birthday." There was a brief pause while the chief looked at her, and she added, "Marc described it perfectly to me, and I think he'd started to cotton on to why I was asking. He might warn Step about it."

Sheens's expression was unreadable at first, and then he said, "Right. We'd better get over there."

STEP CONTI'S HOUSE looked just as picture-perfect on a gloomy day as it had in clear sunlight, though there was a keen, cold wind blasting across from the heath that hit Jonah and Hanson hard. It had snowed again out here, too, a hardened layer that had immediately frozen on top.

Jonah couldn't help laughing slightly as he and Hanson both slipped and nearly fell at almost the same time, and then moved flat-footed across the icy driveway toward the front door. They both looked, he suspected, a little ridiculous, and not much like the stern forces of justice they represented.

He waited for the two uniforms from the squad car to catch up with them before he rang the bell. One of the officers was already heading to the side of the property to make sure Step didn't do a runner out of the back.

Step Conti's expression was contained as he answered the door. It was hard to tell whether he felt under pressure as Jonah greeted him.

"We've been given some information about a gift you received for your birthday," Jonah said. "A knife. Do you have it with you?"

Step looked from Jonah to Hanson, and then behind them to the second uniformed constable. And then he said, "The one Alex and the guys gave me? Sure. Come in."

Jonah caught Hanson's gaze as Step moved to let them in. She looked wary, which matched his feeling. He nodded to her, a silent agreement to be on their guard.

Step led them through the sitting-room door this time. Jonah remembered how he'd nearly taken them into this room during their last visit and then changed his mind.

They found themselves in a large space with exposed brickwork and bifold doors at the far end. The left-hand wall was mainly given over to a series of display cabinets, built around a big flat-screen TV.

The locked cabinets were all full of weaponry, most of it old-fashioned. Old muskets or fragments of them. Ceremonial swords. Daggers. And, at the far end, a much shinier collection of blades that looked to be new. It was no wonder, Jonah thought, that Step had hidden this from them on their first visit.

Step went straight to the far end and waited while Jonah and Hanson caught up. Jonah could feel the constable at his heels, and hoped he was on his guard. Their suspect was standing in front of a whole arsenal. But Step made no move to open the case.

"It's this," he said, gesturing.

And there, sitting neatly between two less elaborate hunting knives, sat what looked to be their murder weapon. Only this one was clean, unbloodied, and gleaming.

33

Louise descended the stairs again, a little self-conscious in her very low-cut black dress. She dropped her rucksack down by her feet and tried to grin at April.

"Great," April said. "You look much more like you again."

"I'm still me when I'm wearing a dressing gown," Louise countered.

"No, we're all slobs in a dressing gown," April argued. "This—this is the strong, mouthy, fun person I know. This is Louise."

"I don't feel strong," Louise said. And then she pulled a face. "Sorry. I sound like a self-pitying idiot."

"That is exactly why we need to get you out of here." April gave her a grin that was full of mischief. "A change of scene is going to do you so much good. We can book you a massage, drink cocktails crazy early, and then party. OK?"

"That sounds good," Louise agreed.

"So you're ready?"

"Yes, I . . ." Louise paused. She didn't really want to ask April this. She didn't want to break the spell. "Look, there's something I need to know." She hesitated, still dreading the consequences of this, but then plowed on. "When we went clubbing last summer, and I said I thought I'd seen Niall. I . . . I did see him, didn't I? I know it was him."

April pulled a wry face. "Ah. I . . . Sorry." She gave Louise a doubtful, slightly humorous look. "That was the first time I saw him with Dina. I didn't know whether to tell you. I was just—I was so goddamn angry with him that I stormed over, but when I got there, they weren't kissing or anything, and I overheard them talking about money. Dina left the moment she saw me, and Niall begged me not to say anything. He said she'd offered to get him a job. That it really, genuinely wasn't more. And I thought, you know, that might have been what I heard." April sighed. "I told him to get out of there, but I said I'd be keeping my eye on him. I felt really crappy for lying to you, but it sort of seemed more like a business arrangement than a date. You know?"

Louise studied her for a moment, and then said, "You still basically trusted him?"

"Yeah, I did." And April nodded. "Ever since I first met Niall, I've thought he was decent. You know, the first time we met, out in Dallas, he thought I was in trouble, and he just straight off tried to help. It wasn't sleazy like every other guy in the world. He never flirted or made any moves on me. He just—saw a human being suffering, and he decided to try and fix it." She gave a small smile. "I mean, he was flat-out wrong. I didn't need any help. But it made me like him. And I've always liked the way he tries to help you too."

Louise gave her own sigh. "I suppose he does. Up to a point. So . . . when you told me on Friday about seeing them together . . ."

"Oh, I'd seen them again, like I said," April replied. "She was just all goddamn over him like a rash. Whatever political maneuverings in the world of pharma may have been going on, he was clearly enjoying it. I felt so torn about telling you. I thought maybe I should just give him a warning and see which way he jumped. And then you told me you were going to get pregnant. . . ."

Louise could feel herself blushing a deep red. "Oh God. I don't know what I was thinking."

"You were thinking it was how you'd sort your life out," April replied with a shrug. "And if Niall hadn't been lying to you, then maybe it would have fixed things."

Louise shook her head, mortified. "A child would never have fixed our fucked-up marriage. It was over years ago."

April pulled her into a fierce hug. "I'm sorry, honey. But you're going to find yourself a really great guy. One who knows you'll be an awesome mother, and who hasn't got some crappy ex-wife Rebecca-ing in the background without having the good grace to be dead."

Louise found herself caught between laughing and crying. She took a long breath in, trying to tip herself toward laughter, and said, "Thanks, April. For everything."

"You're welcome," April said, releasing her with a half-smile. "Shall we go?"

"Yes," Louise said. "Let's go."

34

tep Conti was the picture of unruffled calm. Even while he was stuck in a low armchair, with the DCI in full attack mode and two uniformed officers loitering in the background of his sitting room, he was calm and clear-headed. Hanson found herself wondering idly whether this was how Ben would be under interrogation.

Step explained that he had only ever had one copy of that knife. He also hadn't shared with anyone where it had come from.

"I couldn't have done, because I didn't know myself," he said. "Alex just told me he'd had it imported from Poland, and I didn't try to find out. It's beautiful as it is, without needing any history."

Hanson wasn't positive that she believed him. As strange as it might be to buy a second version of a very distinctive knife in order to kill with it, it wasn't beyond the realm of the possible.

The DCI seemed to be thinking along the same lines and carried on with his questioning. Midway through, he suddenly changed tack.

"Tell me," he said. "Did you have feelings for Alex Plaskitt that went beyond the purely friendly?"

And at that point Step had finally shown some kind of reaction.

"Feelings for him? But I'm not—no, of course I didn't." He shifted in the armchair and looked from Hanson to Jonah and back. "I've never fancied anyone male, and the only person on earth I'd get jealous about is through in the kitchen."

"Why were you so angry with him about kissing a woman at the club, then?"

Step shook his head. "Obviously because he was risking everything for something stupid and meaningless. I was angry because I know how much Issa means to him. Look, he's screwed up before, and it was awful for both of them. Alex felt . . . If you'd seen how broken he was after he cheated on Issa . . ."

"So you were acting as his conscience," the DCI said with heavy skepticism. "Why is Issa so distrustful of you?"

Hanson expected Step to become frustrated, but he gave a slightly weary smile. "Issa thinks I encouraged him the last time round, or maybe even matchmade him, because I was the one who put them in touch. Alex and Sarah. I had zero idea anything would happen. I'd just met her at work, and she'd told me she was unhappy with her weight and fitness." He shifted very slightly again, leaning forward and resting an arm on each knee. "If Issa wants to believe that Alex's straying only happened because of me, then in some ways I'm happy for him to think so. Alex just had fleeting moments when he wished he'd fallen in love with a woman instead. Deep down he knows—he knew—that any acceptance from his family would be hollow, and he wanted to make a life with Issa."

"So you didn't feel jealous when he hooked up with someone?" Hanson asked.

"No," Step said, back in control now. "Alex was a really wonderful friend, and I miss him like crazy. But I never in a million years thought of him as anything else."

Step asked if they'd checked the time of his return on Friday evening with his wife, which Lightman had done previously. But the chief asked Hanson to put the question to his wife again, so she left them in the sitting room while she went to find her.

Karen Conti was trying to bake cookies with two kids who

seemed more interested in eating Smarties out of the packet. She answered over her shoulder, looking worried by the question. But she seemed quite definite that Step had been home by twelve-thirty.

This all meant there was no justification for bringing Step into the station. Given that his own knife was sitting there, unused, and that they had little more to point at him than an observation from April Dumont, they had to leave it.

The other members of Step and Alex's group knew about that weapon, too, Hanson thought. That was where they needed to look.

As soon as they were back at the station, Hanson opened up the data file from Alex's phone. By Step's account, the knife had been given to him on the nineteenth, so she set her date range from January the tenth to the nineteenth.

She vaguely heard Lightman tell the DCI, "Issa Benhawy was in Blue Underground on Friday, looking for Alex. One of the bar staff spoke to me."

Hanson's head snapped up. She hadn't thought about Alex's husband in some while. He seemed such an unlikely violent killer: a pacifist who hated any kind of aggression. So much so that his husband had hidden that he was buying a knife for Step.

But his pacifism could be as hypocritical as the next person's, Hanson thought. He might believe in nonviolence until pushed, and it sounded as though Alex had done a lot of things his husband might have objected to that Friday night.

"Issa has also been spending a lot of time hanging around Saints Close," the chief said. "O'Malley had him back there this morning, until April Dumont arrived and chased him away."

"Did we check for his car reg on the ANPRs?" Hanson asked.

"We did," Lightman said. "His car wasn't flagged anywhere on Friday night, but I'm going to check Alex's car too. He would have had access to it."

There was a pause, and the DCI said, "OK. I'd like to look at him more closely. There could be reasons for his behavior other than grief."

Hanson nodded, and returned to what she had been doing with a new sense of significance. If Alex had sent a message about the knife before they'd given it to Step, Issa might have known about it. Particularly if, as a jealous husband, he was looking at Alex's phone to see if he'd cheated again.

There were thirteen WhatsApp strings on Alex's phone on the right dates, she discovered. He'd been a fairly heavy phone user.

Several of the strings she dismissed immediately. One to Issa she hesitated over, but then moved on. Alex wouldn't have sent his husband a photo of a knife he was hoping to hide. It made no sense.

And then she saw a group chat from the twelfth with the names Marc and Chez, and she opened it with a feeling of buzzing excitement.

There were only a few messages on it. The first was from Alex to the rest of the group, and said:

Look at this Polish beauty! Absolutely psyched for Saturday.

Beneath the words, an icon showed that there was an image attached. Hanson clicked on it and sighed as her screen was filled with a large photo. The knife was identical to their murder weapon.

With perfect timing, the phone on her desk rang the moment she opened her mouth to tell the chief.

"DC Hanson," she said, trying not to sound irritable.

"Hi," a woman's voice said. "It's—it's Phoebe Plaskitt. I hope it's OK . . . I have something I really want to tell you."

There was a shake to Phoebe's voice, a sense of stress that cut through Hanson's annoyance.

"Of course. Anything you have to say is helpful," she replied, pulling her notepad toward her.

"I've been looking at Alex's videos," Phoebe said. "I got— I actually got a little bit obsessed with the trolls. Some of them are repeat offenders, and the things they say are really vicious. One of them started a little while before the row I had with Issa about Alex stopping it all. It's got a ridiculous username but . . . but I looked back through the posts from that account, and there was basically nothing much before the trolling, but the account's been up awhile." She took a shaky breath. "I looked at the comments this person had made three years ago, when it was first opened, and they're totally different. A couple of nice comments on some music. And one of them is on the music of a friend of mine, and I remember that comment. I read it at the time, but the username was different."

"You recognized it?" Hanson asked.

"Yes. Because it was a band I recommended to Issa and the comment was from him." She gave a strange, tight laugh. "The troll was Issa."

TWO THINGS HAPPENED rapidly after Hanson finished her call with Phoebe Plaskitt. The first was that Lightman found Alex's car on the ANPR file. It had been driven down London Road at three minutes past one on Friday night, and then past Asylum Green at 1:37. He reported his findings quickly to Hanson and the DCI, whose expression was distant and, she thought, slightly troubled.

Before the chief had said anything, his phone buzzed, and he switched it to speakerphone before he said, "Domnall. Anything to report?"

"I'm afraid so," O'Malley said, his voice tinny. "April Dumont has managed to smuggle Louise Reakes out of the house. She drove past me a good ten minutes ago and I'm positive Louise is no longer in the house. I'm ready to pursue, but I have no idea at present where they've gone."

"I'll get Heerden's team on it," the chief said, and rang off. As he was striding back toward his office, he called, "I'd like you to get Issa Benhawy on the phone and find out where he is too."

Hanson nodded, her hand already going to her mobile. She could sense Lightman's eyes on her as she made the call and waited through eight full rings before it went to voicemail.

"No reply," she said.

IT WAS CHIEF Inspector Yvonne Heerden's team who tracked Issa down. It took them eight minutes to flag him on a traffic camera at the junction with the M27 eastbound. Two minutes later, as Jonah and Lightman were walking toward the Mondeo, Heerden called to inform them that April Dumont's car had been picked up slightly farther along the same road.

"They're headed in the general direction of Portsmouth," she told him. "And they're about fifteen seconds apart on the camera. It looks like pursuit to me."

As soon as she rang off, Jonah dialed through to O'Malley, who was already on the correct side of town. "Get after them if you can."

"Thanks, Chief," O'Malley said. "I'm sure I can close the gap, Lotus or no Lotus."

"We shouldn't be too far behind you," Jonah said, picking up his coat. "We're going to leave now."

"Do you have any thoughts about what Issa Benhawy is trying to do?" Lightman asked him after the call was done.

"Lots of them," Jonah said grimly. "And none of them are good."

"DONE," APRIL SAID, leaning in through the driver's door to pick up her suede handbag. The car was full of the smell of petrol, a scent Louise had always loved. "Need anything from the store?"

"Vodka?" Louise asked.

"Hell yes!" April replied, and maneuvered herself back out of the car. She slammed the door hard enough to make Louise's head ring. For some reason April seemed incapable of closing doors quietly.

Louise followed her progress across the petrol station forecourt, hugely relieved to trust her again. What April had told her about that strange moment in the club had rung true, not least because April had been endlessly loyal to her from the moment they'd met. She, unlike Niall, had proved herself over and over.

April passed by a young guy, probably in his twenties, as she stalked her way in, and he stared after her with obvious admiration. The April effect.

Louise smiled and then yawned. She was beginning to feel genuinely tired now. She guessed the adrenaline was finally wearing off. There was no longer any reason to feel keyed up. She was out of the city and accompanied by her best friend.

She cranked her seat backward and then shifted until she'd found a comfortable position. She felt as though she might, finally, sleep. Her eyes were half closed as she looked lazily at the rearview mirror and watched an old Ford Fiesta pull into the station forecourt behind them. She could see the driver looking ahead as he pulled into the small queue of cars waiting to fill up. She caught his face just before he turned and vanished behind the bulk of a Qashqai. Sleepily, she thought she recognized him.

It was Issa, she realized, with a sudden jolt. What was Alex's husband doing here?

Then she remembered that she had flirted with Alex. That she had, in all probability, gone home with him. That his death was her fault.

She turned to look behind her, and saw Issa climbing out of his car. There was something really wrong in his expression. Something that went beyond grief. And he was holding something under his jacket. Something bulky.

She was suddenly no longer sleepy. Not sleepy at all.

She hurried to undo her seatbelt, and then pushed the door

open. She scrambled out in a crouch, hoping to be hidden behind the SUV until she could make a run for the shop and the tills. She could feel every inch of her flesh crawling as she scooted forward and around the front of the car, not caring that a woman leading a small girl back from the shop was staring at her.

"Hey!"

It was Issa's voice. He'd seen her.

She stood up and ran for the shop. She didn't notice a car trying to exit the petrol station until she was already in front of it, and she gasped as it jolted to a stop. But she ran on. And then she cannoned into the heavy swing door, feeling the time it took to open as if it were an age. But she was through, into the shop, where April was. Strong, dependable April, who would somehow stop whatever it was that Alex's husband was trying to do.

Except that there were only two customers in the shop, and neither of them was April.

35

"**W**e're coming up on Junction Eight," Jonah told O'Malley.

"I've already passed Nine," O'Malley answered. "I haven't seen either of them yet. Are they still on the M27?"

"I'll check with Yvonne's team." Jonah rang off and listened to the phone ring four times. "Come on," he muttered.

And then Yvonne Heerden was there, telling him they had the two cars thirty seconds apart going past Junction Nine. "They were still on the road eight minutes ago, but we haven't picked them up since."

THE TOILETS. APRIL must be in the toilets. And there were locks on the doors. They could hide if they had to.

Louise saw an open door at the rear left of the shop and ran toward it. She almost tripped on the mop and bucket that were propping it open, but then was through.

She was so busy running forward, totally fixed on escape, that she was slow to realize there were no toilets here. They must have been through another door. Out here there was just a small staff kitchen and a storeroom. Boxes of confectionary spilling out into the hall.

There was nobody here, and nowhere to lock herself away.

She could feel her pulse twitching madly in her chest and neck.

Shit. What do I do?

There was a way out. A heavy gray door with a bright green lever. She barely paused before bolting toward it. She slammed it open, and felt as if she were leaving some form of hell behind her as she ran out into the bright sunshine again.

She closed it behind her as quietly as she could, and then moved to her right, along the blank back of the shop. What next?

She took a breath, knowing she just needed to stay calm and try to find April.

But at the thought of moving past the bins and round to the front, a vivid image of Issa stalking toward her struck her, and she leaned back against the wall for fear of falling.

O'MALLEY SLOWED JUST before the entrance to the petrol station, his eyes scanning the forecourt. He was almost past it by the time he saw the back of April's Lotus. It only became visible as a large vehicle pulled out from behind it.

Cringing at the thought of being rammed, he stepped on the brakes and felt the car begin to skid as he turned the wheel. The Astra hung for a moment, as if unsure whether to let him live through this or not, and then suddenly gained grip and lurched toward the forecourt. He pressed the brakes harder and managed to bring the car into a controlled entry with a few feet to spare.

Breathing hard, he drove around the queue waiting to fuel up and dumped the Astra in the space reserved for putting air in the tires. A quick glance showed him that the Lotus was empty. He tried to remember what kind of car Alex Plaskitt had owned. The one Issa might be driving.

His eye fell on the Fiesta sitting two spaces behind the Lotus. It was empty, too, despite the fact that the driver hadn't made it to a pump.

O'Malley checked his waistband for his baton, and then jogged toward the shop.

THE CLUNK AND squeak of metal as the back door opened was one of the most terrifying sounds Louise had ever heard. She should have moved. She should have gone around to the front of the shop.

And then Issa's quiet voice said, "Louise," and her flesh crawled. She was trying to remember. To remember if this was the voice she'd heard that night, even while she pushed herself away from the wall and stumbled away from him.

"I'm so sorry," he said.

And Louise found herself stopping. Turning. He was crying again. She could only remember ever seeing him in distress. Even when he'd been angry with her.

He was putting his hand into his pocket, and she tried to back away farther. Had he armed himself with another knife? With a gun?

And then he pulled his hand out and it wasn't a knife. It was a box of some kind. Dark wood inlaid with gold.

"I found this in Alex's car," he said.

He was holding it out to her, and she didn't want to come closer to him. It must be a trick to get her to come over, so he could attack her. The knife would come out from another pocket, and he would kill her.

But watching him hold it out to her with such pathos, she found that she couldn't refuse to take it. She took two steps and stretched to cross the gap between them until it was in her fingers.

And then she opened the hinged lid while trying not to stop looking at him.

What she saw made no sense at first. There was nothing in there but hair. Strands and fragments of hair, all of them dark. Two of them so dark as to be almost black. All of them coiled up and slotted into neat squares.

And then her hand went to her own hair, and she suddenly understood.

"You must have been one of many," Issa said quietly. "You must have been just one of a long list. It wasn't your fault."

Louise took a large, shaky breath. "It is my fault. I was angry. And hurting. And I flirted with him." Her vision had become fragmented as her eyes filled with tears. "I sat at the bar with him for half an hour. An hour. I'm not sure. And I sank drink after drink with him and I laughed at everything he said, and I put my hand on his knee, and I told him—I told him that I'd like to take him home with me." She gave a great, heaving sob. "And I didn't even mean it. I didn't mean it."

Issa's jaw moved. For a moment he looked angry. But then he said, "I think he would have followed you anyway."

There was a long silence, which wasn't really silence because of the rush of cars from the motorway.

"I think I killed him," she said a little later, remembering the slick feeling of hot blood on her fingers. Remembering that he had made a strange laughing sound that had turned into a groan. "I think I killed him."

And Issa, to her profound sadness and humiliation and relief, said, "It's OK."

The back door of the shop opened so hard that it banged back against the wall, and the rotund police sergeant cannoned through it, followed quickly by April, who looked so terrified it was almost funny.

"It's all right," Louise said, holding out a hand. "He just needed to show me something."

And then April flung her arms round her, and Louise felt as though her legs had turned into string. Perhaps harp strings. And she laughed as she slid through the embrace and sat heavily on the tarmac.

. . .

"WE'LL NEED TO know about Friday night," Jonah told Issa an hour and a half later. "You went to find him, didn't you?"

"Yes," Issa said. "I thought he might cheat again. When he didn't reply to my messages on Friday, I called him, and a woman answered instead. So I went to find him. I couldn't get my car out so I took his. I should have told you . . . but I never found him. I looked for him up London Road, and then between there and home. But I didn't catch sight of him." He put his hand onto the table edge, very carefully. "I must—I must have driven right past them, mustn't I? While he was attacking her."

"It's possible," Jonah agreed. "They would have been out of sight."

"Why do you think he ended up at her house?" Issa asked, his gaze fixed on his own fingers. "Do you think she ran and he kept following?"

"That's the most likely explanation," Jonah agreed. "Alex may even have forced his way into the house after she injured him fighting him off. We think he might have taken her driving license earlier on. So he would have known where she was. But by that point he had suffered extensive blood loss. Whatever he planned by way of revenge or . . . well. It may not have happened."

Issa gave a small, hiccupping sob. "It's—I still feel so sad that he—that he just curled up and died. Alone. And I don't know how I can feel that now that I know . . ."

"It's still possible to feel for people," Jonah said gently. "Even those who have done terrible things."

Issa looked up toward the ceiling, but he nodded.

"Do you have any idea why Alex might take hair from these women?" Jonah asked. "Was there some reason for it?"

"I don't—I suppose all these women were—they looked a little like Alex's mother." He rubbed at each of his eyes in turn. "I think he felt more betrayed by her, when she turned on him for his sexuality, than he did by his father. Maybe they all represented her. Or just . . . the women he told himself he should desire. I don't know."

There was a silence in the interview room for a few seconds, and then O'Malley, his voice full of sympathy, asked, "Could you explain to me, too, why you were trolling your husband?"

Issa's empty expression briefly shifted. Fleetingly, he looked as though he hated himself.

"I wanted him to take it seriously," he said quietly. "I was so frightened that something would happen to him. I mean, I was frightened for myself, too, but he was the one who was going to get recognized. He'd—he'd done some TV appearances and it looked like he might get to be a regular fitness adviser on a life-style show. It was all dangerous for him." He gave Jonah a long stare out of gleaming eyes. "I know it was an awful thing to do. And it didn't even work. He was a lot tougher than I am, I guess. Or maybe he just knew he was capable of—of hurting people."

Jonah nodded, and then said, "We'll need to hold on to Alex's car for a few days." When Issa said nothing, he went on, "We'd also like your help with a few dates from Alex's diary. To make our search for the women whose hair he had easier."

"We have a shared diary on our phones. You can—can you see it on Alex's?"

Jonah glanced at O'Malley, who said, "Yes, we should be able to. Thank you."

There was another silence, and then Issa said, "Do you think he . . . hurt . . . any of them?"

Jonah knew he was asking whether Alex might have killed anyone, a question Jonah badly wanted an answer to as well. All he could say in reply was, "We'll find out."

HANSON FELT FLAT. Flatter than she had felt at the close of any case.

She had been wrong about Alex. Really, truly wrong. He

wasn't a kind, supportive person. He was a bloody monster. A man who had stalked and abused women out of, what, a warped revenge on his mother? And then had kept trophies of them in his car. Memories of his victories.

Their job now, hers and Lightman's, was to find them. To find the women he had attacked before. And that was depressing too. Scanning case after case to find women who might have been Alex's victims rather than anyone else's.

It hadn't taken her long to find one who seemed to fit. Just over a year ago, a student named Gianetta Jilani had been left huddled in a heap in Portsmouth with almost no memory of an assault that had left her bleeding. The one thing she remembered was a knife.

That attack had happened on Step's birthday, six days after Alex had sent a photograph to the WhatsApp group. Six days after he'd talked about the knife as a Polish beauty.

36

The inevitable flurry of work that came with trying to tie up their investigation kept the team at their desks until late. O'Malley and the DCI spent a good hour shut away with DCS Wilkinson, going over and over the upsides and downsides to pursuing a case against Louise Reakes. Lightman spent the time writing up a preliminary report, which would be used to create a press release the next day. Hanson, meanwhile, finished compiling her list of assaults, rapes, and murders across Southampton and major cities within a potential day trip or overnight distance, and started comparing Alex's diary and messages with them.

Gianetta Jilani's attack was almost definitely a match. The database revealed that the student had originally gone to Rain in Portsmouth. Earlier in the same WhatsApp thread where Alex had posted the photo of the knife, she found that this was the club his group had arranged to meet at.

She'd found other possibilities too. One of which she didn't quite want to connect to Alex. A thirty-four-year-old Londoner named Laura Stevenson had last been seen at a bar in Camden Town in May. Her body had been found in the canal four days later. She had been stabbed twice in the back.

She'd had long dark hair, like Louise Reakes. Like Alex's mother. It was much like all the hair they'd found in that box. And blood tests had showed traces of Viagra in her system.

Alex had, it turned out, been away that night. A lads' night in London. It matched up too well.

Hanson sent McCullough a summary of the report and asked if she could look at the postmortem. They needed to know whether the weapon that had killed Laura Stevenson might have been the same as the knife that had killed Alex.

Their theory on the knife was that Alex had ordered a second one shipped to a different address. They were confident they would connect him to another order in the end, even if it meant going to the original makers of the knife in Poland and checking up with them.

At nine-fifteen the DCI announced that he'd spoken to the Crown Prosecution Service. The CPS were not enthusiastic about charging Louise Reakes with either the more severe charge of murder or the lesser charge of manslaughter. There was an ongoing debate about whether the perversion of justice charge should go ahead, but they had two more days in which to make a decision.

"I know what she did was pretty sneaky," Hanson told them all, "but I hope they let it lie."

"I hope you aren't expressing a personal opinion that isn't in line with the letter of the law," O'Malley said, giving her a grin.

"Of course not," Hanson replied, deadpan. "Wouldn't ever."

"So with that, I think it's time to call it a night," the DCI told them. "I'll see you all in the morning."

Hanson ended up walking down to the car park with Lightman, who asked, once they were on the stairs, how she was doing.

"I'm OK," she told him with a shrug. "Feeling a little flat at the outcome of all that, but not as anxious about Damian and all his bollocks. Having talked it all through has helped a lot. So thank you."

Lightman nodded. "We should have a plotting session," he

said. "Tomorrow or Wednesday. A plan of action for dealing with the ex."

"That sounds good," she said, holding the door for him as they walked outside. "Thank you."

They stepped outside, and then Lightman paused on the pavement. "He, um . . . he was here when we got back from the service station. Damian. He was hanging around out here, presumably in an effort to scare you."

"Shit," Hanson said. She shuddered, an involuntary reaction she wasn't proud of. And then she asked, "Are you sure it was him?"

"Yeah, I looked him up yesterday," Lightman said with a trace of a smile. "I dug up *all* the dirt on him."

Hanson gave a shocked laugh. "You didn't use the police database for this, did you?"

"I haven't so far," Lightman said. "But I'm bearing it in mind if I feel he merits further investigation."

Hanson glanced around and tried to ignore a crawling sensation up and down her spine. "I hope he's got bored and buggered off."

"Well, he didn't hang around," Lightman said, carefully not looking at her, "after I had a quick word."

"*What?*" Hanson realized it had come out a little sharply and pulled a face. "Sorry, but . . . What did you say?"

"I addressed him as Damian, and he reacted, so I asked if he would like to come inside and talk to us or vacate the premises. He chose to leave." He shrugged. "The DCI was about five feet away, watching, so I think he felt a little outgunned."

"Right," Hanson said. "Right." She wasn't sure if she thought this was high-handed or actually the best thing anyone had ever done for her.

Lightman looked at her, his eyes clearly trying to read her expression. "Was that all right? I really don't want to interfere. I just . . . well, I hoped it would help. Make him realize you aren't on your own."

Hanson thought about what Damian had probably wanted to say to her. She had no doubt that he'd wanted to see her reaction to his shit. To everything he'd told Jason. He would have wanted to crow over it. She could imagine his smug, awful smile without needing to see it.

"No, it was a great thing to do. A great thing." Then she gave a small tilt of her head from side to side and added, "Surprised you managed it, to be honest."

Ben grinned. "Glad you salvaged that one. I was worried you might have actually said something nice to me."

"Nah, you know me. Only ever a compliment sandwich." But she went on, "Thanks, Ben. I'll see you tomorrow."

Ben made his way across the near side of the car park, waving briefly as he went. Hanson's car was parked almost at the far end, away from the bright lights of the building. It was in such darkness that she felt the need to switch her phone on to flashlight mode and check between the cars as she walked past.

She fully expected to find her tires slashed again. If Ben had chased Damian off, there would be some kind of revenge. She was certain of it.

But the car was fine. Perhaps Damian had been worried about doing it at the police station. She knew there would be some kind of retribution on the horizon, though. Something petty and damaging. It made her feel weary.

LOUISE HADN'T EXPECTED to be allowed to leave. Not now they knew what she'd done. However kind to her they were, she knew that she had to face the music on this one. That she had killed a man. She'd done it in fear for her life, and in what could be termed self-defense, but she'd still killed him. That memory of hot blood spilling onto her hands was real.

Patrick had been with her from the moment she walked back

into the station, and she'd felt such uncomplicated relief at seeing him this time. There was nothing for him to suspect her of anymore. Nothing except what she'd done, and she might have killed Alex Plaskitt, but she hadn't gone home and slept with him. She was, in some bizarre sense, cleared.

He'd put a hand on her arm when he first saw her. His touch had been firm. Reassuring.

"We'll get this sorted," he said.

"Thank you." She grasped his hand, just for a second. And then she found herself asking, "Is Niall all right?"

Patrick gave her a funny little grin. "He's fine. And relieved that you're OK."

And then, a matter of hours later, they were suddenly releasing her. Patrick told her she could go home, and that he was happy to drive her there.

"Am I not under arrest?" she asked.

"Technically, you still are," he explained, "but with no fresh charges, the situation reverts to your previous bail conditions."

It took no time at all for his Jaguar to drive them the few miles home. The roads seemed absurdly quiet, but then she remembered that it was nearly ten P.M. on a Monday. Of course it was quiet.

Patrick climbed out to help her with her overnight rucksack, which had gone with her to a service station and then back without being opened. And then he gave her a brief hug and told her to get as much rest as she could. It was only as he'd backed away again that he said in a low and surprisingly uncertain voice, "You know, I felt tempted to say earlier, but . . . I never liked Dina. At all. I was very glad . . . when you and Niall got together. I would very much like to think there was still a chance for you two."

She couldn't find any response, but she nodded at him, and he smiled before getting back into his car. She felt a trace of sadness after he left. Niall's best friend had turned out to be a great deal more loyal to her than she'd had any right to expect.

She let herself into the house, and wondered, suddenly, whether she would continue to live here. Whether she might find herself in jail, or whether she and Niall would sell the place in order to go their separate ways. And all those uncertainties were far too much now, so she dumped the backpack and let herself into the music room, where her harp was waiting for her.

She sat and leaned it against her shoulder, and felt its comforting weight for a moment. And then she started to make music, a flow of unwritten melodies that seemed to pour out of her without thought.

It was still hard for Hanson to feel safe in her home, but it unquestionably felt better than it had. Sharing all of it with Ben had given her more comfort than she could have expected.

She glanced up at the mock CCTV camera over the door, with its big, bulky black box and its cable that actually didn't go anywhere. She'd tucked it back in on itself within the box before she'd mounted the thing. There was another one on the first floor, too, looking out toward the road.

Hanson went through her usual routine of locking up, though less quickly, and decided that a glass of wine and catching the end of *Last of the Mohicans* was in order. And then sleep. Hopefully good sleep.

She dozed off quickly, keeping thoughts of Damian firmly away and thinking instead about the work she would do tomorrow. How she would go on tracing other women who had been victims of Alex's need for revenge. How she would also reengage with drug dealing in a pub on the Highfield estate on O'Malley's behalf. There was a lot of catch-up to do on their other casework.

The thoughts were satisfying, if not actually cheerful. They soothed her. Though just before she slept, she found her mind drifting briefly to the image of Ben talking to Damian outside the station, with Ben as unflappable as ever and Damian suddenly on the back foot. No longer in control. It made her smile.

And then she was awake. Fully awake and half out of bed, because there had been a sound. A sharp, loud, heart-clamoring sound from downstairs.

She staggered as she tried to stand, her body not yet catching up with her mind, which knew that the sound had been the kitchen window shattering.

Weapon, she thought, hearing sporadic crashes of glass as more fell out of the pane.

She'd got this one covered. She'd been sleeping with her truncheon next to her for months now. She'd rehearsed this situation for months too. She picked up a pillow off her bed and clutched it in front of her, an instant guard against knives when she had no time to put on her stab vest.

She knew, without question, that the intruder was Damian, and part of her was glad. Whatever he was trying to do, she'd back herself in a struggle over him. He was taller and perhaps a little stronger, but also out of condition. Too self-indulgent to keep himself toned or to go to any of the martial-arts classes he'd always talked about.

She opened her door as silently as she could, determined not to flinch with every fresh sound. Was he in the kitchen? Or had he already moved into another part of the house?

She became aware, as she went slowly down the stairs, of a strange light and smell. It was a hot, Bonfire Night smell, and the colors on the walls were a faint, unsteady orange.

Shit.

She ran the last few steps and dropped the pillow in order to open the hall cupboard and haul out the foam fire extinguisher. She kicked the cupboard door back out of her way and walked into the kitchen, where little sprays of fire were burning away merrily on different objects. The fridge. The table. One of the chairs. The sink.

In the center of the floor was the source of it all, a fiercely burning heap of glass and petrol that was melting the linoleum.

And she dropped the baton without regret, pulled the pin out of the extinguisher, and began to douse every one of those little fires.

She was lucky that there wasn't more flammable material in the kitchen. Lucky, too, that the Molotov cocktail had landed centrally and not any closer to the hallway. The carpet had remained untouched, and once she'd drowned everything in foam and stopped spraying, there was silence.

She looked around at the burned and blackened room and smiled grimly to herself.

37

"You look perfect," April told her. "Stop fiddling and drink." Louise applied another smudge of eyeshadow before she put the brush down on the bathroom counter and picked up the glass of Prosecco.

"Something doesn't look right," Louise said, looking back at the mirror.

"It *all* looks right." April was definite.

"But it doesn't look like me," Louise said, trying hard to pinpoint what was wrong.

"You know what I think?" April said, coming to put an arm over her shoulder and giving Louise's reflection a considering look. "I think you're normally drunk when we get ready. What you're seeing is Sober Louise in her going-out clothes, and it's freaking you out because you've never seen her like this before."

Louise gave a laugh and wondered if April was right. She studied herself again, and thought about all the times they'd done this, when she'd looked at herself through a haze of alcohol and felt fantastic.

She realized that she wasn't smiling, either, and that was a wrong note. Drunk Louise always smiled. She was fun and she never cared if her lipstick wasn't just right.

Sober Louise took the Prosecco and swallowed a large mouthful. "I'm not going to be Drunk Louise tonight, but I definitely don't want to be Sober Louise." She gave a small belch as the bubbles came back up and laughed again. "Allow me to introduce you to Tipsy Louise. Tipsy Louise is a lot of fun, too, but she knows her limits."

"I want to be like Tipsy Louise," April said, and then drained her glass. She was already pouring another one before Louise had managed a second mouthful. "Only, I guess I don't want it that badly. . . ."

Louise watched her thoughtfully. At this point in the evening it had always been about April bringing Louise out of herself. It was always her lively, dominant friend insisting that they needed to drink so that Louise could feel better. And for the first time, Louise wondered if that was really why April brought wine over and ordered round after round of tequilas.

"How are *you* doing?" Louise asked. "What's going on with you?"

"Oh." April gave a shrug. "All OK."

"You don't seem . . . happy, now I have time to think about it."

April laughed, but then she tipped the glass back again and swallowed, and Louise had the impression she might be swallowing back tears.

And then she said, "I don't know. I guess I've just been . . . missing my sister. And worrying that things are changing without me somehow." She shook her head.

"You haven't seen Dee for a long time, have you?" Louise asked her gently.

"No," April agreed. "No. Not for a long time. I had a dream about her the other day, about going on a road trip with her, and when I woke up, I felt . . . bereft, I guess." She gave a frustrated sigh. "I'll get over it. I'm good at picking myself up."

"You don't have to get over it, you know," Louise said gently. "You can talk about it properly, if you want."

April rolled her eyes, but said, "Thanks, honey." She put her arm round Louise and pulled her into a hug. Then she reached for her phone. "I want a photograph. To commemorate this fine occasion."

She held the camera out at arm's length, studying them both on the screen for a few seconds before she smiled and took the shot.

"You know," Louise said, "Tipsy Louise loves you just as much as all the other Louises. And she'll still be here for you."

"I know she will." It looked like April might say something else, but she looked at her phone instead. "OK, the cab's here in five. We'd better drink up."

Louise felt a twist in her stomach. She wasn't sure she was ready to do this. However much she wanted to tell the horrors of the last week to go screw themselves, the idea of going to another club on another Friday, of seeing men there who might want to flirt with her . . . it was horrifying. It had been hard enough going on her own on Sunday, before she knew for certain that an apparently kind man had pinned her down and raped her.

But April was a firm believer in getting back in the saddle. She'd rebooked the hotel they'd never made it to on Monday, and had insisted on paying for Louise to spend two full hours on a massage table. She'd also booked them a VIP area at a club that was run by a friend of hers.

"We won't be standing at the bar with everyone else," April told her. "You'll have a safe space at the table to retreat to if you feel bad, and if it's awful, we'll just go." She'd raised an eyebrow. "But this is going to be a night we'll remember for years. I can feel it."

"Oh, will it?" Louise had said, and then found herself capitulating. April was essentially right. She shouldn't be hiding away because some psycho had attacked her. She was stronger than that.

But she could still feel the pounding of her heart as she put her coat on and looped her large handbag round her, holding it close in front of her like a shield. And she wondered, a little wistfully, whether Drunk Louise would have been a little tougher.

. . .

FOR THE FIRST time in six weeks, the team did pub night. The DCI always took himself off after the first forty-five minutes, in some sort of deference to them wanting to kick back and enjoy themselves. Before he left, however, he caught Hanson on her own.

"I don't want to pry into anything," he said, "but it's come to my attention that you may be having a few issues with an ex-boyfriend."

Hanson could feel her cheeks heating up from the moment he started speaking. But it was right that he should know what was going on.

"Unfortunately he's been stalking me, slandering me, and vandalizing my property, so I've had to report him," she said.

Hanson guessed that Chief Inspector Heerden had mentioned the case to the chief. Heerden had probably felt that she had to. Hanson was eager, however, for the whole situation to be handled by the uniformed police. The idea of it landing somewhere within CID, with the people she worked with every day, was agonizing.

There shouldn't be any need for them to get involved anyway. There was little investigating that needed to be done. Jason had written a summary of his conversation at the pub, including all of Damian's allegations about her. It had been awkward asking him for it while they existed in such an unresolved state, but he had been eager to help. Ben had, of course, provided an account of Damian's presence on the evening of the arson. And Hanson also had her own diary entries, detailing almost all of the grim reality of being harassed.

None of which might have been enough if Damian hadn't petrol-bombed her house. She still found herself smiling whenever she thought about it. It was the one real mistake he'd made, presumably triggered by anger that she still had her job and was being protected by her colleagues.

She'd asked for a quiet chat with Lightman the morning after. It had been hard not to grin at him as she shut the door of the meeting room behind her. Despite a large hole being smashed in her window and a similar hole bored through her night's sleep, she'd felt more energized than she had in months.

"I'm going to report Damian," she said. "Today, if possible. Would you be able to write up the conversation you had with him outside the station yesterday? I'd like to link his behavior with it."

"What behavior is that?" he asked.

She told him, in a few words, about the nighttime vandalism.

"Which means we've got him," she said, her eyes bright with exhilaration. "I caught the whole thing on camera, by making him feel clever."

Lightman narrowed his eyes at her. "The fake cameras . . ."

"I opened them up and put real ones inside." She laughed with total glee. "It cost me a fortune, but I knew it would work. He's such a smug, egotistical arsehole that he was congratulating himself on knowing they were fake. The best bit is, they're the same ones he put up when we lived together in Birmingham. He knew for sure that they were fake because he recognized them and was too arrogant to realize that I knew exactly what I was doing."

She held out her phone, which featured a close-up image of Damian's face. He'd actually turned to look in satisfaction at what he believed was the fake camera over the doorstep.

"The upstairs one got his car, too, and his approach to the house. Add that in to the lesser crime of smashing my security light, and we've got a pattern of violent and destructive behavior."

"God," Lightman said, taking it with one of the largest and most open smiles she'd seen him give. "That's absolute genius."

She'd filed her report with the crime desk three and a half hours later. And although she hadn't felt quite as upbeat since— had, in fact, had moments of squeezing anxiety at what Damian might do when he found out about the charges—she'd generally felt as though she'd been cut free from a heavy weight.

"Well," the DCI said to her now, with an expression that was somewhere between wary and warm, "I may not be able to get involved, but that doesn't mean I can't offer support. Just tell me if you need time, or space, or a rant, or—I don't know, alcohol—to get you through it."

Hanson gave him a grin. "Thanks, Chief. I will. And, um . . ." She shifted a little before going on, "thank you for the, er, help with the emails he sent. Ben told me about it. It means a lot. Knowing you have that kind of faith in me."

"Well, you know," Sheens said with a shrug, "I sort of had to. Otherwise it'd make me look like I made a bad hiring decision, so . . ."

She gave an out-and-out laugh at that. "Yeah, true. Well, thanks anyway."

JONAH WAS ENJOYING the pub more than he'd expected to. He generally had trouble relaxing in these situations. He was too conscious of being the boss. And despite liking his team a great deal, he half expected them to exchange a look about something he'd said, or to quietly hint that he should go.

But tonight he was finding his team's company genuinely helpful. The lack of resolution to their case had made him dissatisfied. He couldn't quite let go of it all. Something in him didn't really want to believe that Alex Plaskitt had been so twisted, and he'd found himself picking over it all with a feeling of depression.

The moral gray area over Louise Reakes's actions had also left a sour taste in his mouth. He supposed it was in his nature to look for certainties and endings. To keep pushing until an investigation felt rounded off. Closed. Finished. And yet, as he well knew, life was rarely like that. There wasn't always a definite conclusion about who the bad guy was. And when there *was* a bad guy, there was usually a reason. Like Alex Plaskitt's awful parents, or Louise

Reakes getting drunk because of a faithless husband and then lashing out as she was attacked.

The great thing about his team was that they understood. They got that he might feel a little melancholy right now, even though it seemed like time to celebrate. Their expressions were full of that same feeling, and it soothed him.

But at quarter to nine his phone buzzed with another text from his ex-fiancée.

Did you get my text last Saturday? I really need to talk to you.
Can you ring me, please?

He felt strangely depressed reading it. He really didn't know what to do. Ignoring Michelle felt like unnecessary cruelty, even if she was angling for nothing more than an ego boost. But talking to her felt like a betrayal of Jojo. And worse still, it reminded him uncomfortably of how badly he'd slipped when he'd seen his ex four months before. Of how stupid he'd been to sleep with her.

He looked at it for a minute and then put his phone away. He'd call her tomorrow. Tonight, he needed to see his girlfriend.

HANSON WATCHED THE DCI go, thinking it a shame that he couldn't stay out and be one of them.

"It must be lonely," she said to O'Malley, "being the chief."

"Ah, you'd think so," O'Malley agreed, "but don't feel too sorry for him. He has a burning-hot girlfriend and a house that's three times the size of yours." O'Malley leaned forward. "And a proper pension too."

"OK, fair point," Hanson agreed, picking up her beer. "He's clearly an arsehole. Who's getting the next one?"

LOUISE HAD ACTUALLY made it to a club again, one that looked not unlike Blue Underground. She wasn't blind drunk, and she was almost having a good time. The "almost" part of it was less to do with anxiety, as she'd expected, and more to do with the fact that drunk people turned out to be incredibly annoying.

It was strange to think that she'd never really seen other people getting this drunk before. Sober Louise had always headed home before it got too late, and Drunk Louise didn't seem to see anything that wasn't rose-tinted.

"Oh my God, look at the state of him," she said to April, safe in their little cordoned-off area and watching as one of the other punters staggered over to the bar and then managed to drop all the cards out of his wallet onto the floor. He'd already tried to slobber over some poor girl and been told to sod off. "Please, please tell me I'm never like that."

April glanced over at him stooping to pick the cards up, seemed to weigh it up, and then said, "Hell no. You're way less coordinated."

"You can go fuck yourself," Louise said with a laugh.

One of the bar staff came over and asked if they wanted anything, which felt bizarre to Louise. This was a crowded club. They ought to be elbowing their way to the bar. This VIP thing was strange.

"I'd like another screwdriver," April said. "You should have one too," she added to Louise.

Louise looked at her doubtfully. "I'm not—I'm probably OK. I had the Prosecco."

"You sure?" April asked it a little slyly, as if the only right answer was to change her mind. The inevitable pressure drinkers applied to those who were not drinking.

Louise let out a sigh. Truthfully, she felt a bit over-sugared. The three non-alcoholic cocktails she'd sunk had all tasted like variations on fruit punch and she would really have killed for something to cut through it a little.

"OK. A single gin and tonic. But that's all. That's me done for tonight."

"Great," April said, and then, to the guy taking their order, "Is Charlie here yet? He's supposed to come say hi."

"Oh yeah," the guy said, glancing around. "I think he's here. I'll tell him."

"I'd love you to," April said, giving him a look that was one hundred percent Predator Mode.

The guy grinned back at her as he walked away, and Louise shook her head. "I don't think he's your type."

"But that's the thing," April argued. "Maybe my type needs to change."

Louise narrowed her eyes at her. "What about this Charlie, then? Your friend? You seem quite keen to see him?"

April gave her a slightly wicked grin. "Oh, he's a doll. But I was thinking of setting the two of you up, honey. He's Chez. The guy you kissed at the wedding."

"No, April," Louise said with a rush of horror. She tried to be firm. "I really don't want to see him. And anyway, there won't be any of that. I'm in this . . . non-situation with Niall, I'm still shaken as hell over someone assaulting me, however little I can remember, and . . . and the rest. We're not going to do any setting up. Not for a long, long time, all right?"

April tutted. "If you say so." She sat back a little. "But I bet he won't even remember that whole kissing and running thing. It'll be like you just met."

"WELL, HERE's TO almost having put a case together," O'Malley said, raising his glass of tonic a little unsteadily. It was wonderful to Hanson how he could simulate drunkenness with the rest of them without ever touching a drop. He told her that he never consciously modified his behavior. He just got drunk on *their* drunkenness.

"Ugh, thanks," Hanson said, lifting her glass. "I just spent five hours today trying to prove that Alex Plaskitt had the knife in time to kill a young woman in London, and I can't seem to do it.

He didn't order two at once, and the only order that's anywhere nearby was made after she was killed. And given a similar weapon was used, I may have to accept that he didn't do it, even though every other thing fits."

"But he didn't have that knife on the night of January the nineteenth either," Lightman pointed out, "as he'd given it to Step. We're positive he was the person who attacked Gianetta Jilani. She specifically mentioned a knife. Maybe he was using something else for quite some while, but eventually decided he wanted something more like Step's artistic one from Steel and Silver."

Hanson hesitated for a moment. "Yeah, or . . . or what if he took it off Step on the nineteenth? Offered to look after it and then used it, cleaned it, and returned it?"

She put her glass down onto the table quickly, and pulled her phone out of her pocket.

"Um . . . It is Friday night, you know," O'Malley said. "You're not actually supposed to be working."

"It'll only take a second," Hanson said, grinning.

She took her phone out of the warm pub and into the cold street. It was another arctic night, and there was a sharp, all-penetrating wind tearing down Shirley Road. She regretted leaving her coat on the padded bench inside but made the call anyway.

Step Conti picked up warily, and she didn't blame him. Finding out that your best friend had been at the very least a serial rapist would have made anyone wary. Each phone call from the police so far had revealed a darker and darker truth, and she felt a twist of guilt that she was now in the process of pinning a murder on Alex too.

"Step, hi," she said. "DC Hanson here. I'm sorry to call you on a Friday night, but there's something we need to check with you. It's about that night that Alex and the guys gave you the knife. January the nineteenth."

"If you'll just give me a second . . ." There was a brief toddler screech in the background. His daughter, she guessed, up later than she was supposed to be. After that came the sound of a closing door. "OK," Step said. "Yes."

"I just wanted to know what happened to the knife right after you were given it," she asked. "Did you hold on to it yourself? Or did someone else look after it?"

"Um . . . oh," Step said. "I left it behind the bar. Marc's brother, Charlie, owns the club we went to, and he offered to keep hold of it."

"Marc's brother," Hanson said. "So that's Charlie Ruskin?"

"Yes," Step confirmed.

"Does he own any other clubs?" she asked, trying to make the question sound as if it had no importance at all.

"Yeah, he has three. We normally go to the one in Southampton but we did an overnighter in Portsmouth for my birthday."

"Oh, right," she said, aware that her voice sounded not quite right. "The one in Southampton, is that Blue Underground, where you were last Friday?"

"Yes, that's the one."

Hanson was aware that she was shivering, and that it had as much to do with the adrenaline that was suddenly coursing through her as it had to do with the cold. She tried to keep her head. To ask all the relevant questions.

"Did you take it home at the end of the evening? The knife?"

"No," Step told her. "Charlie wasn't around when I left so I got it off him the next day."

"That's great, thanks," she said. And then she added, "So it couldn't have ended up with Alex?"

"No," he said firmly. "No, it couldn't."

APRIL SWUNG HERSELF to her feet and grabbed her handbag. "I'm going to pee and redo my lip gloss. You coming?"

Louise shook her head, determined not to be a tag-along. Not to be needy, anxious Sober Louise anymore. "I'm good here, thanks."

But as soon as April was gone, she regretted not going with her. The club turned from a comfortably dim place into a shady, crowded cavern. The men dancing down on the floor took on a predatory shape, and she found herself staring at the closer ones.

One of them glanced round and gave her the smallest of smiles, and she looked away, quickly, ashamed of how wobbly she suddenly felt.

She pulled her bag onto her lap, the big, comforting shield, and pretended to be rooting around in it. When she looked up again, the dancing guy was facing away from her, as though nothing had ever happened, and she sighed.

For fuck's sake, get a grip, Louise. Nobody's looking at you. Nobody cares.

She wondered whether she should have just one more drink. Another gin and tonic. Just to ease the panic.

She looked over toward the bar, which she realized wasn't even that crowded. It was still only eleven-fifteen. Early for a club. It wouldn't turn into a real crush until later, at pub kicking-out time.

The barman April had flirted with was speaking to someone, but there was no queue behind them. She could get over there, get herself a drink, and get back before April returned. A small victory for independence.

She stood, pulling her bag strap over her head, and began to walk over. She saw the barman nod in her direction and the guy who'd been talking to him turned toward her.

And as she took in his face, her whole body felt like it was tipping sideways into some kind of void.

"You've got a fucking nerve."

Hanson swung round, the phone still close to her ear, even

though she'd rung off. There was urgency thrilling through her, and the person she cared least about just now was Damian. And of course, *of course,* he had followed her to the bloody pub. And of course he'd chosen now to confront her.

"What exactly do you think you're going to get out of this shit?" he asked her. "Do you think you're going to get me put away? Because I've done nothing the fuck wrong, and you're going to look like a total tit in front of your precious new colleagues."

She'd thought so many times over of the things she'd love to say to him if she were to confront him. She'd fantasized about it for days. How she'd laugh at him and tell him to talk to her solicitor. Or she'd ask how he'd liked being caught on camera.

But in the end there was no time for anything she had to say. And when she thought about it afterward, there couldn't have been a better way of pulling the carpet out from under him than what she said instead.

"Sorry, but I don't have time for your bullshit right now."

And she pushed through the heavy swing door of the pub and said, "We've got everything, *everything,* wrong."

IT WAS STRANGE how quickly hours and hours of memory could suddenly replay themselves. Louise was standing in a bar in Portsmouth with her bag over her shoulder and had faltered for only a second. That was the truth of it.

And yet the truth of it was also that she had been sitting at another bar for almost an hour while a tall, handsome Italian bought her drinks. While he charmed her. She couldn't quite remember his name. And she felt as though he was familiar somehow, but she wasn't sure how and had somehow missed the part where she should have asked.

She had also been thinking about Dina and Niall. Specifically, about Dina's hand on Niall's knee, and she had rested her hand on this man's leg, imagining that she was Dina. That she had that sort of power. And the handsome man had given her a long, slow smile and said, "Drink up."

And then she'd been leaning too heavily against the bar. She'd felt too drunk. Sick drunk. She'd become suddenly frightened of it and of herself, and she'd stood up, unsteadily. She found out only then that the man's hand had been right at the top of her thigh. And she was no longer sure that she even knew who he was. What had she been thinking?

"Are you leaving?" he'd asked. And she'd tried to focus on his face. He seemed to be giving her a smile that wasn't quite right.

"Yes," she'd told him. "Sorry. I need to—to go home."

She picked up her handbag and went staggering out into the hall, weaving almost from wall to wall as she went.

And she was still in that second of frozen time on the dance floor, but she had also spent what felt like hours trying to stay steady on her feet and on her stupid fucking heels as she stumbled up London Road. Somewhere during those hours, she'd glanced behind her and seen that not-quite-right smile following her, and she'd felt frightened.

She'd pulled out her phone but somehow had been unable to unlock it. Her fingers weren't working. They had become someone else's. And so she'd started trying to run.

And then, without any time passing, she'd been on her face in the earth, sobbing into the ground as he pressed a knife into her lower back. And she recognized his voice this time. She'd heard the Sheffield lilt back in the club, back when he'd been saying nice things to her.

"Please don't," she'd told him. "Please. Please."

"Shut your fucking mouth."

Her hair had been over her face as he'd turned her over, and she'd felt like she might vomit through it. She felt dizzy. Unwell. Nauseous.

He was pulling at her underwear, but he couldn't be. This

couldn't be happening. She must be able to fight, but it was like a dream where her body wouldn't work. Nothing worked.

"Hey!" It was another voice. A deeper one. One that was full of a different sort of threat. "What the hell do you think you're doing?"

The tugging at her underwear had stopped, and the weight that was on her eased momentarily, though there was a sharp pain in her left arm still. She could feel his hand pressing down on it.

"Get—the fuck—out of here," the man who was on top of her said. "I'm not fucking around." Louise managed to free a hand and pulled the hair out of her eyes enough to see something. She twisted to see the face of this man pinning her down. The smile had gone, because he was wearing a balaclava now. He'd become faceless. Awful.

There was a tall figure standing a little farther away, one that loomed over them both.

"I don't care who you are or what you think you're doing. You need to get off her. Right now."

"Mate, I told you to go." There was such coldness in that cheerful Northern voice. "This has nothing to do with you."

"Please," Louise sobbed. "Please don't go."

There was a brief silence, and then the tall figure strode forward. The weight on her arm lifted abruptly as the figure above her was hauled away. And then there was a sickening noise as her attacker swung a fist at the tall stranger.

She heard a noise of pain and then a roar. The taller man brought his fist up so quickly that there was no time for the balaclava-clad man to dodge. It connected with a crunch, and then the taller one was kicking and shoving her attacker away, so that he was scrambling backward. He was fleeing and trying to shield himself all at once.

It was quiet for a moment after that. He'd gone. The awful man in the balaclava had gone.

She could hear the tall man breathing, and then he said, "Are you OK?"

And then suddenly she was crumpling in on herself and sobbing. Sobbing so hard that she couldn't breathe.

"Shhh," he said, and he was sitting next to her. "Shhh. It's all right. It's going to be all right."

He helped her to her feet, and once she was in front of him she saw that there was something sticking out of his abdomen. She reached out. She touched his dark-stained T-shirt just below it, and when her hand came away, it was warm and sticky.

"You're hurt," she said. "You're hurt. He hurt you."

He gave a laugh, but it ended in a groan.

"Ah, s'OK," he said, after that, and she looked into his face for the first time and realized that she knew him. Had spoken to him. He'd been in the club too. "I'll get it . . . doctored. . . . Just let me walk you home first."

He sounded so sure that she nodded, and started to lead him home. Flakes of snow were beginning to fall around them, and everything seemed unreal.

And it was a while later, but all in that same second, that she was up in her room, and kicking her shoes off so she could climb into bed. She was still shaking, but she curled up facing him and felt better because he was there.

He sat heavily on the bed, making her tip and bounce as the mattress moved.

"I don't . . . Is it all right if I lie down?" he asked. "Just for a minute?"

"Yes," she told him. "Lie here."

He lay down, his face toward her, and he gave a sudden, sharp intake of breath. And then he was struggling with something, until he gave a gasp of pain and relief. It was a knife that had been in him. A knife. She could see it in his hand and a small voice was telling her that this was wrong. That she needed to do something.

But even while it told her that, she was shutting down. Losing consciousness. Losing the world around her in favor of a softer one somewhere beneath all of this.

"I'm cold," he said, and she opened her eyes again, and saw that he was pale. So pale. And his eyes were frightened.

She reached out to his face and began to stroke it. "It's OK," she said. "I'm here. I'm here."

38

The scene was so very familiar to Niall. Another hotel bar, with Dina waiting for him, long-legged and intensely glamorous in her short black dress, her hair pinned in a loose bun so that most of it fell in artful dark-brown curls.

She was looking at her phone as he arrived, a drink already in front of her. It was always like this. His ex-wife would always be waiting, perfectly arranged for maximum effect.

He shook his head slightly and closed the last few feet between them. She looked up and smiled at him, her expression rueful this time.

"I'm glad we get to see each other again," she said. "I hated being told not to talk to you."

Niall sat, slowly, and then said, "We won't be seeing each other again, Dina."

Dina's gaze settled on him for a moment, and then she laughed. "Don't be ridiculous, Niall." She picked up her martini and took a very careful sip. "We're free to do what we want now. Everything's all out in the open."

Niall laughed in return, a sound that was totally unlike her relaxed chuckle. It was a bitter sound.

"You're right," he said. "Everything *is* in the open. Who you are, and what an idiot I've been."

He saw Dina roll her eyes. "You aren't angry with me for

obeying orders, are you? What was I supposed to do? Tell her no, we had our own plan?" Dina shook her head, the expression in her eyes a little harder. "You know it doesn't end well for people who do that."

"There's not a chance in hell those were orders," Niall said flatly. "Everything you've tried to do from the moment she brought you in . . . wriggling your way into the middle of it all, to get one up on me . . . has been a ridiculous game. And, of course, playing me at the same time. Telling me you missed me, that you regretted ever walking out. Chipping away at my chances of happiness. And for what? To feel like you've *won*?" And then Niall stopped, closing his mouth deliberately. "Actually, forget that. I don't need to know why. I don't care anymore. I'm here to pick up what you have to give me, and then I'm going."

Dina gave him a long look, and then she shrugged. She put a manicured hand out to the handbag that was hooked over the back of her chair and drew out an envelope.

"It isn't as much as you're hoping," Dina said. "Certainly not enough to see you out of debt."

Niall took it with a shrug and slid it into his pocket without opening it. He wasn't going to give her the satisfaction of seeing his disappointment. "It doesn't matter. It's all done."

"Nearly," Dina said as he rose. "She has a few loose ends to tie up, she said."

Niall paused, his feeling of certainty wavering. "What does she mean, loose ends?"

JONAH HAD ALMOST made it out of Southampton by the time Hanson's call came through.

"I'm so sorry, Chief," she said. "But it looks like—it looks like Alex Plaskitt never attacked Louise Reakes. It was the nightclub owner, Charlie. He's Marc Ruskin's brother, and he was at Rain for Step's birthday, the night Gianetta Jilani was attacked in January of last year. And he had the knife for safekeeping."

Jonah found his mind slow to process all this information. "Step's knife?" he eventually managed to ask.

"Yes," Hanson said. "He was also at Blue Underground on Friday. I've called the staff there and it turns out he wasn't actually working like he implied. He was on the other side of the bar, and one of the staff can remember him flirting with Louise Reakes. He's sure it was her because she came back in asking questions later. Charlie had told him to lie if anyone asked, and say he'd been working. And the bouncers were told to support the idea that he'd been punched by a punter. They thought he actually had been, after Charlie tried to walk home then came back to put ice on it."

"Right." And he was turning the car across the cross-hatching, swiftly and illegally. He switched the flashing blues on. "Did they say where he is?"

"In his Portsmouth club," Hanson replied. "Rain. And . . . Niall Reakes called me. He's frantic with worry for Louise because she's apparently in danger. He says we need to track her down, but he can't raise her or April Dumont, who he's sure she's with."

"Right, that's . . ."

"The thing is," Hanson went on, "Niall found out they're going to Rain. Where Charlie is."

He thought back to Louise's accounts of their night out, and how the venue had been April's idea. He felt a run of cold up his back.

"Was it Portsmouth they were going to on Monday when we picked them up at the service station?" he asked.

"Yes," Hanson said. "I think so."

And that had been April's idea too. If Issa hadn't disrupted everything, they would have been off for a night out in Portsmouth. To a club. He was willing to bet he knew which one they'd been headed for.

"OK. I'll be there in five to drive you, provided you've only had a couple of drinks. Tell Domnall to take Ben and go. Now."

THIS COULDN'T BE *happening again. It couldn't be.*

And yet it was. Louise had made no conscious decision to run. By the time she'd surfaced from the terrible waking dream, she was no longer close to the bar. She was running, skidding down the corridor that led to the way out, with her handbag banging uncomfortably into her leg.

There were bouncers on the door. They could help her. She could tell them what was happening and they could protect her until she could call a cab and get hold of April.

But then, as she drew level with one standing in the doorway, she remembered what April had said. Charlie owned this place. Charlie, whom she'd wanted to set Louise up with. The same man Louise had once fled from at a wedding, with a better instinct than she'd had when she saw him again, years later.

Fuck, she thought. *Fuck. They work for him.*

And so, as one of them gave her a coldly amused look, Louise ran past them, and out onto the road. A terrifyingly empty road.

She'd expected to find people here, but it was drizzling now, and nobody seemed to be out in it. She looked frantically for some kind of shop that might be open, but all she could see were estate agents and dry cleaners, their lights off and shutters down.

What's wrong with this place? Why didn't you stay at fucking home, Louise?

She saw an alleyway to her left, and she scuttled into it. She could at least be out of sight while she called for a cab. She ducked behind a large blue wheelie bin that stood against the near wall of the club. God, it was cold. She wasn't dressed for this. The overhang from the roof above was so small that it barely kept any of the rain off her, and the wind kept picking it up and hurling it around.

She reached for her phone, and then felt her heart drop. A terrible, lurching fall.

Her phone was still in her jacket pocket, all neatly folded up on the padded bench of their booth.

Fuck. She wanted to hit something. Herself. The bin. Anything. *What the fuck were you thinking, Louise?*

But she had to stay quiet and think. She had to get herself out of this mess.

Could she just go back into the club? She might be able to find a group of people to protect her.

But she remembered all of the men and women in there, how drunk they were already. Would they even stop him if he came and dragged her away to somewhere quiet? Some part of the club that only he knew about?

There were voices somewhere on the road and she froze, trying to catch what they were saying. But whatever had been said had been over too quickly for her to understand.

And then she heard footsteps, and she knew that the bouncers had told him where she'd gone. She'd been too close to them when she ducked down the alley. Of course she had been. She'd done everything wrong.

And while she stayed absolutely still, hoping that he might somehow walk past her without seeing, or turn around and go back to the club, she started to talk to her husband again in her head. She imagined writing to him, safe and warm in their house. She imagined getting out of here and surviving somehow, and she promised herself that she was going to write it all down. All of it.

I'm going to see you again, Niall, she thought.

The footsteps were painfully close. He was walking past the bin. There was no way he could fail to see her now.

She could feel her hand shaking, and she shoved it into her handbag. The handbag that had no phone in it but was still unbelievably full and heavy in the way of every handbag she'd owned, despite her having cleaned it out and organized it earlier that evening.

"Louise . . ."

He said it so quietly. So gently. And Louise felt her body try to sob in fear, but she wouldn't let it.

Charlie was suddenly there, in front of her, looking at her, but it was somehow better now that he'd found her. This was the worst it could get, and she wasn't going to die cowering behind a fucking bin.

She stood up straight, and she looked back at him.

"There you are," he said, and his eyes flickered over her and over the bin, and he smiled.

She understood the smile. He was thinking that she'd brought him to the perfect place. Because after he'd killed her, he could simply tip her into the bin and come back for her later.

"I'm so glad you came," he said with a cheerful little laugh. "I can't believe it's been quite this perfect, but . . ." He glanced over her face. "You do remember me now, don't you?"

Louise nodded, and said, in a voice that wasn't as steady as she wanted it to be, "You're the one who has to drug girls in order to fuck them."

His mouth moved. Tightened. His grin went a little awry.

"Just as much of a bitch as I thought you were," he said. "You should watch that, Louise. Men don't like it."

And here it was. The feeling of strength that Louise had been looking for. She'd pissed him off, and she was going to keep doing it. She was going to make him angry, because she was so very, very done with being afraid.

"Did you enjoy getting thrown around by him?" Louise asked. "By Alex? He totally owned you."

Charlie gave a laugh that had no humor in it. "Yeah, well. He should have stayed out of it like I told him to. Because I totally killed him."

She could see in his expression that he was thinking of what he was going to do to her. She watched him, tensely, waiting for his move. Was it going to be a knife this time? Had he brought one?

He looked right and left, up and down the short alleyway, and he seemed satisfied. He stepped toward her, and before she'd had time even to think, his hands were round her throat.

"Bye-bye, bitch," he said as he lifted her up off the ground with his hands.

It was the worst thing she could remember feeling. It made her want to vomit and kick out at him. And it hurt. Jesus, it hurt.

Her hand was still in the bag. But it was holding a rubberized black handle, as it had been for some minutes. And in spite of the pain, she put every ounce of her consciousness into that instead of her desperate need for air. She was nothing more than her hand on the handle, and she drew it out and across in the small space between them, and then she drove it up and sideways into the flesh below his armpit.

There was a long second while he did nothing, and then, just as she started trying to pull the knife out, he suddenly let go of her. She fell, gasping desperately for air, but she didn't lose her grip on the handle, and she could feel it levering downwards as she dropped to her knees.

Charlie let out a howl. And then he started to kick her, his feet connecting hard and painfully with her thighs. Her stomach. She once again thought she might vomit, and wondered if her throat might be too swollen to let it out. But she stayed kneeling there and grabbed on to the handle with her other hand too.

And then she remembered how Alex had died, and with a strangled roar, she yanked on the handle and felt the blade come clear of his flesh. The feeling was followed by an awful pain in her head. He had hold of her hair and was lifting her up by it.

"What the hell?"

She heard the voice. Her friend's voice. April's voice.

At the sound of it a sudden rush of fear ran through her.

She brought me here. She wanted to set me up with him. . . .

She'd planned all of this. April had planned all of it.

"No," Louise said.

But the pain in her head stopped. Charlie was slumping backward, and it was April whose arm was round his neck.

"Get off her! Get off her!"

Charlie spoke, but it wasn't quite his voice anymore. It was a gurgling, cracked sound.

"She—fucking—stabbed me!"

He stumbled backward, and April shoved at him until he fell. She looked him over coldly. And then she met Louise's eye for a moment. She gave her the strangest smile.

"Goddamn right she stabbed you. She's a stone-cold badass."

THERE WAS LITTLE left for Jonah's team to do except deal with the aftermath. They arrived an hour too late to stop Louise Reakes stabbing someone for real this time. Fifty minutes too late to help Charlie Ruskin, who went into arrest before the two paramedics managed to get him to the ambulance.

And when one of the uniformed constables from Portsmouth City asked if he'd really wanted to save an attempted murderer, Jonah had rounded on him and told him of course he bloody had. That a human life had been lost tonight, and another one probably ruined.

Though at present, Louise actually looked the happiest he'd ever seen her. Her neck was already red and purple with bruising, her left leg had a bandage on the knee, and she was holding an ice pack to her right wrist. But she gave Jonah what was definitely a smile when he went to speak with her.

"The crew tells me they want your wrist and neck checked," Jonah said. "Let's get you taken to Portsmouth General and we can talk later."

"You can talk to *me* right now," April said from her perch next to her. Jonah was glad she had stuck around. There was an awful lot he wanted to ask her.

"Thank you," Jonah said. "Perhaps we can take your statement."

THERE WAS NOTHING in April's account to suggest that she'd had anything to do with the attack on Louise Reakes. Nothing to suggest that she might be involved in Niall Reakes and Dina Weyman's drug trafficking either. Nothing, in fact, to give him any reason to take her into custody. At least, not yet.

And counting in her favor was the fact that she'd been the one to call an ambulance, and the one to drag Charlie Ruskin off Louise. She was also determined to come to the hospital, and Jonah told her to ride with him, rather than the paramedics. He shut her into the car, and then watched alongside his team as the ambulance carrying Louise Reakes drove away.

He breathed out in a long sigh. "What an utter mess."

"I'm sorry," Hanson said, looking wretched. "I should have thought of asking Step earlier. Ben said—well, he was the one who thought of it."

Jonah shook his head. "Honestly, I'm not sure yet whether this was our mistake or not. We'll undoubtedly spend a lot of time over the next few weeks trying to work that out. Regardless, you actually *did* work it out." He gave her a tired smile. "Which puts you a whole step ahead of your wrong-headed chief."

He told O'Malley to drive Hanson home, then took Lightman to the hospital along with April Dumont. He glanced frequently in the rearview mirror at April, but there was nothing in her expression except grim determination.

April stayed with Louise until Niall Reakes arrived, ash-white and frenzied and desperate to see his wife.

There was a curious moment, though, when Niall and April

came face-to-face. Niall faltered, and then gave her a very small nod.

April raised an eyebrow and asked, "So you're here for her now? I can trust you with her?"

Niall Reakes's voice was very quiet and very raw as he said, "Yes. You can."

April smiled, jumped up from her chair, and announced that she was going home.

"We'll need you at the station tomorrow," Jonah told her.

"Sure thing," April said. "Just don't make it too early, hey? See you, Niall."

"Is Niall there?" Louise called from behind the curtain. "I want to see him."

And Niall Reakes had surprised Jonah by crying as he cuddled his wife. He had kissed her again and again and told her he was sorry.

Patrick Moorcroft surprised Jonah almost as much by coming to advise Louise in person. He was waiting at Southampton Central by the time she'd been discharged at one in the morning.

Niall had followed his wife to the station and agreed to wait in the relatives' room for as long as it took. Though Louise had told him to get some sleep if he could. That he looked exhausted. She had suddenly seemed like a parent looking out for a child, and it had been a strange thing to watch.

What followed was the first interview in which Louise seemed unafraid. She sat up straight in her chair, apparently unaffected by tiredness or injury except for the huskiness of her voice. And she was calm and rational as she told them what she'd finally remembered about that Friday night.

"I'd seen Alex's face so many times. I looked him up online, watched some of his videos . . . and I suppose, without realizing it, I started to overlay him onto other things, so when I began to remember sitting at the bar, I just assumed it was with him." She shook her head, her mouth tight. "Probably partly a guilty con-science at work."

She explained to them April's idea of going out in Ports-mouth, and her own terror of being attacked again.

"I just thought . . . that I would never have survived last time if I hadn't got my hands on a knife," she said. "And it made me feel like I could face going if I knew I had one." She gave a short laugh. "I can't tell you how little I actually believed that I'd use it. But I suppose I became the same as every other terrified knife-carrying adult out there."

"Weren't you afraid of what you might be capable of?" Jonah asked her. "You thought you'd killed Alex Plaskitt. Did you not think you might kill again, but without cause?"

Louise shook her head and said, very clearly, "I was thinking of nothing more than surviving. I'm sorry." She frowned after that. "Though I'm not, really. I wouldn't have made it if I hadn't taken it with me, would I?"

And then she'd told them about Charlie's attack on her, and how stupid she'd been from the first.

"I panicked, and I did the wrong thing," she said. "I should never have left the club. I should have gone to the ladies' and found April."

Jonah gave her a thoughtful look before he asked, "Do you feel that you can trust her? She's explained that she knows Char-lie. It's possible that . . . well, that she invited you to Portsmouth so he could silence you."

Louise gave him a smile. "I thought that for a minute too. When she turned up at the scene. And then instead of helping him, she hauled him off me and was in no hurry to stop the bleeding. She cared a lot more about if I was OK than about him. Until I said I didn't want to be facing a murder charge." Her mouth twisted. "And I do know that I'm facing one now. I do know."

Jonah could only nod, feeling inwardly furious that she had

avoided one false charge for killing Alex Plaskitt, only to find herself forced into killing Charlie Ruskin. It seemed desperately unfair, and he wondered what going through all this did to a person. Ironically, he now strongly suspected that the Louise of over a week ago would never have reacted violently. They had all, between them, somehow created a new version of her.

The strange thing was that their wrong assumptions had helped her. Without them, she would almost certainly have been dead before April Dumont arrived. It was possible that April would have been killed shortly afterward too.

That said, he still wasn't sure what to make of April Dumont's involvement. She had insisted that setting up Charlie and Louise had been her own idea, not Charlie's, and that it had all been the worst coincidence. She said she'd had no clue what Charlie was capable of. She'd thought, like the rest of them, that Alex Plaskitt was the killer.

She'd also insisted that setting Louise up had been a secondary part of the evening. "The main thing was to make her feel like she could go out and be herself," she'd explained, with her customary firmness. "I didn't want all of this to end up changing her for good."

They'd also found out that April had known Charlie for longer than she'd known Louise. But a lot less well, she said. He'd run the bar at a conference she'd been to several years running, back when she worked in pharma. They'd got on well and managed not to ruin everything by sleeping together. Jonah had tried not to smile at that. A world where not sleeping with a friend seemed surprising was a very different world from Jonah's.

"You really weren't aware of any of Charlie's crimes?" Jonah had asked her, watching her very closely.

"Of course I wasn't," April said. "Jesus, you think I'd try and get my best friend together with him if I knew he'd sexually assaulted her before and stabbed a guy? I love Louise." She fixed him with a very direct gaze. "I would probably have killed him for her if it would have saved her life. She's the only one—the only family I have, and it doesn't matter that we aren't blood-related."

And asked whether she was involved in organized crime, April had laughed, and said of course she wasn't. That she had enough trouble organizing her own life.

Discussing it with Lightman after Louise had given her statement, Jonah admitted that he at least partly believed in April's ignorance. Charlie Ruskin had successfully convinced the world that Alex Plaskitt had died poetically at the hands of his own victim. The last thing he would have wanted was to meet Louise. The chance of her recognizing him was too high.

The conversation had tailed off in uncertainty. Jonah wanted to grill April again the next day, though he suspected she'd be a tricky customer. Louise, at least, had told them everything readily, and then had been given an overnight cell with as many comforts as Jonah could get organized at that time in the morning.

After that, Jonah had finally headed home. He had to wind the windows down for most of the drive. His eyes were desperately heavy and he was seriously concerned about nodding off. He drew the car into Jojo's driveway as quietly as he could and got himself ready for bed downstairs to avoid disturbing her. And then he climbed the stairs and slid into her very new Egyptian-cotton sheets beside her.

He thought about Alex as he started to drift off. About what a good man he had been, and the unfairness of Charlie Ruskin and alcohol conspiring to kill him.

But at least everyone would know now. Everyone would know what he'd done.

39

By the time Saturday evening came round, Jonah felt like walking right out of the station and not coming back.

It had been a grueling day, made up of difficult conversations and extensive paperwork. He'd reported to the DCS first thing on Saturday morning, and after a long silence, Wilkinson had asked to meet him for a proper conversation. That second conversation had been probing and difficult, and had made Jonah feel like he'd failed everyone.

In the end Wilkinson had sighed. "My personal feeling is that you made the best decisions you could at each stage. I honestly don't think anyone could have been more careful, Jonah."

"Thank you," Jonah said, already braced for what was coming next.

"But as DCS, I'll have to put this all under review. We need to dig into everything and show that we weren't lax in allowing a serial offender to almost kill the woman who might identify him. We need to show that there were no failings. And perhaps we'll all learn something from the process too."

"Understood."

He'd had to call on Marc Ruskin after that, with Lightman, and inform him of his brother's death. Marc, who was a shorter, milder version of his brother, had gradually become pale and silent, and had then gone to be sick for some while in the bathroom of his home.

On his return, he had sat down in front of Jonah, fixed his gaze on the carpet, and said, "It wasn't his fault. That he was like he was."

"Did he . . . was there something in his past?"

"It was our mum," Marc said, his voice unsteady. "She . . . we were both abused by her. She used to make us do things . . . Charlie was older, and he often used to talk her into leaving me alone. So he got the worst of it. The worst of all of it. I knew it had messed him up, but I thought that we'd—that we'd come through it."

Jonah thought of the box planted in Alex Plaskitt's car and asked if his mother had been dark-haired.

"Yes," Marc said. "She had long dark hair. She used to make us brush it, before . . ."

Jonah did his best to get the full story out of Marc as gently as he could. He eventually left the house with a heavy feeling in his chest.

April Dumont had been due in to see them after that, but they'd been unable to raise her. Her phone was, in fact, no longer connecting. And when they'd eventually sent someone round to her flat, it was to find her husband distraught. April had left him a full twenty-four hours before, removing her stuff before she'd picked Louise up to head to Portsmouth. She'd told him she was unhappy, and that she wasn't sure if she would see him again.

It became apparent that April had wound up every part of her life. She had closed down her bank accounts, or at least the ones her husband knew about, and had left her passport in the hotel room she and Louise had booked in Portsmouth.

And somehow Jonah knew they wouldn't find her again. That she was far, far too clever for that. And that she must have had an escape route planned for years.

"At least it answers a few questions," Jonah told the DCS, with an attempt at positivity. "I'm pretty sure it was April and her ex-husband who recruited Niall Reakes. I have a strong suspicion that she was doing a lot more too. My guess is that the whole drugs operation was her brainchild, and under her management. And now that she's gone, Niall will probably be happy enough pointing the finger at her."

There was nothing much else for Jonah or the DCS to do about April, except to pass her details to the National Crime Agency and make tracking her down their problem.

Later, in the early evening, Jonah and Lightman had arrived at Issa's house. They'd come to sit amid his brightly colored cushions and tell him that his husband hadn't been a killer after all.

"Oh my God," Issa had said, his hand to his mouth. "You're sure? You're sure?"

"Yes," Jonah had said. "We believe that it was Charlie Ruskin. His friend, apparently."

"Charlie?" Issa asked, his face blank.

"We think Alex happened on him while he was attacking Louise Reakes," Jonah told him. "Charlie was masked and unrecognizable. Alex stepped in to stop him. Louise is now certain that that's what happened, and that the killer stabbed him and ran."

Issa was listening to this intently. "So . . . so he tried to save her."

"Yes," Jonah said, and he added quietly, "I'm so sorry we were so wrong about him."

Issa's eyes moved back and forth a few times, as if he was trying to compute all of this. "But how did he end up back at her house?" His voice sounded anguished again. "Why didn't he go for help?"

"We think it's because he was very drunk and didn't realize how badly injured he was," Jonah said. "And also because he wanted to make sure Louise got home. She says . . . he put her to bed, and then asked if he could lie down, because he felt unwell. Louise did her best to comfort him, not realizing that he was dying."

Issa's mouth twisted, and then he nodded. "What about—the box? In his car."

"It was Charlie's, not his," Lightman said, taking over. "We think Charlie had a stroke of good luck. Alex had left his bag at the club, and so Charlie had access to his car keys. He planted the box in Alex's car at some point during the early hours of the morning, once you'd driven it home and parked up. And then we think he posted the keys through your front door."

Which was something Jonah had realized for himself, when he'd finally remembered how Issa had struggled to open the front door to receive news of Alex's death. There had been a set of car keys jamming it, apparently having fallen from the table in the hall, but, in fact, shoved through the letterbox.

"They were actions of desperation," Jonah added, "designed to cast doubt if Alex survived, and to frame him if he didn't."

"We also have accounts of the killer talking to Louise Reakes for some time at the club," Lightman added. "And we've placed him at three scenes where other women have been victims of assault."

"So you think it'll be enough for the court?" Issa asked, his expression suddenly and markedly eager.

"It's certainly enough to be conclusive," Jonah agreed. "Unfortunately Charlie died late last night in circumstances we're still looking into."

For a moment Issa looked as though he might crumble again. But then he breathed out a shuddering sigh and said, "Good. He deserved to die."

There wasn't much more to tell him at this stage. It wouldn't have been appropriate to explain the events of the night before, so they took their leave. But as they reached the front door, Issa said, "Please say thank you. To Louise. For—for comforting him. It means such a lot to know that he didn't die alone."

Jonah nodded. "I will."

. . .

HANSON FINALLY MANAGED to get some exercise on Sunday, tired though she was from the day before. She ran until she felt wobbly and slightly sick, and enjoyed the sensation hugely.

Lightman messaged her late in the afternoon to suggest they go for a drink. She wondered whether he was just looking out for her, or whether he wanted to talk something through. It was unusual for him to suggest anything sociable.

They met at the Marriott, the same hotel where they'd last had a drink together. It had seemed the natural place, though she then felt awkward at having suggested it. That last drink had been on uncertain terms. She'd never been quite clear whether they'd purely gone as friends.

She took a good look at him as she approached his table. She thought he looked tired. And possibly, just possibly, like he was sad. It was admittedly hard to tell. She'd known cappuccino art that was more expressive than he was. But she decided she was going to be brave and ask him before he had a chance to sidetrack the conversation.

"How are you?" she asked, putting her bag down and sitting quickly. "How was yesterday? How's your dad doing?"

Lightman looked up at her and broke into a grin. "Do you want me to answer all those at once, or shall I take them one at a time?"

She grinned back at him. "Well, the most important one really is how you are. But I thought that might be affected by the other two."

He tilted his head back and forth a couple of times, as if allowing that that was fair. "Everything's all right," he said, and glanced at her as if checking to see that she believed him. She made it obvious that she didn't. But he went on anyway. "It was a long day yesterday but the chief did a great job of talking people round."

"How did it go at the hospital? With Louise Reakes?" It wasn't really the question she wanted an answer to, but it seemed like safer ground than anything personal.

"It went weirdly," he said, giving a slow nod. "Her husband turned up and was, to everyone's surprise, desperately upset about what had happened. And of course I wasn't intentionally listening, but they were only behind a curtain. . . ."

Hanson grinned. "You can admit that you find people's love lives as interesting as everyone else does, you know. Come and tell me at the bar."

"All right." Lightman rose and walked with her, speaking quietly as he went. "He did a good begging act. All about how much he loved her and how much of an idiot he'd been, lying to her for so long. He told her it was all about this drug-running mess he'd got himself into. And he added what an awful person Dina is and how much he hopes he never has to see her again."

"Hmm," Hanson said, thinking inevitably about her own situation. About Jason. "Do we believe him?"

Lightman stopped with his hands on the bar and looked at her for a moment. A look that could have meant anything. "It's hard to say. Tense situations can make people think they care more than they really do."

"I suppose so." Hanson flagged down the bartender. She ordered them both gin. It seemed like a gin kind of day. And then she asked, "How did Louise respond?"

"Somewhere between won over and wary," he said. "I'd imagine she'll give him another chance."

Hanson pulled a face and said nothing for a while. They both watched the bartender pour Tanqueray into a metal measure, and then she said, "I don't know what I'd have done, in her shoes. Whether there was enough trust."

Ben nodded next to her. She could feel his eyes on her, but it was easier to keep watching the bartender.

"I suppose what it really comes down to is happiness, isn't it?" Ben said. He leaned farther over the bar, resting his elbows on it. He was at her level now. "My theory is, that's the only thing that matters. Does having that person in your life make you happier than not having them in it? And if the answer is yes, it's simple."

Hanson gave a small smile. "Yeah, well. I've pretty much always got that one wrong myself." She gave him the very briefest of looks. "Maybe I don't *want* to be happy."

"You should work on that," Ben said, and then gave the ghost of a smile in return.

The bartender deposited their drinks in front of them. Hanson paid, and then lifted her glass. "Well, I'll drink to it anyway. To not choosing to make your life more shit."

"Cheers to that."

They were in perfect unison as they lifted the glasses and drank.

IT WAS ACTUALLY on Sunday night that Jonah's worst conversation happened.

He was back at his desk, trying to provide the CPS with sufficient reason to dismiss the case against Louise Reakes. The sound of his phone ringing was a relief at first. He didn't recognize it for what it was, not even when he saw the name of his ex-fiancée on the screen for the third time that week.

He still didn't know what to do. But something in her insistent contact struck him as unusual. Michelle might be in some kind of trouble. Something could be badly wrong.

The ringing took on an urgency he found hard to deny. And so he picked up.

"Jesus, Jonah," she said, sounding somewhere between angry and tearful. "Could you just have replied to one message?"

"Sorry," he said, easily maneuvered into guilt. "I've had a really intense case. Are you . . . all right?"

"No, not really," she said. "I'm . . . well, in a bit of a state, to be honest. We fucked up. I'm four months pregnant."

There was a beat while Jonah's mind did the math, an instinctive checking to make sure he understood what she was saying, and then he said, "Oh. Fuck, that's . . ."

"A massive balls-up," Michelle agreed, and then he heard the sound of her crying down the phone at him, and he wasn't sure he had it in him to comfort her. Not when he could feel everything falling apart.

40

LOUISE

t's time for you to read all of this. Everything I've written to you. Everything I wrote up until the night that almost killed me. It's all here.

There isn't a lot to add from the last few days. Except that I'm honestly not afraid.

That doesn't mean I'm deluded. I know the CPS is bringing a manslaughter charge against me, and I know it's possible that I'll be convicted. There are a lot of women who have been convicted for killing their attackers in the past. The stats are actually quite frightening now I've looked into it.

I don't know how much Patrick has told you about the case. But he tells me a lot will hinge on my decision to take the knife with me, which implies premeditation. However, he hopes that any jury will understand I had no idea I was going to meet my attacker and was purely thinking defensively.

The other bonus is the trauma I'd already gone through. Legally speaking, that is. I can speak openly and honestly about that when my time comes. Nothing anyone says will change how frightened I felt. Patrick thinks I should allow myself to look vulnerable when the time comes. This is something I am now struggling with, and it's the strangest feeling. I keep somehow coming across as too strong. Too together. What happened to the old Louise?

April has managed to be our star witness even in her absence. The statement she gave was pretty conclusive. Apparently there's no case being pursued against her at present to make that statement doubtful, which is lucky for me. The National Crime Agency is looking into her, but Patrick tells me she's done a remarkably good job of disappearing. I suppose that's the advantage of planning it for a long time. I just feel strangely grateful that she risked it all to spend one last night out with me. It's obvious to me now that it was a farewell.

It probably seems strange to you that I feel the loss of her so intensely, given how much she hid from me, and how responsible she was for all the shit you got into with Dina. I know that she essentially blackmailed you into running drugs for eight years. I understand that nobody made her do any of it, and that she must have made unbelievable amounts of money off you, Dina, and every other person dragged into her scheme. And I know that you're still angry as hell with her, for all sorts of reasons.

But I miss her, Niall. It's clear to me that she's cared about me for the past five years more than anyone else, even you. I'm sad that I'm going through this without her now. I'm sad, too, that I won't get to hear her stand up in court to say her piece. I know she'd have done a great job tying the prosecutor in knots. Though I don't feel scared of it. I don't feel like I actually need her to fight my corner anymore, however much I might enjoy it.

I found out a little more about her from the National Crime Agency. They asked me if I knew her by any other names, and then they asked if the name Abigail Jones-Rounier rang any bells. She was April's age, the daughter of a Tennessee doctor whose wife left him. Abigail brought up her sister, Dolores Jones-Rounier, pretty much single-handed, and then lost her to a drunk with a gun one New Year's Day. Abigail vanished soon afterward, but not before the drunk had been beaten senseless with a scaffolding pipe.

So maybe you could argue it wasn't really me she loved. It was her baby sister, Dee. Everything she felt for me might only have been a shadow of that, it's true. And yet I felt like April saw me and understood me like nobody else. Like I hope you will.

There's one more thing for me to tell you about April. I had a card that's clearly from her, even though it isn't signed. It called me "honey" and apologized for her terrible lack of judgment in Charlie's character.

There was a key taped into it too. For a Big Yellow storage facility. It has the address on the fob. And she'd circled it and written "not to be opened until your next, next birthday."

I'm pretty sure I know what's inside it. That she's left me a comfortable life, and the option of clearing your debts if I want to. I'm not sure yet whether we should take it. Whether I should just leave it and everything to do with April behind.

I'll certainly have to leave it until after all the court proceedings are done, and even then, it might get me into a lot of trouble if anyone finds out. Taking the proceeds of crime. But I'm still glad she sent it. And equally glad that she's out there in the world, unarrested and probably kicking ass.

Anyway, I think that's enough about April. This is supposed to be about us.

Such an awful lot of strangeness has come out of all this. Your fear for me. Your respect for what I did. And your sudden, absolute hatred of Dina for betraying you when things got tough. I actually think you calling her a manipulative cow might have been the most wonderful thing I've ever heard you say. I fully recognize that that's a petty victory, but it doesn't lessen my enjoyment of it one iota.

There was the other thing you said too. About how worried you'd been that I couldn't cope with a child. How stupid you'd been, in fact, because I'd just coped with something a lot harder, and come through it just fine. You said you should have seen that capacity in me before, but in fairness to you, Niall, I never truly saw it either. It was hidden from both of us.

Perhaps the strangest thing of all is suddenly thinking we might have a future again. And actually *wanting* us to have one. It's still only a *might,* of course. There's a lot of shit that the two of us have to deal with. Two probable prosecutions and potential jail time in each direction, though Patrick says Daniella's working incredibly hard on a plea deal for you.

We also have a lot to work through and explain and apologize or get angry for. Or to just . . . forgive. But it feels like we might get to build this again, on solid foundations. That maybe, just maybe, if we fight hard enough for it, we might end up the family I've always wanted us to be.

And I want to tell you that I'm looking forward to the fight.

Acknowledgments

A book is created by so many people. It is never, ever just one author sitting alone and writing.

Felicity Blunt is, was, and always will be the reason that this book happened at all. My wonderful human dynamo of an agent, you rock in every possible way.

I also have the best editors in the world. Joel Richardson ran with my sudden change of idea for this book here in the UK, and helped me turn the idea into a real, wonderful reality.

Andrea Walker is my U.S. editor extraordinaire, whose faith in me is wonderful, humbling, and inspirational. I am so proud to be working with you.

To the fabulous cover design team at Random House, you have surpassed yourselves once again. I've been so lucky to have such beautiful covers on all my books, and I know just how important covers are in making people pause to pick the books up.

To the wonderful reps, who are the reason my books end up on any shelves at all: I am so fortunate to have your faith in what I write, and for that to turn into the amazing reality of seeing it in countless shops all over the country.

Allyson Lord and Katie Tull are the publicity and marketing team who help thousands of readers across the United States find and connect with the books: brilliant, creative, and utterly lovely. Huge thanks.

To Emma Caruso and the whole wonderful copyediting team: You provide such smart, insightful comments with an attention to detail that bowls me over. I am so proud to have you take such a careful interest in the books.

To Chris Haines, the policing mastermind I go to whenever I want to ask about how some aspect of the forces work: You are fantastically patient and helpful. It's so heartening to have you there, and I just hope I managed to ask all the right questions in order to avoid any unintentional errors. Any of those are obviously mine.

To my fabulous family and partner, who are still the most incredibly supportive bunch: I hope you have the patience for it all with the next books too.

To Colin Smith for all the cheerleading, support, and epic procrastination: This book would genuinely have been written more quickly without you.

And to all the wonderful members of the crime writing community I have gotten to know over the past three years, who are too numerous to name but who have been the most welcoming, fabulous and entertaining bunch: Who knows how such lovely people write such horrific things?

Glossary of British Policing Terms

CID: Criminal Investigation Department. CID sits within police headquarters, and is the home of most of the plainclothes detectives within a regional police force.

DC: Detective constable. A DC is the lowest rank of detective, but one who has already previously trained as a regular officer and been promoted to the rank of sergeant. They therefore have some experience of policing prior to working with CID, but in a detective team might expect to do most of the lower-level work, such as knocking on doors, flyering, and conducting initial interviews.

DCI: Detective chief inspector. DCIs are senior officers who will generally lead high profile investigations and will run a department or team. Their duties include liaising with other parts of the force.

DCS: Detective chief superintendent. A DCS is a very senior officer, and will lead multiple teams and areas of command. They also carry responsibility for strategy and/or policy, meaning that their junior officers will seek their advice when it comes to difficult decisions. A DCS can also do a great deal to smooth the way for other officers, and will be actively involved in high-profile investigations or critical incidents.

DI: Detective inspector. A DI is the next rank up from DS. Detective inspectors generally have the freedom to undertake investigations the way they see fit, and might oversee other members of a team, such as detective sergeants or detective constables.

DS: Detective sergeant. A DS is the rank above a DC, and has authority over DCs. They take on more of an organizational role in most teams, and might deputize for a detective inspector if they work with one.

PSCO: Police community support officer. A member of the force with no powers of arrest, who specializes in building links with the community, helping to patrol, giving crime-prevention advice, and assisting victims of crime.

Station: The police headquarters as a whole. This can also refer to any individual, smaller base from which the police operate.

PHOTO: © TOM ADAMS

Gytha Lodge is the author of *She Lies in Wait* and *Watching from the Dark*. She studied English at Cambridge University and received an MA in creative writing from the University of East Anglia.

imperfectsingleparent.blog
Facebook.com/gythalodge
Twitter: @thegyth